Sign up for our newsletter to hear
about new releases, read interviews with
authors, enter giveaways,
and more.

www.ylva-publishing.com

Other Books by Emily O'Beirne

A Story of Now Series

A Story of Now (Book #1)

The Sum of These Things
(Book #2; Coming December 2015)

A

STORY

OF

NOW

Emily O'Beirne

Ylva

Acknowledgements

The author would like to thank Astrid, Sheri, and Sandra at Ylva for their help and support. Thank you to those who read and offered their thoughts on the book in its earlier stages. Especially to Shannon, for her friendship, fun, and invaluable feedback along the way.

For all the girls who fell for a girl.

CHAPTER 1

Claire has it down to an art. It starts at the entrance of her house, where she knows that, with a careful turn of the wrist and a firm grip, it will open without a sound. Then, with just the right amount of pressure from her shoulder, the thick wooden door will slink open and no one will hear her come home.

Silently, she kicks off her boots and picks them up. She takes a moment to adjust to the dark, then pads across the downstairs carpet.

She stops at the entry of the living room and listens carefully but hears only the hum of the refrigerator and a car as it passes slowly on her street. She bolts for the stairs but then pauses, one hand on the banister. Chocolate. She wants chocolate. No, scratch that. After that shift at work, she needs chocolate. She performs a quick sweep and grab of the pantry, stuffs the chocolate into her back pocket, and prepares to attack the stairs.

And this, right here, is the problem with the fact that she lives at home.

It's bad enough that she's still within the radius of her parents' will and their many, many ideas about how she should be running this thing she loosely calls a life, but lately, her efforts to avoid them have made it even worse. Every single night is like this, a furtive exercise in getting inside, up the stairs, and to her bedroom without being seen or heard.

Even her father is gently offering solutions to get her out of her crappy job. A few times now, he has suggested she come and work as an admin at his office. What he can't seem to get into his head is Claire has no plans to *ever* master the spreadsheet—unless they magically help immunise babies in third-world countries or single-handedly defuse bombs or something. Then maybe, for the sake of humanity, she'll consider it. But even then *nothing* will induce her to learn to touch-type.

She freezes at a small sound coming from upstairs. As she clutches the banister and waits, she debates the merits of flight or fight, should the need arise. When she doesn't hear anything else, she begins to breathe again. She sets her shoulders once more and tiptoes up the carpeted steps. The next part is critical—getting past her parents' bedroom. She grasps her keys tightly so they don't jingle and steps carefully on the very outside edge of the creaky step, second from the top. She can hear them talking from behind the closed bedroom door—well, she can hear her mother talking. Her father is probably doing what he always does—listening. Or, rather, pretending to listen.

Claire ducks into her room, shoves the door shut behind her, and congratulates herself on another successful mission. She flicks on the lamp, drops her bag on the floor, and flops onto her bed. Reluctantly, she picks up the paper left on her pillow and readies herself for her mother's latest onslaught of "opportunity."

This time, it's a brochure for an information night at the law faculty. Claire sighs and rolls her eyes. This is one of the regulars. Every time a university schedules one of these nights, the notice appears like clockwork. Sometimes in her room, other times on the kitchen counter. As if Claire doesn't know enough about lawyers already. Does she really need an information night?

Her mother has something for all the other days too. Nearly every night for the past month there has been something different—an advertisement for a job or a brochure about some sort of practical skills course that would make her more "rounded" and employable. Last week, she even found a list of handy buzzwords to use when writing a resume. After their last battle *royale* over her life choices, when Claire threatened to move out, her mother switched tactics. The brochures are her new, non-intrusive way of showing Claire all the options she could exercise, instead of studying for a flaky arts degree and working a crappy job. This is how her mother backs off. It won't last, and it's still annoying, but it's definitely better than full-attack mode.

She tucks her hand under her head and idly reads the flier even though she has no intention of going. Of all the options her mother has presented, this is the one Claire is least likely to take up. Mostly because it's the one her mother would most like her to pursue.

There's a soft tap on her bedroom door.

Claire jumps, sighs, and frowns in a rapid chain of reactions, and then sets her jaw and hauls herself off the bed. Experience tells her it's better to answer the door than to let her in, because once her mother is in, it's next to impossible to get her out. The best technique is to open the door slightly, then lean out and block the entrance. That way, the exchange takes place in the hall, and her mother can't invite herself in, sit down, and initiate a heartfelt conversation. If she makes it over the threshold, she'll stay until Claire convincingly pretends to agree with whatever her mother wants this time.

She checks her watch and pulls open the door a fraction. "Mum, I'm kind of tir—"

But it's not her mother. And it's not her father either. It's her stupid, beautiful brother grinning at her. She flings open the door, lets out a small whoop, and throws herself on him.

He staggers backward into the hallway, laughing.

"Hey!"

"Sssh!" He pushes her into her room, clearly not wanting their mother to hear any more than Claire does. "I taught you well. I nearly missed hearing you get home."

"Dude, you need a haircut." She backs into the room and affectionately pulls at his floppy mane, grown unruly while he's been gone.

"Trust you to get straight to the life-and-death stuff." Cam chuckles and combs his hair with his fingers.

"Okay, so what are you doing back, and what are you doing *here*?" She sits cross-legged on her bed and takes in the welcome sight of Cam, ridiculous hair and all. She hasn't seen him for four weeks. They'll be sick of each other within days, but right now, in this moment, it's really good to see his face.

He parks himself on her chair and rubs his face, clearly exhausted. "Well, I'm back in Melbourne because the training is finished, and I am here because Elana is mad at me for going."

"What? She's mad *now*? But you're back?"

"Oh." He grins ruefully. "She was mad before I left. She was mad the whole time I was gone, and she's mad now that I am back." He sighs. "So, she kicked me out the minute I arrived."

Claire shakes her head. Cam has a thing for difficult women, and this Elana girl is insane. Claire loves to tell him he's looking for a replica of their mother. That was a favourite until Cam started telling Claire that *she* is just like their mother. It's the perfect endgame for any argument, so she's stopped mentioning it and so has he. Now that they both know the power of the just-like-Mum taunt, it has negated itself.

"How was training?"

"It was okay. A bit hairy sometimes, though," is all he says, and that is all she asks. He'll tell her when he's ready.

"I'm glad it was okay." She picks up the forgotten chocolate and tears it open.

"So am I." He grabs a book from the pile on her desk and flicks through it. He holds it up. "This is not in English, Claire."

"Well, freaking duh." She pops a square into her mouth. "That's the point."

"What does one *do* with a degree in French, anyway?"

"Oh shut up." She puts another piece of chocolate in her mouth before she swallows the first. "Mum asks that at least once a week."

"How is everything? Still working in that trashy bar?"

"Nope. Working in a different trashy bar."

"Mum's still playing career counsellor?"

"And *how*." Claire holds up the flier, rolling her eyes. "Found this on my bed tonight."

Cam laughs. "You've got to give it to her. She never gives up. No child left directionless with Christine Pearson." He holds his hand out for the chocolate.

"Yeah. I need to move out." She sighs and breaks off another hunk from the bar before she throws the rest to him.

He catches it with one hand. "Maybe you *should* go. Not move out, but to the info night, I mean."

"What?" Claire raises her eyebrows, mouth open. "Wait. Why?"

"I don't know." He breaks off a piece of chocolate and throws it back. "Because you might actually like it. I know you. Even though you act like a princess, you're tough. You're quick-witted and you *love* arguing."

"Shut up." She shoots him an evil look and lies back on the bed. "And go away now. I am officially over your return and no longer happy you survived training."

He laughs and gets up. "That's got to be a record." He pulls open her door. "Want to go for breakfast in the morning?"

"Yeah sure, but you're paying."

"I expected nothing less."

A light flicks on in the hall behind him. Claire freezes. Before she can warn him, their mother appears in the doorway, her blonde hair pulled back in a headband, her face slick with night cream.

"Could you two please keep it down out here?" She sighs and puts her arm around Cam's waist. In her best mumsy voice she adds, "*Some* of us have to work in the morning." She smiles to soften the nag.

This is clearly a concession to Cam's recent return. Any other night, there'd be no such smile. Instead, there'd be the classic ten-minute this-is-not-a-hotel speech.

"Sorry, Ma." Cam wraps an arm around her shoulder. "I was just saying hi to the Claire-monster."

Her mother turns to Claire, arms still around Cam's waist. She's so short she only reaches his shoulder. "Sweetheart, I didn't realise you were home. How was your night?"

Claire shrugs. "Fine."

"Were you out? I thought you were at work?"

"I was." Claire frowns, wondering where she's going with this. Her mother is always going somewhere with her comments.

Her mother looks her up and down, frowning right back. "You wear *that* to work?"

"What?" Claire looks at her outfit, a simple black top and jeans.

"It's a little grungy, isn't it?"

Here we go. Claire clenches her jaw.

Cam catches her eye; his face is blank, but his eyes issue sympathy.

"Mum," she drawls. "In case you haven't noticed, I work in a boring uni pub, not some Southside yuppie bar. No dress code applies."

Christine just stares at her.

It's incredible. Just when she thinks her mother couldn't look any more disapproving, she manages to kick it up a notch.

"Still, you could make a little effort," Christine concludes briskly. "Then maybe you'd find a better job."

Claire takes a slow breath and tells herself not to engage. There is no way she's discussing this tonight. She wants to sleep sometime.

Cam steps in. "She looks great, Mum. Leave her alone."

"Hmm." Her mother taps her nails against the doorframe. "Right, I must get to bed. Keep it down, my babies." She Jekyll-and-Hydes her way sweet again, smiling and patting Cam on the sternum before striding off down the hall.

Cam grins at Claire. "See you in the morning for coffee?"

She nods.

"And Claire?"

"What?"

"Turn the light on before you get dressed tomorrow, okay?" Cam grins. "Don't embarrass me," he adds in his best Christine voice.

Claire shoots him a withering smile and kicks the door shut in his face.

CHAPTER 2

Claire is hauled from sleep by sunlight hitting her square in the eyes. She was so distracted by her mother's pre-bed appearance she forgot to close her blinds before crawling under the covers. She tries to find her way back to sleep, but it's too late. Her brain busies itself with thoughts.

Then she remembers. Cam is home.

She has to admit, she's kind of happy to have her brother here. Cam is a pain, but he's *her* pain, and she likes to know he's alive. And, of course, there's the added bonus that the return of the Prodigal Son might divert the parental spotlight for a while.

She rolls over and finds her mother's brochure on the other side of the bed. She picks it up and frowns. She can't believe Cam chimed in, saying she should go to this information night. It's enough to cope with the twinned expectations of her parents—her mother's desire for her to find "direction" and her dad's deceptively simple, yet infinitely more difficult, desire for her to be "happy." Claire can't cope with her brother pushing his imagined version of her future on her as well.

She sighs. Law. Now that's a possibility Claire isn't sure she can allow. She has no desire to march in lockstep down the family line as if there's no other choice.

Well, it's not as if there aren't other options. It's just that Claire can't figure out what fits with her idea of herself in the world. And there are times when she's tempted to follow her parents simply for the ease of not having to make a decision. But what if she turns out to be the only Pearson who was lousy at law? Even her brother—though he gave it up to work for the police—did well enough to be offered honours upon completing the course. She isn't sure she could face the humiliation of not matching them. And most of all, she doesn't think she could handle the disappointment—no, the disapproval—from her mother if she fails.

Her mother simply doesn't believe in failure. Christine Pearson believes that success is well within a person's own power if she puts in the effort and plays her cards right. Claire isn't so sure.

At first, when she graduated, Claire didn't care that she hadn't come out of high school with a solid, specific strategy. Many of her friends have tedious, add-water-and-stir, three-step life plans that include degrees, weddings, and babies. Claire wants the same at some point, but why is everyone in such a hurry? She also doesn't care because she doesn't need the world. But it's not so great to discover the world doesn't need her, either. Not unless she *makes* it need her.

But the problem is she has no idea where to start. She loves studying French. Being able to read a book in another language is a source of ego-stroking pride. She also knows her studies are barely a step up from doing nothing at all. Lately, the ambitious, highly achieving part of her—the part that was wrangled into being by virtue of residing in the Pearson household—shudders at the thought of leaving university no better off and no more qualified than when she started. Claire was raised to *do*, and she feels the inexorable pull to do *something* as she works her way through her course.

She just has to figure out what she wants to do. She sighs and lets the brochure drop to the floor. Right now, though, it's definitely not law, no matter what her family says.

CHAPTER 3

Claire stands at the end of the narrow bar, staring idly into the dimly lit cavernous pub. Vintage lamps dot the walls and tables without adding any actual light. Work is particularly slow and painful tonight.

Nina calls out from the other end of the bar, "Seriously, come check this out."

Claire wanders over and looks where her friend is pointing.

"Would you look at what those douche bags are doing," Nina mutters, hands on her hips.

The guys by the pool table are deeply invested in some obnoxious game where they shut their eyes and try to pinch one another's nipples through their hockey shirts. From what Claire can tell, it's a stupid, drunken-frat-boy version of pin the tail on the donkey. If someone hits the mark, they yell "Nipple cripple!" and drink.

And it's only Monday.

Claire sighs. "See, I need to record this or something." She leans against the bar and crosses her arms. "Then every time my mum says I should go to university full-time, I can show her this as an example of why I shouldn't. This is the kind of company I'd keep." She shakes her head as one of them scores a hit. "Our old dog had more brain cells."

"That's not too hard."

"Why do we work here again?" Claire wipes down a bottle she's already wiped twice tonight.

"Better hours. No evil boss breathing down our necks. No getting sexually harassed on the job. Free knock-off drinks," Nina recites, still staring at the game as she fixes her hair into a high ponytail. "And we wanted to work in a place where we'd never hang out, remember?"

"Oh yeah."

It was Nina's idea that they should find a bar somewhere around the university, near Nina's flat. Just a regular bar with no deafening house music or pretentious idiots in their poorly chosen, all-money-no-taste suits and ties. A place where they could stay safely tucked behind the bar making drinks. A place where they might get the pick-up lines but not the grabby hands.

"Now, instead, we have all this." Claire flicks her cloth in the direction of the idiots.

Nina nods grudgingly.

The problem, Claire quickly discovered, is that it doesn't matter if a place doesn't have house music or suits. There are plenty of annoyances to replace them. In fact, this bar offers up a veritable Pick 'n' Mix of stupidity—particularly on the quieter weeknights. There are the nipple-crippling, dimwit jock types. The usual hipsters come in, too, looking for the cool, no-frills ambience of this place. They go gaga over the "real authentic jukebox" one minute and complain about the music selection the next. There are the cynical and needy hospitality workers who come here for after-work drinks. Some nights, there are even a few crusty, overly earnest hippies, drawn in by the sign saying they have vegan beer on tap. Claire doesn't get that one. Since when is there animal in beer anyway?

The pub is a motley place, and Claire is pretty sure she doesn't like it any better than the last job. When it's not weird, it's boring. Especially on quiet nights like tonight. Aside from Team Douche, there are about six other people in the place, and she and Nina have been pretending to clean for hours in case the owner, Andrew, comes downstairs. But there are only so many times she can clean a bar that's already as clean as it's ever going to be, which, as it turns out, isn't very clean. This place has the ingrained grot that comes from years of drinking embedded in it, the kind that won't be lifted with a wet cloth and sanitiser spray.

But at least she won't run into any of her old high school friends here. That's one bonus.

"I'm thinking of finding a few shifts somewhere else too, though." Nina checks the state of her eye makeup in the mirror behind the shelves. "Somewhere more exciting."

"What?" Claire pulls a rack of clean glasses out of the washer. "Don't leave me here. What is it with you? I've known you for three months, and you have had four different jobs already."

Nina grabs a towel and picks up a glass to dry. "Yeah, well, it's not like I should stick around for the pay raise. Besides, I need fodder for my memoir. That's what's going to make me rich one day."

"A book about your crappy jobs?" Claire raises an eyebrow. "Sounds like a real best seller."

"It will be. And you know what it is going to be called?"

"What?" Claire isn't sure she wants to know.

"*From Behind Bars*," she announces proudly.

"Oh wow. I see what you did there. Hilarious."

"No, Claire." Nina flicks the rag at her. "It's genius."

"Genius like that game." Claire tips her head in the direction of the douche brigade and their nipple crippling.

Nina smiles as if it washes right over her.

And Claire can't help smiling too. Nina is such a damn optimist. One of the things Claire likes most about her, though, is she doesn't care what she does. Nina doesn't care about university or getting a high-paying job. Nina just wants to live. She doesn't quietly judge Claire or constantly remind her about what Claire should be doing. There aren't any little comments like she gets from her high school friends or her parents. For Nina, Claire is what she is, taken as a fact and not a lack of promise.

"You staying at ours tonight?"

Claire nods. "Is that okay? Mum is on leave this week. Yesterday she left an ad for a temping agency on my bed. Can you believe that is the height of her aspirations for me right now? That is how low I have set the bar," she says wearily.

Nina laughs. "Sure, our couch is your couch. You know that."

"Thanks."

They polish glasses in silence for a while, idly staring at the television on the shelf above the door. Just as they finish, the door swings open for the first time in an hour, and a couple of people walk in. They drag some of the chilly night air with them. They wander to the far end of the bar and pull up two bar stools, all while laughing quietly. Once seated, they take books, notepads, and pens out of their bags. Claire puts the glass on the shelf and frowns and then picks up another. She can never understand why anyone would want to study in a bar.

"I'll go." Nina trots off to their end of the bar and starts chatting with them in that guileless, affable way she has with the customers. That's what earns her all the tips, while Claire is lucky to get any. Claire knows she could make more if she were nicer. And if she had to pay rent like Nina, she might consider it. But while she can still call her parents' house home, she can't be bothered.

When she is done with the glasses, Claire drops her polishing cloth, carries the empty tray to the end of the bar, and slides it back in the rack.

"We totally deserve a beer, right? After that shift?" A guy with dirty-blond curls and shaved sides nudges the girl next to him.

She nods, head down, as she digs through her bag.

Nina leans on the bar, smiling. "Which beer?"

"What have you got?"

"Ah, we've got—"

"Really?" Claire interrupts, her eyebrows raised in disdain. "You're going to make her list all the beers in the place?" She can't help herself. It's her pet hate.

He purses his lips, tips his head to the side, and looks at Claire thoughtfully. "You're kind of rude," he muses, as if it's more noteworthy than objectionable. "But you do make a good point. Who am I kidding?" He turns to Nina. "We'll have two pints of the cheapest drinkable beer you have, please."

Nina nods and goes to the taps.

"Classy," Claire mutters as she wipes down a shelf, revenge for the "rude" comment.

"Rich coming from someone working in this high-end establishment." He puts his pen in his mouth, chews the end, and looks her up and down. He has dark-brown eyes, which contrast weirdly with his blond curls and pale skin.

"Rich coming from someone doing his homework at the pub."

"Actually, we're not studying," he tells her cheerfully. "We're working on our definitive ranking of nineties-era heartthrobs."

Claire raises her eyebrows again, but before she can fashion a suitable comeback to that particular piece of insanity, the girl pipes up.

"Uh, your definitive ranking." She slips on a pair of glasses and waves her book at him. "I'm actually trying to study."

They're the first words she's spoken in front of Claire. In fact, it's the first time her gaze has parted ways from her bag or her book. Claire notices what an odd couple they are. He is kind of a rocker, with his shaved sides and band T-shirt with the sleeves hacked off. She is dressed simply in a blue top and jeans. Her only adornment is a chain around her neck with a long, delicate, silver pendant hanging from it. Where he is short, she is long and skinny. Not in the underfed, needs-a-cheeseburger way but in a naturally slender way. A curly mess of dark hair falls behind her shoulders. The only similarity is their dark-brown eyes. Except his are wide and hers are slightly sleepy and catlike. But it's enough to make Claire wonder if they're related.

The boy scoffs at her response and taps her hand with his pen. "What do you mean, Mia? Your input has been invaluable. I mean, if it wasn't for you..." He taps the pen harder to get her attention.

She complies, a patient, amused expression on her face as if she's completely used to his shtick.

With her attention won, he continues, "If it wasn't for you, dear friend, I would have forgotten Christian Slater actually straddled the eighties *and* nineties, which would have thrown everything off. And, your statistical know-how has been fundamental to this endeavour."

Mia says nothing. She shakes her head at him, pats his arm placatingly, and returns to her book. He grins and delivers a smacking kiss to the side of her head.

He turns back to Claire. "So *that* is what I am actually doing."

"The fact that you're making that list and not studying doesn't make you any less weird," Claire tells him as she wipes a spot on the bar near his elbow. She returns his faux-sweet smile with one of her own.

"We're absolutely fine with that." He nudges Mia with his elbow. "Aren't we?"

Mia shrugs and flips over a page in her book. Then she leans her chin on her hand and gives him a slow smile. "Well, I admit I wonder what would happen if you used your considerable brainpower for good, instead of for crazy."

He just smiles at her.

Nina returns with the beer, takes their money, and makes the change. She takes Claire by the arm and drags her to the other end of the bar. "Please, don't insult them," she mutters. "If you haven't already."

Nina knows her too well. "Why not?" Claire narrows her eyes. "He's a smart-ass."

"They work at Leona's."

"I have no idea what that means."

"The café I was telling you about before," Nina whispers. "It's amazing, and I plan to take you there. So behave."

Claire can't even remember talking about this café. Nina talks so fast and so much that, even when she's trying, Claire can only absorb about a third of what she says. "All right then." Claire throws her hands in the air, more to shut Nina up than anything else.

"And he's kind of hot."

"Who's hot?" Claire asks, trying to catch up.

"The one you were fighting with." Nina tosses a stray coin into the tip jar.

Claire looks back toward the other end of the bar. The boy is waving his skinny arms around as he chats animatedly to his friend. She listens with a half-dubious, half-amused look on her face, her hand holding a place in her book. "Dude, he's a runt. Not to mention gay."

Nina looks up, wide-eyed. "Noooo." She stares at them.

"Uh, yes."

Nina's shoulders fall into a dramatic slump. "How do I never, ever get that?"

Claire laughs. "In this particular case, I honestly do not know." She shakes her head and pats Nina's shoulder.

* * *

Later, Claire returns to their end of the bar, as far from the nipple-cripple douches as she can get. She leans against the counter and gives up all pretence of cleaning. She wants the night to be over so she can take off her shoes, lie down, watch TV, and eat pizza in Nina's living room far away from the idiots next to the pool table. In the last hour, the boys have taken turns hitting on her each time they order beer. They throw out idiotic pick-up lines at random. It's gross and depressing. In response, she simply stares, her face frozen in a perfectly composed, blank expression until the douche of the moment gives up and walks away.

Now they're teasing Nina, who has gone to collect some of the empty glasses from their table. Claire wonders if she should go help but decides

Nina can take it. She can be surprisingly feisty when she wants to be. That's another reason Claire likes her.

One of the guys finds the jukebox. He slaps the side of the machine, flicks through the choices, and drops in some coins. Claire cringes in anticipation. Yup, next thing she knows, some stupid cock-rock anthem starts, and they whoop it up, playing air guitar with the pool cues, and singing. They all join in on the chorus, fists flung in the air. She sucks in a deep breath and releases it in a disgusted sigh.

"Uh-huh."

She looks up. It's the girl, Mia, sitting by herself. She pushes her glasses closer to her face and watches the idiots. Looking back at Claire, she shakes her head with a sympathetic smile that stretches all the way up to her almond-shaped eyes. "Real mental giants."

Claire nods slowly and gives her a this-is-what-I-put-up-with-all-the-time look. Mia smiles wryly and tucks a curl behind her ear as she flips to the next page. Surprised by Mia's unexpected friendliness, Claire wanders away.

Later, when Claire goes back to the pair to collect their empty glasses, they're both watching the action near the pool table. The music seems to have reignited the douches' passion for the game, and the boys are deep in another round of nipple crippling.

The boy rubs his hands together. "They should really up the ante now, go for below the belt."

"Then at least there'd be a risk of accidental injury. Or even sterilisation," Mia says. "And it's got to be a plus for the rest of humanity if they can't procreate."

Claire snickers. She can't help it. Mia looks over at her and catches her eye. She smiles at Claire before she turns away again.

The boy suddenly leans forward and slaps his hands on the bar. He stares at Claire, eyes wide. "Ooh, that was nearly laughter! It has a sense of humour. Who'd have thought?"

Claire turns to him. "It also *accidentally* spills beer in laps sometimes." She hangs air quotes around "accidentally."

Mia looks between the two of them, highly amused, before going back to her book.

"Wow, you are *such* a bitch." He shakes his head. He sounds more admiring than anything, though. "And the best part is you don't even care." He leans on his elbow, staring at her as if in awe.

Claire smiles sweetly. It seems she's met her match.

"I guess it's lucky you look like you do."

As he says it, Mia looks Claire over quickly, a blank expression on her face. Then she goes straight back to her book.

Claire walks away and wonders why she is more insulted by Mia's casual dismissal than by anything the smart-ass boy has said all night.

CHAPTER 4

They eat chicken salad.

They always eat salad.

Claire's mother likes to say she doesn't believe in carbohydrates. It's not true, but that's what she does in public. And Claire plays the game when they eat lunch in one of these boring, ultra-modern little cafés. Her mother likes the style, all clean lines and surfaces—as if choosing no décor is better than choosing the wrong décor.

Claire goes along with it because it's easier. For every battle she fights with her mother, there's a handful she can't take up. If she did, she'd never have time for anything else.

They've been shopping. This is one activity they usually get through without an eruption between them, so it's how they spend most of their Christine-designated "quality" time.

Claire sighs as her mother slices neatly through the chicken breast perched on top of a rainbow of leaves. For as long as she can remember, they've been locked in this mutual charade of watching what they eat, ordering salads, and making conspicuously healthy choices. Claire would rather eat whatever the hell she wants and not think about food as a social statement.

On the other hand, Christine believes she really is that disciplined and health conscious. Claire remains complicit in the fantasy because time and experience has proved that it decreases the chance of her mother initiating another conversation about how Claire looks. There have been enough of those.

Her mother has this mysterious capacity to notice the slightest shift or flux in Claire's weight—faster than Claire herself. She also instantly picks up on any small changes in her hair, the way she dresses, or how she applies her makeup. Even though Claire has always fallen on the slender side of average, any gain comes with a swift reminder that, if her mother can stay trim on the march toward fifty, Claire should be able to do so at her age.

The thing is Christine complains if she goes the other way too. Months ago, when everything went to hell with Brendan, Claire was so miserable she wasn't even compelled to eat her feelings. She came out of those depressing weeks bored of her own misery and a few kilos lighter. Suddenly, instead of snide comments about weighing too much, Christine switched to snide comments about nobody liking women who are too skinny. That was confirmation of what Claire already knew—there's no reason to try since she can't do anything right in her mother's eyes.

Claire forks a piece of cucumber drowned in dressing into her mouth and idly watches the waiter zip over and top off her mother's water glass. Her mother gives the waiter a brief nod and takes an obedient sip.

"I am still not sure about that jacket," Christine says as the waiter places a coffee in front of her. "It's a bit tasteless, don't you think?"

Claire sighs. Of course her mother doesn't like the jacket because Claire loves it. It's a snug, waist-length, black-leather jacket that will take her through the cool nights of spring. More importantly, it looks good. She loves the way it makes her feel both hot and armoured as if she's protected somehow.

"It's not tasteless, Mum. It's just not your taste." She picks up her fork again and frowns as she spears a piece of tomato. Claire doesn't even like salad very much. It's not that it doesn't taste good. It's just so exhausting. All that chewing for so little payoff. And then she has to eat all over again a couple of hours later.

"Well, anyway, it's nice to finally spend some time with my daughter," Christine says, casual, as she pulls the coffee toward her.

Claire doesn't respond because she's learned to ignore comments about her supposed neglect. This is one of the smaller battles she ignores.

As expected, her mother goes in again. "I just feel like I don't get to see you much these days."

"Well, I'm working a lot." Claire scoops more leaves onto her fork. "Saving."

A lie, of course. Luckily, her mother doesn't know anything about the contents of her bank account—especially not after the jacket. She says "saving" because she knows her mother will approve.

"I do wish you'd find a nicer place to work, sweetheart." Christine sighs as she takes the bread from the side of her plate and tosses it into the basket—a show of self-discipline. "That bar sounds positively seedy."

"It's not that bad, Mum. It's just a regular old pub." Claire folds her napkin and drops it on her plate. "Andrew, the boss, is nice."

"Did you know he was arrested for drug possession a few years back?"

"How would I know that?" Claire frowns, irritated by her mother's ability to turn every conversation into a well-planned interrogation, how she always drops in little bombs to shake things up. "And the more obvious question is how do *you* know that?" she snaps. She can't help it. She's pissed, and there goes the path of least resistance.

"I had him checked out."

"Why did you do that?" Claire sits back against her chair and glares at Christine. "Jesus, Mum!" She really shouldn't be surprised, though. Her mother would get a background check done on the postman if she were suspicious enough. The lawyer in her never rests, and her father's old police friends are always ready to do a favour.

"I wanted to know what kind of establishment my daughter is working in. So I checked." Christine sips her coffee calmly. "Concern is a natural part of being a mother, Claire. You'll find out one day."

"It's part of being the mother of a *child*, Mum. Not someone who is nearly twenty."

"Well, I don't see an adult anywhere." Christine gives her that exhausted look she favours whenever this conversation starts, as if she doesn't know what to do with Claire anymore. "An adult would be planning her future, thinking about her career, not wasting time in a place like that."

And, because this conversation is the backing track to her life, Claire gives it a nod and moves the hell on. "As ever, I do apologise sincerely for the unbearable wretchedness of my existence, Mum. So, what was it?"

"What was what?" Christine frowns and pushes her plate to the side.

"What was my boss caught possessing?" Claire picks up her coffee. "Something tells me it wasn't meth."

"It was marijuana." Her reply is grudging. They both know that a little bit of pot is hardly indicative of a criminal life. Claire smirks into her coffee. Besides, it kind of explains Andrew's general dopiness.

Christine moves on, clearly aware of the weakness of her last attack. "And will I ever meet this Nina girl? The one you stay with in town?"

Probably never, Claire thinks but doesn't say. Instead, she shrugs and pretends to inspect a fingernail.

"I don't like the thought of you spending so much time with strangers."

"She's not a stranger to me, Mum. And if she ever finds herself out in the deep burbs, I'm sure she'll drop by."

"What does she study again?"

"She doesn't." Claire sighs. Her mother knows the answer. This isn't the first time she's asked.

"Then what does she do?"

"She works in the bar."

"But what does she *want* to do?"

"I don't *know*." She's not going to tell her mother about Nina's supposed memoir. Christine's not likely to be assuaged by that prospect. Besides, Claire has never seen Nina write a word.

"Surely she doesn't want to work in bars for the rest of her life?"

"I don't know, Mum," Claire repeats with a sigh. "I don't ask. It's none of my business."

"By the way, speaking of your friends, Michelle called the house the other day. Why isn't she calling your phone?"

Claire shrugs. She really should call her friend. It's been a month. "Michelle's not so bright," she jokes. "Can we go now?"

"Now that's not true." Christine whisks her bag off the back of her chair and pulls out her purse. "At least she's working toward her future. She'll have a job when she finishes her degree."

"Yes, she will, Mum." Claire ignores the bill the waiter left on the table. Her mother can get it. Payment for pain and suffering. "And I bet she'll have that job for, oh, roughly three years before she's married and pushing out babies instead."

"There's nothing wrong with making the choice to leave work and raise a family, young lady." Her mother slaps some notes on the bill tray. "Not everyone wants or can manage work and a family, you know."

Claire hears the silent "like I did" at the end of that sentence and fights the urge to roll her eyes. Only her mother could make that defence of Michelle into an actual ego stroke for herself. Her mother is a master at making herself look good—in the eyes of her employees and clients. That's how she has gotten so far. If Claire and Cam gave her performance reviews, maybe she wouldn't do so well.

"Well, don't worry, Mum," Claire says cheerfully as they leave the sterile café behind. "I'm much tougher than Michelle. I'll keep working in the bar right up until I give birth to Andrew's crack baby, okay?"

CHAPTER 5

The skinny boy is back. And apparently he's Nina's new best friend.

Claire looks down the length of the bar, cloth in one hand, glass in the other. Nina, for some reason, is leaning over the end of the bar, her arm turned at some crazy angle and laid flat along the surface. He's kneeling on a stool, taking snaps of her arm with his camera.

Claire has absolutely zero idea what they're doing. And if she wasn't so busy watching a couple on one of the most awkward dates ever, she'd probably go find out. For now, though, she has something slightly more entertaining to do.

It's another quiet weeknight in the bar, and Andrew is upstairs watching TV, so they're free to work as little as possible, knowing that he won't pop out of his office at any moment. He'll turn up at the end of the shift, bleary-eyed and cheerful to count the till and lock up.

To stave off complete boredom, she polishes a rack of wine glasses as she surreptitiously watches this guy and girl try to make conversation. They turned up forty-five minutes ago, ordered a bottle of red wine, and sat down in the booth. And for forty-five minutes, Claire has watched, enthralled, as they struggle to find something to say. Maybe, if it wasn't dead tonight, and if the skinny boy wasn't hogging Nina, this date wouldn't be quite as fascinating. For now, however, it's like one of those awful reality shows on late-night TV. Inevitably, she tunes in about halfway through an episode and finds herself idly captured until the end—mostly because she wastes that much time trying to figure out what the hell is going on.

It took her a little while to figure out this was a first date. The bottle of wine threw her off initially. Claire would never make the mistake of ordering a bottle on a first date. She thought everyone knew to always choose a drink that can be disposed of quickly. That way she can get out fast if she needs to. The bottle had to be the girl's idea, too, because he's pawing the glass as if he's never held anything smaller than a pint glass. Totally classy. The girl fills in the many silences by checking her phone and playing with her hair, while he stares longingly at the group of students drinking beer and watching some sport crap on the TV. Yep, their first mistake was coming here.

And now Claire is trying to figure out which of them is going to make a break for it first. When Claire went by before, she took her time to wipe down the table next to theirs, and he was talking in this kind of stupefied drawl as though he's been hit in the head one too many times. Probably a footy player. The girl was politely pretending to be interested, clearly much more socially generous than Claire would ever be. Everything about their interaction, even from this far away, suggests that this date is dead in the water.

She shakes her head and picks up another glass. She would never let it get this far. If she's learned one thing, it's when to cut and leave. Just a few weeks ago, she went out with one of Michelle's friends. The guy was so congenitally boring that she feigned cramps and left nothing but a Claire-shaped dent in her seat before an hour was up. No point wasting time dancing around the edge of something that she's already decided is never going to happen in a million years.

This girl should take a leaf from Claire's dating book. At least that's what she's thinking when the curveball comes. Suddenly, he leans in and says something to the girl. The girl tucks her hair behind her ear, smiles, and nods back at him. Next thing she knows, they pick up their drinks, throw down the last of them, and reach for their belongings. He takes up the half-empty bottle and holds it down low at his side, out of sight. He checks to see if anyone is watching.

Claire quickly glances away. If they are about to do what she thinks they're about to do, suggested by the mutual head-nodding, smiling, and drink-downing, she figures they're going to need as much alcohol as they can get. Who is she to get in their way? *Good freaking luck*, she thinks as the pub door closes behind them.

She shakes her head. She didn't see that one coming. Not one bit.

Now that her entertainment has departed for the night, she wanders to the other end of the bar. Nina is still with the skinny boy, who now seems to be taking photos of her shoulder pressed up against the mirror fixed to the wall.

"Don't worry, Neen, all the glasses are clean. I took care of it." She shoots her friend a dirty look.

"Oh sorry, babe." Nina faces her, contrite, her shoulder still pressed to the mirror. "I'll take out the bins, later, I promise."

"You better." Claire leans against the wall and checks her watch. There's an hour left until they can start to pack up.

The boy takes shots of Nina's shoulder from above. He notices Claire watching them and nods a greeting at her.

"Why are you so weird?" Claire asks him.

"Why are you so judge-y?" He grins; his eyes never leave the viewfinder.

"Because you're so weird." Claire folds her arms. *Obviously.* "So, what are you doing, anyway? Do you purposely come in here for your insanity projects? Or is your whole life like this?"

"Actually, this time I am doing homework," he mutters, staring at his camera's screen. "I'm making the familiar strange."

"Tell me now, am I destined to never know what you are talking about?"

"Probably." He moves around to the entrance of the bar to take a different shot. "But that won't be my fault." He grins again as he captures the silhouette of Nina's shoulder and neck.

"Yes it will."

He ignores her and turns to Nina. "Can you lift up your arm and hold it until I tell you to put it down?"

Nina obediently complies. Claire leaves them to serve a customer and then returns to the scene of the crazy. Nina is still holding up her arm, wincing a little but remaining stoic. He takes a few more shots and then sets the camera on the bar.

"You can put your arm down now. Thank you so much, honey."

Nina lets her arm drop. "That kind of hurt. But it's all in the name of art, right?"

"Art?" Claire is doubtful.

The boy ignores her and sits on his stool. "It's for class, actually. We have to take photos that make parts of the body unrecognisable. Totally conceptual," he says in a faux-wanky art voice. "You probably wouldn't get it." He gives Claire a look that says he's fully aware she probably does get it, but he can't stop digging at her.

"I gotta do some work." Nina rubs her shoulder and wanders away.

"Yes." Claire glares at her. "You do."

"I'm Robbie, by the way."

Claire nods.

"I think you're supposed to tell me your name. Just a suggestion. Social niceties and all."

"You don't seem to be into them, that's all."

He chuckles. "Fair enough."

She caves. "I'm Claire." She can't help it. She kind of likes this guy even if he is a smart-ass.

"Claire," he says, contemplative, as though he's considering whether he'll accept it as a suitable name for her. Not as if he doesn't believe her, more that he's trying to figure out if it sounds right. Then he nods and shrugs slightly as if he finally, silently, accepts it as her name.

"Where's your friend?" She empties a few of the glasses that Nina has stacked on the bar in front of her and puts them in the rack. "The geeky one who reads in bars?"

"I don't know." He sips his beer. "Probably at home studying because she's way more well behaved than me."

"Yes, she did seem very well behaved."

"Don't judge her, missy." He holds up his glass, a silent request for another beer. "She is one of my favourite people in the whole world."

"Yeah, but she's not mine, so I can." Claire takes his glass and pours him another. "Besides," she says over her shoulder. "Anyone would seem well behaved sitting next to you."

"Except you maybe."

Claire smiles. He's probably right.

"So what do you do, anyway?" Claire asks as she returns with his beer.

He holds up his camera. "I do this. I study photography."

"You're going to do it for a living?"

"I hope so." He scrapes his blond hair back with his fingers. "Though I'll probably have to work a crappy commercial job to support it, you know?"

Claire nods, although she doesn't really know anything about photography. "What do you take photos of? Body parts?"

"No, that was for class. We're working on form. I like taking pictures of people." He sips his beer. "Whole people. What about you? What are you going to do?"

Claire tips her head back and sighs. "I just spent the day with my mother, and that was the subject *du jour*. Please don't ask me that. Something easier," she begs.

"Okay." He laughs. "Let's start small then. Star sign?"

CHAPTER 6

Bored, Claire fades out of the conversation. Instead, she stares out the window of the university café and watches the world shuffle by. She stifles a yawn and hopes this will be over soon. The catch-up lunches Michelle organises are becoming less and less fun.

Claire already knows she needs a life plan. As a matter of urgency. Now she is also starting to think she might need some new friends too.

"Hel-lo? Claire?"

"What?" She's yanked back to the table and to her three friends staring at her.

"Where did you go?" Michelle asks.

"We were asking why you quit working at that bar in the city?" Kate checks her teeth with her phone's camera.

"I don't know." Claire shrugs. "Mostly because the boss was evil, among other things."

"Oh." Kerry frowns. "Pity. Now we can't get on the door list anymore."

Claire shoots her a look. "So I should stay in a crappy job just so you can get discounted drinks, should I?" She throws her napkin onto her empty plate.

Kerry, suitably contrite, shakes her head and looks down at her plate. "Of course not, I just—"

"Hey, how great was that place where Tara had her drinks the other night?" Michelle cuts in with a change of subject, always the one to defuse any tension. "I loved it."

"Me too." Kerry's eyes brighten. "I loved…"

Claire stops listening again as Kerry pipes up. Why should she listen? She wasn't even there. She was at work. As usual. She pushes her plate away and looks around the room, bored again.

This is exactly why she hardly ever bothers to meet them anymore even though they continue to invite her. All they talk about is what they did last night or about their mutual friends. And Claire was fine with that in high school, when she actually did the same things as them, but now...

If she wasn't so bored with the idea of going to clubs with them, she'd probably feel left out. The other three are doing the same course in business and majoring in tourism—mostly because Kate and Kerry are such freaking sheep they wouldn't know what they wanted without Michelle. Even now, in their second year, they still take nearly all the same courses.

She watches them talk but can't bring herself to tune back in. She won't know who or what they're talking about anyway. They have less in common all the time. The fact that Claire studies something else is just one more wedge between them. Last year, when Brendan still came home on the weekends and Claire didn't work as much, they all saw each other more, clinging to old high school social formations. Now, with the list of things they have in common shrinking by the moment, there's not much left. They stubbornly hold on to each other for the sake of a shared history, but one that is undermined by a growing, mutual disinterest.

Claire knows she shouldn't be surprised. Not if she really thinks about it. Their friendship in high school was created around their shared schedules and similar social rankings. Of all them, Claire only genuinely likes Michelle. Their friendship consolidated in the last years of high school when they started going out with Brendan and Jack who are best friends. Michelle is nice and smart and funny, and sometimes, when they're together in a small group, Michelle actually has something to say.

But Kate and Kerry? They just came with the Michelle package, and Claire put up with them—puts up with them—because she has no choice. It kills her that those two twits look down on her and her degree. Even with their brain cells pooled, Claire could outsmart them in a second. Still, they seem to think what they're doing is better than what she's doing. Maybe it's because there's the certainty of a job after graduation. It doesn't matter if they barely make it through their studies or if the job is in a partitioned cubicle inside a shiny building somewhere. Just because they can scrape a pass in Fundamentals of Finance doesn't make them better than her.

She looks at their outfits as they talk and shakes her head slightly. At least they give her plenty of fodder to make fun of them. Recently, they dress as though they work in an office already. They put on fitted skirts and jackets for class, trying desperately to look the part. Kate, of course, takes it too far as usual. She bypasses corporate wear and lurches directly to borderline business slutty with her partially unbuttoned shirt and porn-length skirt. And Kerry, who barely breaks the five-foot barrier, looks more like a kid playing dress up.

"Claire, what are you up to this weekend?" Michelle tries once again to drag her back into the conversation.

"Working. And catching up with Cam. He's back from that training thing."

In truth, she probably won't be hanging out with her brother because he's back to work after the week's holiday, on night shift. She just wants to mention him as payback to Kerry, who has harboured a mammoth crush on him for the last three years. Squat, blonde, and bland, Claire knows Cam wouldn't look twice at Kerry, and that's if he actually registers her existence at all. Kerry is too sane for Cam.

But she also tells them that because she has too much pride to admit she'll probably do nothing.

"Well, if you're around on Friday, come to Steph Habic's party with us." Michelle scoops up another forkful of her pasta.

"Maybe." Claire barely remembers Steph from school.

"I can't stay too late, though, because I have to hit the road early in the morning," Michelle says as she puts down her fork. Then she flinches and sneaks a look at Claire. "Sorry."

"It's fine." Claire frowns. "You can say you're going up to see Jack. I'm okay."

Certain she's blushing, Claire looks down at her hands in her lap because she doesn't want to meet anyone's gaze. Pity about why she broke up with Brendan actually feels worse than the actual breakup.

"I know, but still..." Michelle falters.

"It's been months." Claire raises her hands to stop Michelle. "I'm over it," she tells them, unsure if it's the truth or not.

"Really? You were going out for, like, over two years." Kerry raises an eyebrow.

Claire glares at Kerry. Why is she always so *annoying*? Besides, what would she know? She's never even had a proper boyfriend. "I know that." She throws her a look. "I was there, remember?"

"Anyway..." Michelle reaches over and plucks at her sleeve. "Trust me; she's not even close to as good looking as you. And she's kind of—"

"What?" Claire lifts her head, surprised, and stares at Michelle. "You've met her?"

"Uh, yeah," Michelle says as she tucks her dark hair behind her ear. "Because of Jack and Brendan. I, uh, see her sometimes when I go up and visit."

Claire stares for a moment as she absorbs this disturbing new piece of information. She draws in a deep breath to steady herself. Why hasn't she considered this possibility? Of course Michelle's freaking double dating with Brendan's new girlfriend. They're probably friends by now too. That was how Claire and Michelle became friends, wasn't it? Why should it be any different with this girl?

Claire breathes slowly, trying to dull the roar of blood in her ears. She cannot believe she was so busy getting over Brendan's betrayal that she didn't think of this smaller, yet equally significant act of disloyalty at the hand of her closest friend. "So, what? Do you all go out together?" She narrows her eyes. Michelle won't be able to lie to her. She's terrible at it.

Michelle drops her hands to her lap. "Uh, well, we've been out to dinner a few times and to some parties, I guess."

"You guess?" Claire shoots back. "Exactly when did you meet her?" For a moment Claire's mind flashes back to a day, years ago at her mother's work, when her mother had placed ten-year-old Claire at the end of a large table as she interviewed one of her clients to prepare him for court. Claire watched, enthralled as her mother launched questions, one after the other, until the poor guy was dizzied and exhausted. Her mother had wanted the answers, though. Claire isn't sure she does. But, driven by her hurt, she doesn't know how *not* to ask them either.

"I don't know." Michelle shrugs, helpless now. "A while back?"

"So you are just, what, hanging out with her now?" Claire looks out the window as anger and embarrassment build a great red wall around her. Tears threaten, pricking the back of her eyes. She cannot look at Kerry or at Kate, who she knows are watching carefully, probably equally alarmed and excited by this hint of drama. "And you didn't think you should tell me?"

Michelle doesn't respond straightaway. She looks terrified as if she might be about to cry too.

"Hey, Claire, come on, quit making her feel bad." Kate leans forward. "What is she supposed to do? She's—"

"Stay out of it." Claire growls at her.

Kate slides back in her seat as though she's been stretched out on a sling and shot into the chair. She obediently shuts her mouth.

Claire turns back to Michelle. Whether she likes it or not, Kate's defence has somehow enticed her to pull the reigns. She musters the last shreds of her Pearson dignity and pushes her chair back. "You know what? Do whatever you want." She says it quietly as she pulls money out of her pocket. She points at her so-called friend. "Just know that I would never, ever do that to you without telling you. You should have *told* me." She blinks fiercely at the embarrassing slick of tears. She puts her money gently on the table and strides out of the café without another word.

And no one calls after her either.

When she makes it out the door and onto the street, she doesn't stop walking. She numbly pushes through the crush of people trying to get back to work, not caring who she knocks or who knocks her. She bites down on her lip and wills away the tears—tears that have sprung as much from humiliation as from hurt. She will not give in to them.

She feels like a complete idiot. And she hates to feel like an idiot. And she really, really hates to look like an idiot. Not only has Michelle broken the girl code, but she also gave the other two a new reason to look down their cerebrally challenged noses at her.

Great. She flinches as a suit bumps her in the side as he charges down the street. Now, not only do they think she's a loser for waiting on people and for not really knowing what she wants to do with her life, but they also feel sorry for her because her ex-boyfriend is a giant asshole and her supposed best friend doesn't care enough to show a little loyalty. And that is something she cannot bear.

CHAPTER 7

Exhausted, Claire and Nina march along the damp street, faces not yet entirely clear of last night's makeup. A shared umbrella partially protects them from the relentless drifting rain. The sky is a sodden mass today. It sags around their ears like a ceiling of endless grey over the city. It's not too cold, but it is miserable enough to match their moods.

Claire could really use a few more hours of sleep. And she shouldn't be in the city either. She's supposed to go home and get ready for a lunch at her aunt Lucy's, but she can't bring herself to go anywhere near her mother just yet. She knows sudden, un-caffeinated contact with Christine will not end well. So Nina, ever helpful, is finally taking her to the coffee place she's been raving about to fortify Claire for her afternoon of family fun.

Last night at the pub was a late one. By the time they shut the doors, trudged back to Nina's flat to watch some crappy TV, and then fall asleep, it was the early hours of morning. Then, just to make the situation worse, Claire woke up a couple of hours later when Nina's boyfriend, Josh, barrelled into the apartment, drunk and raucous, some time just before dawn. He didn't notice her ensconced on the couch at first and had turned on all the lights and the television. When he realised she was asleep there, he backed into the bedroom and apologised profusely. It was the most he'd said to her in ages.

Josh is always a bit weird with her. She's not sure why, but he mostly ignores her. Or when he does talk, he barely says three words. Maybe he doesn't like how often she stays. But Claire doesn't worry too much because Nina tells her Josh has no say as he barely pays rent. He doesn't get to care.

And anyway, Claire's happy to ignore him. He's an idiot who studies personal training, and he's obnoxious and full of himself—one of those types who thinks he doesn't need charm because he's got a six-pack and a car. He doesn't realise none of this negates the fact that he's a giant tool.

And the weird thing is Nina seems to know he's an idiot. At least she always calls him one but in a fond, long-suffering way. It's as if she knows her boyfriend is less than desired, but she can't be bothered to do anything about it. Claire isn't sure if it's because Nina likes to have a guy around or because she doesn't expect better for herself. Either is kind of sad, really, especially considering she's great. Claire's pretty sure she could do a lot better than this human void.

"Here we are." Nina yanks open the door of the café, and they hurry out of the rain. It seems everyone else had the same idea, because the place is packed. The café is a long, narrow, white space with high ceilings, crammed with bench tables and metal stools—every seat seems to be occupied by the damp crowds drinking coffee. The windows are completely steamed up, blocking the view of the street outside. It feels as if they've entered a loud, crowded cave.

"It's kind of full." Claire thrusts her hands in the pockets of her new jacket. "Should we go somewhere else?" Not that she really wants to go back out in this weather.

"It's always like this." Nina cranes her neck to scan the length of the room. "Let's see if there's room closer to the back." She leads them through the room, squeezing between tables as she moves toward the counter.

"Hey!" It's Robbie. He grins as he holds several coffees expertly in his hands. He looks as conservative as he probably gets, wearing clean black jeans and a black T-shirt with the café name on it in white letters. "Come for coffee? There are some seats by the machine." He gestures to the area behind him and then holds up the coffees. "I'll take these and be right back."

They find seats at the end of the long counter and climb onto the stools. Claire presses her hands to the back of the machine, absorbing its warmth.

"How are you, honey?" Robbie is back, hands free, and wrapping his arm around Nina's shoulder. "Glad you came."

"I've been telling Claire how good the coffee is, so I brought her." Nina leans her arms on the counter.

He turns to Claire and slowly raises an eyebrow. "I didn't think you'd be able to go out in the daylight. I thought you'd turn into a little pile of ashes." Then he grins and leans in to give her a kiss on the cheek.

"Hilarious," she mutters, simultaneously rendered shy and slightly flattered. She's not used to people like Robbie, for whom affection seems to be second nature even with people he doesn't know that well.

He turns to Nina. "I'm buying your coffee. Payment for modelling the other night." He stands on his tiptoes and looks over the coffee machine. "Hey, Mia?" he calls. "You remember these two from the bar? You know, the place on Monteith Street?"

The girl who came into the pub with him last week sticks her head out from behind the machine. Her hair is tied back into a neat ponytail. "Yeah, I know the one. I don't go to quite as many bars as you, remember?" She turns and smiles warmly at Claire and Nina, her eyes crinkling. "Hi there."

"Yes, Mia," he snarks with a grin. "You *are* better than me in every way possible. Anyway, I owe Nina, so don't charge them, okay?"

Mia nods and ducks behind the machine.

"I better get back to work." Robbie whips a pen from behind his ear. "Tell me what you want, and I'll put your order in. The guy working your section is useless." He rolls his eyes. "Beautiful, but useless."

They order their coffees, and he leaves them to it and disappears into the mass of tables.

Nina is telling Claire about the trip she has planned to visit her giant hippie family in Northern New South Wales when Josh turns up. He slides his arms around Nina's shoulders and kisses her loudly on the neck.

"Hey." He growls in a voice he probably thinks is sexy. He nods at Claire.

She nods back and tries not to roll her eyes at his sudden, unwelcome appearance.

"Hi," Nina croons as she wraps her arms around his waist. "You got my message. I thought you'd still be asleep."

"Nah, I wanted to see you before I go to training." He takes a hold of her ponytail and kisses her again.

Claire sighs. That's it. Intelligent conversation over. She turns the other way. These two are huge fans of gross, prolonged PDAs, and she's been a reluctant witness to enough of it to know what to expect. She sips her coffee, which is as good as Nina promised, and checks out the stickers and comics stuck to the back of the machine.

"Hey, mind if I sit?"

Claire looks up. It's Mia. She stands next to the last available stool in the row by Claire with a tiny cup in her hand.

"Break," she explains.

"Yes, please." Claire rolls her eyes. "Save me from this grotesque display." She tips her head toward Nina and Josh.

Mia unties her apron, puts her cup on the counter, and climbs onto the stool. Then she leans over and rests her chin on her folded arms.

"Over it?" Claire asks her. It can't even be midday yet.

Mia nods without lifting her head. "You know what the worst part about this job is?"

"What?"

She turns to face Claire and frowns. Mia has a small smattering of freckles across her nose and cheeks. "Having to make hungover, tired, and needy people feel better when you are hungover, tired, and needy yourself."

Claire smiles. She knows this game well—the hospitality whingefest. And she has plenty of ammo too by now. "Yeah, well, in my job, you watch people being all happy, getting drunk, and having a weekend when you want to be happy, get drunk, and have a weekend. That also sucks."

Mia nods. "But at least they're happy customers. Some days I see half of Melbourne before they've had their first coffee. And let me tell you, this city is moody in the morning."

"Well, you know," Claire counters, always happy to go for the one-up in the my-job-sucks game. She and Cam play it all the time. "Sometimes a person can get too happy, you know? I've seen someone so happy with the combination of margaritas and a Friday that she vomited in her own shoes." Claire leans forward. "Not on, Mia. In."

"Oh okay. Gross." She sips her coffee. "This game of who's got it worse could go on forever, but maybe we should just agree our lives of servitude mutually suck."

"Or we could just agree that I won, because grumpy, coffee-deprived people have nothing on vomit in shoes."

Mia grins at her.

And Claire grins right back. "Just saying."

Mia nods slowly, conceding to Claire's win. She tips her head back and drains the last of her coffee.

"I don't want to get all up in your business, Mia, especially considering we just met." Claire pulls a face and points at her cup. "But maybe if you are so exhausted, you should consider graduating to a big-kid coffee?"

Mia contemplates the teeny espresso cup as she spins it around on the counter. "Yeah, but if I had a bigger coffee, I wouldn't be able to drink as many in a shift. I'm not sure what a caffeine overdose would be like, but I bet it's not pretty."

"Probably not."

"So I'll stick to small doses and lots of them, thanks."

"Drip feed. Fair enough." Claire is stirring, anyway, because this girl seems up for it. And Claire's always up for it.

Claire's just about to ask what Mia does when she's not working when a tall guy with some seriously stupid facial hair comes around the counter. Claire can't help staring at him. He must spend hours with his shaver. Seriously, where do some people get their ideas about what looks good?

"Uh, hey, Mia, I just wanted you to know that I adjusted the grind," he says in this kind of worldly, hipper-than-thou monotone. "So you might notice, you know, that it's pouring a touch slower, but I think you'll find you're getting more *crema* on the pour."

"Okay, thanks." Mia smiles politely at him. "I'll be back in a couple of minutes."

"No problem, take your time." He disappears behind the machine.

"Should I have any idea what he was talking about?" Claire asks.

"He was just talking about the coffee."

"So, you like, actually make the stuff? That's like top of the café pecking order, right? What do they call you people again?"

"A barista—if you want to be a giant wanker." Mia rolls her eyes. "And some people really are when it comes to coffee."

"It is Melbourne. We are known for being a city of coffee snobs."

"Yeah but some people," Mia looks around as if she's afraid hipster boy might hear, "act as though making a decent latte is the highest form of art. It's not." She rests her chin on her hand and frowns. "It's just basic science, compensation between pressure, heat, and volume. That's all."

"Wow, Mia. Just...wow." Claire giggles. "That was an awesomely nerdy way of asserting your superiority."

Mia laughs and climbs off her stool. "I like to have both a heightened sense of superiority *and* inferiority at any given time. Keeps me balanced. I better get back to work." But she just stands there as if she's reluctant to leave her break just yet. "What are you doing today?"

Claire sighs. "I'm going to lunch at my aunt's. Which basically means three hours, give or take, of watching her and my mother argue."

"The whole time?"

"Yeah, pretty much, if you include the parts when they pretend they're not arguing. We might get anywhere between ten minutes to half an hour of peace at the start, but then it will be game on for sure."

"What do they fight about?"

"Anything. Everything." Claire sighs. "Well, after much workshopping, my brother and I have decided it's basically all part of one big meta-fight over who is the better daughter, sister, mother, and human in general."

"Wow, that sounds—"

"So, how many names has she called you?" Robbie stops behind Mia and leans his chin on her shoulder.

"None, actually, that I can remember." Mia frowns, reaches up, and pats his cheek. "Oh no, I lied—she called me a nerd. But it was kind of justified."

"Shush. Don't tell her she's right," Robbie says to Mia and winks at Claire. "I suspect it only feeds her." He strides away.

"He's so charming."

"Yeah, no wonder you two get along so well." Mia picks up Claire's empty coffee cup and saucer.

"Excuse me?" Claire cocks an eyebrow at her.

"You two are kind of alike."

"Shouldn't you be going back to work?" Claire says pointedly.

"Yes, yes, I should. See you. Have fun at your aunt's," she tells her, a parting return shot.

"Oh, now that's just mean." Claire groans. She checks her phone. Yep, it's time.

CHAPTER 8

It's as if they're caught in a bizarre staring triangle. Claire wants to laugh, but she's pretty sure now is not the time.

Her mother stands behind her chair, staring at Leo with her hands on her hips, nostrils flaring. Leo, however, focuses on Claire. Well, Claire's hair to be exact. He picks up the brittle strands, runs them between his fingers, and then drops them again. Claire simply leans back in the seat, arms folded across her chest. She stares at both of them via the mirror and waits.

"So, can you do something?" her mother asks as she taps her boot against the floor. Claire fights the urge to roll her eyes. Why does her mother have to be such a drama queen?

Leo doesn't answer straight away. He examines her hair closely, his lips pursed and his brow furrowed.

Claire watches him as a way to avoid looking at her hair. She'd never admit it to her mother, but it looks awful. Really awful. Yesterday, she had her regular hair, the long light-brown, almost-but-not-quite-blonde hair, hanging down past her shoulders the way it has since she was a small girl. Today, she has a hot mess of bleach-damaged blonde pretending to be hair. And it's not a consistent blonde either. It runs a rainbow of shades, from white to straw yellow. There are even some parts where the bleach missed and her old hair shows through. Not to mention, it's taken on a strange new frizziness. It's *not* pretty.

"Why, Claire? Why?" her mother asks wearily for the eighteenth time this afternoon.

"I don't know." Claire shrugs for the eighteenth time this afternoon and stares mutinously at the mirror. "Because blondes have more fun?" she suggests because she knows it will irritate her mother.

It does. Christine lets out a huff and turns sideways. She closes her eyes for a moment as if she can't even bear to look at her.

Actually, Claire did it because Nina was dying her streaks at the apartment yesterday and asked if she could experiment with Claire's hair. And Claire was bored and hungover and pre-menstrually frustrated enough with the epic sameness that is her life to say yes on a whim. Annoying her mother is a pleasant, surprise side effect.

Christine doesn't like the new look one bit. Exactly ten minutes passed between her laying eyes on Claire's newly bleached tresses and making an appointment with her own hairdresser to fix the "appalling, cheap mess." Two hours later, Claire was at the salon being presented to Leo, a middle-aged, rounded man with perfect, bleached hair.

"Leo," Christine asks again, eyes still closed. "What can you do? It's a mess, isn't it?"

Leo continues to inspect Claire's hair. "We have options here," he tells her through the mirror. "The problem is how much the bleach damaged it. We can cut it back, dye it, and start again. Maybe a new pixie do or something?"

Claire looks at him wide-eyed and shakes her head. She does not want to lose *all* her hair for this dumb mistake. "Or?" she asks.

"We dye it properly, treat the hell out of it, try to get it back to some semblance of healthy looking, and give it less of a cut."

"I don't really care, just make her look like a child I raised," Christine says impatiently. "Whatever it costs."

Leo turns to her mother and takes her arm. "Christine, hon, don't worry, I'll take care of it. I've always taken care of you, haven't I?"

"Yes, but then I've never done anything like that...that atrocity." Christine jabs a maroon fingernail in Claire's direction.

Claire shakes her head. Someone would think she shaved a swear word into her head or something the way her mother is acting.

"No, of course you haven't." Leo soothes as he places a hand on her shoulder. "But I'm sure you did something foolish when you were young. We all did. Listen, this is going to take a couple of hours. Why don't you go run some errands or go get a relaxing massage? We'll call you when it's done. No point you being made to hang around here."

Claire stares hopefully at her mother's reflection as she considers this option. Eventually, Christine turns to her and wags her finger again. "I'm going to do some shopping. Call me when you're done. And you do as Leo advises, okay? We know what happens when *you* make decisions about your appearance." She gives Leo a wave and heads for the door.

He waves back, smiling widely as she stalks out of the salon, and then turns back to Claire. He rolls his eyes and lets out a sigh.

Claire's eyes widen. She wasn't expecting *that*. She thought Leo was her mum's obedient hair lapdog, especially after the way he has been tut-tutting over her hair.

"Sorry." He places his hands on her shoulders. "I couldn't think straight with her breathing down my neck."

"Welcome to my life."

"Okay." He places one hand on his hip. "So what do you want, Claire?"

She sucks in a deep breath and lets out a voluptuous sigh. "Not to have done this to my hair?"

"Well, that's a given. But you know, Oprah or someone said a crisis can be an opportunity in disguise. So, if you've been feeling like a change, now is your moment to go big. With supervision this time, of course," he adds hurriedly.

Claire chews on her lip. Of course she feels like a change. That's what got her in this mess in the first place. She just doesn't know what she wants to change to.

"And if you're not sure where to go, I have an idea for you."

"What?"

He trots over to the coffee table at the front of the salon and hunts through the pile of magazines in the centre until he finds the one he's looking for. He flicks through the pages as he walks back. "Here." He holds the open magazine in front of her. "This would be fantastic on you."

It's a picture of a model with a longish bob that falls halfway between her jaw and her shoulders. Her hair is dyed a deep reddish brown, and her fringe is cut in a straight line over her eyebrows. Claire likes the fierce look instantly.

"You could definitely carry that dark colour—but no darker, probably." Leo scrutinises her via the mirror again, still holding the magazine in front of her. "And that warm colour would be fabulous with those blue eyes of yours."

She stares at it longer, even though she has already pretty much decided. She wants to look like *that*—sleek and dramatic.

"My mum is probably *not* going to like it," she says warily.

Leo gives her a conspiratorial grin. "Show me a haircut that woman *has* liked, sweetheart, and I'll show you the unicorn eating grass in our backyard. It's your hair. Will you like it?"

She stares at the image. "I'll like it."

"Are you game?"

Claire nods. *Why the hell not?* "I'm game."

CHAPTER 9

Claire doesn't recognise the small, green, hire car parked behind her mother's in the driveway. In fact, all she really registers is the annoying fact that the blue car means her mother is home.

She sighs, turns off the ignition and drops her head against the headrest. She needs a minute to prepare herself for a Sunday morning dose of her mother. She is not in the mood. Not today.

Last night was another crappy night. At work it was so busy they had to scramble to get through the shift even with Andrew's help. Then afterward, they went to a party hosted by one of Josh's friends. Claire didn't want to go, but Nina begged, and because she needed her couch for the night, Claire caved. The party wasn't bad, no worse than many she's gone to lately, but it wasn't great either.

After the party, though, everything went to hell. Drunk and exhausted, Nina crawled straight into bed the minute they got back to the flat. But Josh didn't. In fact, he went from his usual silent act to being all friendly and insisting he was too awake to go to bed and that they should watch a film. Next thing Claire knew, he opened a beer and settled onto the other end of the couch, remote in hand. Claire didn't feel as if she could refuse because it was more his apartment than hers. But she definitely did her best to let him know she was not into the idea at all.

Instead of being the mute, grunting freak he usually is around her, he got all chatty and friendly and tried to make conversation. She's not sure if it was the booze that unlocked his jaw, but it was incredibly annoying. First, it was just generic chitchat about school, about sport, about anything. And no matter how much Claire, taken hostage by this sudden social assault, tried to freeze him out, he talked and talked and talked while she covetously eyed the blankets folded up in the corner.

Then to make things worse, he suddenly moved into disturbing, over-share territory. He talked about Nina and how he was tired of being in a long-term relationship and how he and Nina probably weren't right for each other. To top it off, he threw her meaningful looks between these confessions, looks that confirmed that what Claire thought *might* be happening was *definitely* happening. Claire ended the situation right then and there.

Claire stares at her parents' brick, suburban house. It's impossible for her to fathom his level of stupidity. He has exactly the right combination of mammoth ego and lack of brainpower to actually believe she'd be into him. And he took it as fact that she would go behind a friend's back for the opportunity. It's as mind-boggling as Josh is repugnant.

She reaches for her bag on the passenger seat floor and shakes her head. The thing that Claire can't figure out is how many girls must've given this guy the right amount of ego strokes for his head to get this outsized.

Both grossed and freaked out, she considered getting up immediately and driving home, but she knew she drank way too much at the party. Instead, she let loose the *bitchkrieg* on him in the loudest, most threatening whisper she could muster. She told him he was a creep, and that, given his complete absence of brains and charm, he should consider himself lucky to have landed someone like Nina, let alone managed to keep her. Then she graciously informed him that, if he shut the hell up and went to bed right that moment, she'd consider not telling Nina. That was the last she saw of him.

When she woke on the couch this morning to that grossly uncomfortable memory, she got up as quickly as possible and got the hell out of there before anyone else surfaced.

She didn't want to see Nina, either, because now she has to decide whether to tell her about it. Not just that he'd come on to her but about the way he talked about Nina, about their relationship. How can she tell a friend something like that and still stay friends?

She sighs, clutching her keys in her hand. Why the hell hasn't Nina figured this out for herself already? She pushes the car door open, climbs out, and drags her feet up the driveway. She shoves open the front door and lets it fall shut behind her. No point being quiet at this time of morning. Her parents are both well and truly up by now.

She tosses her bag on the couch and heads straight for the coffee. Not even the voices coming from the kitchen—one of them definitely her mother's—is going to stand between her and caffeine right now.

The minute she sees Claire in the doorway, Moira is out of her seat like a shot, hurrying over and enfolding her in a tight hug.

"Hello," she croons, stepping back and appraising Claire, her bright-green eyes affectionately lit. "How's my girl? You look well."

"So do you." Claire smiles widely. If she'd known Moira was in Melbourne, she would have come inside faster.

And her mother's best friend does look good, a little rounder, maybe. She hasn't aged like Christine has of late, gathering lines around her eyes and mouth. Moira's hair is still that rich red, shot through with only a little grey.

"And would you look at that hair?" Moira runs a hand over Claire's sleek new bob. "It's fantastic."

"You should have seen it when she first had it done." Christine taps her fingernails against the coffee machine. "It was *awful*."

Claire gives her mother a look. Even though it's the weekend, Christine, of course, looks immaculate, dressed in crisp jeans and light blue shirt with her blonde hair tied in a pert ponytail. All she needs is a sweater thrown over her shoulders, and she'd be perfect for the part of soccer mum.

Moira ignores Christine's comment. She presses a hand against Claire's cheek, smiling warmly at her. "Still as beautiful as ever." She climbs back onto her stool. "Oh, why didn't I have a daughter?" She sighs and shakes her head. "All those boys."

"I don't know, Moi." Christine pulls a carton of milk from the refrigerator. "There was a few moments there when I'd have taken on all three of those boys over one fifteen-year-old girl."

Moira smiles at her and turns back to Claire. "How's your brother?"

Claire opens her mouth to tell her about Cam's return from police training, but her mother interjects again. "He was staying here," she says, busily opening and closing cupboards. "But we haven't seen him much this week. The kids treat this place like it's a hotel."

Claire rolls her eyes, but Moira acts as though she didn't even hear Christine and pats the stool next to her. "Sit with me a minute, sweetheart. Tell me what you've been up to."

"Nothing much at all, I'm afraid," Christine says.

"Oh, pipe down, you," Moira chides. "I'm talking to Claire."

Claire giggles as she sits on the stool and leans her arms on the counter. Thank God for Moi.

Moira takes the cup Christine slides over to her and heaps in a spoonful of sugar from the bowl. "Thanks, Chrissy. How are your studies, Claire?"

"Good," Claire says as her mother puts a coffee in front of her.

"And your mum says you're working in a pub in town?"

"Yep," Claire glances at Christine. The less she says about it in front of her mother the better.

Just as Christine sits down with her own coffee, her phone rings. She frowns, abandons the cup, and snatches up her phone. With the phone to her ear, she walks out of the room, talking in that clipped, serious voice that tells Claire it's work on the other end.

"Your mother told me about Brendan."

Claire sighs. *Really?* Why did her mother have to talk about her business?

"Little dickhead." Moira shakes her head and blows on her coffee.

Claire can't help but laugh. She forgot about Moira's mouth, always "colourful," as her dad used to say. And that's why Moira is one of Claire's favourite people. Moira has a sense of both reality and comedy that Christine lacks. Claire has to admit that it feels good to hear someone call Brendan a dickhead even six months later.

"And let me guess, your ma is hounding you about dropping to part-time at uni?"

Claire nods. "I just couldn't focus."

"I know, hon." Moira pats her hand. She stares out the sliding glass door into the thready morning sunlight. "Don't worry about your mum. Just keep doing what you're doing, which is fine."

Claire nods, aware that Moira is thinking of one of her own boys. Sam, probably, who has "gone off the rails" in Adelaide, as her mother calls it. He lost it after his father's accident, and he never got it back, apparently. The last time Claire saw him, a couple of years ago, he barely said a word, a complete stranger from the cute, bigmouthed ginger he used to be.

"So, what are you doing in Melbourne?" Claire asks. "Are the boys here too?"

"No. I'm here for work, to help set up the holiday program at the new community centre. The boys are back home with my mum."

"How are they?" Claire thinks about the boys, who were like cousins when they were all younger, when Gary was still alive and they lived two streets away. They stayed at the holiday house together every summer. She misses them. But she misses Moira especially. She is the perfect antidote to her own mother.

"They're fine," Moira says simply.

"What are you and Mum doing today?" Claire changes the subject because clearly they are not fine, and Moi doesn't want to talk about it.

"We're going to the gallery and then to lunch. Want to come with us? Get some culture?"

"You have no idea how little I want to do that with Mum." Claire rests her chin on her hands. All she wants to do is go back to bed and maybe watch a movie.

Moira chuckles and nods.

"I am happy to see you, though."

"Oh, it's good to see you too." Moi wraps an arm around Claire's shoulder. "What are you going to do with your summer?"

"I don't know really. Work. Save some money?" She has no idea what she'll do this summer. All she knows is she cannot wait for it to come.

"They need a ton of help at the new centre if you find yourself at loose ends."

Claire nods. "Okay." She slowly traces the marbled pattern on the kitchen counter with her finger. "You know, Mum still wants me to transfer into law."

"Of course she does." Moira chuckles as she climbs off her stool and takes her cup to the sink. "The question is, do you?"

"I don't know."

"Well, it should be up to you."

"I know." She's just about to ask Moira about her new job when her mother marches into the kitchen and picks up her abandoned coffee. She tips it into the sink.

"Shall we get going?" Christine asks briskly.

"Yes, we'd better," Moira agrees.

Christine turns on Claire as she pulls out her sunglasses and puts them on her head. "And what are you going to do with your Sunday, young lady? I hope you won't be lying around all day."

"I'm—"

"Oh, leave her alone, Chrissy." Moira scoffs. "Stop nagging. She's nineteen. She's young. She can lie around on a Sunday if she wants to. All day. Let's go."

Christine doesn't say a word. She just hooks her bag onto her shoulder and gives Moira a look. Claire grins. Moira is the only person in the world who can shut her mother up.

Moira comes around the counter and folds Claire into another tight hug. "Ignore your mother," she says, loud enough for Christine to hear, and kisses her on the cheek. "It's wonderful to see you."

CHAPTER 10

The hangover that set in upon waking made a swift mess of Claire's day, and it's only midday. It doesn't help that it's been a day sans caffeine. That's never good. She has no idea how she even made it to uni on time.

That's the beauty of nights spent on a sofa. Even if she were willing to skip class, it's difficult to have a luxurious sleep-in on a lumpy, narrow couch. Even more difficult given that she woke to dry-mouthed, head-aching horror.

When she found out that Josh was away visiting his brother, Claire agreed to hang out with Nina, knowing there would be no awkward encounters at the end of the night. She hasn't told Nina about what happened with Josh last week, and she probably won't. Nina needs to figure it out for herself. Or maybe Claire doesn't know how to bring it up. Either way, she's said nothing, and she's reasonably certain Josh hasn't either.

So, last night she let Nina drag her out. Apparently, it's perfectly normal to go out on a Monday night and get messy. How did it take her until second year to learn that?

And now she's paying for the lesson.

Her first hour at uni is spent in a lecture. Fortunately, that means watching a documentary about the Industrial Revolution in Britain. The last part of class is spent listening to their crusty old lecturer explain that the term "Industrial Revolution" is a misnomer. *Way to bury the lead.* Claire smirks to herself, one eye held open in case he says something important.

She has French class straight after, and it's not as easy to hide. She tries to maintain a low profile as she writes down everything, yet takes in nothing. When she's asked a rapid-fire question in French, she becomes confused and gives the wrong answer completely. Cue red face. People snicker, and her teacher looks at her as if that's all he expects of her anyway.

That's all she expects of this teacher, too, though. Middle-aged and perennially bad tempered, he seems to exist in a constant state of unimpressed. And Claire is too disappointed in him to care. She has gone from being a star in her high school French class, to adequate in first year, to being barely tolerated in second year. To make it worse, her one friend in this class—a sleepy sounding, quietly hilarious exchange student from the States—went home because his semester-long visit was done. Now she's on her own, and she can't be bothered to try to impress this teacher. She'll just do what she did last year, study like hell and ace the exams. Then it won't matter what she does in class.

As soon as she's released from the stuffy room, she makes a beeline for the student-run coffee cart in the courtyard. Again she asks herself why she thought it was a good idea to go out on a Monday? This is one time when she should have listened to her mother.

Crap. Instead of a pumping little coffee business, all she finds is an empty courtyard and a locked-up cart. There's a sign, scrawled in black pen. *Gone fishing, back tomorrow.* Smart-asses. She sighs and turns in the other direction. Steeling herself for the longer walk, she cuts across the grassy quad and squints into the sunlight that she's usually happy to see this time of year. It's almost hot, and she's already starting to sweat. If she'd looked out the window this morning, instead of just stumbling into the daylight, she might have dressed properly.

At first, when she hears her name being called, she thinks she's imagined it. It's not a stretch given the state of her brain after much tequila, four hours of sleep, and two classes. Then she hears it again. She scans the crowds of students scattered across the broad stretch of green grass, making the most of the spring sun. Mia waves at her, looking like a human island in the sea of her textbooks. Claire hasn't seen her for a while. Nor Robbie. Not since the last time they came in for a drink after work, and Claire had been too busy to talk much that night.

Claire grimaces and veers from her trajectory to where Mia is sitting.

"Hi. I almost didn't recognise—" Mia starts to say as Claire drops onto the ground next to her.

"I do not like today. Not at all." Claire groans as she pulls at the sleeves of her sweater. "I'm hungover. The coffee place is closed. And it's *hot.*" She shields her eyes from the sun with her hand.

"Hello to you too." Mia turns her face to the sun. "And what do you mean? It's beautiful." She's wearing a tank top and jeans, her narrow shoulders already beginning to brown. If Claire did that, she'd burn in a minute. She shuffles back into the shade of a tree, yanks off her jumper, and immediately feels better.

"What are you doing?"

"What does it look like?" Mia waves her pen over the array of open books.

"Okay, smart-ass," Claire grumbles. She's about to ask for specifics when a lanky guy in shorts with an almost-cool haircut strolls up with two coffees in his hands.

"Thought you'd be here." He offers Mia one of the coffees a little too eagerly. "I owe you one."

Smooth, Claire thinks but doesn't say.

"Thanks." Mia is clearly a little surprised. She carefully takes the coffee.

The guy turns from confident to awkward in about two seconds flat, obviously not sure what to say now that he's delivered the planned line and beverage. "Uh, okay, well..." He runs a nervous hand through his hair. "I'll see you at lab later?"

"Yeah, see you." Mia gives him a parting smile and puts the coffee on the grass next to her. She points at it. "And thanks again."

Claire watches him stride away, quickly putting distance between himself and his backfired manoeuvre. "Cute. The move, not the guy, of course. Though he's not bad, if you like them earnest." She turns to Mia. "You were supposed to ask him to sit, you know."

Mia just shrugs.

Claire covetously stares at the abandoned cup. "I'll give you every cent I have for a sip of that coffee."

"You can have it." Mia passes it to her. "I just had one."

"Seriously?" Claire raises one eyebrow. "You're giving away caffeine?"

"Seriously. Just never tell Pete."

"Done." She clutches the coffee and takes a long, long drink. Lying down on the grass, she rests the cup next to her and throws one arm over her forehead to shield her eyes from the glare. "So, you with Mr. Coffee?"

"Nope. We hang out sometimes."

"Oh, sleeping with him?" Claire grins, thinking Mia is being coy.

"Nope."

"What?" Claire frowns and lifts her arm from her face. "Then how did you get him to do that? Am I not seeing something here?"

"I don't know. I bought him one a few weeks ago." Mia screws up her face. "I guess he thought he'd pay me back."

"Just out of the blue like that? Wow." Claire shakes her head and appraises Mia's angular, makeup-less face and her mess of dark, wavy hair. "I mean you're hot and all, in a kind of casual, no-fuss way, but hot enough for unprompted beverage deliveries from a non-boyfriend? That's impressive pull."

Mia raises a warning eyebrow. "You want to give that coffee back?"

"No."

"Then shut it."

Claire obediently shuts her mouth. For a minute, anyway. "He's totally hot for you, though. You know that, right?" She smirks at Mia.

"I'm well aware of his interest, thanks." Mia leans over and plucks at Claire's hair. "You know, I nearly didn't recognise you. I was looking at you thinking, 'How do I know that girl?' When did you change your hair?"

"A week ago."

"And what prompted this radical makeover, if I may ask?"

"Well, Mia, I was running out of ways to disappoint my mother. And then it came to me."

Mia laughs and drops Claire's hair.

Claire pulls a strand over her face and examines the new shade again. She's not used to it herself. Though, she has to admit, she kind of loves it. She never thought she could have dark hair. And she never thought she could wear bangs, either. It's so much more exotic than the boring long, straight hair she had all her life. Even better, her mother still doesn't quite approve. She probably would have only been satisfied if Leo had returned it to exactly what it was before.

"You look like that girl from that movie."

"That's what everyone has been saying. Only no one can remember which girl from which movie."

Mia tips her head to one side and stares at her. She laughs. "Neither can I. You know, it *actually* looks good," she teases as if maybe it shouldn't.

"Uh, well, thanks, Mia." Claire throws a twig at her. "Do you have classes today? Or are you just hanging out on campus for fun?"

"Classes." Mia checks her watch and stacks her books. "Soon, in fact."

"What are you studying, anyway?"

"Biomedicine."

"Really? Wow." Claire raises her eyebrows and looks at the books again. She figured Mia was studious, what with doing her homework at the pub, but she didn't expect anything as hard-core as that. "How do you even have a life?"

"I honestly don't know." Mia puts her glasses in their case and shoves them into her bag. "Actually, I *do* know. I don't have a life," she declares. "I live at home with my parents so I can afford to exist on one or two shifts a week at the café during the semesters. And I only go out on weekends."

"Sounds kind of sad."

"I love it, secretly. Well, except for the lack of social life. What about you? I didn't realise you were studying here."

"Arts. French and English lit." Claire sits up because Mia looks as though she's about to leave. "Just to keep my parents off my back while I figure out what I actually want to do. If I study, I can stay at home and I don't have to pay rent."

"Fair enough."

"Are you going to be a surgeon, like on *Grey's Anatomy*?"

"Not sure yet." Mia shakes her head. "Medicine would be cool. I'd also love to do forensics. I have to decide."

"Forensics is dead people, right? *CSI* stuff? Why would anyone want to work with corpses?"

"Why is it everyone references TV shows when they ask about it?" Mia ignores the last question and slides her books into her huge bag. "But yeah, kind of like that, but not at all."

"Why are you studying medicine, then, if you're going to work with dead bodies? Makes zero sense to me."

"Because they have the same parts as live ones, dummy."

Claire shrugs. Whatever. She's newly impressed by this information. She wouldn't have pictured Mia picking that for a career. She seems so... sunny. Doing something geeky like science, yes, that explains all the study. But forensics? That's kind of creepy-cool.

"And I can't do any of those things until I finish this degree. Then I'll probably have to do another."

"Wow. How long will you be studying?"

"Forever." Mia plays with the silver chain around her neck, the same one with the long silver pendant she wore the night Claire first met her.

"Couldn't you have done something easier?" Claire picks up a dead leaf and crushes it between her fingers. "I've heard undertaking is a good, reliable career. And you'd still get to be with the corpses."

"That's *exactly* what my dad said just last week." Mia laughs as she does up the clasps on her bag.

"They aren't doctors?" Claire wonders if Mia is also following a family tradition like she's expected to.

"Nope, Dad does research—climate change stuff—and Mum teaches biology."

"Oh." Claire wrinkles her nose. "Wow, that's quite a tradition of geekdom. You're just one-upping them, I guess?"

"I suppose." Mia doesn't appear to be even slightly bothered by Claire's teasing. "I don't know. I love it."

"You'd have to. I cannot even imagine what you people do for all those years at uni. I mean, do you really just cut up people and look at their insides all day?" She suddenly re-assesses. "Actually, that'd be kind of cool."

"Sometimes." Mia stands and brushes the grass off the back of her jeans. "No cutting people up today. It's a lecture, but it's a pretty awesome one. What are you doing now?"

"Uh, nothing? Being a hungover, futureless arts student until it's time to go to my crappy job?"

"Come with me?" Mia grins, a challenge in her brown eyes.

Claire looks at her, eyebrow raised. "To a lecture?" Claire says it as if it's a dirty word. She's already suffered a lecture today in a language she can understand.

"You'll like this one. I promise."

Claire tips her head, eyes narrowed, amazed she's even considering it. "Is the lecture theatre comfy? Can I nap if I get bored?"

"Sure."

"Why not?" Claire surprises herself by climbing to her feet. "Can I bring my coffee?"

"*Your* coffee?" Mia raises her eyebrows. "You can bring anything." She drags her heavy bag onto a shoulder and winces. "But hurry up." She heads across the uni lawn in a direction Claire has never been. The straps of her bag dig into her narrow shoulders.

Claire follows. "See, Mia, here's another reason to study a slacker degree," she tells her, waving her lone textbook gleefully in the air as she struggles to keep up. "Look at what I have to carry."

"Yeah, yeah."

CHAPTER 11

When they walk into the bright, modern lecture theatre, a thousand times removed from the dusty, uncomfortable one Claire was stuck in this morning, she follows Mia to a seat in a middle-back row. Mia tosses her bag on the seat next to her and throws her long legs over the back of the chair in front as if she's staking out her territory. She whips out a notepad and barely stops scribbling for the whole hour.

Claire parks herself in the seat next to her and watches the other students trickle in. She treats the whole thing like an anthropological exercise. This is where all those ambitious, nerdy kids from her high school ended up, she realises. She recognises the type but not the faces. If she'd known they were potentially as fun as Mia under all that geekdom, she might have made more of an effort back then.

The lecture is strangely entertaining. Claire's not sure if it's the hangover or the random otherness of it all, but it doesn't matter that she doesn't understand any of it. The gross bits of video, the lecture slides, and the unnaturally excited man delivering the lecture make it kind of interesting.

When the video shows the first scalpel cut into flesh, Claire grimaces at Mia, completely grossed out. Mia grins right back and returns to her note taking. Later, when they start slicing into whatever they've removed from the body, Claire grabs the pen out of Mia's hand and scrawls in the margin of her notebook. *What the hell is that, anyway?*

Mia grabs the pen back. *Kidney.*

Claire pulls a face and takes the pen again. *That is freaking disgusting.*

Mia smiles. Claire hands her the pen and sits back to watch the rest, enthralled. When the hour is up, they walk out of the lecture theatre, blinking into the sunshine.

"I have no idea what that dude was talking about, but that was weird and gross and kind of awesome."

"Told you."

"Does my kidney look like that?"

"Yep, probably. Both of them." Then Mia tips her head to the side. "Well, maybe a little younger."

Claire wrinkles her nose. The less she thinks about that one, the better. "What do you do now? Go cut one up yourself?"

"Nope." Mia shakes her head. "I get free coffee from work, if the boss isn't there, and then go to another class in an hour. Come? For a coffee I mean, not another class. I don't think you'll go unnoticed in the labs." She squints at Claire. "One of the boys is likely to spot the odd girl out, even if we found you a white coat."

"Coffee, yes." Claire nods and follows Mia across the campus.

They go to her café and drink free lattes, and the remains of Claire's hangover ebbs with the second round of caffeine.

Mia tells her about the first dissection she ever did, and Claire teaches her how to say "That's the worse pick-up line I've ever heard" in French. Mia learns it quickly, but her accent is awful.

"Just curious, if you don't really want to do anything with your French, what do you want to, you know, do later?"

"I really don't know. Everything I think of doing, I see the endgame, the career, and I go meh." Claire pushes away her empty coffee cup. "See, Mia, I have lots of potential, but I lack direction. I lack ambition."

"Said all your teachers, right?"

"Oh, no, they didn't really notice. Said my mother."

"What does she want you to do?"

"Be a lawyer, like her. And my dad, and his dad," Claire recites. "Oh yeah, and my uncle-in-law. *And* my brother's godfather."

"Wow, that's some family line."

"I know." Claire rests her chin in her hands. "Hence why I kind of don't want to be a lawyer."

And Mia nods as if she gets it.

When the hour is done, they traipse out of the café.

"That was fun," Mia tells her outside as she once again hauls her elephantine bag onto her shoulder. "Hey, are you coming to Robbie's show next week?"

"Don't know." Claire slides on her sunglasses. She doesn't know anything about it. Besides, she doesn't even know if Robbie really likes her that much, let alone if he would want her to come to something.

"It's with a few other students from his photography class. They're doing this group exhibition thing at a gallery near here. His stuff is amazing. Here." She digs in the side pocket of her bag and pulls out a flier. "Here's the invite. You and Nina should come."

"Maybe." Claire takes the paper and reads it. "But it's on a Thursday, Mia. I thought you said you don't go out on weeknights?"

"It's for Robbie. I make exceptions for Robbie." She rolls her eyes but smiles at the same time. "I make too many exceptions for Robbie."

Claire checks her watch. It's not that long until she has to get ready for work. "I better go. Uh, thanks for a strangely fun and educational afternoon."

Mia grins, hand on hip. "So you want to switch to medicine now?"

"Not a chance." Claire screws up her face. "I can barely commit to my two classes. If I had to go to a lab right now, I'd be pissed. See you."

She gives Mia a wave and strolls off down the street in the direction of Nina's apartment. Nina's not even at the bar tonight, but she won't mind if Claire shows up there to change before work. She hurries through the congested traffic, across the road, and down a small side street. It's lined with listing trees, heavy with their burden of crimson bottlebrush flowers. Even though the afternoon is fading, the sun gives a kind of offhand, casual warmth. It's as though it's trying to convince people that they imagined the last rainy, dull months of Melbourne winter, that it's always been like this.

All around her, people slow to a stroll as they soak in the gentle heat on their way home from work. A couple of passersby catch her eye and smile, a sudden generosity born of this turn in the weather. And Claire smiles back. Because why not? It turned out to be a pretty good day considering the start she had. It's weird. She spent the afternoon with a virtual stranger and had more fun than she's had with any of her friends, aside from Nina, in ages. That's it, she decides. Nina doesn't know it yet, but Claire's going to make her go to this exhibition with her next week.

* * *

It's near the end of her shift, and the bar has emptied out. Claire cleans the last of the glasses as she waits until it is time to lock the door. Andrew is in his office, pretending to count money or something. Really, he's avoiding the work of closing up. Claire doesn't mind though. His extra hands would mean listening to his boring stories. And she's heard them all a gazillion times already.

Hearing the squeak of the door opening, she sighs, frowns, and looks up.

"Hello to you too" Robbie says, echoing Mia's exact words of earlier.

Claire really needs to work on her greetings, it seems. "Sorry," she mutters. "I thought it was more customers, and I'm about to close."

He ignores her comment and lets out a whistle. "Ooh, I like the hair! It's super hot."

"Thanks." She throws a glance at the office door before reaching for the tequila bottle. She grabs a couple of glasses, quickly pours two shots, and passes one to him.

They silently clink glasses and drink them down. *Hair of the dog*, Claire tells herself as the hot burn of the tequila recalls last night. She reaches into the tip jar, counts out enough to cover his, and throws the money in the register.

"Where's Neen?" He rests his arms on the bar.

"Sick," Claire says loudly as she glances at the office door and then whispers, "Working at another bar."

Robbie nods. He pulls a clump of papers out of his pocket. "I just dropped in to give you guys an invite to my exhibition next week." He holds one out.

Claire pulls out the one Mia gave her earlier and dangles it in front of him. "Snap," she says.

"Where'd you get that?"

"Mia."

"Where'd you see her?"

"At uni."

"Oh. God, I love that girl. So, will you come? Free drinks. Cheap, nasty champagne. But, like I said, free."

"Shouldn't your art be the selling point?" Claire puts their empty glasses into the last rack.

"Let's not kid ourselves, woman. People come for the alcohol. Then they look at the photos and moan that they'd love to buy one. Of course, they can't afford it because they can't even afford decent alcohol." He rolls his eyes. "Such is the story of my artistic life."

Claire smiles sympathetically and picks up her polishing rag.

"Will you be there?"

"Sure." Claire plays nonchalant, but secretly she is pleased that he cares if she comes or not.

Robbie slaps his hands on the bar. "Great. And you'll tell Nina, yeah?"

"Of course."

"Great, see you next week, if not before." He runs a hand through his unruly blond curls. "Besides, there's something you'll want to see." And then he is gone.

CHAPTER 12

Claire misses the days when she used to feel invincible.

Sometimes she craves those confident, cocky times—particularly the last year of high school. Freedom was coming, she nearly always had a good time, and the social order was in place. All was right in her universe. Back then, she didn't have to work so hard to feel as if she could face off against the world and win nearly every time. It just happened.

That feeling lasted pretty much through her first year of uni, too. This year started out smelling of potential but turned into raw anger and hurt before it withered into something bloodless and divested of colour. Now those invincible days don't come like they used to. Some start with the promise of that feeling, but it never quite goes the distance.

She's getting that invincible feeling back. At least she thinks she is. But sometimes all it takes is a small blow—another "Claire's future" argument with her mother, or an awkward exchange with someone in class because they don't get each other. Or maybe it's another apologetic, pleading message from Michelle that reminds her of the current, sad state of her friendships. Any one of those can cause any assurance she's rallied to dissipate. Without so much as a warning, she's back in that grey, depressing place.

This time it's the re-appearance of Brendan.

Fuck Brendan. And fuck him for throwing himself like a grenade into a week that started with promise. On Monday life looked good. Her mother went away for the week for a court case, Melbourne's forecast called for a few solid days of spring sunshine, and there was even the potential of some new people in her life. And she had a plan for Thursday night that didn't involve going to work.

But the week she envisions is shot down by a missed call. She discovers it on Monday afternoon as she walks out of the lecture theatre. The sight of Brendan's name on her phone throws her into a stunned tailspin. She nearly walks straight into an information desk as she stumbles out the door, staring distrustfully at the phone. Mortified by her extreme public clumsiness, she shoves it in her pocket. Claire heads home, unable to fathom a single reason why he might want to contact her.

He didn't leave a message, but it doesn't matter. The damage is done. Even though she's reached the point where his new relationship isn't a constant, painful presence in her mind, he once again inserts himself into her world. And he does it with just his name on a screen, a call she will never return.

Instead of enjoying a halcyon week, she mulls and stews and revisits the bitter ground of their sad, sorry breakup. So begins a shitty week of lying around the house between classes while she tries to ignore the pervasive question of why he decided to contact her after months of silence.

And, of course, it means the epic return of all the debilitating self-doubt that comes with thoughts of him and what he did. It's not just the betrayal that depresses her. It's the relentless, merry-go-round tedium of these feelings—feelings that aren't even really about him. It's about how the whole situation causes her to feel. No, she isn't prepared for this week, not for this small backslide to this depressing place. And now she wants out.

She doesn't tell anyone, either. Who would she tell? *Toughen up and don't let on.* That was her mother's advice back when it first happened. In fact, that and *just apply yourself* are her mother's advice for everything. She dispenses her wisdom in two finely whittled-down pieces of cure-all guidance that she tosses out during her brief appearances in the land of motherhood.

And sure, that's great advice for when she's out in public, and it's advice Claire learned to take on in order to leave the house in those first weeks. But it does nothing to help with the long hours she spends alone in the privacy of her room in the aftermath. It does nothing to ease her through the hurt, humiliation, and anger. Her mother never told her how to deal with that part. No one did. And no one told her how long it would take to get back even a fraction of the assurance she used to have. Now, just when she's finally feeling the capacity to move on, he happens again.

So Claire decides he's not going any further into this week with her. Especially not today. It will *not* be one of those days. This just might be one where she gets to feel good about herself. She has a new jacket, she has new hair, and she has somewhere to be tonight. Also she has new people to hang out with—people who don't know anything about the Claire she used to be. She can spend time with them because they are not her old friends. With them, she can always detect the traces of their kind but irritating sympathy over the fact that she is no longer untouchable.

So tonight she's going to do whatever she can to find a sliver of that old confidence. And right now, she's finding it in the form of eye makeup.

She has no real idea what to wear to this show, but going on Robbie's comments about cheap booze and cheaper attendees, she decides to go casual in jeans and a top. And eyeliner. There must always be eyeliner, her second favourite form of armour.

"Hey, person vaguely resembling my sister."

It's Cam, already making himself comfortable on her bed.

"Where have you been?" She leans toward the mirror and carefully applies the pencil to her lower eye.

"At work."

"For a week? You can't be sleeping there. Elana?"

"Sort of."

"Lucky her."

"I'm just trying to make it up to her." He picks up Claire's wallet from the bed and starts idly picking through it.

She holds out the mascara wand and turns. "Get out of my stuff."

"No." He grins. "I'm checking for fake ID."

"Hey, idiot boy." She gently swipes away a teeny smear of black from her eyelid. "I'm nearly twenty, remember?"

"Oh yeah." He chuckles and continues his rifling. He examines every single receipt, card, and coin. "I forgot."

She leaves him to his knee-jerk detective work and focuses on the task of long lashes. She has nothing to hide, anyway, except an embarrassing student ID photo. And he's already seen it.

"What are you doing tonight that requires all that war paint?"

She frowns into the mirror. She's not wearing *that* much makeup. She hasn't even put on lipstick yet. "Going to an exhibition opening."

"I don't even know what that is." He holds up a card and reads it.

"It's a party where they lure you in to look at the art and maybe buy it on the promise of free alcohol."

"Ah." He nods. "Now I get it. At first I was thinking you...and art?" He gives her a dubious look. "But you and booze? That I understand." He returns the card to her wallet and tosses it onto the bed. Within seconds, though, he picks up one of her school notebooks and looks through it. She shakes her head. Cam just can't help himself. No wonder he wanted to be a cop so badly.

She grabs her brush and runs it through her hair. "Brendan called me."

He frowns. "What for? What did he want?"

"I don't know. I missed the call." She puts down her brush and turns around. "And no way am I calling him back."

"Good. Don't, Claire."

"Don't worry, I don't plan to," she can't help snapping. Who does Cam think she is? One of those desperate girls who'd return to a guy who is too gutless to tell her he's fallen for someone else? That kind of feeble crap is more Cam's bag. He's the one who crawls back to Elana even though she's kicked him out at least half-dozen times since they started dating. Sure, she's supermodel hot, but seriously? Cam has zero willpower, especially when it comes to that psychotic...whatever she is to him. Guys can be so spineless sometimes.

"You know, that offer to kill him is still open."

Her irritation is replaced with a smile. She's got to hand it to her brother. He's incredibly annoying, but he's loyal as all get out. "Thanks. You're very sweet. I think ignoring the asshole will suffice for now." She stands and pulls on her jacket. "But I'll let you know if I need you to get out the tire iron, okay?"

"Who else is going with you to this thing tonight? Michelle and her sidekicks don't seem like the art-loving types. Unless it's prints from IKEA."

"Nope. I'm going with Nina and some other people. A friend of hers has photos in the show."

"You're hanging out with photographers now?" Cam runs a hand through his hair. He finally had a haircut, thank God, and looks normal again. Well, normal for Cam.

"So what?" She stands and looks at herself in the full-length mirror behind her door. She'll do, she supposes. "Maybe I don't want the extent of my social life to be trashy nightclubs like those girls."

"Yes, you do." He picks up her phone and turns it over and over in his hands.

"Okay, sometimes." She whips the phone out of his hands and tucks it in her back pocket. "But not all the time."

"You're full of it." He squints at her and delivers his best I-know-you look, because calling each other out on their crap is one of their favourite things to do. "Let me guess, this artist is some hot guy you're chasing?"

"Nope." She grins and then tips her head to the side, considering Robbie. "Well, he actually is a little hot. But also very gay." She turns toward him. "What are you doing tonight?"

"Some club with Vito."

"See." She rolls her eyes as she zips up her jacket. "Boring."

"Well, that training was plenty new and exciting for me. I'm kind of happy to go with predictable for a while, you know?"

Claire nods. She'll give him that. "Fair enough." She straightens her collar in the mirror and asks, "How do I look?"

He looks at her, raises his hands in the air. "How would I know? You look like Claire. Only with magazine hair."

"Gee, thanks." She picks up her wallet and shoves it in her jacket pocket. "Now get out. I have to go."

CHAPTER 13

The gallery is a mob scene with people spilling out onto the pavement. As she approaches, Claire shoves her hands into her jacket pockets and slows her pace. Nina is supposed to be here somewhere, but that doesn't mean she will be. Nina is always late. And Claire is always painfully on time. She can't help it. It was drilled into her. She wishes she were better at that casual, party's-already-started arrival, because the fear of standing around on her own makes her nervous. Like now.

As she nears the mass of people already gathered—mostly students and a few proud-but-beleaguered parents—she knows she made the right choice about what to wear. Everyone, except the parents, firmly embraced the dressing down.

She stops at the fringes of the crowd and wonders how she's going to get inside. She edges closer to the wide, glass doors and stands on her tiptoes to get a glimpse inside. All she can see is bodies. How does anyone even manage to see the art at these events? She steps to the edge of the pavement, out of the way of the steady stream of people weaving in and out the door.

She considers elbowing in so she can find someone she knows or at least get a drink. Either would alleviate the social anxiety that is taking firm hold of her. Before she decides, a hand clutches her arm. She spins around. It's Nina.

"Hi!"

"Hey."

Nina dyed her hair again, a darker blonde this time. Nina is always changing her look. It's a constant work in progress. *I like change*, she tells Claire. Raised in a huge, vaguely hippie family, Nina learned to go with any kind of flow. It's a source of envy for Claire. She'd like to be that free and easy but knows she'll never find anywhere near that level of calm. Nina's carefree behaviour can also be annoying, because it's difficult to pin her down. Claire can never count on her to be where she's supposed to be at any given time.

"I like your hair this week."

"Thanks," Nina says as she runs her hand over her head and smiles self-consciously. "I still like yours too. It's awesome."

"Yeah, better since I got it fixed."

Nina doesn't respond to her dig about the botched bleach job. Instead, she says, "Josh has gone in to find drinks."

Claire nods, chewing her lip. She forgot Josh might be here. Awkward.

"Have you been inside?" Claire asks.

Nina shakes her head. "Too hard to get in." She glances at the teeming crowd. "I'm going to wait a bit and then try. Let's find somewhere to sit."

They end up on the curb with their feet in the gutter. A lot of people do the same and line the edges of the street with drinks in their hands.

"Classy," Claire grumbles as they sit.

Nina smiles, not bothered in the least by their position or by Claire's complaint. Josh finds them eventually. He clutches a bottle of bubbly and a small pile of plastic cups. He pours them each a glass, hands one to Claire with barely an acknowledgement of her presence, and sits on the other side of Nina. At least he seems to have returned to his old grunty ways. She hopes he stays that way. She sits back and sips her—as promised—disgusting champagne. She watches the people around her, all dressed to appear as casual as possible, a look that probably took just as long as anything fancier would have.

She stares idly down the street, half listening to Josh talk about a sporty obstacle course he's doing on the weekend, and spots a guy who looks kind of familiar. She runs through a list of ways she might know him, trying to figure out if he's in one of her classes at school or maybe a customer at the bar. When he gets closer, she notices Mia walking next to him, dressed in jeans and a loose red top. That's when Claire realises that the vaguely familiar guy is Mia's coffee boy.

Mia's clearly mid story, talking animatedly while he listens avidly. Claire smirks to herself and wonders if he's gotten anywhere with her yet. As they get closer, Mia spies her and waves. She veers over to where they sit.

"Hi! You came."

"Hey." Claire smiles. "You know Nina, right? And that's Josh." She flaps a hand in his direction.

Josh nods at them and holds up the bottle and glasses.

"Nice to meet you." Mia nods at the proffered bottle. "Thanks."

"It's disgusting," Claire warns her.

"I'll risk it." She turns to her friend. "This is Pete."

He says hello and wanders away to talk to some people on the other side of the street.

"Coffee Boy, hey?" Claire teases.

Mia is about to say something when Robbie appears. He folds Mia into a tight, one-armed hug, holding his drink aloft in his other hand.

"You're here!" he sings. He looks great tonight, with his hair high. He's in black skinny jeans and boots, and a bright-blue T-shirt with the sleeves cut off.

Claire wonders if he cuts the sleeves off everything the minute he buys it. She also wonders what he wears in winter.

"Of course I am." Mia presses a hand to his cheek. "I just got here, though, so I haven't been in."

"Don't bother." He clutches her arm as if for protection. "It's packed, and you can't see anything anyway." He steps gently on the tip of Claire's boot. "Hey. You came too."

She pulls a face at him and then smiles.

"Yeah, we're waiting until we can actually get in the door. You're popular." Nina shades her eyes and looks up at him. "How is it going?"

"I'm freaking out a bit, actually." Robbie leans against Mia. "Some of our teachers turned up, even though it's not a school show. I was not expecting that. None of us were."

"Do they like your stuff?" Mia immediately shakes her head and corrects herself. "Well, of course, they do, but did they say anything?"

Robbie gives her a bashful look. "I don't know. I might have hidden from them."

Mia sighs. "You're an idiot." She jabs his chest with her finger. "Shouldn't you be trying to promote yourself?"

He stares at the ground. Mia shakes her head again and slides her arm around his narrow waist and holds him against her.

"What about you?" he asks her. "Get that anatomy thing done?"

She nods and kind of waves it away as though she's done thinking about it.

Claire watches them, struck by how they are so worn into their intimacy, how much they seem like brother and sister. Their devotion to each other—even though they are so different—is cute.

"I better go back." He sucks in a deep breath. "The owner said that someone might, *might* be interested in buying one of my pieces."

"Really?" Mia turns to him immediately, eyes wide. "That's amazing. Get back in there, then." She pushes him away.

"Okay," he whines. "I hate doing this stuff."

"You want to live off your work?"

"Yes." He sighs as though this is a conversation they've had many times before.

"Then go back in there."

"Yes'm," he mutters but leans in and kisses her forehead. "I'll come find you guys when it's quieter, okay?" He points at Claire. "I want to show you something." Then he turns and strides away.

Claire frowns. It's the same thing he said last time he saw her. She looks up at Mia. "What does he want me to see?"

"He'll show you," she says with a smile.

"Want to sit?" Claire slides closer to Nina. "It's very comfortable, as you can probably imagine."

"Sure." Mia drops down next to Claire.

"How did you guys meet, anyway?"

"Me and Robbie?"

Claire nods.

"At work. Last summer. We both started working there around the same time and, being the new kids, they put us on the early shift together." Mia shakes her head. "Nothing will make or break a friendship like a couple of months of 6am starts."

Claire smiles. She can imagine. "Coffee Boy's here."

Mia nods. "Coffee Boy's here." She looks over at where he's talking to two other guys.

"I thought nothing was going on with him."

"That's not what I said." Mia turns the plastic cup between her hands, staring at it. "I just said I hung out with him sometimes."

"Oh yeah, that's right." Claire smirks. "And that you weren't sleeping with him and yet he still brings you free beverages. So, did it pay off?"

"Nosey, aren't you?" Mia gives her a look. She doesn't seem too upset, though.

"Yeah, I am. Habit. It's all the lawyers in the family. But I get it. We don't have to talk about it."

"It's not that big of a deal. It's just...unconfirmed, you know?"

Claire nods. She does understand. Besides, it's none of her business, and Mia clearly keeps these things to herself. Claire is used to Nina, who will talk about anything. In the few short months they have known each other, Claire has learned Nina's entire history—family, romantic, *and* sexual. On the other hand, Claire is kind of private about her business, and Nina makes her seem like the most closed person in the world. She changes the subject. "Is it exciting being out on a Thursday, Mia?" She turns and flicks her eyebrows up and down at her. "Feeling dangerous?"

"Oh yeah." Mia takes a sip of her drink and gasps. "Whoa. Confirmed, disgusting."

"Told you. Besides, should you be drinking on a week night? Surely that's not in the rules?"

"Exams are coming, and I am determined to enjoy everything while I can. Life will be hellish soon enough."

Claire hasn't given much thought to exams yet. Mia's right, they're not far away. "How many do you have?"

"Six."

"Ouch. I only have two."

"Lucky." Mia wraps her arms around her legs again. "Do you worry about how you'll do? Your grades?"

At first, Claire goes to act as if she doesn't care, but she thinks Mia probably isn't the kind of person to judge. "Yeah, I do," she admits. "I was raised by perfectionists. Can't help it. You?"

"I stress. Getting into the good postgrad courses is really competitive."

"But you seem so chilled."

Mia seems so relaxed and cheerful—and in a surprisingly un-annoying way. Claire thinks it would take a lot to ruffle her.

"Wait until exams," Mia warns her.

"Oh God, are you talking about exams?" It's Pete, Coffee Boy. He sits next to Mia and grins at Claire. "Don't talk to her about exams."

"Why?"

"Hush, you," Mia tells him at the same time.

"Mia was a wreck last semester. And she nearly lost her mind when she had to do her GAMSAT." He bumps his shoulder against hers.

"The medical entry exam," Mia tells Claire as she elbows him back. "I wasn't that bad."

Claire detects the high note of defence in her voice and smiles. Pete's probably right.

"You kind of were." He turns to Claire and shakes his head. "You should have seen her. She was a mess." Before Mia can respond, he adds, "And, of course it turned out you didn't need to stress at all, did you?"

Mia doesn't answer. She turns to Claire. "I thought I had a good reason to worry. I need really good results. Did you know only ten percent of biomed students get into postgrad med courses in Australia every year?"

"No, Mia, I did not," Claire tells her, playing along, somewhere between sarcastic and serious. Why in hell would she know that?

"I read it on Wikipedia, so it might be true."

Claire laughs.

Pete shakes his head. "I, on the other hand, did know that, because she's told me about six hundred times."

Mia throws him another look but doesn't say a word.

They sit in the gutter and drink a second, awful bottle of champagne and trade stories. Claire tells them about how Cam and his partner were called in to arrest a woman for not returning a football after the neighbour's kid had kicked it into her yard a thousand times. When she got fed up and refused to give it back, they had to come in and threaten arrest.

Mia's eyes widen. "You're kidding. They can do that?"

"Apparently it constitutes petty theft."

"That's nuts," Pete scoffs.

"The law is a weird, weird thing." Claire thinks of some of the courtroom tales her family has told her through the years.

Pete starts to tell them about his brush with the law when Robbie appears again.

"Hey, guys, the gallery has cleared a bit if you want to come and look." He sounds as if he's not sure he wants them to.

"Yes, please!" Nina jumps to her feet and brushes off the back of her skirt.

"How sad to leave our prime position," Claire mutters.

Mia chuckles and stands. She holds out her hands to Claire. "Oh, come on." She hauls Claire to her feet. "You're sitting in a gutter, but admit it, you're having fun."

Claire ignores her. Mia already knows she's right. Besides, Claire is having fun, more than she's had all week.

CHAPTER 14

Robbie leads them inside. The crowd has thinned, and Claire can actually see photographs on the walls. Large, moody landscape shots of a fog-bound airfield hang in the front room.

"So, where's your stuff?" Nina asks.

"In that room." Robbie points to a doorway. "And that one." He points to another.

The others head for the first room. Claire goes to follow them, but Robbie catches her wrist and pulls her back. "Hey, come in here for a sec."

He pulls her along behind him and leads her into the second room. As soon as he turns the corner, he releases her wrist and takes her by the shoulders to position her a short distance from a large photo that occupies a narrow section of wall on its own.

It's a photo of her.

Robbie rests his hands on her shoulders as she takes it in. It's a black and white shot of her working at the bar. Well, not working exactly. She's standing at a distance from the camera, at the other end of the bar, in profile. Her arms are folded over her chest, and she's staring intently at something beyond the frame. The neon sign above the door serves to backlight everything but her face. The effect darkens her features almost to the point of silhouette and creates a hazy halo of light around her upper body. Her hair is long in the photo, pulled into a knot at the base of her head. Loose strands hang around her face.

"I don't even remember you taking that." She cannot stop staring, incredulous. She's unable to comprehend that there is a picture of her hanging in a gallery, even though she is standing right in front of it.

"I sneaked it that night I was taking photos of Nina. It was a lucky shot. I only took the one, but I love it. You don't mind, do you?" He sounds slightly nervous.

Claire doesn't say anything for a minute. She just keeps staring at it. And she doesn't mind. Not at all. Even she can see the subtle beauty and mood of the photo beyond the confronting fact that she's in it. There's an atmosphere that has nothing to do with her and everything to do with the moment Robbie captured. There is something both pensive and transitory in the way she is standing. She's so far away from the camera, surrounded, but not touched by the bar, her mind clearly elsewhere. The way her chin is slightly dropped and her arms are folded makes it slightly defiant too. *Anywhere but here*, it says. She feels a welling of something caught between pride and gratitude, a reminder of her potential to be someone who should be looked at.

Claire shakes her head. "No, I don't mind. It's a great photo. You know that," she tells him quietly, still staring.

"Good. Because, look." He points at the small red sticker stuck next to the photo. "I sold it."

"Really?" Claire shakes herself out of the shock of the photo and turns and to him. "That's awesome. Congratulations."

"Thanks." He smiles dazedly, as if he's amazed by the fact. In this moment, he's more genuine and serious than she has ever seen him. She realises this is something he can't be flip about. "I sold another one too."

"That's really great." She feels a flash of envy because he has this thing that he *knows* he wants to do—is compelled to do. And it's something he's good at. Why can't she figure out that thing for herself?

The others trickle in and, suddenly wrought shy by the thought of them staring at a picture of her, Claire ducks out to the other room.

And all of his photos are great, of course. As he told her, they're all portraits, but they all manage to be somehow more than the people featured in them. Now, after seeing these, Claire gets it. Even knowing nothing about photography, she understands that Robbie is talented.

She wanders around the other rooms, less interested in all the other people's work but biding her time before she goes back into the room with her photo. When she does, they're all standing in the middle of the room with a bunch of other people, presumably Robbie's friends.

As she rejoins them, Mia turns to her. "Do you like it?"

Claire shrugs, still feeling shy. "It's kind of weird, you know?"

"I can imagine." Mia looks at the picture and then back to her. "But it's really, really beautiful."

"You already knew, didn't you?" Claire blushes as she remembers how Mia brushed off her questions earlier. "You could have warned me."

"I saw the smaller prints when he was choosing which photos to use in this show."

"To Robbie!" someone calls out. Slowly, everyone catches on and raises their glasses.

"To Robbie!" the room responds.

Claire drains the last of her warm champagne.

"And to actually selling art," a voice adds. A few people laugh.

"There's going to be a picture of you in some stranger's house." Nina comes over to stand next to her. "That's so weird."

Claire freezes for a moment to contemplate this new, incredibly freaky thought. "Thanks, Neen, I hadn't actually thought of that." She wrinkles her nose. "And now I have." And it *is* weird. But before she can mull it over any further Robbie comes over.

"Hey, a few of us are going to go to dinner and celebrate—just dumplings or something cheap. Will you guys come?"

Nina nods. "Of course."

Claire nods too, secretly pleased to somehow, suddenly be considered part of this weird little group. These people are nothing like the people she's always considered friends. But she also knows that maybe, just maybe, this is a good thing.

They make their way down the streets in a tight throng, headed for a Chinese restaurant. Robbie falls into step with her. "Thanks for coming tonight." He hooks his elbow through hers.

"Thanks for inviting me." She stares idly at the motley little crowd walking in front of them. There's a girl in a hat who pretends the curb is a tightrope, with her arms out. Nina slaps someone on the arm and laughs. Pete rests his hand on the back of Mia's neck as they walk. The mood is loose and happy and infectious, and Claire feels a sudden pang of longing for the summer.

Robbie turns and gives her one of those looks she has grown accustomed to, as though he finds her highly amusing. "I guess it'd be kind of rude not to invite the talent."

"Oh shut up."

He laughs.

CHAPTER 15

She's picking her way through the bodies scattered around the university lawn, looking for a spot to kill the next hour when she sees them.

Mia and Pete are sitting in a patch of sun strung between the spring-fattened shadows of two trees, a stack of books and a couple of coffee cups between them. Claire considers stopping to say hello, but feels awkward. She decides she should leave them be. Even from this distance, she can see how animated they are with each other. They probably don't want a third wheel butting in on their little sunshine coffee date.

Instead, Claire walks a little further away and finds her own sun-dappled patch of grass and drops down onto it. She slips her French textbook out of her bag, slides on her sunglasses, and lies down, using her bag for a pillow. She flicks open her book and tries to read, but it's difficult to concentrate with all the cheerful banter around her and the lulling warmth of the sun. In minutes, she drops the book to her chest and mellows out to the light breeze and the scent of freshly mowed grass.

She thinks about the possibilities posed by the coming summer. She'd love to take a trip during the break, but she can't decide where to go. Every travel agency she passes, she stops and looks at the fares. She muses over the delicious possibilities of the destinations on offer. Europe tops her list. The two short trips with her parents when she was young left her with vague memories of beautiful, beguiling places that she wants to see again.

She'd love to wander through those cities, only at her own pace and without the constant behest of a guidebook or, worse, a guide. On those early trips, the guide was inevitably harried by Christine's relentless interrogations. She seemed convinced that the only way to seem intelligent was to ask a litany of questions more designed to show off her own knowledge rather than learn anything new from the guide. Those childhood holidays were fleeting introductions, but they weren't enough. Claire wants to explore places that exist outside the increasingly small world of here. And she wants to know each more intimately because those destinations offer the potential for her to be another Claire, an anonymous Claire even she doesn't know yet.

She's knee-deep in contemplating the lure of being someplace else and maybe somebody else, when something nudges at her boots. She's drawn back to the university lawn and to the question of who is trying to wreck her peaceful moment of sunshine daydreaming. She shades her eyes and looks up, ready to growl.

It's Mia. She stands over Claire, her long hair hanging around her shoulders. "Didn't you see me waving?"

"What? No. I only see someone ruining the serenity," Claire mutters, playing innocent, She sits up on her elbows and blinks into the sunshine. "When?"

"Just before."

"No." And at least it's true. Sure, she saw them sitting there, but she didn't see Mia wave.

"Oh, well, that's okay then. You weren't ignoring me, I won't be offended." She hooks her fingers onto the straps of her bag and swings it slightly from side to side. "So, what are you doing?"

"What does it look like, Mia?" Claire shoots her a withering look and waves her book in the air.

Mia tips her head to the side and delivers a knowing grin. "You were *not* reading. You were napping."

"Maybe." Claire sits up and pushes her sunglasses on top of her head. "So what?"

"So, tell me, what are you doing now you've caught up on your beauty sleep?"

"Meeting my group to prepare our French conversation exam." Claire rolls her eyes as she checks her wristwatch. "Soon. I am not looking forward to it. I got put in a group with completely uptight folk. Very high maintenance and stressy."

"At least those types get good marks." Even as she says it, Mia screws up her nose in a way that tells Claire she knows it won't make the experience any more tolerable.

"I guess."

"Then what are you doing after?"

"Going to work. Because my day isn't wonderful enough already."

"Oh." Mia frowns. "I'm going to visit Robbie before my next class. It's his afternoon to babysit the exhibition. I was going to see if you wanted to come."

"Want to. Can't. What about tomorrow? Are you around? I've got a lunch thing, then a class, but I'm free after that?"

"Robbie won't be at the gallery, but we could hang out?" Mia suggests. "I have a break between three and four."

Claire nods. "I can meet you at three."

"Great." Mia smiles, her brown eyes narrowing a little. "Meet you here?"

"Here."

"Awesome. I'll see you then." She taps her foot against Claire's boot one more time and turns on her heel.

"See you." Claire watches Mia stroll away. She is so long and lanky, but there is a kind of casual grace to the way she moves, weaving her way among the other students scattered across the lawn. Claire feels enlivened by the fact she seems to be making a new friend. Of course, Mia seems so warm and indiscriminately sociable it's kind of difficult to tell if her geniality is by default or if she really is making friends. Either way, Claire is relieved to know that someone is acting as if she genuinely wants her company. Their random hangout last week was surprisingly fun, so she is looking forward to tomorrow. And, as an added bonus, it's something to look forward to after her dreaded lunch tomorrow.

For some stupid reason, Claire agreed to meet Michelle for lunch. To talk. Clearly sick of Claire avoiding her calls, Michelle showed up at the bar last night, a jarring and discomfiting visit that told Claire she was not going to get away with this...thing that wasn't quite a fight with her friend. Not without a conversation about it at least.

Claire had been busy, but she spotted Michelle within a second of her arrival. She was way too neat and tidy and clean not to stand out.

"Hey," Michelle squeaked timidly. She rested her fingers on the edge of the bar and smiled nervously at Claire. "Cool place," she said.

"No, it's not."

When Michelle's expression fell, Claire instantly felt bad. There was no reason to torture her.

"What are you doing here?" Claire asked with a not-quite smile meant to soften the question.

"I came to see you." Michelle tucked her hair behind her ear. "You weren't answering my messages."

Claire shrugged and pressed her lips together, partly because she didn't know what to say, but also because she knew it was bad form. During the past month, Michelle hadn't given up. And having listened to those messages, Claire is fully aware that Michelle, who is ridiculously kind-hearted, is incredibly sorry about what happened. In fact, that's probably the reason she said nothing about hanging out with the new girlfriend in the first place. As much as it upset Claire, she knows Michelle doesn't deserve to feel this bad. But Claire left it alone for so long that she has no idea how to deal with it now. When she doesn't know how to deal with an issue, she simply doesn't. Avoiding is what she does best.

"Do you think we could, you know, meet? And talk?" Michelle asked, her face hopeful as she clutched the edge of the bar.

And Claire found herself saying yes—if for no other reason than to end the awkward exchange and get Michelle out of the bar. Besides, she couldn't have handled the expression on Michelle's face if she'd said no.

Claire stuffs her unread textbook back inside her bag and sighs. At least now she has something to look forward to.

CHAPTER 16

At three o'clock, Claire finds Mia exactly where she said she'd be, under the tree on the west side of the lawn. She's sprawled on her stomach, arms draped over her bag, holding a paperback in front of her face.

Claire sits down on the grass next to her.

"What? No homework? No textbooks? Might that be actual leisure reading?"

Mia looks up, smiles, and pulls off her glasses. "I *should* be studying," she says with a sigh. "But sometimes you just have to rest your brain, you know?"

"I rest my brain with trashy TV, not—" Claire reaches over and pushes the book toward Mia's face so she can get a look at the cover. She lets the book go, grimacing. "Early twentieth-century literature."

Mia raises an eyebrow. "How do you know that?"

"Because I'm a genius." Claire opens her water bottle and takes a nonchalant sip.

"It does seem that way." Mia dog-ears the page and closes the book.

"We might have studied it last year. Pretty depressing *first* feminist novel." Claire hangs air quotes around "first." "Lady marries dude. Lady falls in love with another dude. Lady feels too guilty to be with other dude. Lady kills herself. Totally depressing."

Mia sighs and tosses the book on the grass in front of her. "Way to spoil it, Claire."

Claire slaps a hand to her mouth and giggles. "Oops, sorry!"

Mia shakes her head and laughs.

"You know," Claire tells her apologetically. "It's short. You would have found that out in, like, thirty pages. Besides, you deserve to be spoiled. You dog-ear the pages. That's, like, book vandalism."

"Yeah, yeah," Mia grumbles. But she's smiling so Claire is ninety-nine percent certain she's not actually mad. "How was your day? Ruin anyone else's yet?"

"Probably. And if not, I've still got time." Claire lies on her back in the grass. "It was okay. I had lunch with a friend, which was weird."

"Lunch is weird? What do you usually do when you hang out with your friends?"

"That's not what I meant." Claire flicks a blade of grass at her.

Mia brushes it off her arm. Claire stares across the lawn and thinks about her lunch with Michelle. She chews her lip and wonders if she and Michelle will see much of each other from now on.

Lunch was as awkward as she thought it would be. But at least by the end, they'd come to some sort of peace. Weirdly, the worst part was trying to fill in the silence after they sort of kind of talked it out. Particularly considering they were avoiding all Brendan-related territory. It was exhausting. But it's been exhausting for ages, having to work so hard to seek out common ground all the time. Claire could not wait to leave that horribly clunky, silence-punctuated meal. Walking away felt like freedom after a jail sentence.

"Are you going to tell me why your lunch was weird?" Mia asks. "Or should I just sit here and watch you pout?"

Claire thinks about Michelle and about Kerry and Kate. "Girls are weird, you know, Mia? In fact, girls are stupid."

"I'm a girl, in case you hadn't noticed. On behalf of the rest of us, I'd like to say thank you so very much."

"You're nothing like these girls. In a good way."

"And do you want to be more specific about why girls are weird? Or are we working in sweeping generalisations today?"

Claire smiles. She debates brushing it off, changing the subject, but when she looks over and sees Mia looking at her, seemingly receptive and ready to listen, she tells her about the lunch. And, of course, why the lunch happened. Then, the story of Claire and Michelle becomes the story of Claire and Brendan. How could it not? And the next thing Claire knows, she has told the whole stupid, sorry little tale while Mia lies there on the grass and listens. She doesn't say a word until Claire's done.

"How did you know?" Mia asks when Claire finally finishes.

"I don't know how I knew, exactly." It feels incredibly weird to talk about this. She hasn't confided in anyone in any real way—a little with Cam, maybe, when it first happened. Even before she knew Michelle is hanging out with the new girlfriend, she couldn't bring herself to discuss it with her. It was too close, and thus, too raw. Besides, she couldn't risk letting Michelle know just how bad she felt because Michelle would tell Jack, and Jack would tell Brendan. Claire's pride wouldn't allow it.

"I just felt like that connection between us wasn't as strong. At first, I thought it was the not being able to see each other. I had to stay in Melbourne more and more for stuff on the weekends. He started making all these new friends. And then when I did go and see him, I could feel it, like...like an absence, you know? I don't know. I could just tell his attention was elsewhere, if you know what I mean."

Mia nods. "What did you do?"

"Well," Claire says wearily. "I avoided dealing with it. Because apparently that's what I do best. Then, after about a month or two of quietly freaking out, wondering if maybe he'd met someone, but too gutless to ask, I thought I could...I don't know...just go and spend some real time him and remind him why we were so good. So I drove up there one weekend to stay. I changed my shifts, got out of a family dinner, and ignored a French test. But when I got there it was like he barely registered my presence." She bites her lip. "It was too late."

"He cheated?"

"No, he never cheated. He wouldn't do that." She gently plucks at a single blade of grass and tries to ease it up out of the ground without breaking it. "But it didn't matter. He didn't cheat, but he was already completely into this girl. He just didn't have the balls to tell me. Until finally I asked outright."

"Oh."

"Yeah." Claire rolls over onto her stomach so Mia can't see her face, because she can feel the vague choke of impending tears in her throat. And crying would be completely humiliating right now. "That's right, oh." She blinks hard. This is why she doesn't talk about it. The hurt and the embarrassment come back. In this case, there's also possible double humiliation of crying in front of a potential new friend who doesn't need to know how pathetic she actually feels about all this.

But Mia doesn't say anything. Nothing at all. She just rolls over onto her stomach too and nudges Claire's foot with her own, a small but reassuring gesture of sympathy.

"The worst part is," Claire continues, "I was almost angrier at Michelle about this than I was at him. I am over it...well, maybe I'm not completely. But I am over being angry and upset. It's over and I don't have the energy for anger and sadness. But her..." She frowns. "I thought she was my friend."

"What did she say about it today?"

"She just said that she's really, really sorry and that she didn't mean it to happen, but circumstances made it hard to avoid hanging out with her, blah, blah. I don't know. It's like, I get it. I do. It would have been awkward for her. But I'd never, ever do that, not without telling her first at least." She stares across the tract of grass. "And now, I really don't know if I can be friends with her anymore, not like before, anyway."

Even as she says the words, a small, guilty part of Claire wonders if it's really her lack of desire to maintain their dwindling friendship that's the issue and not Michelle's supposed betrayal.

Mia suddenly sits up. "That seems so unfair, having that happen with your best friend and your boyfriend like that."

"Yeah, but you know, I don't even know if Michelle and I were that close, or if it was just because Brendan and her boyfriend, Jack, were best friends. But still, I expected more loyalty from her, you know?"

And again, Mia is silent. For a minute, Claire wonders if she's gone on too long, overshared. Mia's probably bored. It is only the third time they've hung out, and she probably doesn't want—or need—to hear all Claire's problems. She's trying to think of a way to change the subject when Mia leans forward.

"I think every friendship has its limits," Mia says. "And sometimes a friendship runs its natural course too. I don't know. I'm not friends with half the people I was close with in high school. We just don't have anything left in common, or we don't have enough time for each other. You just can't hold on to everyone. Maybe it's a part of moving on with the next stage of life."

Claire nods, contemplating what Mia is saying, grateful for some perspective and for insight that explains the difficult—painful, even— lunch and its probable outcome.

"I mean, the people who count, the ones who I really care about, they're still around. That's how you know they're the keepers, right?" Mia tips her head to one side, staring past her.

Claire nods again, even though she doesn't really know. The way she's going, she won't have any friends left from high school. Besides, Claire hasn't had a friend like that—a keeper—since Beth, her best friend who moved away at the start of year ten and left Claire adrift in the social world of high school. And that feels as though it was decades ago now.

Mia straightens her legs, reaches into her bag, and pulls out a sandwich. She slowly unwraps it, then offers half to Claire. Even though Claire isn't hungry, she takes it, appreciative of the gesture. She sits up on the grass, inspects the insides of the sandwich, and takes a bite.

"What about you and Robbie?" she asks, between chews. "He's a keeper, right?"

"Yeah, of course. But even we have our limits."

"Like what?" Claire asks, curious. She figured he and Mia are in friend love.

"I love Robbie, but it's hard with him sometimes because he just disappears."

"What do you mean?"

Mia chews slowly, a thoughtful look on her face. "I mean that he just... there have been times when I've needed him, and he's not around, you know? I would get hurt in the past, but now I'm getting used to it. And I've learned not to depend on him to always be there." She stares at her sandwich. "And you know, I don't think that he doesn't want to be there, or that he wouldn't if I asked. Or that he doesn't care. He's just flighty. He'll be everywhere for a while, and then he'll just kind of be gone."

"Where does he go?"

Mia breaks off a piece of crust and tosses it to a sparrow that has been edging closer to them since the appearance of food. "New guy, new photo project, new friends. Any or all of the above. Also, sometimes, I think he just goes into hiding. Like he puts himself out there so much that sometimes he has to retreat so he can focus or rest or something."

"Oh." Claire watches the bird dart forward and pull the crust backward across the grass with its beak, unable to pick it up. It covetously pecks at the bread, moving quickly, as if wary another bird will discover the treasure before it can finish. "That would be hard."

"I don't mean to make him sound like a bad friend. He's awesome and beautiful. I just had to learn to not always depend on him being there exactly when I need him to be. I mean, when he's there, he's there, you know. But sometimes he's just...gone." She shrugs.

Frowning, Claire tosses the last crust of her sandwich to the handful of birds that are gathered hopefully on the grass near them. "Is he your best friend?"

"He's definitely become one of them. My friend Kristen is my oldest and closest friend. She's in Sydney, though, studying."

"How long have you known each other?"

"Since forever. She and her brother grew up a street away from me. I miss her. We talk all the time, and she's here some holidays, but it's not the same."

Claire nods. She tries not to feel envious. And she's not sure what she's more envious of, Mia having two really close friends, or Mia's close friends themselves. Claire misses feeling important to someone aside from her brother. He's the only person she can think of who wants her around enough that he actually misses her when she isn't there. Maybe Michelle would have in the past, but now she doesn't know what Michelle thinks of her.

As though she can read her mind, Mia reaches over and plucks at Claire's sleeve. "Anyway, maybe it's not so bad then, that you have some space from Michelle? Not that I'm saying you should just cut her out, or that it's not worth it. Only you know whether you should do that, but maybe you just need some time...some space."

"Maybe. I feel like my whole social world just came apart, you know? One day I knew exactly how everything worked and who my people were. And the next day, not a single freaking clue."

"You have Nina. And you have us."

And before Claire—both embarrassed and warmed by this sudden, confident declaration of friendship—has to say anything in response, Mia checks her watch and sits up. "Damn, I've got to go. Class in ten."

Claire reaches out and grabs her wrist and looks at the time. "Me too. I have to meet my brother."

They scramble to their feet. Mia groans as she hauls her heavy bag to her shoulders. When it's on her back, she thrusts her hands in her pockets and looks at Claire. Claire smiles at her, feeling weird and shy and slightly embarrassed from all this sharing.

And Mia returns the smile. But hers, of course, is open and easy and tells her she doesn't have to worry about what Mia thinks of her.

They stroll slowly across the campus together, mutually reluctant to leave the peaceful cocoon of the university lawn for the thrum and impatience of the real world.

"You know, on paper, you don't sound like you actually *are*," Claire tells her.

"What?" Mia screws up her face. "What do you mean?"

"Well, if you said to me, sporty science geek, wears glasses, into old books, I wouldn't imagine you."

"Um, what makes you think I'm sporty?"

"Actually, I don't know." Claire appraises her as they walk. "Maybe your long legs?"

"Believe me, I'm not sporty." Mia laughs.

"You *look* sporty."

"Well, you make no sense, either. At work you're completely hostile, but outside you're actually nice. You give everyone hell, but you're completely sensitive yourself. You act like you don't care about stuff, but I can tell you do." She gives Claire a look. "All kinds of conflicting information there too, so I don't know if you should judge."

"But I always judge, Mia. That's what I do."

"Besides, what you really meant is that I sound like a giant geek on paper, while you're probably used to hanging out with all the shiny party kids." Mia shrugs. "You're surprised that you like to hang out with me." She gives her an I-know-you-grin.

"Maybe." Claire laughs.

Mia is silent for a moment as they walk. "You know, I don't really care what I sound like on paper. If being a geek is doing what I am doing, then I don't care. I'm pretty happy with who I am most of the time."

Claire fleetingly wonders when it is that Mia isn't happy with who she is. Claire could say she's happy with herself about half the time on a good day. She can't imagine Mia feeling less than satisfied with who she is, though. How could someone so smart and funny and friendly and liked be unhappy?

Claire shakes her head. "I'm telling you now, I don't know if I can hang out with someone so well adjusted."

Mia grins. "It doesn't matter. You have no say in it. We're friends. Even if I didn't want to—and I do—it wouldn't matter because Robbie loves you."

"What?" Claire nearly stops in her tracks at that revelation. "He doesn't act like it."

"That's just how he is with you. If he didn't like you, trust me, he'd just ignore you. Besides, do you think you're particularly friendly? Remember that night at the bar when we met?"

Claire blushes a little against her will. "I thought you weren't paying any attention." She was pretty feisty that night, even by her own standards.

"No, I was just letting you guys fight it out. I knew you would either destroy each other or become friends. And either way, it would be entertaining for me."

Claire doesn't quite know what to say to that. "Whatever, Mia."

"Like I said, you two are cut from the same cloth. Two thoroughly charming jerks."

Claire blinks. She was not expecting Mia to pass judgement so swiftly and so damningly on them both. "Jerks, huh?" She shakes her head and laughs.

Mia just grins and changes the subject. "What are you doing with your brother today?"

"I'm meeting him at Robbie's gallery. I told him about the photo, and now he wants to see it." Claire shakes her head. "I don't know why. He knows what I look like."

"Oh, you know why." Mia smiles. "What's your brother like?"

"He's...I don't know. He likes beer and sports and shooting stuff—real stuff because he's a cop. He's good at figuring out problems and making others laugh, and he makes terrible decisions about people with pretty faces and boobs. I guess he's a regular guy."

Mia laughs.

"And people with pretty faces and boobs seem to like him even though he's an idiot."

"Wow." Mia stops at the end of the long path leading out of campus. "I feel like I know him already."

Claire pulls out her phone and looks for his last message to see how far away he said he was. Before she can check, though, Mia has taken her phone out of her hand and is tapping away.

"What are you doing?"

"Messaging me." Then she passes it back to Claire. "Now you have my number. Call me or something if you want to meet up." She checks her watch. "See you soon," she says as if it's the most natural, inevitable thing in the world. Then she turns around and hurries away, the set of her shoulders tells Claire her mind has already turned to the next thing on her list.

Simultaneous bursts of both admiration and envy for Mia's effortless vitality and her social ease run through Claire. It is something Mia simply has, but Claire always feels she is trying so desperately to muster.

Maybe if she spends enough time around it, she can learn something from her.

CHAPTER 17

Claire has only slept with four guys in her life.

Four.

One was the guy she lost her virginity to back in year ten when she decided she was drunk enough for it to go. One was Brendan, of course. Repeatedly. And the other two were similarly drunken one-off incidents in the aftermath of Brendan, just for the possibility of forgetting. She tried to move on by getting drunk and randomly hooking up. It didn't work, though. The awkward one-night stands simply set off another maelstrom of regret.

Four guys.

That hardly makes her a slut. In fact, it barely makes her interesting. So how in the hell is she left here feeling like a complete skank? How come she feels like that when she didn't do anything wrong?

Claire stalks down the street, her hands jammed in her pockets and her collar up around her ears. It's a miserable day, the first in a while, featuring a particularly whippy, biting wind. She picks up speed because she's already a little late.

And being late doesn't help when Claire is in the foulest mood she's been in for a long time—one that's going to make this meeting with her mother more unbearable than usual. She frowns into the wind and crosses the street, dodging around the stalled traffic at the busy intersection.

Going back to Nina's after Josh's birthday party last night had been a stupid, *stupid* idea. She knows that now. In fact, going to Josh's birthday party at a club after work was the first bad idea. But Nina begged her to go. Hamstrung from being able to offer a sensible reason not to—like the fact that she'd rather stay at home and watch crappy television than celebrate the birth of a giant sleazebag—she agreed, against her better judgment.

But why hadn't she thought of how Josh would react? Of course, a guy like him would think, because it was his birthday, he could do whatever the hell he liked.

They got back to the apartment, and Nina, who was completely wasted, crawled straight into bed, because that's her usual post-party MO. Meanwhile, Claire was left with a drunken Josh. One minute she was at the kitchen sink, kicking off her shoes and downing a giant glass of water to prevent her imminent hangover, and the next Josh was pawing at her while Nina slept in the next room.

It turned out, however, that Nina wasn't sleeping. In fact, she was wide awake and on her way to the bathroom when she came past the kitchen. Next thing she knew, Nina was screaming in rage at both of them. But mostly at Claire.

Suddenly that feistiness Nina wields against irritating sleazy customers—the feistiness that Claire has long admired—was directed at her point-blank. It was horrible. Nina was livid, in a borderline-hysterical fit, and Claire was too shocked to defend herself. Instead, she got the hell out. She grabbed her shoes and bag and headed for the street where she hailed a taxi that took her on the expensive drive back to the suburbs and away from Nina's rage.

Josh just stood drunkenly in the corner and muttered over and over, "I'm so sorry, babe." Fucking toddler. But Nina paid him no attention. She focused only on Claire.

This morning, she's finished with crying. Now, she's angry. How dare Nina automatically assume Claire had instigated it? That Claire would betray her with that stupid pig? In the next room? While Nina was sleeping? She's so engrossed in her thoughts she nearly misses the turn toward her mother's office block.

How do these things happen to her?

Back in year ten, in the period not long after her best friend moved away, Claire was tentatively starting a friendship with this girl Katrina. One night, Claire and Katrina went to a party and spent a half hour talking to this one vaguely normal, non-douche guy. Then, all of a sudden, Katrina let loose on her. She accused Claire of trying to steal this guy she'd set her sights on. Claire was completely baffled and hurt. She hadn't known Katrina liked him—and suspected later that he didn't either—or that she was stepping on toes by having a normal human conversation at a party. Clearly, she'd been wrong.

Claire would *never* knowingly steal a friend's guy. The first rule of the family Pearson—loyalty in everything.

After that, they were no longer on speaking terms, and there were rumours swirling around the school that Claire had done something shitty to another girl. It was difficult to come back socially from that kind of perceived betrayal in girl world. That was the point when, hurt, she decided it was better to be a loner than to try to negotiate the unsteady friendship terrains at school. She spent her social time with the guys she dated or even Cam and his friends.

She became a girl who only hung out with guys. Because it was safer. Guys didn't have these weird unspoken rules and undercurrents. By the time she met Michelle, who actually wanted to be her friend despite all the gossip, the hurt had faded, and she remembered why she liked female friends.

Claire pauses to let a man carrying an armful of catering boxes cut in front of her and frowns. Now she's in this mess again, only worse. What is it about her that makes people think she would be so traitorous, that she's some kind of man-eater who'll go behind her friends' backs? She never has, and she never, ever will.

She does *not* get it at all.

* * *

"And this, sweetheart, is why I like working in a world of men." Christine pulls a sweater from the rack and examines it. "Men are simple. Men are straightforward. It's easy. They're easy."

Claire frowns. It's weird to hear her own thoughts come out of her mother's mouth. She trails her mother through the store, where they are ostensibly looking for an outfit for her cousin's birthday but really seem to be on the hunt for clothes for Christine.

"Women, on the other hand...most women are defensive, and they will betray you in a second if they think you're a threat to their territory."

"Glad to see the feminist movement left a mark on you, Mum."

"You don't need feminism, sweetheart. You don't need solidarity or any of that nonsense. You just need to look after yourself." Christine flicks a dismissive hand in Claire's direction and moves to the next rack. "Look, if you say you didn't do anything with this idiot of a boy, I believe you—I certainly hope I raised you with better taste, at least. But honey, there's no point getting all weepy about a girl who claims you tried to steal her boyfriend. Who needs that in her life? Just move on and find a nicer friend to spend your time with."

Claire sighs. And this is why she hardly ever tells her mother anything. She probably wouldn't have today if the wounds hadn't been written all over her face when they met outside the store. Just one look and Christine started firing questions that Claire didn't have the mettle to dodge. She didn't ask her mother for advice, either. Not that it matters. Whenever her mother encounters any of her problems, she delivers some simple, cutthroat solution. Then she dismisses it as if it's solved. When it's over in her mother's mind, it is over. Full stop.

She trails slowly behind her mother as she picks up folded blouses from shelves, investigates them, and then re-folds them as neatly as she found them. The thing is she has no intention of doing what her mother advises. She doesn't want to lose Nina to the situation. Sure, she's mad as hell at her for thinking Claire would do that, but she also knows that maybe it's a little her fault too. If she'd told Nina about Josh last time, this probably wouldn't have happened.

Her mother wraps a blue-patterned scarf around her neck, inspects the effect in the mirror against her work blazer, and then tosses it back onto the pile.

"Aren't we supposed to be shopping for Lisa?" Claire reminds her, bored of watching her mother shop and in no mood to do any browsing of her own.

"Well, yes, but your father and I have that seminar in Canberra next month. There's going to be a million boring social engagements too, and I need some new clothing to wear. It won't take a minute, then we'll find something for Lisa and have a nice lunch."

Claire continues her sigh-a-thon and follows her mother to the next rack where Christine quickly dismisses the selection of shirts. Claire leans against a nearby wall and yawns. Her phone vibrates in her pocket and she checks it, both hoping it is and is not Nina at the same time. It's not. It's Mia. *Hey. Are you around? Coffee?*

Claire shoves her phone back in her pocket without responding. No one but the woman who brought her into this ridiculous world should have to deal with her mood today.

"Though I will say, darling," Christine suddenly pipes up again, a manicured finger directed at her, "I do think it's about time you moved on from that awfulness with Brendan, don't you? You need to get yourself out there again." She lays a dress over her arm. "If you had a boyfriend of your own, these things wouldn't happen, would they?"

"I suppose," Claire mumbles. Sadly, she thinks it might be true.

"I think you've moped long enough, don't you?" She turns in the direction of the dressing room. "I'm just going to try these on. Won't be a minute."

Christine hurries off, the spikes of her heels digging into the department store carpet. Claire parks herself on a stool, resigned to wait.

Her mother is wrong. Claire is fully committed to moping right now. She doesn't want to lose her friend—one of the only friends left standing. The saddest part is, whatever happens, Claire knows it's not going to be her decision to make.

CHAPTER 18

Claire's been hiding in her room so long she's become sick of the unbearably familiar four walls.

Restless, but unwilling to go anywhere other than class or work this week, she has stayed put. Better for everyone, she guesses. Tonight she doesn't have to work, and Nina called in sick for both her shifts so far. In fact, she wonders if Nina will go on calling in sick until she goes home to her family next week. Claire wouldn't be surprised.

She walks through the empty house, aimless and bored and sick of her own noisy, self-hating thoughts. Her parents have both been working late, as usual, and Cam has reinstalled himself at Elana's permanently, so she's spent most of the week alone.

In fact, Claire feels as though she's spent way more time in this house alone than she ever has in company. Especially during the last five or six years when her parents clearly decided she and Cam were grown enough to fend for themselves. At that point, her parents busied themselves with their climb up the career ladder. They stopped hiring the babysitters and housekeepers who populated their early years, leaving Claire and Cam on their own. It was a new form of benign neglect—they were given pocket money, a schedule, a strict set of rules, and a healthy fear of what would happen if they did something wrong.

Mostly, that suited Claire just fine. But sometimes she craved her parents' time and attention. And she knows Cam did too. Instead, they had each other. When her mother was around, it took Claire roughly twenty-four hours to wish her mother would go for another promotion and leave her the hell alone. Then, of course, she regretted ever wishing for maternal attention.

Claire stops in the kitchen, opens the fridge door, and inspects the contents even though she isn't hungry. She closes it just as quickly and wanders into the living room. Tempted by the golden, late-afternoon sun, she opens the sliding door and steps onto the terrace. She hears the sound of hammering that means her father is home.

She walks slowly down the long path to where a tall, wooden building sits, nestled among apple and pear trees in the backyard. She stops at the door and peers inside. Her father has changed from his suit into old jeans and a sweater. He fixes yet another handmade shelf to the wall. She parks herself on the step, pulls her knees to her chest, and rests her chin in her hand as she stares out into the yard. Some of the fruit trees are still blossoming, and Claire smells the softest hint of their pinkish, light perfume. Spring has sprung in the yard.

The hammering stops. First, she hears footsteps and the quiet grizzle of his voice and then feels the hand placed momentarily on her head.

"Claire."

"Hey, Dad."

He leans on the doorpost next to her, his gaze turned outward as he appraises his yard. His kingdom.

She feels as though she hasn't seen him for an age. He's always so late after work, later than her mother sometimes. Other nights, he's in bed by the time Claire comes home. And now that the afternoons are getting longer, when he does get home at a reasonable time, he goes straight to the yard. Or to his shed, where he tinkers at his eternal project.

"Still not finished with this dump?" She peers around his legs into the dimly lit shed.

He chuckles, because they both know it's not a dump. It's beautiful. Probably the nicest shed anyone ever built in Melbourne. From the outside, it doesn't look like much, just a regular wooden structure, but the inside is a work of wooden art, all burnished timber, high ceilings, and polished floors. He even installed high-up windows near the attic-style roof to let in the light. Claire used to tease him about them. *What, so the tools can enjoy the morning sun?*

He's been working on it for years, but he'll probably never be finished. It doesn't matter, though. She knows it's less about the end product and more about the process. This planning, this methodical building, this constant attention to detail, they are his version of meditation, of finding daily peace in the quiet act of doing.

It's the same at the holiday house. When they were younger, she and Cam rejoined the army of kids who hung out there, and her mother joined her own group of lake mothers who collectively socialised and neglected over never-ending bottles of *sauvignon blanc*. Her father, however, contented himself with working all day at his various projects. He built their elaborate and much envied cubby house and later the bunkhouse for when the number of visitors stretched the house to its limits. After that, it was the coveted sleeping porch at the side of the house, the holy grail of spots on the hottest of summer nights. The projects were endless, and he doted on each of them until they were done.

Claire knows these projects are testament to what makes him a good lawyer. Strategy and method, they are his normal. They are his strength. Unlike her mother, for whom negotiating the levels of power is the product of her intense social masterminding, he quietly slides upward, hefted by his ability to strategise and manage big cases that succeed on the underpinnings of his quiet and calculated planning.

She also knows that this shed is his sanctuary from the world. And sometimes, she feels the urge to come and borrow his peace for a minute.

"What have you been up to?"

"Nothing much. Studying for exams," she lies, staring out into the wealth of bloom and leaf. "The garden looks great."

"There'll be plenty of fruit. Your apple bloomed magnificently this year."

She looks at the apple tree, still shedding the last of its pink blossoms. She watches petals freefall as the tree wavers in the light breeze. It *is* her tree. When she was six, her father told her she could choose any kind of fruit tree she wanted to plant. He was slowly turning their neat, shrubbed, uniform suburban backyard into some sort of crazy market garden. He built vegetable patches along the back fence and filled in the lawn—except for one section near the terrace, which her mother demanded he keep "normal" for guests—with an army of fruit trees of every variety that could survive the Melbourne weather.

At six, Claire had no imagination for trees and no real heed for the possibilities of nature, so she picked the only fruit she liked at the time, an apple. Claire still remembers the lush smell of the garden centre, the feel of her father's hand with his wiry, hairy fingers clutching hers. And she remembers the feel of damp soil that passed through her hands as she sprinkled it around the young tree, pressed it around its narrow little trunk, and tucked it into its new home by the garden path.

For the next year, she helped tend it, which largely meant watering it every so often. But its inherent hardiness and independence meant it needed nothing else from her. She forgot about it for a couple of years until her father took her out into the yard and pointed out the tiny fruit finally beginning to grow. They clung to the spindly branches of the adolescent tree. That's when it became part of the fabric of their backyard for her, a ceaseless, predictable cycle of leaf, bloom, fruit, and fall—a cycle that he watches and nurtures, but she only notices every now and again when she takes a moment out here or when he brings her the first ripe apple from the tree.

"You know, I'm thinking of getting rid of the pool at the end of summer," he says—a reminder to her that he's still standing behind her, also enmeshed in contemplation of the backyard.

"Why?" The small aboveground pool next to the terrace is still covered from the winter.

"Because you kids don't use it anymore. And your mother would like a paved area on the lawn for entertaining."

Claire rolls her eyes. Of course it's what her mother wants.

"So, anyway, how are you? You doing okay?"

"I'm fine." She knows he's asking because she hardly ever comes out here and he's curious about this unprompted visit. She tells him she's fine because, even though her mother's the one who puts the effort into making Claire fine, she most wants to be okay for her father. Since she started uni and supposedly became an adult, he's the one who stands back and lets her do what she wants, however unexpected. Unless she threatens a too radical departure from the Pearson normality, he keeps quiet and lets her go, something she appreciates more all the time.

But she feels his quiet concern sometimes. And he looks at her, too, with a fondness tempered by a mild helplessness. It's as if he's not quite sure what to do with this alien person he's raised, someone so unsure of who she wants to be. Because of the quiet but unflinching way he cares and never questions, she doesn't want him to worry about her.

"Don't study too hard." He leaves her to it and goes back to his work.

She sits a while longer and listens to the sounds of him working as she absorbs the last warmth of the sun. The phone in her pocket beeps, and she pulls it out. It's Mia.

Hey, are you working tonight? Robbie and I were thinking of coming in for a drink after work...

She feels a flash of guilt because she didn't answer Mia's last message earlier in the week. Even though she'd like to see her, Claire is glad she isn't working because she's nervous to see Robbie. What if Nina told him about what happened? That would be completely embarrassing. She quickly types a response. *Not tonight. See you soon, though.*

"Hey, Dad, I'm going inside." She dusts down the back of her jeans as she gets up from the step and waits a beat for his response. But he doesn't hear her over the sound of his hammering.

CHAPTER 19

"Dude, that's rough." Cam shakes his head and wipes froth from his upper lip.

She spins her cup on its saucer and frowns. "Yup."

"Have you spoken to her since?"

"Nope. Won't answer my calls."

He shakes his head. "Girls are weird."

"That's what I keep saying."

That's when his phone starts ringing. Again. He picks it up, turns a little from the table, and listens hard. His face shifts immediately to serious. As she waits for him to be done with his third work call during their brief coffee date, she turns and looks around the café. It is less busy than the first couple of times she's been there, with just half the tables full. The waiters stand around the counter and chat instead of running around, frantic, like they usually do. And Mia is toiling away behind the machine, a small frown of concentration on her face as she works. She doesn't seem to have noticed Claire is there.

"Crap, I've got to go. Sorry, sis." Cam tucks his phone into his back pocket and pulls on his jacket. "Work."

Claire nods, long resigned to these constant work interruptions. This is the story of her life, her family jumps ship every time work calls. "Great to see you for, what, twenty minutes?"

"I'm sorry." He squeezes her shoulder. "And I'm sorry about what happened with your friend. That sucks. Anyway, thanks for showing me where the hipsters drink their coffee." He grins. "I'll see you later."

She gives him a sarcastic wave. When she finishes her coffee, she makes her way to Mia. Claire waits a beat as Mia presses a lid onto a takeaway cup and passes it to a customer, and then she steps forward.

"Hey." She leans against the counter and smiles.

Mia looks up, surprised. "Oh hey." She's clearly a little flustered by Claire's sudden appearance.

"How are you?" Claire asks, slightly thrown by Mia's reaction.

Mia flashes a glimmer of a smile and then returns to frowning over the coffee machine. "I'm okay."

Claire wonders if she shouldn't be bothering her at work. She pushes herself away from the counter, suddenly feeling awkward. "I was just going to see if you had a break coming, but you look a little busy. I'll leave you to it."

"Oh, no, it's...um...yeah." Mia pours milk into a shot of coffee and quickly glances at Claire, her eyebrows knitted. Then she takes a breath and smiles. "I might be able to in, like, ten minutes? But you probably don't want to wait around," she adds hurriedly.

"No, it's totally fine. Come join me whenever."

Claire returns to her seat. She still feels uncomfortable, as if she shouldn't be here, but she's committed now. She thumbs through a magazine left in the middle of the table and idly looks at pictures until Mia arrives with a coffee in her hands. A big coffee this time, Claire notes as Mia parks herself on the stool opposite Claire.

"I can only take ten minutes. The boss wants us to pack up early because it's quiet, and she has a hair appointment she 'simply can't be late for.'" She rolls her eyes.

"That's okay." Claire closes the magazine and pushes it away. "Should I not talk to you while you're working?

"What? No, of course it's fine. I was just somewhere else when you came up."

"Oh good. I wanted to say hi. Sorry I didn't get back to you when you messaged the first time. It was a...weird week."

"That's okay." Mia stares at her coffee. "I didn't mean to bother you or anything. You're probably busy with other stuff, I shouldn't—"

"What?" Claire reaches over and prods her in the arm, surprised by Mia's response. "No. You weren't bothering me. Why would you think that? Like I said, it was just a weird week, and I really wasn't fit for human consumption. I didn't think anyone should have to put up with me."

"Is everything okay?"

"Yeah, fine," Claire fibs, because Mia heard enough about her personal dramas last time they saw each other. She doesn't need to hear any more, especially on her break. "How was your week?"

"It was okay."

Claire looks for something to talk about and comments, "It's quiet."

"Yes, thank God. It's was busy all morning."

"And how's Pete? Not that I am being nosy," she hurriedly adds as she remembers Mia's slight caginess the last couple of times Claire brought him up. "I just mean, you know, he seems like a nice guy, and I'm wondering how he's..." She trails off.

Mia smiles at her mini rant. "He's okay, I think. I haven't really seen him much lately." She picks up her spoon and stirs slow circles into her coffee. "I ended it with him, actually."

"What? Really?" Claire leans in, surprised. They seemed so easy and fun together at the opening. "How come—if you don't mind me asking, of course."

"I don't know." Mia shrugs. "It just didn't feel right. I think I just want to be friends."

"Fair enough. You know how you feel."

Mia nods but doesn't say anything.

"Did he take it okay?" Claire asks the question tentatively, not quite sure where to tread with Mia and her personal life.

"I think so. He made like it was okay, but it was kind of hard to tell."

"Guys love to be all cool about this stuff, don't they?"

"I guess."

"Will you really still be friends?"

"I hope so." Mia rests her cheek in her hand. "He's one of the genuinely fun people in my course. I mean, everyone's nice and stuff, but they can be kind of...socially limited."

"He'll be fine," Claire says in an attempt to lighten Mia's mood. "He'll find some other hot science geek to hook up with and get over it, and then you and he can be friends. But don't feel bad. It's not like you did anything wrong."

"I don't know. Maybe I'm a horrible person. I should have figured it out before."

"I don't know you that well yet, but I bet you're not a horrible person." Claire pokes her in the arm again. "And I bet you weren't horrible about it when you told him. Besides, it would be worse to keep pretending if you don't feel it."

"I guess." Mia frowns for a minute as she plays idly with a knot on the wooden tabletop. She seems really low.

Claire leans forward. "Hey, are you okay?"

"Yeah," Mia finally replies. She gives Claire a watery smile. "I'm just a bit...I don't know. There's this thing with Pete, then exams are coming, and I have a heap of work to do, and remember how I told you about Robbie's disappearing acts?"

Claire nods.

"He's doing one of those. I'm just feeling a little overwhelmed, I guess."

Claire bites her lip and looks at her for a minute, not quite sure what to do with this slightly down, stressed version of Mia. This is the first time she's seen her less than together. And while she feels bad for Mia because she's clearly had a shitty week, part of her is a teensy, selfishly bit glad to see Mia isn't always *so* upbeat and at ease.

"Hey, it's okay, you know. You did the right thing with Pete. And I'll bet you'll kill your exams. There's still a few weeks and then study break. Heaps of time." She drops her hand on Mia's wrist and squeezes it until Mia looks up at her. "Just breathe, okay?" she tells her, because that's the only advice she knows to give.

Obediently, Mia takes in a big breath and lets it out, shimmying her shoulders as if shaking it off, and then gives Claire a near-perfect *I'm okay* smile. "Was that guy who was here before your brother by any chance?" she asks, changing the subject.

"Yup, that was the sibling. I thought I'd take him for a decent coffee. He'll drinks crap all day and then complain about it. I thought I'd show him it isn't that hard to find a decent one near his work."

Mia glances at her watch. "Damn, I have to go back already." She picks up her cup. "But thanks for coming and saying hi. And I'm sorry I'm such a mope."

"You don't have to say thanks or sorry. You heard all of my woes last week. It's totally your turn."

"Thanks for letting me have my turn. I'll see you soon?"

"For sure. See you."

Claire waves, glad to see her feeling even a teensy bit better as Mia heads back behind the counter for the rest of her shift. Maybe she's not as shitty a friend as some people seem to think.

CHAPTER 20

This is not what Claire had pictured, not at all.

This party, in this apartment, with these people? Nope, this is not what she expected. Robbie invited her via text message halfway through her shift to demand her attendance. She stands in the open doorway. All she can think is these people don't look like the kind of people Robbie would hang out with. And they look nothing like the kind of people who were at his exhibition party either. The effort gone into this night, with the decorations, food, and even a DJ, makes it look more like a party that her old, moneyed, school friends might have held—albeit in a much cooler inner city apartment.

As she takes in this scene, she wonders what the hell she's doing here with the kind of people she's been avoiding lately. As she pulls off her jacket, she searches the room for a familiar face, feeling completely and utterly adrift. She's nervous to walk right in without the security of a destination and really wishes everything hadn't gone to hell with Nina. At least then she'd have her here.

But there's no point wishing that. Claire only came to this party because she knows Nina won't be here. It's the week of Nina's big trip home, and that's what gave Claire the freedom to finish work, change her top, reapply makeup, and head for the address Robbie sent. If Nina had been in town, unspoken social rules dictate that this party falls into Nina's friendship territory. Claire would have to back off.

She takes a few steps in and pauses by a generously laden food table and scans the crowd. She feels an almost embarrassing surge of relief when she spots Mia on the other side of the room. Relieved, Claire makes an instant beeline for her.

She's leaning against the kitchen counter, chatting with Pete, holding a beer, and laughing. She's wearing what Claire has come to think of as

Mia's uniform. The look never changes. A top or a tank or maybe a shirt if it's cooler. Always simple but in colour or with a small, interesting detail. Jeans. Always jeans. Always blue. Boots. Her hair down, tangled loose around her shoulders, unless she's studying, and then it's always tied back. She never wears earrings or bracelets, but there is often a pendant hanging from the long silver chain. Like her personality, her sense of fashion has only one setting—effortlessly casual as if she doesn't have time to care about how she looks. It doesn't even matter. Guys still notice her. It's not just that she's attractive but because she's also approachable and fun. There's a vitality about her. She seems as though she'll give a minute of her day to anyone, unless the other person proves not worth it.

Claire wishes she had that kind of ease, but even when she's at her most confident, she doesn't. She never will. She doesn't have it in her personality or in her style. She doesn't know how to leave the house without looking as if she's made an effort, without at least the protective barrier of eyeliner and a carefully chosen outfit. Even tonight, she spent a good twenty minutes touching up her makeup and hair before she felt she could go out among people without the distance of the bar between herself and the world. She envies Mia's ability to easily exist without all the trimmings. And it's just plain unfair that she's still so lovely without them.

As Claire fights her way through the crowd, she exchanges dirty looks with underfed girls swaying on the fringes of the dance floor. Mia spots her and waves when she emerges on the kitchen side of the room. She looks a hell of a lot happier than she did a week ago at the café.

Claire raises her hands and gives her a frowning why-the-hell-are-we-here look as she closes the distance between them.

"I know, right?"

"Where's Robbie?" Claire leans on the counter next to her. "I demand answers."

"He's not here yet. He just messaged me to say he's not far. Thanks goodness for these guys." Mia nods at Pete and his friend, a short guy in a cap. "They promised to wait until he got here."

"This is really not my scene." Pete shakes his head. "In fact, this might be what my personal hell looks like." His friend nods in ardent agreement. "Now that Claire's here, can we go?" He smiles at Claire. "No offence, you understand?"

Claire laughs. "None taken at all."

He then turns back to Mia, broadening the grin. It seems he's taking their split pretty well. Well enough to hang out with her at least.

"You can go." Mia grabs his arm and laughs. "Thank you for waiting with me."

"No problem. Thanks for the party. The, uh, the walking here part was fun." He grins at Mia and gives Claire a wave. "See you."

"Bye."

They make their rapid exit through the crowd.

Mia faces Claire and smiles. "I didn't know you were coming. It's good to see you."

"The jury's out on whether I'm glad to be here."

Mia laughs. "How's life? Aside from the fact we're here."

"It's pretty sucky right now." Claire folds her arms over her chest and leans back against the counter. "Yours?"

"Fair to middling." Mia swigs her beer.

"Pete seems okay."

"Yeah, he does, actually. He's been pretty cool about it. Hey, are Nina and Josh coming?"

"Most definitely not."

"Why not?"

"Because Nina's away. And because she hates me right now."

"What?" Mia turns to look at her. "Why?"

Claire sighs and fills Mia in on the whole sad, sorry saga that is Nina and Josh and, by no choice of her own, Claire.

Mia listens, eyebrows raised.

Claire frowns. "The worst part is, not only did she automatically blame me, but I can't get her to talk to me. He's gross. I wouldn't touch him with a ten-foot pole because he's her boyfriend, and he's a freaking douche bag. Seriously, such a douche bag." She turns to Mia to beg for support on this one. "You've met him, right?"

Mia nods. "He didn't seem like the most charming person I've ever met. Or the brainiest, either."

"Crap." Claire sighs. "Maybe I should have told her. Maybe I'm a shitty friend for not telling her she's going out with an idiot."

"I think she's bound to figure that out for herself eventually, so don't feel too bad."

"I'm great, aside from the fact that the person I'd call my closest friend thinks I'm a boyfriend-stealing slut who'd betray her in a second—which I would never do, Mia." Claire jabs a finger in the air to emphasise her point. "I *don't* betray my friends."

"Okay." Mia holds up her hands as if to defend herself. "I promise I won't ever accuse you of trying to steal my boyfriend, okay?"

"Good. Thanks," Claire grumbles. "Anyway, besides being tried and found a boy-thieving ho who's only allowed at this party because Nina is away, I no longer have anyone to stay with in the city. That means I have to spend every single night at home in the company of my mother, who is driving me nuts. Oh yeah, and did I mention I hate my job? But then that's always a thing."

"So, you're not really in the party mood then?"

"No, sorry." Claire frowns. "I bet you want your friends to come back now."

"No, that's okay." Mia chuckles. "I get it. That all sounds bad. I'd feel pretty crappy about being the accused too."

"I may not be in a party mood, but I am in a drinking one. Seriously, where is Robbie? He said he was bringing the booze."

Mia passes her a beer. "That's all I've got, but what's mine is yours."

"Thanks." Claire takes a swig and hands it back. They stand in a comfortable silence for a while and pass the beer back and forth as they watch the party gather steam around them. The volume rises and the dance floor swells into the kitchen area.

"These are really, really not my people," Mia muses as a bunch of girls in barely there dresses drop their handbags into a pile and begin to dance around them. They shuffle from side to side in their heels and look around the room as they gossip.

"That speaks very highly of you, Mia."

"Do you ever wonder what everybody is talking about all the time?" Mia passes her the last of the beer.

"I know exactly what they are talking about." Claire slugs the final mouthful and puts the bottle behind her on the counter. "I've been to this party a gazillion times. They're all talking about each other or they're talking about themselves. Not necessarily in that order."

"These are your friends?" Mia scrunches up her face, confused.

"Not these people exactly." Claire looks around at the people dancing near them and then at the people making drinks in the messy kitchen. It could have been any of the parties she went to in high school, with everyone just fast-forwarded a year or two. "But people a lot like this, and I kept hanging out with them because I'm an idiot."

"I could have told you that."

"Thanks, Mia."

"No problem."

They exchange smiles.

"Well," Claire says. She's had enough of feeling maudlin. "You know what I always found was the best remedy for sucky company—present company excluded, of course?"

"What?"

"Dancing."

Mia nods as if to say she could see how that might be a good idea.

"Just drinking, dancing, and ignoring them. And we have nothing left to drink, so, do you like to dance, Mia?"

"Oh, I like to dance, Claire."

Claire grabs Mia's wrist and drags them into the sweaty, teeming interior of the dance floor.

And that's where they stay forever. They dance without stopping. They dance through the good, the bad, and the cheesy, and they dance with abandon because they don't give a crap about the people around them. Nothing is too cheesy for Claire anyway. She unashamedly likes mainstream pop when she's on a dance floor. And Mia dances as if she doesn't care either, making her Claire's favourite partner in crime. She doesn't judge—she doesn't even look at anyone else around them to investigate what they're doing in that self-conscious, side-eyed way insecure girls do. When the music is good, they move as if they like it. And when the music is bad, they move like it's hilarious. Together it turns out they are a match made in dance-floor heaven. It's all ridiculous fun and, for a while, Claire manages to forget how craptastic everything has been lately.

She forgot how much she loves to dance. It used to sustain her, to carry her through the vapid empty clubbing nights and the parties when she couldn't be bothered with the talk, with getting caught up in all the gossip, the idle chat, the crap. This—the beat and the mindless task of simply moving. This used to be her escape.

And so she keeps dancing. Every now and then she accidentally knocks some girl and gets a filthy look for her troubles, or some guy comes edging in, playing the sleaze game. But Claire smiles and turns toward Mia. Tonight, nothing is going to touch her.

She has no idea how long they have been caught up in the epicentre of the steaming, milling mass of bodies when Claire feels an arm wind around her neck and a stubbly face press a kiss to her cheek. She's just about to shove the arm off her shoulder when she realises it's Robbie, grinning from ear to ear with one arm slung around each of their necks.

"Both of you!" he yells. "It's Christmas!" He lets go of them, reaches into his bag, and pulls out a bottle of tequila and a handful of shot glasses. Claire throws her head back and laughs. Only Robbie would be classy and unclassy enough to carry shot glasses around in his feral, little denim bag.

He somehow manages to wrestle some of the clear liquid into one glass without getting bumped or spilling any. He passes it to Mia. He pours two more and hands one to Claire.

"Whose party is this, anyway?" Claire shouts in his ear as she wipes the sweat from her neck with her free hand.

"My friend Megan's. We were in photography together. But then she quit to model. She's doing really well."

"I bet she is," Claire mutters, then downs her shot. Only a model could afford this apartment at her age. She looks at Mia, one eyebrow raised.

Mia laughs, drinks hers, and winces.

"Stop it, you snob!" Robbie wags a finger at Claire and then pours another shot into her glass. "She's a sweetheart, and she's smart too. Kind of." He laughs, tips back another slug, and shakes his head violently. "I'm going to find her and say hi." He eyes the room as he thrusts the bottle at Mia. "You take care of that. By that I mean drink it. I've had way too much already." He grabs them both by the neck again, kisses their cheeks with relish, and disappears into the crowd.

Mia holds up the bottle and makes a face as if to say "What am I supposed to do with this?"

Claire snatches it from her. She knows she can dance just as well with or without a bottle in her hands. She perfected the art through the years. And they keep moving, Claire with one hand firmly around the neck of the bottle.

At some point, Claire has been dancing so long she's worried she's never going to find her land legs again. It's not long after that they completely run out of steam and depart the dance floor in search of air and somewhere to sit.

Mia finds a vacant armchair, a decadent, beige monstrosity lodged between the front door area and the edge of the dance floor. It's covered in discarded jackets and coats. Mia squashes up to one side, with her knees pulled to her chest, and pats the cushion next to her. Claire backs in, flops down, tucks the bottle in between them, and puts the glasses on the arm. They are so close to the dance floor that Claire could nearly reach out and touch the wall of moving bodies if she wanted. Instead, she turns inward a little, toward Mia, and leans her head against the back of the chair, spent and sweaty.

She stares across the room while she catches her breath. She spots Robbie near the wall on the other side of the door talking to a redheaded girl, his hand on her arm. It must be Megan, the model. She's super tall and skinny, but she doesn't look that pretty. The best models never seem to. Claire's learned that from the embarrassing amount of *Next Top Model* she's consumed over the years. The weird looking ones always win. They are all gawky and awkward and then turn beautiful in front of a camera.

Mia pours them another shot each. They throw it back in unison and tuck the bottle back into the sofa cushions between them. Too exhausted and now too drunk to get up, they stay put, snuggled around the bottle.

"So, what would you be doing if you were here with those old friends you used to party with?" Mia asks, playing with her shot glass.

Claire looks out at the swell of bodies around them and shrugs. She tries to recall all those parties through the fog of distance and drunkenness. She doesn't remember much, just a sameness shaped by routine rounds of drinking and dancing and gossip—gossip about things that seemed so vital at the time and are so forgettable now.

"Same as everyone else, I guess." She notices a girl on the dance floor looking at them. She turns and says something to the one next to her. The other girl glances at them briefly and nods. "I'd probably be wondering why those two weirdos are perched on top of a pile of coats on that chair in the corner."

Mia laughs and leans back against the seat. "I think I prefer to be the weirdo."

"What would you be doing tonight?" Claire asks, curious. "If you weren't here?"

"Maybe watching movies with Pete and his housemate like they were planning before I dragged them here. Or studying for exams."

She tips her empty glass against Mia's. "Well, I, for one, am glad you're here suffering with me instead of toiling over your books or watching sci-fi movies."

"You're not suffering. I saw you on the dance floor."

Claire laughs. She hasn't really been suffering at all.

Mia pokes her in the leg. "And sci-fi movies? What makes you think that? Just putting us firmly in your science-geek box and shutting the lid?"

"Maybe. What would you be watching?"

Mia rolls her eyes. "Probably some really niche indie film or an undiscovered gem of a famous director. Pete's housemate is a total film freak."

"So, still geeky then?"

Mia ignores her jibe. "I'm glad you're here. I probably would have left pretty soon if you weren't." She corrects herself. "Actually, I know I would have. No fun following Robbie around at these things."

"Thanks for staying on my behalf, Mia." But it's only a part joke because it does, sadly, warm her that she's deemed worthy of sticking around for.

"I couldn't leave you on your lonesome with these people." Mia gives her a smart-ass grin. "You might have been re-infected."

"Yeah, yeah. Anyway, I kind of needed this—weird as this party is."

"Me too."

They smile at each other, slow smiles of recognition and something else, something like mutual sympathy. With that, Mia pours them another shot, and they drink it down with sober ceremony.

They debate dancing again, but the music has taken a turn for the worse. Instead, they share random memories and fill the huge gaps in their knowledge of each other. Then, as they dissolve into tequila drunkenness, they play a game. Taking it in turns, one of them picks someone from around the room, and the other one has to make up a story about him, to invent dramas, or concoct secret fears and habits. It's dumb and pointless, and they are just drunk enough to get a complete stupid kick out of it.

After Mia finishes telling her all about the random middle-aged man who just walked in, and his penchant for the feet of young girls, it's Claire's turn to make something up.

"Pick someone!" She slaps Mia leg.

"Ow, okay. No need to brutalise!" Mia winces and rubs her thigh. She scans the room. Finally, she finds what she's looking for. "Them." Mia leans her head sideways on the back of the chair. Her hair tickles the side of Claire's face as she points through the dance floor to a couple standing by the food table, inspecting the contents.

For a fleeting moment, Claire wishes she hadn't drunk so much and felt like taking advantage of the free food, because it looks really good from here. The couple have their backs to her, and there are twenty people dancing between their chair and them, so it's difficult to get an idea of what they're like, except they look basically the same as everyone in the room—brand-named, moneyed, and boring. Eventually, the girl plucks a carrot stick from the array of food and turns slowly to look over the room. Claire is about to tell Mia how she will be off to the bathroom in minutes to purge the carrot stick, when she gets a look at her face.

It's Kate.

"Oh shit," Claire moans. She turns her head quickly toward Mia and buries her face into the back of the chair.

"What's wrong?"

"Girl I went to high school with," Claire mumbles. She swings her head back and forth, veering wildly between wanting to hide her face and wanting to see where Kate is, in case she comes anywhere near their private armchair kingdom. "I have never, ever seen her alone, without the other two." Claire catches another glimpse as Kate closes in on the snack table again. "It's like seeing a guinea pig in the wild. I mean, you only ever see them in cages. I've never seen one in the wild."

Mia laughs and pokes her clumsily in the arm. "I'm not sure that it's completely owing to my state of drunkenness that I have no idea what you are talking about right now."

Claire watches Kate accept a glass of champagne from the guy she came in with, a wide, tall guy with curly hair. She gives him a simpering smile of thanks. Claire just stares. She cannot believe Kate has turned up here, a completely unexpected and irritating intruder in what has turned out to be the most random of fun nights.

"See, I knew it was that kind of party," she moans and presses her face against the sofa as Kate eyes the room again.

"That kind of party?" Mia laughs. "You make it sound totally sinister. Like we're going to be injected with drugs against our will in darkened rooms and induced to perform bizarre sexual acts." Still, she's clearly sympathetic because she pours them each another shot, which they slug quickly. Then she picks up a jacket and holds it in front of Claire's face.

Claire giggles. "Thanks." She positions her head right in front of the jacket. "No, I just mean full of boring vapid idiots like her."

"That's okay then." Mia looks over at the couple and then turns back to Claire, her brown eyes shining. "You want me to make up a story about her? Will that make you feel better?"

"Sure." Claire settles into the chair behind her protective shield.

And Mia, with a surprisingly evil glint in her eye, goes off in a long-winded tale of debauchery and punishment, where nothing good has ever happened to Kate and her date. Sadly, it actually does make Claire feel a little better. Well, at least it makes her laugh.

And the game continues, accompanied by more shots of tequila and even more hysterical, face-numbing laughter. Claire shakes her head at her mental image of them in their corner. Who knew the highlight of her night would be stuck behind a jacket in a corner on top of a pile of coats? The game escalates and the stories grow stupider, with more laughing than actual storytelling. It's as if the whole night is this deeply funny joke, and they are the only ones in the room who get it.

Then it happens. She has no idea *how* it happens or who started it. In fact, if she were questioned in a court of law, she's not sure she could answer truthfully. And when she looks back at it the next day, via the lens of her mind-blowing hangover, it looks like a series of grainy jump shots from one moment to the next. There is no necessary cause and effect, no incident and consequence. One minute they are downing another shot and laughing hysterically, Mia's elbow resting on Claire's knee as she continues to hold up the jacket to hide her. Then, for a split second, they just look at each other. And then, mere seconds later, in a clash of hot breath, lips, tequila and tongue, they are kissing.

It's not a long kiss, but long enough for the jacket to be dropped and hands to start grabbing for leverage. And it ends when Mia accidentally pulls at her hair, and Claire is yanked back to reality. She snaps her head back, eyes wide. And staring straight back at her is Mia, her eyes equally wide.

Then suddenly Mia begins to laugh as she pulls herself up to sit on the arm of the chair. "Umm..." Mia folds her arms over her chest and pulls an *eek* face. And before Claire can say anything, Mia grins. She leans down close and points at her. "So, inappropriate, drunken make outs are generally a solid cue for me that it's well over time to go home. Which means I am out." She sighs and hands Claire her glass. "See you."

Claire takes the glass and nods, still too speechless to respond.

Mia swings her long legs over the side of the chair, picks out her coat from the pile, and disappears into the crowd by the door.

Stunned by both the impromptu kiss and the rapid departure, Claire stays nailed to her seat, both the glasses clutched in her hands. She has many, *many* questions.

Her most pressing being, what the hell just happened?

But she knows no one can tell her because she was right here, and she has no idea.

The second question is does that mean she should leave too? Claire's done plenty of inappropriate kissing in her time. It's part of the fun of parties like these, being messy. Never with a girl, though. That part's definitely new. Maybe it *is* time to go home. Claire nods to herself. She must be very, very drunk.

Third, how did that even happen? Who the hell started it? She shakes her head, rests her cheek on her hand, and frowns.

And fourth, did it really mean that Mia had to bolt like that? Did she have to leave her stranded on a chair, a Claire-shaped pile of stunned and drunk? That's no fun. Surely they could have just gotten over the awkwardness and gone back to the dance floor and forgotten about it? She sighs. How the hell did a night that started out so lame and then turned so freaking fun, catapult itself somehow to outright bizarre?

But before she can get any further along in her stunned and somewhat circular self-interrogation, a body flies over the arm of the chair and lands in her lap. It's Robbie.

"Where have you been? I need tequila."

Claire blinks at him for a second. He clearly didn't see what happened. "I've been right here," she grumbles as she reaches under his legs for the bottle. "And you're sitting on it."

He snatches the bottle and the proffered glasses. "Shall we drink?"

Claire shrugs. She might as well, right?

"Where's Mia?" Robbie asks, unsteadily pouring tequila into the glasses. He hands one to her.

"Gone home."

"Boo. Want to dance?"

"Why not?" Claire snatches the glass and throws back the shot. Might as well carry the night all the way to ruin.

CHAPTER 21

And that's exactly how she wakes up. In ruins.

Actually, she wakes to the sound of quiet strumming, a sound that immediately begins to somewhat violently compete with the symphony of *ouch, ugh,* and *what the hell?* going off in her own head.

She opens her eyes to daylight, winces, and closes them just as quickly. The world hurts, and that sound coming from outside her skull is not helping one bit. She also has the instinctive feeling that whatever she's about to see will only cause her to hurt more.

Before she finds a way to make the sound stop, she has far more pressing concerns, like whether or not she's wearing clothing. This is something quite difficult to ascertain without making any actual, physical movement—particularly given the current state of her brain. But this is a question that must be answered before she greets whatever remnant of last night she is about to face.

It takes a moment of sheer concentration to focus at the surface level of her skin. Then, slowly, she registers the cling of denim at her hips, and the space where her top has ridden up slightly at her lower back, retreating from the hem of her jeans. She wriggles her toes gently. Hell, she's even wearing socks. Checklist complete.

Yes. She'll take that as a win.

The light strumming continues, then stops, and then starts again a moment later.

Time to deal. She opens her eyes halfway and mutters into the unfamiliar brown covers. "Tell me I did not spend the night in the bed of someone who plays guitar. Acoustic guitar."

She hears someone chuckle and then the thrumming thud of the guitar being put down on the floor. "Two chords. That's all I can play, if it makes you feel any better."

"Not really." She remains under the covers. She knows she should look for a way to get the hell out of here, but it's kind of cosy and way less nauseating to lie very, very still in this strange bed.

"It's not even my guitar," the voice continues. "It's a friend's. I'm looking after it. His girlfriend was furious at him, and he was scared she'd smash it or something."

"What'd he do? Play it?"

"Wow, you're sharp this morning."

"Are you trying to suggest that last night I was *not*?" She finally commits to opening her eyes all the way. It has to happen sometime.

He's sitting on the bed—which is a mattress on a floor—leaning against the wall, a lanky guy wearing a faded green T-shirt, with honey-brown waves of hair that fall below his ears. She can only see him in profile, but he's *kind of* familiar. No name floats to the surface of her memory, though. In fact, nothing much at all surfaces.

"Oh no, you told me last night that you were a hippo." He laughs. "I think you meant an elephant. And you don't forget a thing, so not to lay a hand on you once you got in my bed because you'd remember."

"I did?" she mumbles. "Well done, me." She tries to think of a way to ask for a glass of water without revealing just how hungover she is. She needs to go to the bathroom, too, but that is terrain she's not sure she can negotiate, not without knowing if there are housemates, or family, or pets. Too difficult. Too dangerous.

All of a sudden, he climbs off the mattress. The movement sets off a wave of nausea through her. "I'll be back in a sec." He disappears.

She takes this minute to assess the situation, to double-check. Lifting the cover and her head, she looks down. Wow, she's not just dressed, she's, like, *impressively* fully dressed. Only her jacket and her boots are missing. She gazes around the room. Her jacket is hanging neatly on a chair at the end of the bed, with her boots just beneath. She crawls out of the covers, grabs her jacket, and checks in the pockets for her phone and wallet. Both are present and accounted for. *Well done, me.* So far so good in coming out of last night intact.

Relieved, she lies down again and allows a second surge of nausea to abate. She may have all her belongings and some of her wits about her, but this is not going to be a fun hangover. No chance.

She lies back down and tries to recollect whatever fragments of last night she can gather from her cloudy brain. Tequila. And dancing. Lots of tequila and dancing. Maybe she found him on the dance floor? Her little game of memory is interrupted by his return. He's carrying a glass of water, and she prays it's for her. He sits on the edge of the mattress and passes it to her. Grateful, she takes it.

"Thanks." She drinks it down quickly and puts the glass on the window sill next to her. The sun is shining outside, easing in around the dark-brown curtains, a fabric that nearly matches the colours of his equally ugly bedspread.

She realises she has absolutely no idea what time it is. She pulls her phone out of the pocket of her jacket. It's just after eleven. And there are already a ton of messages and missed calls.

The latest one is from Robbie.

I think this can be fixed with bacon. We're going to try, anyway. Come? Ike's in half an hour?

"So, last night was fun." Mystery guy yawns and stretches his arms above his head.

"Was it?"

A phone starts ringing in the hallway. Then a dog starts barking. He sighs. "Hang on, I'll be back." He leaves the room again.

No hurry, she thinks.

She considers meeting Robbie. The thought of food is slightly off-putting, but it might be nice to commiserate over how awful she feels. She assumes he shared in whatever fun happened last night because dancing with him is one of her few scattered memories. She checks the time of the message. Twenty minutes ago. She could make it. "We" must mean Mia is coming as well.

Mia.

And then she freezes, remembering. The dance floor. The game. The beige armchair. The kiss.

She bites her lip. Oh yeah. How did that happen again?

And, even more pressing a question, how did last night just keep on going after that little episode of randomness? Surely that was enough craziness for one night? She was so drunk, she's not sure how she went from drunkenly kissing her friend—a *girl* friend—to ending up in this guy's bed. The problem is she can't remember much beyond the time on the armchair. She knows Mia went home because of her own somewhat stunned, drunken reaction to that moment. Claire knows Robbie made her dance again. But just how long did she stay out?

She wonders if Mia remembers the kiss too. That could make a hungover breakfast date kind of awkward. And Claire's already facing one ghost from last night. Can she really face another right now?

Before she can decide, he comes into the room again, stands by the door, and smiles. He actually seems kind of nice, which is a bonus, she guesses. And she's sure there was probably some drunken making out if she felt it was okay to use his bed at the end of it.

And he did bring her water. That says something. She remembers one horrendous morning, after one of those unfortunate post-Brendan one-night stands, when the guy didn't even talk to her. He just grunted from over his controller, fixed on the screen that was positioned, sadly, at the end of his bed. She made a hasty departure back then. This guy and his cheekbones are clearly perched a few steps up the evolutionary ladder.

She wishes she knew his name. Hell, at this point any biographical detail would be good, aside from the fact he doesn't seem to use a vacuum, and he is overly fond of the various shades of brown. And yeah, those cheekbones.

"You want breakfast?"

She actually kind of does. Well, she wants the coffee that comes with breakfast. But where, and with whom? She quickly assesses the potential levels of awkwardness between each breakfast option and makes her decision. "Uh, no, I actually have to meet my friends."

Better the potentially uncomfortable devil she knows. That's what she tells herself as she climbs slowly out of bed and pulls her top down to meet her jeans. "So...where are we?" She acknowledges her lack of memory of last night. She has to get out of here somehow. She quickly scoops up her jacket and her phone.

"Near the corner of Mason and Ascot. You know it?"

"Yep," she mutters. Good. She's near the university, at least. And Ike's. She can make it there in time.

He flops down on his bed again, sits against the wall, and crosses his legs. "What are the chances of you giving me your number?"

"None to...none." She shrugs on her jacket and pulls up the zip.

"No problem." He grins at her. "Was just checking. You already gave it to me last night."

Wow, she must have really liked him last night. She doesn't say a word. Whoever he is, this guy is too alert for her this morning. Her brain is still at the reboot stage and cannot do this level of nimble right now.

He picks up the guitar again and starts strumming.

That's her cue to leave. "Uh, well, thanks for half your bed." This is the best she can muster for manners right now.

"Half might be a stretch. You're quite the blanket thief." He plucks at the strings and smiles up at her.

"Stop trying to be charming." She pulls her hair out from under her jacket collar. She can't help giving him a small smile, though, as she shakes her head. "Nothing is going to work this morning."

"Okay then," he says, casual. "Well, see you later, Claire."

Damn. She also told him her real name. Oops.

"See you." She makes for the door, hits the pavements, and leaves the small, white worker's terrace behind. Taking a deep breath, she heads for what she hopes is Ascot Street. She walks as quickly as her tender head allows and pulls out her phone. There is a little bit of battery left. Enough to see that there are also two missed calls from Robbie. And three messages that came in before the invitation to breakfast.

The first, sometime in the early hours of this morning.

Where did u go? Don't u know you shld never, ever leave me it a party along. I do stupid tings.

She smiles. Like forget how to type? Well, doesn't he know he should never let her leave a party with random, floppy-haired strangers?

The next came in two hours ago.

So, I want to die. How r u? I have, I can announce, finally located the right adjective for this hangover.

And then, ten minutes later.

Okay, u didn't ask, but I'm going to tell u. Adj: diabolical.

She smiles and then immediately frowns. Should she go to breakfast? Now, out in the harsh reality of daylight and her monstrous—she opts for monstrous—hangover, she's second-guessing her decision to meet them. Mostly because she has no idea where to put that random kiss with Mia in the scheme of her night—let alone her life.

But then maybe she doesn't need to, not if Mia isn't weird about it. Maybe they can just put it down to a drunken party thing. Claire makes these types of hot-mess decisions when she's drunk. She just has no idea how Mia will be about it. Mia doesn't strike her as someone who does stupid trashy things that often. Then, she did make a comment about random inappropriate make outs, so maybe she is. Maybe Mia has some debauched potential Claire hasn't discovered yet?

She might as well go to breakfast. It's better than going home and facing her parents and however they'd like her to spend her day. She walks to the nearest street corner, gets her bearings, and heads for the café.

CHAPTER 22

She finds them in a booth in the back corner, already armed with coffee and a large pitcher of water.

"Hey!" Robbie says. He has pulled his hood over his head. Bright strands of hair curl around the edges.

"Hey." She flops down next to him, groans, and leans her head on his shoulder.

He pats her cheek. "You came."

"Just. It hurt to walk here."

Mia pours a glass of water and slides it over to her. Then she smiles.

And it's just a regular Mia smile. Not a weird or freaked out or uncomfortable we-made-out-last-night smile. *Maybe she doesn't even remember*, Claire thinks. That would help. Or maybe she does, but it's no big deal. Either way, she's not being weird. Claire decides to take her cue from that.

"Hey, thanks." She grabs for the water. The glass sleepover dude gave her didn't even touch the sides of this hangover's rampant thirst.

"How are you?" Mia asks, smiling as if she knows the answer already.

Claire grunts into her glass and keeps drinking.

Robbie laughs. "That good, huh? Me too. Last night was messy. Fun, but messy."

"Agreed," Claire mutters.

Mia leans forward. "And I must say you are rocking quite the panda eye this morning."

Claire hurriedly swipes her thumbs under her eyes. They come up black. Oops. Maybe she should have looked in a mirror before she left that guy's place. She uses the reflection on her phone screen to inspect the damage and clean up the worst of it with her fingers.

"Hang on a minute." Robbie tips his head to the side, looks her up and down, and then narrows his eyes at her. "You're still in your clothes from last night. And you didn't stay with Nina. Could this be a walk of shame, missy?" He sniffs at her as if he's going to be able to tell just from that.

She punches him in the shoulder. "Get away, you creep." She slams back the rest of the glass of water. "And no. It's a walk of shamelessly using a guy for his bed. To clarify." She points at him. "Shamelessly using his bed *without* putting out. There is a line at which I will stop, shell out for a cab, and simply return to the bosom of the family McMansion."

Robbie nods. "Good to know. Sadly there is no such line for me."

Claire picks up a menu and briefly tries to make sense of the written word. "He was kind of hot, actually. Wish I remembered meeting him. Do you remember any of it?"

"Not a thing after the second party."

"The second party?" Claire's jaw drops. She possesses no recollection of any second party.

Mia laughs and shakes her head. "I am so glad I went home."

Robbie nudges Claire. "Yeah, remember? Megan ditched her party and took us to the other one at that warehouse? Maybe he came with us, or maybe you found him there?" Robbie shrugs and turns back to his menu. "Anyway, I can't keep a handle on my own night. I sure as hell can't help you with yours."

"Fair enough." She tries to read the menu again but puts it down. Too hard.

"I wish I could remember this guy, though," Robbie suddenly says.

Claire narrows her eyes at him. "Why?"

"Curiosity." He shrugs. "Given what a bitch you can be on first meeting, for a guy to be into you, he either finds you so hot he can't resist. Or charming. There's no mistaking you're hot. But charming?" He shakes his head. "That'd have to be an acquired taste."

"Wow," Claire mutters. "Did you get me to come here just so you could drop truth bombs on the wreckage of my night?"

He laughs and flips the menu around between his fingers. "Anyway, I personally find you very charming."

"Just not hot."

"Yeah, sorry." He nudges her shoulder again. "That's an acquired taste problem."

They order their food. Claire wings it and asks the waiter to bring whatever breakfast option has the most bacon in it. Somewhere between waking and now, she has developed a hankering for grease and salt. Lots of it.

Robbie reads them their stars from the paper while they wait. "Ooh, mine says to relax after a busy week and to lock down some time with friends. Win! I shall do as it commands. Now, Mia." He runs a finger along the page.

"It's okay," Mia mutters. "I can pretty much guess how today is going to turn out."

"Too bad." He leans over the page. "You are amazing, incredible, and beautiful, and you are so gifted and intelligent you don't even need to study for your exams. Instead, you should spend all your time with your dearest friend Rob—"

"Hush and tell me the real one, you idiot." Mia reaches over the table and slaps his wrist.

He laughs and takes a hold of her hand. "But it's boring. It's time to reflect how far you have come with attaining your goals, you should exercise self-discipline, yada yada yada. You already do that stuff."

Mia pulls her hand back. "Told you."

"Now, Claire."

"What?" She resigns herself to the worst.

"You should have some financial gains this week."

"Oh goodie." Her savings are still looking a little sad.

"This week should also be about hard work and setting goals for yourself."

She nods. "Yeah, like not getting so drunk."

Mia snickers.

"And you should beware of taking advice from family members."

She leans over and jabs at the paper. "That should be in there every week. I hope my mother reads that." Not that she would. Her mother doesn't believe in astrology, of course. Neither does Claire, really. How can all the people in the world be divided up into twelve types, ruled by twelve sets of advice? She's terrible at math, but she knows that can't possibly work statistically.

The waiter arrives with their food. Claire takes a tentative bite of her BLT, chews, and swallows. So far, so good. She's almost ready to brave a coffee.

Mia spreads butter on her serving of toast.

"That's really sad you know, Mia," Claire tells her as she stares over at Mia's barren plate.

"It's for the best, believe me."

Robbie heaps his fork with French toast and pours syrup straight on it. "You're quiet today, Mee."

Mia shrugs. "Feel sick."

"At least you left before everything went pear-shaped. Why'd you leave so early anyway?"

"Drunk."

"You're such a lightweight," he tells her fondly.

"Or just sane. At least I can kind of remember my night."

Claire pauses with her BLT halfway to her mouth. Does that mean the kiss, too?

Robbie wipes his mouth with his napkin. "What are you guys doing for the rest of the day?"

Mia leans back against the booth and yawns. "Preferably IV fluids and bed rest. I should study. But somehow, I don't think it's going to happen until later. Much later."

"Claire?" Robbie asks.

"Avoiding going home for as long as I can. Mum gets kind of chirpy on Sundays. She doesn't seem to know it's supposed to be a day of rest. And I already have to go to dinner at my cousin's with her later."

"Well can I suggest lying around and watching vapid teen films at my place? With junk food?"

"And Gatorade?" Claire asks.

"And Gatorade." He nods. "Definitely."

"The yellow one?"

"The yellow one."

"Then I am in."

Robbie turns. "Mee?"

She nods. "You had me at lying around."

CHAPTER 23

Robbie's flat is tiny. And freakishly spotless. Everything in the room—books, papers, clothes—is arranged neatly. The walls are mostly bare, with only a few unframed photographs pinned in random, light catching spots on the fresh, white paint.

Claire frowns at the immaculate bed. "Did you stay here last night?"

"Yeah, why?"

She shakes her head. "No reason." Wow. He even made it this morning, as hungover as he claims to be. Cam makes his bed about four times a year. *Seasonally*, he likes to say. She sniffs the air. It even smells good in here.

She watches as he lays a selection of movies out on the bed.

"Which one?"

Claire takes a cursory look at the covers as she unzips her jacket. She's seen most of them. Not that it matters. "Don't care." She lays her jacket neatly over the back of the chair. "Nothing that will tax my brain, though."

"I don't plan on taxing anyone's brain today, not after last night. Exercise in futility. Mee?"

"Whatever, I don't mind." She stares at a photo on the wall. "I like this."

"Good, then I'll pick." He plucks one from the pile and puts the rest neatly back on the shelves.

Claire smirks. "Do you alphabetise your DVDs? I'm getting the feeling you might be the type."

"Shut up, you." He freezes, DVD in hand. "Oh shit."

"What?" Mia kicks off her shoes.

"I just remembered I might have done some inappropriate making out with a guy from my photo theory class at the first party."

Inappropriate making out. Claire snaps her head up. Mia's exact words last night. She steals a glance at Mia. And Mia looks right back at her. They both burst out laughing.

She definitely remembers. And given that they are both laughing, it seems to be okay.

"What?" Robbie eyes them both.

Claire shakes her head. "Nothing."

"Did you see it happen?"

"No." She looks back over at Mia, who is still grinning as she perches on the edge of the bed.

"Seriously." Robbie puts the DVD in the tray. "Don't make me insecure. I am extremely fragile today."

Claire lies against the pillows. "Really, it's nothing. We both just remembered something. Nothing to do with you."

"With who, then?"

Mia kicks her legs over onto the mattress. "Just a couple of people making drunken idiots of themselves last night."

"Ooh, who?" He throws himself down on the bed between them. "Will it make me feel better about myself?"

"No, probably not." Claire laughs. There's no way she's going to tell him. She glances at Mia. She gives Claire a small, sly smile and looks away. Clearly Mia isn't going to either.

"Okay." He reaches over Claire and picks up the remote control from his bed stand. "Then let's watch this damn movie."

* * *

Three movies later, Claire is forced to go home. Prompted by a reminder message from her mother that they have a family dinner tonight at her aunt's, she reluctantly gets ready to depart Robbie's cosy apartment.

Mia decides to leave too. "I've still got at least six hours of studying to do." She sighs.

"Six hours?" Claire frowns as she yanks on her boots. "Six *hours*? You're really going to do that much study now? Today?"

"Yep. Have to."

"You poor thing." Robbie checks his watch and climbs off the bed. "I better get ready too."

"What for?" Claire asks.

"Got a thing on tonight." He starts to grab clothes out of drawers.

"You're going out again?"

"Yup."

"Wow." Claire shakes her head. These people have way more stamina than she does. If she had her way, she'd just get right back to bed when she gets home.

Mia and Claire leave Robbie to get ready and trudge slowly back to Union street in the gathering dark.

Mia zips up her jacket against the late afternoon chill. "I actually feel a bit better."

"Me too. I'd still rather not go to this dinner, though. That will still hurt."

"Is this the aunt that fights with your mother all the time?"

Claire smiles. She can't believe Mia actually remembers that piece of information. "Or the one that my mother fights with. Depends which week it is. But yep, the very one. Aunt Lucy."

"Good times."

"Oh yeah."

They reach the corner and look at each other for a moment in a protracted, slightly awkward silence. Claire wonders for a minute if Mia is going to say something about last night. But she doesn't. Instead she smiles at Claire, her face still hangover pale, even in failing light.

Claire gives her a bashful grin, but she can feel the heat of a slight blush. She wants to be supercool and nonchalant about last night, one of those chilled girls who does stuff like that as though it's nothing. But she's way less adventurous than she'll ever let on. And now, when it's just the two of them, she does feel a little strange. "Good luck with your studying," she tells her. "I hope the six hours isn't too painful."

Mia thrusts her hands into her jacket pockets. "Same with your family dinner. I'll see you soon?"

"Sure. Soon," Claire agrees. "Bye."

Mia gives her a small wave and turns on her heels.

Claire heads for the bus stop, relieved that there's no real fallout from last night and that nothing needs to be said about it either. Because she'd have no idea what to say.

She climbs onto a bus and moves to the back. As the bus pulls out into the traffic, Claire sees Mia striding down the street. Mia doesn't see her, though, as she stares straight ahead into the night, turned back in on herself now she is alone.

Claire slouches in her seat and feels pretty damn pleased with herself. She's not sure she's ever had such an enjoyable hangover as today. Of course, they're not supposed to be fun. They're supposed to be the punishment for fun. But today was surprisingly, out-of-left-field good.

And, added bonus, she didn't do anything too stupid last night. She didn't accidentally sleep with the random dude with the guitar, as hot and oddly nice as he was. Hell, she might even answer his call if he does ring. Maybe. *And* she made out with a girl, something new for the history books, with the bonus prize of no one being too weird about it. It was also kind of ridiculously fun, those hours on the armchair with Mia, laughing like maniacs in their own private world.

And she has two awesome new friends who want to spend a hangover with her.

Not bad at all, she thinks. Now she just has to get through dinner, and she's home free.

CHAPTER 24

Claire likes being in the bar before it opens. It's all hers.

She's never had to open up the place by herself before, and she's actually enjoying it. It's nice to have a bit of quiet before the music comes on, the customers come in, and the chaos ensues. She can sets up the bar the way she likes it and dream.

That's what she's doing when she hears the sound of the heavy front door being pushed open. The clamour of traffic outside from the street streams in, rupturing the peace. "We're not open," Claire calls out as she wipes a table.

"It's me."

It sounds like Nina. Claire spins around. It *is* Nina. She stands in the middle of the room, her hands adrift at her sides.

Claire freezes, cloth in hand, as a jolt of nerves hits her stomach. She did not expect to see Nina. They aren't supposed to work together for days. She thought she'd have time to prepare.

Nina's hair is brown now. It's not as good as the blonde. It makes her look washed out and tired. *But maybe she is washed out and tired,* Claire thinks as she takes in the redness around her eyes and the way her hair hangs around her shoulders. Nina never just lets her hair hang.

Claire makes her way back to the safety of the bar, not sure what's about to happen. "Hey."

"Hey," Nina says in return. She follows her to the bar and climbs up onto a stool.

"I didn't think you were working tonight," Claire says quietly and throws the cloth in the sink.

"I'm not." Nina hunches over the bar and rests her chin on her arms. "I came to see you."

"Why?"

Nina takes a deep breath. "Claire, I am *so* sorry about what happened. I was such a bitch to you."

With a small surge of relief, Claire nods her acknowledgement—and her agreement. Just because she's relieved doesn't mean she's going to let this go. She raises an eyebrow and folds her arms. "So why exactly are you sorry now?"

Nina stares down at her hands, knotted together. "For a few reasons, but mostly because I realise I was a complete asshole for going crazy at you and then not talking to you or listening to you when you tried to explain, and I know that now."

"Well that's true."

"And because my mother and both my older sisters told me I was being a seriously shitty friend for treating you like that—and for just assuming what happened was your fault..." Nina frowns. "Actually, my sister told me I was the worst kind of feminist alive for doing that."

Claire thinks of her mother and her sweeping demonisation of all women the other day, "Well, there's got to be worse, but it was extremely shitty of you."

"And also..." Nina continues to stare at the scratched bar surface. "I kind of know for a fact Josh is a cheating asshole now."

"Ah." Claire tips back her head. "So that's it." She sighs loudly. "How did you find out?"

"When I got home from my trip, I might have done a bit of snooping. On my sister's recommendation."

"And?"

"I found messages. Some girl in his course. And some other random as well, a picture of them together on his phone."

"Oh." *What a freaking stupid idiot*, Claire thinks. Doesn't even know how to cover his tracks. But Nina probably doesn't need to hear that right now.

"I might have thrown a chair at him."

Claire stares at her. "You threw a chair?"

"I threw two chairs, actually."

Claire almost wants to laugh at her vision of short-ass Nina throwing furniture at brutish Josh. But she doesn't because she can see the tears gather in Nina's eyes. Claire shakes her head. How is it that Nina manages to be so naïve when she's so worldly in other ways?

Yet when it comes to people and their behaviour, Nina seems to retain this bizarre innocence. The more Claire knows her, the more she realises it's because Nina desperately wants to think the best of people. And she has zero instinct for when they're not. It must be that hippie upbringing. Then, when they don't act as she expects, it hits her even harder than it would for people like Claire, who is always prepared for people to disappoint her.

Claire watches her friend unsuccessfully blink back more tears. She pulls down a bottle of whiskey and two glasses and pours them a shot each. She hands one to Nina with a small, sympathetic smile.

Nina smiles her thanks. She wipes her eyes on her sleeve and smears a streak of mascara under one eye. They silently push their glasses together and drink. Claire immediately takes them back and washes them. She's not sure what Andrew would do if he found her drinking before work. Medicinal purposes, she'd probably tell him. And if he saw Nina right now, he'd probably agree.

Nina sniffs loudly. "It's like I kind of knew, but I didn't want to know," she suddenly says. "Which is why I blamed you. Because I really, really didn't want it to be the other way."

Claire nods again. She feels terrible for Nina. She does. Because she knows how it feels. But she also doesn't want to be treated like that again. She leans on the bar and looks her friend straight in the eye. "Never, ever do that again, okay?"

"Never." Nina shakes her head, vehement, eyes wide.

Claire stares at her, determined to make her point. "Because I don't do things like that. Not to my friends. Not even to girls I don't like."

Nina starts to tear up again. "I'm so sorry."

"And Neen?" Claire pulls a napkin from the pile next to the mixers and passes it to her.

"Yeah?" Nina takes the napkin and blows her nose loudly.

"You have got to pick better guys. Maybe I shouldn't have waited so long to tell you this, but Josh is a giant douche."

Nina nods and starts to cry again.

Claire feels the squeeze of guilt. "And as clichéd as it might sound, you can do so much better."

"I am so sorry, Claire. I was horrible to you."

"Yeah, you were," Claire agrees. She grabs a glass and pours Nina another shot. She clearly needs it. "But I'm over talking about it. What I want to know is did you kick him out?"

Nina nods and takes a small sip of her shot. "He's had to move in with his mum. His nagging, crazy, never-leaves-him-alone-for-a-second mother."

Claire smiles and picks up her cloth. "Karma's a complete bitch like that," she says cheerfully and hopes his mother is at least half as annoying as hers. She can't help it. She likes the thought of him suffering.

CHAPTER 25

Robbie brings the new guy he's seeing to the park to eat lunch with them. Eli is short and slender with curly black hair. He speaks eloquently as though he has all the time in the world to tell a story. And he brought Tim Tams to eat, so he's popular.

They lie around on the grass and talk about breakups—their backward-assed way to comfort Nina. Claire can totally see the flaws in this method, but still it's pretty entertaining.

"I broke up with someone by text message once," Eli offers. "Classic asshole act. Couldn't face the real thing."

"Don't do that to *me*," Robbie warns him. "I'll be pissed."

Eli laughs and pats Robbie's leg. "I promise I'll tell you in person when I've had enough of you."

Claire grins. She's glad Robbie's found a guy who's going to pay out on him a little. He deserves it. Scratch that. He needs it.

Robbie laughs. "I may have once just completely stopped responding to calls because I didn't know what to say. He was just too intense. I was like, 'If he's like this normally, what's he going to be like in a breakup scenario?' So I dodged it."

Claire takes a biscuit from the packet and squints up at him. "You're such a wimp."

He smiles blithely as though he knows but doesn't care. "What about you. How'd your last breakup go? Oh God. I'd hate to be on the receiving end of your rage."

Claire shrugs. "I believe it went something along the lines of a simple 'Go fuck yourself.' I can't really remember."

She can remember, though. Vividly. That's exactly what she said. And she remembers his face as she said those words, that look in his eyes of hurt mixed with relief. Brendan was glad that she was the one calling it.

She's not ready to share the details of that humiliating little scene with anyone. She probably never will be.

Nina pipes up. "I cheated on Josh once."

"What?" Claire's whips her head around, mouth open. "When?"

"It was right after we first met. We weren't really an official thing yet. I only kissed the guy, but I felt so guilty I called Josh ten minutes later. I never did anything like that again."

"Maybe you should have," Claire mutters. She checks her watch. "Hey, Neen, it's one thirty. You told me to tell you."

Nina sighs loudly. "Damn. I have to go."

"Where are you going?" Mia asks her. "Work?"

"No, Josh is coming over to get his stuff in half an hour and then, you know, get the hell out of my life."

Mia smiles sympathetically at her. "Good plan."

Nina picks up her bag and sighs again. She looks as if this is the last thing she wants to do. It's the last thing Claire would want to do on this divine day too. Or any other day, really.

Nina stands and looks down at Claire. "See you at work?"

"Yep." Claire gives her an encouraging smile. "Don't take any crap, okay?"

"Hang on," Robbie says suddenly. He sits up on the grass. "You're going on your own?" Then he turns and looks pointedly at Claire.

Nina shrugs.

Robbie keeps staring at Claire. "You shouldn't have to go by yourself."

Claire glares right back at him. "Don't look at me like tha—"

Nina rushes to her defence. "Believe me, if there is one person who is under, like, no obligation to help me out with this, it's Claire." She nods. "She's put up with enough crap from me and that asshat."

Eli tips his head sideways. "Asshat? What's that?"

Claire just shakes her head. She too has no idea what Nina is talking about. As usual.

"Whatever you say." Robbie holds up his hands. "But do you want someone to come with you? I'll come."

"Would you?" Nina asks, eyes wide. "Really?"

Claire can't help feeling a bit bad that she is not the one helping her friend. In fact, if it weren't for this particular situation, Claire would have made Nina stay in the park and done this moving-out supervision for her. But Claire is not putting herself anywhere near Josh. Not even for poor Nina.

"Sure, I'll come be moral support slash security guard." Robbie turns to Eli. "Want to see what an asshat looks like in the flesh?"

"I kind of do." Eli scrambles to his feet and dusts off his jeans. "It was nice to meet you guys."

Claire gives him a perfunctory smile and wave.

Robbie gets up too. "Okay then, I'll see you guys later." He strides off across the park with Nina and Eli.

Claire calls out to Nina. "Remember, he's a giant douche and you can do better!"

Nina turns around and gives her a wave.

As they watch them cross the busy street, Mia taps her gently on her wrist. "Hey, Robbie doesn't know what happened. He wouldn't have said that if he did."

"I know." Claire looks at her watch again. "Do you have to go yet?"

Mia leans over and checks Claire's watch too. She shakes her head. "Not for a bit."

"Awesome. Me either." Claire rolls over onto her stomach. "I could lie here all day."

"Mhm." Mia stretches out on the grass next to her.

Claire thinks about Josh and about Eli and Robbie and their breakup stories. And about Brendan, of course. "Why are guys such pussies sometimes? Why can't they just end a relationship instead of cheating or avoiding? Why are they so freaking scared to just *say* something?"

Mia is quiet for a minute. "Well, I don't know if it's gender specific."

Claire runs her hands through the cool blades of grass and frowns. "I don't know any girls who do stuff like that."

"Yeah, you do."

"What?" Claire turns to stare at her. "You?"

Mia nods slowly, but she doesn't look at Claire.

Claire is instantly curious. "Which one? Cheat or avoid?"

"Both, I guess." Mia drops her chin on her arm. "Is it actually cheating if they're there when it happens?"

"Um, A, I don't know. And B, *what*? What did you do, exactly?"

"Only the worst thing I have ever done." Mia takes in a deep breath. "A couple of years ago I got really, really drunk and kissed another guy at a party. While my boyfriend was standing right there."

"Whoa," Claire says before she can stop herself. But she's a little shocked. "And here I was thinking you were just too darn nice to have a terrible breakup story. I'm assuming it ended in a breakup?"

Mia nods. "And how. The worst part is it was kind of like what you just said. I think I just wanted to break up with him, and I didn't know how else to do it at the time. Then, while ridiculously drunk, it looks like I found a way." She shuts her eyes for a long moment. Then she finally lifts her head. "Now I bet you think I'm an asshole."

"No, I don't," Claire says quickly. She doesn't really know what to think. But she is a little thrown by this information about Mia.

Maybe she's been a little bit unrealistic about her new friend. For some reason, Claire had Mia pegged as the kind of person who does no wrong. She can't be, though. No one is. Besides, it kind of looks as if Mia might be a bit of a hot mess when she gets drunk at parties, going on this story and Claire's experience.

She watches as Mia frowns and plays with the straps of her bag and decides she should at least try and cheer her up. "Anyway, who am I to judge? I may never have cheated, but I've definitely been an asshole plenty of times."

Mia gives her a half smile but doesn't say anything.

"You know what I did once?" Claire asks.

"What?"

Claire bites her lip for a moment as she debates whether to tell Mia this sorry, ancient story. Then she decides to dive in. Even if it doesn't comfort Mia, at least it will distract her.

She laughs, not quite believing she is about to tell this tale. "It was ages ago, and I am still deeply ashamed. I was twelve, maybe thirteen."

Mia lets out a kind of snorting laugh, reaches over, and pokes her in the side. "Hang on a minute. Your 'Claire is an asshole' story happened at age twelve? And it's supposed to make me feel better?"

Claire reaches over and puts her hand over Mia's face to stop her laugh. "Just shut up, Mia, and listen. Maybe you'll learn something."

Mia laughs into her hand.

Claire takes her hand back and continues. "You know how when you get to that age and the social pecking order at school is, like, everything, right? And then when that's established, there's the amateur, prepubescent dating stage? You know, when you first start going out with each other but you barely touch each other or even talk? And your relationships last anywhere from a few days to a week, tops?"

Mia grins and nods. "I remember. It was all such high drama."

"There was this kid in my class. Tom. He was an idiot. Well, at school he was an idiot. Out of school, we were kind of secretly friends. I never talked to him much at school, but he lived on my street, and we'd hang out on the holidays when we were bored. At school he was this total attention seeker. Completely hyper." Claire rolls her eyes as she remembers how even the usually tolerant Ms. Clayton would constantly lose her patience with him. "He was always talking, always interrupting the teachers, and bugging everyone." She turns to Mia. "You know that kid?"

"I do."

"But out of school, he was kind of sweet and chilled, and we'd do totally geeky stuff together like sit in my backyard and make up really long stories about what we'd do if we got to explore the whole world. Totally nerdy." She grins. "You would've loved it."

"Shut up," Mia says dutifully and smiles. "And get on with it."

"Well at some point in grade six, he caught up with me on the way to school and asked me if I would go out with him. Totally out of the blue." She starts giggling, remembering that awful, awkward moment, the look on his face when he asked, and her own answering shock. She tries to take a breath but hiccups instead. It makes her laugh harder.

"And?" Mia jabs her in the arm. "Don't leave me hanging."

"Well, of course, I was so stunned I didn't know what to say. I didn't want to say yes. The only guy I wanted to go out with at that point was Nick Dimas. But he was in a committed, monogamous relationship with his soccer ball. And I didn't want to hurt Tom's feelings, either. I had no idea how to say no, so I said yes." Claire shakes her head. "If I'd been at school, surrounded by my friends, I never would've agreed. But because he got me on my own, I just couldn't. He really was this sweet kid."

"He must have felt like a real Romeo, landing you," Mia teases.

"Shut up, Mia," Claire tells her. "Do you want to hear the rest or not?"

"I really do." Mia grins. "I'm still waiting for the asshole part."

"Oh, it's coming," Claire warns her. "So, that day we go on a field trip to this eco park. And while we're there, learning how to recycle or whatever, I'm still so shocked that I said yes, I tell one of my friends about it. And she is all shocked and horrified, saying, 'You can't go out with him! It's social suicide.'" Claire shakes her head. "Social suicide in grade six? Sad really. But true. So, being a totally weak and self-conscious little prepubescent brat, I don't stick up for him or for myself. Instead, trying to save face, I assure them, 'Oh, don't worry. I only did it so I could dump him later.' Which was so not true."

Mia pulls a nervous face. "Oh dear."

"I know, right? It gets worse. My friend demands to know when I'm going to break it off. She was probably terrified my giant faux pas would have some effect on her social standings. I tell them I will do it when we are all back on the bus. Oh God." Claire puts her face in her hands. She hates the next part.

Mia yanks on her sleeve. "Don't stop now. What happened on the bus?"

Claire takes a deep breath and lifts her head. "I had no idea that my friends had been telling everyone on the bus that I was going to break up with him at two." She shakes her head. "Then, the next thing I know, we're all piled on the school bus. He's sitting right behind us, and I am looking at my watch, trying to figure out a way to discreetly tell him. Then..." She takes a breath. "It turns out I didn't need to."

"Why...not?" Mia looks suitably wary.

"Because at two-thirty, practically the entire bus—everyone except the teachers and the driver—turns around and screams, 'Tommy, you're dumped!' at him." Claire cringes, waiting for it.

"Oh my God." Mia claps her hand over her open mouth. She shakes her head. "That poor kid."

"I know." Claire buries her face in her arms and blushes and giggles at the same time. "It was horrible, Mia."

"What did he do?" Mia gasps, eyes still wide.

"He tried to laugh and stuff, like it was all a joke, but he looked so upset."

"Of course he did. I would have been mortified."

"I felt so, so bad about it." Claire lifts her head and gives her a bashful smile. "I went home and cried," she admits.

"You did *not*."

"Yes, I *did*." Claire blushes. She remembers how she sat in her room and wept mortified tears and plotted how she could avoid the poor kid for the rest of the year.

Mia rests chin in her hand and grins as if she's got her caught. "You're a secret softie, aren't you, Claire Pearson?"

Claire ignores Mia's tease. "And the worst part is he was still my friend after that. He'd still come over and hang out during the holidays." She shakes her head. "I never understood that."

Mia shrugs. "Boys are suckers for pretty girls. Enough to forgive the most terrible crimes. Fact of life." She smiles. "The fact that you are still completely ashamed about it is kind of cute though."

Claire smiles back at Mia. "There. Feel better now?"

Mia chuckles. "Maybe. You know, it wasn't exactly your fault, though. Those little witches you were friends with had a lot to do with it. They were bigger assholes than you, getting a bus full of kids to do that."

"Well you shouldn't be so hard on yourself, either," she tells Mia. "About something you did at a party—how long ago was it?"

"Two years."

"See? And you still feel terrible about it. That speaks pretty well of you. You just did something dumb. And I bet you never do it again. I'd say you're not a total asshole. Maybe just...a recovering asshole."

Mia smiles over at her, squinting a little. "At the risk of sounding kind of Hallmark and mushy right now, how do you always know what to say to make me feel better? In a really insane kind of way?"

"I don't know." Claire feels suddenly shy. "Because I'm a genius?"

"Oh yeah, that's right. Sorry, I forgot for a second."

Claire grins at her. "Anyway, I am starting to think maybe you shouldn't get so drunk at parties. You kind of do crazy things."

Mia looks at her for a second and then clearly registers what she means. She gives Claire a quick, shruggy smile. "Yeah, maybe," She gets up and picks up her bag. "Come on. We better go."

* * *

They're making their way back to uni when she sees him. She never sees her brother at work. Even though she automatically glances into every police car she sees, it's never him.

Then all of a sudden here he is, outside a grocery store in full uniform with his partner, Vito.

"There's my idiot brother," she tells Mia.

When he spots her, he opens his mouth in mock shock and holds out his arms as if to go for the long-lost sibling embrace.

She walks up to him and slaps his jaw shut instead. "Shouldn't you be busy catching criminals or something?" She grins at him. "Hello."

"Nope," says Vito as he gives Claire his automatic sleazy up and down.

"We're on a break, smart-ass." Cam turns to Mia. "Hello," he says in his friendliest who-the-hell-are-you voice.

Claire waves a hand between them. "Cam, this is Mia. Mia, this is Cam."

"Ahem." Vito leans up against the window of the store and folds his arms over his chest.

"And that's Vito," she says grudgingly. Because Mia, like Claire, could probably have lived very easily for the rest of her life without making his acquaintance.

Cam holds out his hand to Mia. "Hi. I'd say I've heard lots about you, but I haven't heard a thing."

She laughs and shakes his hand. "Claire probably didn't want to bore you."

"Oh, I bet you're not boring," Vito says.

Claire serves him a filthy look.

"Are you studying French as well?" Cam asks.

Mia shakes her head. "I'm doing biomed."

"Whoa." He raises his eyebrows and looks over at Claire. "What are you doing hanging out with a beatnik like my little sister, then?"

Claire crosses her arms. "Shut up, Cam." He can be such a dick sometimes.

Mia grins at him and grasps Claire's arm. "Hey, listen, I have to get going. Got to meet some people in the library. I'll see you soon?"

"Yeah, see you later," Claire says. She is kind of relieved to be spared any further embarrassment.

Mia turns to Cam. "It was really great to meet you. See you around." She even extends the smile to Vito.

Claire gives her a wave as she takes off down the street. How does Mia manage to be so polite to people—even to idiots like Vito? Even though Claire knows Mia probably thinks he's a dick already, too.

Cam watches Mia stroll back down the street towards the university. "She seems nice," he muses. "Cute too."

"Uh yeah." Vito raises his eyebrows. "Hot."

Before she can tell them to quit being creeps, Vito starts in on her with his usual come-on shtick. "So, Claire, when are you going to come and have a drink with us one night?" He grins. "You never know, you might learn to like me after a few pints."

"It's going to take way more than a few pints." She shakes her head. In three years of failing to get anywhere with her, he still hasn't figured out he doesn't have a chance in hell.

Cam just smiles. He never stops Vito when he starts in on this crap. Claire's pretty sure it's mostly because he knows she can handle herself. And she's also pretty sure he finds it kind of entertaining.

Vito pretends to pout. "Don't be like that."

She tips her head to the side and pretends to consider him. "Do you know who you remind me of?"

"Who?" He steps in closer. "Brad Pitt?"

She takes a step back. "You remind me of that dick guy character who is in every teen film. You know the douche who is always friends with the guy lead?"

He just stares at her.

"Oh come on," she scoffs. "You know the one? The one who tries to crack onto everything that moves and always epically fails because he is a creeper and has no social gauge at all? And yet," she muses, "he doesn't seem to notice that he never succeeds."

He crosses his arms over his chest again but doesn't say a word.

She shakes her head and holds up her hands. "Dude, some advice. Learn some subtlety. Coming from a girl who has refused your gross advances a gazillion times over the last few years, trust me." She nods.

"Subtlety might just work for you. Not with me, of course," she adds hurriedly. "But maybe with some poor misguided soul."

Vito's mouth drops open, and Cam laughs so hard he doubles over.

She points at Vito. "And you know, I don't know what's more terrifying right now, how much you are like that guy or the fact that I just cast my brother as the male lead in this scenario, which is horrifying. So, in answer to your question, I won't be coming for a drink, *ever*."

She turns to Cam and points at him. "And, Cam," she snaps. "Do not ogle my friends. It's seriously creepy." With that, she leaves them there on the footpath and heads back to school.

* * *

Later, during a less than enthralling lecture, she slips her phone out of her pocket. There are two messages. One is from Cam.

Epic takedown. Vito didn't say a word for thirty whole minutes.

She smiles. The other is from Robbie.

N just told me what happened. I'm sorry. I'm an evil prick. Forgive me.

She quickly types out her response. *xo*

CHAPTER 26

Her lungs are suddenly capable of only the shallowest of breaths. And if her mother's hand wasn't pressed lightly to the small of her back, Claire's not sure she'd be able to remember exactly how standing works.

"They said it's not as bad as it looks, sweetheart." Her mother's voice is quieter than usual. Less shrill.

Claire takes in the sight of her brother. He currently looks more machine than man. From where she stands, she can see how at least three different tubes exit his body, departing from places that previously worked just fine without them. One pushes oxygen in and out of his lungs with terrifyingly robotic regularity.

She thrusts her hands into her pockets and tries to focus on the tasks at hand—standing and breathing. "It looks pretty fucking bad to me."

"Claire," her father says quietly, a warning.

"What?" she snaps.

He doesn't respond.

The woman in a white coat standing over her brother doesn't even react to her language. She's probably used to it. She gives them a small, sympathetic smile as she passes.

At the prompting of her mother's hand, Claire takes another step.

"I'll be right back, honey. I'm going to talk with the nurses."

The hand on Claire's back is suddenly absent. Abandoned by its psychological role in keeping her upright, she fights the urge to fall backward.

So now she's adrift in the middle of the room, a metre or so from her brother, trapped in this panicked, head-spinning, little vortex where everything that *was* this morning, when she had bacon and eggs with him in a shitty café before his shift, no longer *is*.

How does that happen?

His chin is pushed upward, and his arm is stretched out at an odd angle from his body. It looks as if he's been flung against the bed and left there. There's a bandage covering most of his left shoulder, and she can see a deep graze near the line of his jaw. She wonders how much more damage there is that she cannot see.

A light cotton sheet conceals his body as if whatever is underneath can only bear the lightest of touches upon it. The ventilator that breathes for him looks as if it's pinning him down, an aggressively benevolent form of life sustenance.

Claire fixes her gaze on the calming familiarity of Cam's light-brown hair, the one part of him untouched by injury, machine, or bedding. She focuses on her mother's words. *It's not as bad as it looks*, she reminds herself.

"He's in an induced coma," her father tells her quietly as his hand replaces her mother's. "That's why he's on the machine. It looks worse than it is."

Claire nods. It has to look worse than it is.

A nurse strides in, does something to the drip attached to Cam's arm and leaves again. Claire follows her as her mother re-appears.

She needs a minute if she's going to have any chance of taking this in. She needs some air, and she needs silence. Unsure of where she's going, she follows the swift steps of the nurse who just left Cam's room. She follows her back to the nurses' station, situated near a small waiting area.

"How's eleven?" the woman at the counter asks the nurse.

"He'll live." She picks up a can of energy drink and slugs it down. "If all of his major organs hold up."

Claire stops in her tracks. Eleven. Who's in eleven? Is it Cam?

She swallows hard again and heads automatically for a vending machine in the corner. She buys a bottle of water, takes it back to Cam's room, and glances around for a number she doesn't want to find.

* * *

Her parents go home in the early hours of the morning. Claire spends the night in his room. She sits there and listens to the steady sounds of beeps and whirs that fill the ICU and to the hushed hurry of the night shift at work. In these few hours alone, she learns every inch of this room, every shade of colour, and every nuance of its clinical, disinfected odour.

She watches as medical staff march in and out and tend to him in all kinds of ways.

He even has his own nurse, an efficient middle-aged man with more bald patch than hair. He performs an astonishing amount of tasks throughout the night, despite his slow, steady movements. While he's not exactly friendly, he takes a minute to explain to Claire everything he does in concise, one-line briefings.

"Just to stave off any infections," he explains as he sticks a needle into the flesh of Cam's stomach.

"Just checking the wound drain. Large puncture in his leg," he mutters later as he lifts the narrow pipe with one finger and makes a note on the chart. The drain contains fluids in colours Claire didn't know could inhabit a human body.

"We're just taking him for another scan," he announces in the early hours of the morning as staff members wheel Cam's bed from the room.

And then Claire is left in a small, empty square of space alone. The room, divested of its reason for being here, suddenly makes no sense.

* * *

Sometime in that in-between time of night and morning, when the grey predawn makes its appearance through the windows, her parents return.

They wait in the hallway while the doctors are with her brother. Her father pretends to read the paper, and her mother stands at the nurses' station and asks them every single question she can think to ask about Cam's night, questions she's already asked Claire twice over.

Claire picks at the plastic lid of her coffee cup and wishes she could scream at her mother to shut the hell up. She wants to tell her that nothing she says or does will make these people any better at making Cam better. But she doesn't. She just shuts her eyes and stays as still as she possibly can.

Finally, they are introduced to a doctor. Small, fast-talking, and with a lovely singsong accent, he stands there and quickly recites the litany of injuries that earned Cam a trip to the ICU. Claire catches phrases—the lung collapse, a small crack in a vertebra, mild trauma to the liver and a kidney, broken elbow, severe puncture wound in thigh, minor brain bleed. For some reason, she hangs on to the qualifiers, to the *smalls*, the *minors*, and the *severes*. She wonders about their measure, about the difference they make.

"Now we have seen clear scans," he tells them. "We know none of these injuries in of themselves are life threatening, but the combination of traumas, the question mark over the damage to his organs..." He takes a breath and taps a pen on his chart. "Well, now it's a matter of waiting, letting his body do whatever healing it can before we decide if surgery is necessary. The most pressing thing right now is that kidney. The trauma has prohibited some function, and we need to see if this corrects itself. We want him to hang on to it if he can, but it's too soon to tell."

Claire thinks about the nurse and his comment about organs holding up. "Is he going to die?" she asks before she can stop herself.

"Claire." That hand makes its presence known on her back again as her mother tries to play puppet master.

Claire bites her lip and steps away from the hand. She does not care if it's rude to interrupt. She needs to know this *now*.

The doctor turns to her and smiles. "In my profession, we have learned never to say anything with utmost certainty until we are of the utmost certainty. I can tell you this, I feel very, very confident, complications notwithstanding, that your...brother, is it?"

Claire nods.

"That your brother should recover. Everything from now on is about how well and how quickly we can help him get over this."

Claire nods and lets out a breath. The ice in her stomach slowly start to melt. That's all she needs to hear. Everything else can wait. She walks back to his room.

* * *

The house already looks as if it's been abandoned even though her parents were here just last night. It always has a slightly neglected air anyway, clean and spotless and untouched. Right now, though, it's downright forlorn.

She ignores its neediness and heads straight for the undemanding surroundings of her bedroom. It's still a mess from her rush to get ready for work last night. Twelve hours ago, she flung these clothes onto the bed, accidentally knocked the books off her desk, and squirted that final spray of perfume that lingers faintly in the air. It looks as if the scene of something that happened a month ago, already relegated to a shady, half-conjured memory.

She stares blankly at the wall until she finally recalls herself to her task—sleep. She takes her phone from her pocket and throws her jacket across the chair. As she's about to set her alarm, the phone rings. It's Nina. Claire stares at the name flashing on the screen but doesn't answer. She doesn't have the energy to speak.

She sits paralysed on the edge of the bed and contemplates undressing. She decides not to. It feels too permanent, as if she'll sleep and wake to a fresh new day. But that's not true. She needs to retain the feeling of this all being temporary if she's going to return to the hospital and walk back inside the nightmare that awaits. Then maybe that will feel temporary too.

So she crawls into bed fully dressed and squeezes her eyes shut. Her phone begins to ring again. It's Mia this time. Claire blinks heavily and stares at the name on the screen. She wants to answer it. She really does. If there's anyone she would want to speak to, it's Mia. She wants—needs, even—Mia's calm warmth. But she also knows if she's going to make it through this, she can't afford that kind of comfort right now.

Besides, she'll probably just cry the moment she hears the slightest hint of sympathy. And she doesn't want to cry. She slips her phone under her pillow and shuts her eyes. She begs sleep to emerge from behind the wall of caffeine she's built over the last few hours. It's slow to arrive.

They called her at work. That's how she knew something was really wrong.

One minute she was knee-deep in customers and listening to one of Nina's hilarious stories, a fractured narrative continued each time they had a moment between orders. The next Andrew was handing her the phone, a look of fatherly concern on his face. Andrew doesn't do fatherly concern.

That's when the feeling started, the cold dread that crawled into her stomach and stayed there. It staked its claim before she even found out who was at the other end of the phone. And then, only minutes later, she was in Vito's service car on her way to the hospital, the dread freezing solid in her gut.

CHAPTER 27

On the third morning, the perfunctory consultation with the doctors feels routine.

"We're going to keep him sedated for another twenty-four hours, at least," the latest doctor says. "Just to be safe."

They tried to wake her brother again this morning. And again Cam struggled so violently that the doctors, fearful he'd do more damage to his compromised organs, quickly sedated him again.

Claire gives a small exhausted smile at the linoleum floor. How typical of Cam. He's always been difficult to rouse from sleep, so of course he'd be worse during a good old-fashioned trauma and sedation.

Claire yawns into her palm. She wouldn't mind a bit of sedation herself right now. She is so acutely exhausted she can't even remember what it feels like not to be tired. For a place of rest, the hospital is anything but restful. People come and go all day from Cam's room. There are the doctors, the nurses, and the aides—even physios. Then there are Cam's friends, her aunt Lucy, and her mother's and father's superiors waiting just outside the door. Even Elana has appeared, a constant questioning presence, forming a Greek chorus of sorts with her mother and her aunt.

Jangled with fatigue, Claire spends all of her time with Cam in his room, where only immediate family is allowed. She can barely stand to be in the waiting room. She can't handle the constant, repetitive enquiries, the efforts at comforting advice or sympathy, the need to talk when, really, there's nothing to be said. She goes home to sleep for a few hours at a time, but it's choppy and restless and cut up with dreams that wake her long before she's ready.

She leaves her parents with the doctor and wanders through another set of doors to the covered section outside emergency. There is a small crowd of people smoking, looking skittish and anxious, the way people outside emergency centres do. Claire avoids them and stands against a wall by a sad garden bed with some scrubby natives. She checks the time on her phone. It's nine fourteen in the morning. She has missed calls and messages from Mia, Robbie, and Nina. She knows she should call them, but she can't just yet. Instead, she shuts her eyes to the stinging sunlight and tries to be somewhere else for a minute.

* * *

On the fourth day they manage to wake Cam.

He's lucid straight away, but his voice is so raspy and quiet that Claire is the only person who understands what he says. The nurses tell her it's the irritation from his oxygen. Temporary, they assure her.

Claire acts as his translator, making words from his slurring, barely there whisper.

It turns out she doesn't only need to play translator to his words, though. More alarmingly, she also has to translate the world back to him, explaining and re-explaining why the hell he's lying in a hospital bed. It's the pain relief making him forget, his nurse explains, not his head injury. Claire answers the same questions over and over. He's been in car crash. His shift partner, the driver, is fine. The kid is fine. Cam is fine. It's like some horror version of *Groundhog Day*.

She tries not to lose patience. She can't. Every time he rouses slightly and asks her again what's going on, she sees the panic in his eyes. And she recognises that feeling of dread in Cam that she felt when Andrew passed her the phone four nights ago. Only this is way worse and on constant repeat for him.

So, every time he asks, she just takes a deep breath and tells him all over again.

* * *

On the fifth day, they take him to another ward.

Now he's awake, mostly coherent, and breathing on his own, the doctors say he can move to a high-dependency ward. Her mother and father return to work, too, and Claire is left with him during the day. She sits in a corner under the windowsill and studies for exams as he slides in and out of sleep.

They give him his own little remote to administer pain relief.

"I feel like a cyborg, using a remote control to operate myself," he jokes weakly.

"How bad does it hurt?" Claire asks.

"A lot."

Claire pulls her legs up onto the chair and frowns. She's not sure she could cope. She has never hurt herself badly, just a couple of sprains and a broken toe when she was eleven.

"Remember when you broke your toe when we were kids?"

"I was just thinking about that."

"I bet this hurts a lot more."

Claire shoots him a look. "Yeah, you know, Cam, I think this is one time where we don't need to be competitive, okay?"

He chuckles and then groans. "You still have to say I won, though."

Before Claire can say anything, a nurse comes in. She goes over to the bed and checks on the different tubes and bandages. She barely responds to the smile of greeting on Cam's face and leaves without saying a word.

"Geez," he mutters. "What did Mum do? I've been in this ward one day, and I think they all hate me."

Claire flicks her pen between her fingers. "She was...Mum. She treated them like they were guilty of a crime they hadn't even committed."

He lets out a choppy sigh. "I've got my work cut out for me charming these ones, then. Or no treats for me."

"With your social skills that was always going to be an uphill battle anyway." She waits for his comeback, but he doesn't have one. He's sliding suddenly, involuntarily back into sleep again, the way he does. Claire opens her book and smiles. She never thought she'd be so happy to bicker with her brother.

* * *

On the sixth day, she sits in the hallway and tries to figure out what day it is.

She's just decided it's a Tuesday when her parents arrive, fresh from a conference with the doctors. They sit on either side of her. She stiffens, immediately wary of this collective approach. This is never good.

"Sweetheart," Christine says as her father takes hold of Claire's forearm. "We have to leave town tomorrow."

"Leave? Where are you going?" Claire frowns. She wasn't expecting that.

"Canberra," her father says.

"What? Why?"

"Remember that conference we told you about?"

Claire nods dully. *Here we go*, she thinks.

"It starts tomorrow, and your mother and I are running half of the sessions between us. We left it until the last minute to decide, but we think we need to go."

Claire lets out a sigh, not sure what she's supposed to say to this. They seem to have already made up their minds.

"If we don't go, they'll have to cancel our sessions," Christine adds.

"Yeah, and God forbid the lawyers of Canberra don't get the benefit of your wisdom." Claire sighs and shakes off her father's hand and crosses her arms over her chest.

Christine narrows her eyes as though she's about to tell Claire off. Instead, she lets out a little sigh, rearranges her face, and leans in closer. "We thought about cancelling. But, sweetie, the doctor says Cam will be fine. It's just a process of recovery now. And if we're needed quickly, we're only a couple of hours away."

"Which, the doctors assure us, we won't be," her father adds.

"Besides," Christine puts a hand on Claire's arm, "you're quite old enough to look after things here without us."

Am I? Claire wonders. This is new information to her.

"And we'll call you morning and night," Christine continues. "Lucy will be here too. We've asked the doctors to check in with us daily, so you don't have to worry about anything but being with your brother."

Claire rests her head against the wall, eyes closed. There's no point saying anything, obviously. This has clearly been decided, and their departure is now to be treated as fact. "When do you leave?"

"In the morning, first thing. We'll come by here first and then go."

A week. *That's all they could spare for Cam before going on with their lives?* "What if something happens?"

"*Nothing* will happen," Christine tells her firmly, her hand still on Claire's arm. "And if by any small chance it does, I'm sure you can handle it until we get here. You're an adult now," she tells her as if she's bestowing a treat on Claire, like an imminent trip to the zoo or a new car.

Claire sits up taller and inhales deeply. "Yeah, whatever. Go." She yanks her arm out of her mother's possession and stands. She wants them to shut up and go now if that's what they're going to do.

CHAPTER 28

On the eighth day, Claire walks wearily along the bright, fluorescent-lit hospital corridor toward the waiting room. That's when she sees them.

At first, she thinks she's dreaming, or having some sort of sleep-deprived hallucination. But no, the three of them, Robbie, Nina, and Mia, are walking slowly toward her. They look like the promise of summer in jeans and T-shirts, sunglasses perched on their heads. It must be another of those perfect late spring days, when a person can feel the tang of summer and the potential of what's to come. A day when it's finally possible to bare legs and shoulders.

For the first time in days, Claire feels a desire to be away from the clinical stink and climate-control air of the hospital. She wants to experience the unpredictability of real air against her skin and to absorb whatever warmth the sun provides. The glimpses of sun she catches in the cloying, smoky emergency entrance hardly count.

They spot her straight away and pick up the pace in a bashful, approaching collective of sympathetic smiles. Robbie breaks ranks first and strides quickly until he's right in front of her. He enfolds her in one of his relentless, no-choice hugs, and his grip is even fiercer than usual.

"What are you guys doing here?" she asks.

He steps back and squeezes her shoulders. "We came to see how you are, dummy."

"And to bring you a coffee." Mia holds up a take-away cup. "Here." She passes it to Claire and smiles.

"And to see if you're okay," Nina adds.

"I'm okay. Tired."

"You look it," Nina tells her as they step out of the way of some hurrying nurses. "No offence."

Claire smiles in weary agreement and sits on a bank of seats that line the narrow corridor.

Robbie drops down next to her. "How's your brother?"

"He's okay. He's getting his chest tube removed, whatever that means."

Robbie automatically turns to Mia.

"He must have had a lung collapse," she says.

Claire points at Mia. "What she said."

"Gross." Nina grimaces before turning to Claire, contrite. "Sorry."

Claire smiles. "Don't be sorry. It *is* gross. It's all been gross."

"I should probably confess I know more about this from movies than school." Mia frowns. "We haven't got to that stuff yet. Is he doing okay?"

"Yeah, I guess. He's out of intensive care. So that's good."

"Do you need anything?" Nina asks again as she folds her arms over her chest, looking awkward. "Clothes or stuff from school?"

"No, I'm fine."

"You don't look fine." Robbie brushes his finger against her cheek. "I didn't think it was possible for you to get more pale, but you've outghosted yourself."

Claire pushes his hand away. "Thanks, Robbie. No, seriously," she grumbles but is secretly grateful for the way he never changes. "Thanks a lot."

He smiles at her as if he knows it's easier for her if he just treats her like normal.

"Maybe we should go outside?" Mia suggests. She looks down the long white hallway to the sliding doors. "While they're with your brother? It's beautiful out there. It might make you feel better."

Robbie nods. "Good idea. It's pretty awful in here."

Before she can say anything, they stand.

Anchored by fear, Claire almost wants to say no, that she wants to stay here just in case. But the other part of her doesn't have the energy to protest, so she stands too.

They traipse back down the long hallway. Claire stops at the nurses' station and rests her palms on the cool counter.

Lorraine, one of the nurses, comes over. "They're still with Cam, sweetheart," she tells her. "Might be a while longer."

"I'm just going outside for a bit."

"Good." Lorraine nods as she picks up a pile of papers. She looks over at the others. "Put her in the sunshine, kids. I don't think she's seen much daylight for a while." She turns to Claire. "I've got your number. I'll call you if you're needed. Go outside and breath some air, child."

Claire smiles and turns away. She secretly loves Lorraine, with her epic hair that looks as if it hasn't changed since the eighties, and her wiry, comforting competence. Cam has managed to chip away at the reserve of this recent round of nurses, for whom their mother is, thankfully, already becoming a distant memory.

They trudge through the sliding doors and head for the park across from the hospital. When they find a patch of grass, Claire sinks wearily onto it, blinking into the brightness. Nina immediately takes off her sunglasses and places them on Claire's face. Claire smiles her gratitude and lies back on the grass, absorbing the nourishing warmth of the sun.

They sit there in sun-stunned silence for a few minutes.

"Did you know they brush your teeth for you when you're unconscious?" Claire tells them, breaking the quiet.

"Ew," Nina says. "That's weird. What, they just pry open your mouth and brush them?"

Claire shrugs and looks at Nina. "Pretty much. Saw it with my own eyes."

"Yuck," Nina says.

"No, I did not know that, Claire." Robbie flops onto the grass next to her. "Thank you for that invaluable piece of information."

Claire gives him a lazy smile. "Happy to drop some knowledge on you. Anything else you want to know about sedation-hygiene routines?"

"Definitely not." Robbie laughs. "Do they teach you this stuff, Mia?"

"Not really," she says from somewhere behind Claire. "We're, uh, into things at a more cellular level."

Nina sighs. "I don't even know what that means."

And Claire idly listens to the other three banter, glad they don't try to make her talk about the accident or ask relentless questions about Cam's condition like everyone else who visits and doesn't know what to say.

But after a while, she forces herself to sit up, mostly because she's afraid she's going to fall asleep. She hugs her knees to her chest and tries to focus on what everyone is talking about, but it's difficult to concentrate. She's grateful they are here, though, a distraction from the awful monotony of another repetitive day.

Her phone starts to ring, and their talk trickles off as she checks it. It's her mother. She puts it down on the grass next to her. When she looks up again, they're all looking at her.

"It's just Mum." She plays with the laces of her boots. "Probably just to see if they are done. She checks in every five minutes. I'll call her when I get back."

"She's not there?" Nina asks.

"No, Mum and Dad are in Canberra."

Nina frowns. "What? What are they doing in Canberra?"

"Both of them?" Robbie asks.

"Yeah, they were scheduled to lead this big conference at a university. It started yesterday. So they decided to go when Cam got out of ICU."

"Is anyone else around?" Mia asks.

"My aunt Lucy comes to see him every night. And his friends visit lots. And I stay with him in the day. Now that he's out of ICU, they're stricter about visiting hours, though, but I can hang out with him in the mornings and the afternoons." She pulls a small clump of grass from the ground and ties the narrow blades into a knot. "I guess they don't let us be with him all the time because they know he's not going to die now. Which is, you know, good." She tosses the grass away.

"What do you do the rest of the time?" Robbie asks.

"I go to the café or sit in the waiting room and study. No point going home just to come back." She watches kids run into the playground while their mother, laden with shopping, yells at them to slow down.

Mia frowns. "And so you're staying at home by yourself?"

"Yeah, but it's fine." She doesn't tell them that she can't sleep at night by herself. That for the first time in a long time, she actually wishes her parents were there.

Nina checks her phone and sighs. "Crap, I have to go." She gets up and dusts the back of her jeans. "Sorry, Claire."

"Don't be sorry." Claire squints up at her and frowns. "Why be sorry?"

But Nina looks as if she doesn't know what to say to that, and Claire immediately feels bad. "Thanks for coming, Neens."

Nina smiles back, grateful. "Andrew's holding your shifts at work, too, okay?"

"Lucky me." Claire rolls her eyes. "Tell him thank you, I think."

Nina grins.

"I'd better go too." Robbie climbs to his feet and holds his hand out to Claire. "Will you be okay, babe?"

"Of course." She takes his hand and stands. "I'll be fine. Thanks, guys, for coming," she says again, because she doesn't know what else to say. They turn back toward the hospital.

"Don't thank us." Robbie throws an arm around her shoulder as they trudge back across the parking lot. "Of course we came."

And Claire feels a rush of warmth, a solace that seems to come as much from his words as his affection. Of course they came. These people are her friends. These people have become *her* people. She feels an embarrassing prick of tears at the back of her eyelids.

They walk her to the doors of the hospital, and she goes inside quickly before they can leave her. She doesn't want to watch them go, free to walk into that intoxicating sunshine and to the simpler worries of study, break, and work. She, on the other hand, is relegated to her lonesome station in the hallway, waiting for her brother's battered body to heal.

She trudges the long passage, keeping to the sides, out of the way of the busy staff moving between rooms. There's still an hour and a half until afternoon visiting hours, so she decides to go to what she thinks of as her personal corner of the hospital, a little bank of seats tucked away in an alcove at the end of the hall.

She usually has it to herself. There aren't many people around the ward at this time. Most people come during evening visiting hours and then leave. There are only a few who, like her, are left with the sole responsibility of care for someone, or cannot bring themselves to leave until they know everything is going to be okay.

As usual, it's empty. She sits cross-legged on a seat and pulls out her French text. She opens her book, ready to re-read a chapter, but zones out instead. She stares at the wall opposite with its colourful but depressing posters about health care and skin cancer checks and yawns heavily. Her exhaustion feels like something heavy chained to her, and it pulls her slowly but interminably downward. It makes sitting upright feel impossible. She shuts her eyes slowly and slumps in her seat.

"Hey."

Claire jumps and opens her eyes, blinking into the fluorescent light. It's Mia. She stands in front of Claire, her sunglasses still perched on her head, and smiles at her.

"Uh...hey." Claire blinks harder and once again wonders if she's seeing things. "What are you doing back here?"

Mia drops into the seat next to her. "I don't know. I thought I'd wait here with you for a bit, at least until you're allowed to see him. It must be kind of horrible hanging out here by yourself."

"It's okay. You don't have to. I'm used to it now."

"I don't mind." Mia puts her bag on the seat next to her as if she is here to stay.

"I'm fine, you know."

"Yeah, yeah, I know you are," Mia says in that knowing way she has and settles into her seat. She removes an elastic from her wrist and ties her hair into a ponytail.

"Why would anyone want to sit in a hospital if they don't have to?" Claire frowns.

"Well, I'm thinking of studying medicine, remember?" Mia threads the elastic one more time around her thick hair. "Might as well get used to it."

"True." Claire still feels compelled to act nonchalant about Mia's reappearance, but already her presence feels like a salve.

Mia smiles at Claire. She's developed a handful of freckles in this sunny weather, a smattering of brown spots across her nose and cheeks. It suits her. "And you don't have to talk or anything. I know you're really tired."

"I am."

"Have you been able to sleep?"

"Not really," Claire admits. "I can't."

Mia nods, reaches into her bag, and pulls out a huge textbook. "Rest if you want. I've got plenty to keep me entertained." She lifts up the book. "Exams are horrifyingly close."

Claire nods. It's difficult to believe she's missed the last week of classes and that it's nearly study break already. She's been studying as hard as she can when Cam is asleep or between visiting hours. She knows she'll pass. But she's also prepared for the fact she might not do too great. For the first time in her life, she doesn't care.

Mia flicks open her book, pulls out a notepad, and rests it on her knee. She replaces her sunglasses with her reading glasses and busies herself with work.

Claire immediately relaxes, glad Mia doesn't expect her to talk. Claire has nothing to say, nothing to tell anyone that isn't about hospitals and wounds and trauma. She rests her head against the wall and shuts her eyes glad of the simple solace of having someone beside her. The last few days, although surrounded by people, have been a lonely experience.

In fact, the whole week has been an exercise in trying to hold it together. Now she actually feels as though she might be able to breathe a little, to let go. She takes in a long, deep breath and lets it out in an unexpectedly shaky sigh.

"You okay?" Mia's voice is quiet.

Claire nods. Suddenly scared she is going to cry, she keeps her eyes jammed shut and purses her lips. Mia doesn't say anything, but Claire can feel her gaze. She takes another deep breath, holds it in, and tries to stem the tears. She feels fingers slide over her own and take a light hold of her hand. Warmth spreads through her body at the sympathy contained in this touch, at the comfort of being with someone who knows she's maybe only dancing around the edges of being okay. For that, she's incredibly grateful. She gently squeezes Mia's hand, her way of saying thank you. And Mia's only response is to simply hold on a little tighter.

After a few peaceful minutes of sitting there, eyes closed to the inexorable, quiet hospital scurry, tethered to the island of sanity that is Mia, Claire turns and looks at her. Her friend's free hand is busily at work. It flits briskly between writing copious notes and turning the pages of her book. Claire smiles. She could probably use her hand back, but Claire's not willing to return it. It's keeping her sustained right now. She looks down at their hands, at Mia's long brown fingers and neatly manicured fingernails, a stark contrast to Claire's chipped blue polish and chewed-down nails. She exhales another long sigh and rests her head back against the wall.

"Claire?"

"What?"

"Why don't you lie down?"

She opens her eyes and turns her head.

Mia gestures at the bank of seats. "I'll stay with you, and if you fall asleep, I'll wake you when it's time to see Cam."

Claire starts to shake her head, but then gives in. All she wants, all she needs, is to shut her eyes for a while. "Do you promise you'll wake me? At three?"

"I'll wake you." Mia squeezes her hand again, her brown eyes insistent. "I promise."

Claire gives in. She has to. "Okay." She releases Mia's hand, kicks off her boots, and eases herself down across the chairs.

"Here." Mia reaches into her bag, pulls out a sweater, and folds it up. She passes it to Claire. "Pillow."

"Thanks." Claire gratefully takes the proffered sweater. She lays it on the chair next to Mia's leg and lowers her head onto her makeshift pillow. She shuts her eyes and breathes in the comforting, clean scent of washed clothes and something else fresh and light—a smell she's already come to associate with Mia. She tucks her hands under her chin and shuts her eyes, safe to let go of consciousness for a while.

CHAPTER 29

Claire puts her French textbook in her bag and looks over at her brother and smiles.

Today is nearly a good day. Last night Cam's new doctor said if his scans are okay, they'll move Cam to a regular ward tomorrow. That feels like a step closer to Cam being okay again. With that small but precious nugget of good news in her pocket, Claire is able to go home and relax a little.

Today she feels just a little bit human again. As she leaves his room she doesn't say goodbye. Cam is already two-thirds of his way back to sleep, to the place where his body and brain spend most of their time, busy with the steady work of returning him to health.

As she's making her way down the hall, her phone vibrates in her pocket. She sighs and pulls it out, expecting her mother for what will be the third time today.

It's not. It's Robbie. "Hey, where are you?" he asks the moment she picks up.

"At the hospital. Where else?"

"Good. I'm out the front, near emergency. Come out."

And before she can ask what he's doing there, he hangs up, and she heads for the front entrance.

As soon as she hits the outside air, she zips up her jacket all the way to the top. In the spirit of the tempestuous Melbourne springtime, the sun is out, but the wind is whippy and biting, a stark contrast to the caressing warmth of that dream weather when her friends came to visit.

Robbie sits on a bench near the entrance, his camera in one hand and his backpack next to him. An obviously handpicked—or hand-thieved—bunch of flowers hang out of the opening, drooping already. He grins when he sees her and stands.

"What are you doing here?" she asks.

"I've come to take you to lunch." He loops his arm through hers. "It's Sunday."

"So?"

"So Sunday is the time for Sunday lunch, Claire. Get with the program."

"Uh, okay then." She figures it's easier not to question it, not when Robbie is being so willfully cryptic. They walk off the hospital grounds and down the street. The late-morning traffic hums around them.

He pulls out his phone. "Actually, it's a little early. Let's get a coffee first." He makes a quick turn for the crossing. "How's your brother?"

"Better."

"Hey, that's really good." He gives a little skip and squeezes her arm.

"It is. And they say he's really lucky, that so far there doesn't seem to be any real permanent damage, except he might have lifelong trouble with back pain and a slightly screwy kidney."

He laughs. "That's the medical term, right?" He leads her around a corner to a little café Claire never noticed before. He shoves open the door, and she follows him into the tiny, cosy space fragrant with coffee and baked bread. They find a table, order coffees, and sit.

"What have you been doing?" Claire asks him, so ready to hear anything about the world outside the hospital.

"Freaking out."

"What about?"

"School. Everything. I have to write a stupid essay, and I am terrible at writing essays." He rolls his eyes and sips tentatively at his coffee. "It's, like, I know how I feel about certain ideas, certain art, and I am completely confident in my opinions, but I'm no good at organising it into words on a page in that way they want you to structure them. It just ends up being one big tangle, if you know what I mean."

Claire nods. She doesn't have that problem, though. Essays come easy for her. It's just working to a formula. "You know, I'm actually okay at them. I could look at it for you, if you want?" She offers it shyly. She never imagined she could help Robbie with anything. "It might help."

"No, it's fine." He shakes his head and waves the idea away. "You have enough to worry about."

"No, seriously," she insists. "I don't know how much help I can be, but I kinda have a lot of time on my hands. I am actually starting to wish my brother would sleep less and talk to me. And, believe me, that's *not* a feeling I've had often in my life."

He cackles. "I might take you up on it." He grabs her wrist and squeezes it. "Thank you," he says, serious for a moment.

She gives him a sly smile. "But just so you know, Robbie, there's only so much I can do to polish a turd."

"Oh shut up. I'm not that bad!" He lets go of her wrist and slaps it instead.

"I know. I'm joking. What else can I help you with?"

"Can you prescribe anxiety medication?"

"You might need Mia for that. Why?"

"I'm just freaking out about the end-of-year show too," he confesses. "And about the feedback, which is—"

"But everyone loved the last exhibition."

"Oh, no, not that kind of feedback." Robbie shakes his head. "That'd be okay. I mean the formal feedback we get from our professors. They examine our final project, the stuff we put in our show."

"Oh, scary."

"Uh-huh."

"But your stuff is kind of amazing. They'll love it."

"Maybe. I'm scared about this bunch of photos. They are some I took the last time I went home, of my family, and they're, I don't know, they're..." He trails off as if he never knew where that sentence was going in the first place.

Claire frowns. "Where is your family?" She realises she knows nothing about them. "In Melbourne?"

He shakes his head. "I grew up outside Geelong."

"Do you have brothers and sisters?"

"One of each, but they're ten and twelve years older than me."

"Wow." Claire raises her eyebrows. "How'd that happen?"

"I was kind of an accident. I don't think my parents were too impressed, really, having another kid in their forties." He smiles ruefully. "And they were especially not that impressed when he turned out to be gay."

"Really?"

"Yeah. They didn't kick me out onto the streets or anything dramatic like that. But they do refuse to acknowledge it."

"Like, they don't mention it at all?"

He nods. "Just like that. They're kind of religious. And they just don't get it. Or me. And they don't get the photography thing. Neither do my brother and sister. One works in a bank, and the other is a medical receptionist. They're so completely uninterested in anything other than their kids and their jobs and their mortgages. So they ignore everything about me that they don't get. Which is pretty much everything." He shakes his head. "I never, ever want to be like that."

"Me either." She gives him a sympathetic smile. "I'm sorry your family is a bunch of jerks."

He grins back at her. "Thanks. I'm luckier than some. You know, Eli said his ex-boyfriend's parents actually kicked him out when he came out. I didn't even know that still happened to people."

"Wow." Claire shakes her head. She'd have to do something pretty awful for her parents to kick her out.

Robbie sits up. "We better get going or we'll be late."

"For what?"

He doesn't answer. He's already halfway out the door.

They leave the café, continue up the road, and turn down another side street, a narrower, tree-lined strip of old apartment blocks.

"Where exactly are we going for lunch?" Claire asks. They seem to be walking further away from cafés and deeper into pure neighbourhood.

"Mia's." Robbie strides up to a red-brick apartment block.

"What, like, Mia's house?" Claire asks, hurrying to catch up with him.

She hasn't seen Mia today, but for the last few days since they all came to visit, she's been coming to the hospital to keep Claire company when she can't be with Cam. Sometimes they studied in the cafeteria or walked over to the park to sit in the sun. Sometimes they just sat in the waiting room and talked or not talked, and it's felt like a reprieve. Mia made the days pass faster and Claire feel less lonely.

"Yup." He leads her up a flight of steps. When they reach the top, he pulls the flowers out of his bag, a ragtag, but charming, bunch of clashing colours and wide green leaves. He raps loudly on a door. "Mia's house."

A tall brunette woman with her hair tied back in a neat bun opens the door. Claire immediately recognises Mia's brown eyes and clear, not-quite-olive skin. The woman's face is broader than Mia's though, with a more handsome, stern brand of good looks.

"Hi!" Robbie steps up and gives the woman a kiss on the cheek. Her serious expression softens into a smile at his embrace. "I brought my camera and these." He passes her the flowers. "And, as instructed, I brought Claire." He turns to Claire. "Claire this is Mia's mum."

"Hello." Claire is immediately shy and wonders why he's been instructed to bring her here. She always gets timid around other people's parents. They never seem to like her.

Mia's mother smiles at her, clutching the flowers. "Hello, Claire." She shakes Claire's hand. "I'm Tasya. Welcome."

"Uh, thank you." Claire blushes and obediently follows Robbie into a large living room. It's a lovely, alive kind of room, where furniture seems to be an afterthought, forced to work around the brimming bookshelves and leafy indoor plants. It's such a contrast to the sterile beige wash that is Claire's house, where it's always difficult to feel completely comfortable. She likes it already.

Mia appears through a doorway in her jeans and work T-shirt with a dog at her heels. "Hey, perfect timing. I just got home from work." She smiles at Claire and turns to Robbie. "You found her."

"I did," Robbie says. "I'll admit it wasn't too hard."

Tasya walks toward a door on the other side of the room. "I think lunch is close to done. Come into the kitchen when you're ready."

Robbie follows her from the room.

"Okay," Mia tells her and then turns back to Claire. "Sorry for the surprise invite. I told my mum and dad about Cam and how you were there by yourself, and they told me I had to invite you to lunch." She shrugs as if she is slightly embarrassed but can't help her parents.

"It's okay," Claire says. "It's...nice."

"Good. I'm going to get changed. I'll be back in a minute." Mia dashes up the stairs.

The dog wanders over to Claire and gazes up at her. It's a stocky, friendly looking blue heeler, greying around the muzzle and eyes. One of its ears is standing at attention while the other flops lazily onto its head. She offers her hand for it to sniff before she pets the velvety failed ear.

"What happened to your ear?" she mumbles as she scratches his muzzle. "Do you need to be returned to the factory?" The dog licks her hand and leans against her leg. She pets him absently until Mia trots back down the stairs, changed into a light-green top, her hair loose.

"This is Blue." Mia leans over her dog, clutching his snout affectionately between her hands.

"Is he yours?"

"He's all of ours, I guess." Mia rubs the fur across his back. "But he mostly hangs out with me. We got him when I was ten."

"We got a dog when I was ten too. For Cam, though," Claire tells her. "A Labrador. He was so stupid. Like, incredibly stupid. My dad took him to a trainer because we couldn't get him to do anything. And even the trainer said he was dumb."

Mia laughs. "Did he ever learn anything?"

"Only how to get out through the gate when we weren't home. He got hit by a car and died by the time I was eleven."

"Oh." Mia frowns.

Claire sighs. "Mum said she was surprised he lived that long. We stuck to cats after that."

Mia takes Claire into the kitchen and introduces her to her father, John, a tall, impossibly thin, bearded man in an apron and slacks. He paces busily between the stove and counter and chops salad on a board laid out next to a stack of dishes.

He stops momentarily and greets Claire. And immediately she sees the rest of Mia that isn't made from Tasya, her slender, freckled features and her warm, open smile. They are her gifts from him.

They all sit at the table, waiting for John to finish what he's doing. Claire doesn't talk much but listens to the conversation as it flows around her. It's a shock to be suddenly removed from the disinfected whiteness of the hospital and the silence of Cam's room to the patchwork charm of this large, sunny flat. Jarring, but lovely. She wants to let it wash over her in soothing waves of comforting normality before she has to return to her current reality.

Finally, John places dish after dish on the table, fish and vegetables and a delicate, leafy green salad. "Sometimes we're all too busy to get together much during the week." He pours wine into his glass and sits down. "So we always try and eat one meal together on Sunday if we're home."

"Then we can remember what each other looks like," Tasya adds.

"And I sometimes get lucky enough to be a recipient of such feasts." Robbie grins as he spoons potatoes onto his plate.

"Thank you for inviting me," Claire says.

"You're so very welcome. I'm sure you need some time away from the hospital." Tasya serves herself some salad. "And probably a break from the food."

"True." Claire takes beans from a dish and thinks of all the crappy stodge she's been eating lately, all washed down with endless cans of Coke and terrible hospital coffee.

They ask her about Cam. And as Claire answers their questions, she can tell Mia's parents are concerned and maybe even a little bit disturbed by the fact her parents aren't even in town. And part of her agrees. But that other small, defensive part of her, that relentless Pearson pride—the loyalty that never will budge, no matter how much they drive her nuts sometimes—wants to defend their absence. She's tempted to explain how the pressures of their jobs keep them away, but she doesn't.

They each drink a glass of wine during the meal. John toasts to Cam's newest reprieve. Feeling the warm glow brought on by the wine, Claire blushes at their generosity and at the easy compassion of these people she's only just met. After lunch they stay seated at the table and talk. Once again, Claire is confronted with the contrast to her own family, who only stays at the table long enough to eat or finish an argument.

Later, when the dishes are stacked and they've drunk a pot of tea, Mia and her father walk Claire back to the hospital. Blue pads next to them on a leash he doesn't seem to need. Mia and John are on their way to the university. John works in the physics department, a part of the university Claire has never visited. Mia is going to the library.

"Will you be okay?" Mia asks her at the entrance to the hospital.

Claire thrusts her hands in her pockets. "Of course. I'm fine."

Mia smiles. "You do like to say that. How long can you stay today?"

"Just a couple of hours. They close visiting hours at four on Sundays."

Mia nods. "Well, see you later. And call me if you need anything, okay?"

"Goodbye, Claire." John leans in and gives her an unexpected kiss on the cheek. "Lovely to meet you. Let us know if you need anything, okay?"

"Sure. Thank you." Claire blushes and ducks into the hospital.

* * *

After a couple hours of watching Cam sleep and preparing for her French exam, Claire leaves the hospital.

When she gets to the nurses' station, she finds Mia.

Claire frowns. "What are you doing here again, weirdo?"

Mia gives her a bashful smile. "So, this is embarrassing, but Mum *made* me come down here and get you on my way home."

Claire narrows her eyes. "Why?"

"She says you should stay at our place tonight. I think she's freaked out by the idea of you being at home by yourself."

"I'm *fine*."

"I know you are, sort of, but Mum's..." Mia sighs, as if she can't explain it. "Besides, you know, it would be easier for you. It's really close, and you can just stay with us and come back here tomorrow. And it will shut Mum up."

Claire bites her lip. Part of her wants to accept, but she feels kind of dumb too. The thought of going home to the empty house for yet another silent night is pretty depressing, especially after the soothing lunch today in Mia's lovely flat. She glances at Mia, chewing her lip.

Plus, she wants to hang out with Mia. She has this way of making Claire feel closer to normal, closer to okay. She takes in a breath and wonders how to say yes without feeling needy and clingy and dumb.

"We can study together."

"Ooh, exciting," Claire teases, thankful that Mia took the pressure off her in that easy, casual way of hers.

"Oh, what were you going to do? On a Sunday night? Go clubbing? Come on."

"Um, okay, I guess."

"Good, let's go, then." Mia turns and leads the way out of the hospital.

CHAPTER 30

Claire stretches out at the end of the bed in a pair of borrowed leggings, her arm under her head, and reads her French textbook. Mia sits cross-legged at the other end, hunched over her notepad. Blue is prone on his side, snoring quietly on the rug between the bed and the door.

It's cosy in Mia's room with the lamps on and the heat set low as the sun makes way for the night-time chill. For the first time in a long time, infected by Mia's ferocious studiousness, Claire is able to concentrate. Every time she glances over at Mia, she's greeted with the same sight, Mia's gaze glued to what she's reading as one hand scribbles notes. Her glasses repeatedly make the slow, intrepid journey down her nose until she pushes them back with a finger and flicks over a page. It makes Claire smile. Mia's so cute and nerdy and utterly focused. How is it the two of them have managed to become friends?

They eat soup and toast that Mia makes for them and return to their work. Then they study in complete, unbroken silence until Claire's phone rings.

"Sorry," she mutters, grabbing for it.

Mia looks up from her book. "Don't be sorry."

Claire answers, "Hello?"

"It's Lorraine, hon."

It takes Claire a second to work out who Lorraine is. Then it hits her. Lorraine, the nurse. Her heart starts to beat a little faster. "Is everything okay?"

"Of course it is. I just rang because I tried your mother, but I couldn't get through. This is a sneaky call to tell you that they have decided to send Cam to the wards in the morning."

"Really?" Claire leans forward.

"Yes. Good news, isn't it?"

"It is." Claire sits back as she feels the rush of relief. The worst part is over. Now Cam is just a patient in a hospital, a patient with parole instead of a sentence.

"Tomorrow morning when you get in, come and see us and we'll tell you where they've put him, okay? And you know what? It's just my guess, but I think he'll be out of here in a week or two."

"Really?"

"Really. He'll have physio, of course, and need lots of rest when he gets home, but I can't see it taking much longer. The doctors might see it differently, but I doubt it. Don't tell anyone I told you that, okay?"

"I won't, I promise. Thank you, Lorraine," Claire says breathlessly. She has no idea how better to express her gratitude to this warm, generous woman.

"And then I don't want to see you two ever again, okay? In the nicest possible way."

Claire laughs. "Okay."

"Night, sweetheart."

"Good night. And thank you so—" Claire starts to say, but Lorraine has already hung up. Claire smiles and stares at the phone in her hand.

"News?" Mia asks.

Claire nods. "Cam is definitely going to a regular ward tomorrow."

Mia leans against the wall. "That's great."

"It is." Claire sighs, feeling almost gleeful. "I better call Mum and Dad."

She sits on the edge of the bed and dials her mother's number. It goes straight to the clipped, officious cheeriness of her mother's voice mail. Claire sighs and tries her father's number. This time she gets his short, polite message.

She checks her watch. They should be well and truly done with work for the day. Where are they?

She feels the glee dissipate as she tries her mother's number again with the same result. Frustrated, she tries her father one more time. No answer. Claire clicks her tongue. She feels as if she's heard the sound of her parents' recorded voices more in her life than she's actually heard them in person. Why does her mother always veer between being irritatingly in her face or entirely, depressingly absent?

She lets out an annoyed breath. She just wants to be able to tell them the good news. Why can they never, ever just pick up their freaking phones when she calls?

"Hey, what's up?"

Claire sighs. "You know, Mia, I can't even remember the last time I called my parents when I really needed to talk to one of them and they actually answered the phone." She tosses her phone onto the bed in front of her. "Why are they never there?" Against her better judgement, she picks up her phone and tries again. Voice mail again.

She throws her phone onto her bag on the floor. She's done. As she sits there and stares at the deep blue of Mia's quilt, the anger she has kept locked down bubbles to the surface. It makes her throat ache. Why do they get to just leave all this? To leave Cam? To leave her?

Until this moment, she hasn't had room to dwell on her anger at their departure. Her need to focus on Cam has taken up all her emotional real estate. She used to be grateful for her parents' perennial absence. But she never thought it would happen at a time like this. She takes a deep breath and tries to stem the tears she can feel coming. But it's too late. She erupts in a frustrated sob.

Mia slides down the bed until she's seated next to her. She doesn't say anything, though.

Blue's paws clack across the wooden floor as he comes to investigate this change in arrangement and mood. He sits down on the floor in front of them, his one good ear suddenly alert. He rests his snout on the edge of the mattress and stares dolefully at the two of them.

"I'm just so tired and so sick of it." Claire swipes at the tears making a break for it and then strokes the comforting velvet of Blue's smooth head. "And I wish they'd just be here and deal with all this. My mother thinks because she calls me a million times a day and calls the doctors and interrogates them and sends her police friends down to the hospital to check on me every five minutes that it's okay that she's not here." She shakes her head angrily and wipes her nose on the back of her sleeve. "It's not."

Mia goes to her desk and brings a handful of tissues for Claire. She sits beside her again and presses a hand into the centre of Claire's back. And Claire lets her tears fall, released by the permission of that touch. This touch tells her she has a right to feel bad, that she doesn't need to just grow up and get over it.

"I'm so sorry," Mia whispers.

"It's okay." Claire sniffs. Her embarrassment at these tears instantly renders her defensive. "I mean, I'm an adult. I should be able to do this. I am doing this."

"Yeah, but," Mia presses on Claire's back for emphasis, "if anything like this happened to me, I'd totally want my parents to be there."

"Yeah, well, most of the time I don't want my mother there. But it would sure as hell help if she were now."

Mia nods and rubs her hand in small soothing circles on Claire's back. And she does it until Claire finds her breath again and the tears finally stop.

And when they do, Mia makes them tea. They drink it silently on the bed as Blue watches over them, a silent, vigilant sentry. Then Mia carries her books over to her desk and arranges them into a big pile.

"We can't study anymore," she declares wearily. "Want to watch a movie or something? Just chill?"

"Sure," Claire says numbly. She couldn't concentrate on study now anyway.

They lay Mia's laptop on the bed between them and watch a film on it. Claire reclines against the pillows and tries to focus. At some point, her phone lights up, but knowing it's probably her mother, she doles out her small punishment for her mother's neglect and ignores it. She can find out the news from the hospital. Claire does not feel like talking to her now.

But she can't concentrate, either. She stares past the screen and wonders how life is going to go back to normal after this. She can't even imagine it, days where she doesn't carry around this fear and this sadness, or now, this anger at her parents.

Mia turns to her, frowning. "You okay?"

Claire nods. "Sort of. I'm just...I don't know." And before she knows it, she is crying again. Small, manageable tears this time, shed without rage. Now they're just tired and overwhelmed tears.

Mia stops the movie and puts her hand on Claire's arm. "Let's just go to sleep. Then, tomorrow when you see Cam in the regular ward, you'll feel even better."

Claire nods, obedient, glad Mia seems to know what to do because she doesn't have a clue.

"Do you need anything? More tea? Something warmer to wear?"

Claire shakes her head and wipes her eyes. "No thanks, I'm fine."

"Does it bother you if Blue sleeps on the floor? He usually does." The dog raises his head at the sound of his name then drops it back on the floor.

Claire smiles down at him. "Of course not."

Mia pulls off her jumper and climbs under the covers. Claire does the same. She turns over onto her side, and faces the window as the light flicks off behind her. "I'm sorry to be such a mess," she whispers into the darkness. "It all just kind of hit me."

"Shh." Mia's voice is soft as she settles onto a pillow behind her and presses her hand on Claire's back. "You've been amazing at keeping it together. But you get to not be okay. God, Claire, it's not like you're being melodramatic. Cam was really badly hurt. You can be as much of a mess as you want."

Claire doesn't say anything. She can't. She pulls the covers higher over her shoulders.

"And, you know, it will all be okay."

"I hate it when people say that." Claire smiles into the darkness.

"Why? It will be," Mia insists as she shuffles closer to her and winds her arm around Claire's waist. "I know it will. So put up with it."

Claire doesn't say anything. She just leans back a little and settles into the sympathetic circle of Mia's embrace, grateful to be here in the shelter of this room right now. "Night, Mia," she whispers eventually.

"Night, Claire."

"And...thank you."

And all she feels is Mia's arm tighten around her.

* * *

Claire wakes to a world barely different than when she fell asleep. She's still on her side, still encircled by Mia's arm. The only difference is the early light leaking into the room and the fact that she feels almost normal. For the first time in a while, she feels as if she really, really slept. She opens her eyes a little and smiles to herself. And although she doesn't move, her waking must send some current through to Mia because she begins to rouse. She rolls away from Claire, and her arm slides off her waist. Claire listens as Mia yawns quietly and sits up in bed. Blue's claws clatter excitedly on the floorboards.

Claire takes a moment, though, and hides in the pretence of sleep. She wants to stay suspended in this place of comfort before she faces another day that is bound to be like all the recent others. Except now she will take this small respite with her.

She must slide backward into sleep again, because she wakes to a room that is lighter still and empty. She pulls on her jumper and socks and goes in search of Mia.

As she pads through the living room, Blue comes out to greet her. His thick tail wags wildly. She pats him and goes out into the kitchen, where she can hear voices.

Mia and her mother are at the kitchen table. Tasya looks as if she's dressed for work, neat and formal in a skirt and stockings and a jacket. Mia sits in the corner chair, her feet on the seat, in leggings, sneakers, and a giant T-shirt that she's pulled over her knees. Claire can tell from the silence that falls and the way they smile at her when she walks into the room, they have been talking about her.

"Good morning." Tasya gets up. "Would you like some coffee?"

"Yes, please."

Mia pats the chair next to her. Feeling awkward that she has interrupted some sort of discussion about herself, Claire sits down and bites her lip.

"I hope Blue didn't wake you. He kept going upstairs to check on you." She takes one slice of toast from her plate and then pushes the rest toward Claire. "I'll make some more in a sec. You eat that."

"Yes, bossy." Claire takes a bite, glad of something to do.

Mia smiles at her.

"So, Claire," Tasya says as she puts a mug of coffee and a carton of milk in front of her, "when do your parents get back from their conference?"

"Uh, Wednesday night, I think."

"Well," Tasya picks up a pile of papers from the table and puts them in her case, "I think you should stay here with us until they get back."

Claire stops the piece of toast halfway to her mouth. She frowns and starts to automatically refuse. "Oh no, that's o—"

"I wish you would," Tasya says. "It will make life a little easier for you. You'll be nice and close to the hospital, and you won't have to worry about anything else." She closes her case and snaps the lock shut. "You could just come and go as you need, and you and Mia can study for your exams together."

Claire opens and closes her mouth. This level of kindness, of generosity, is both lovely and daunting. "Oh no, that's okay, really," she stutters. "But thank you."

"And to be honest, I really don't like the thought of you staying by yourself right now." Tasya takes her empty mug to the sink.

Mia leans forward. "You should, you know. We can study here, too, when you can't be at the hospital."

Before Claire can say anything, Tasya walks over and puts a hand on her shoulder. "You really are very welcome, Claire."

Mia grins at her. "So, come on, just stop being polite and say yes."

Claire feels as if she's under siege. But in a good way. "Really?"

"*Yes*," Mia insists. "And don't feel like you're putting anyone out or anything. Mum loves to take in strays. Look at Robbie, freeloading every Sunday."

Tasya squeezes her shoulder. "And I insist, actually."

"Um, okay, th...thank you," Claire stutters, utterly bewildered by the constancy of kindness from these people but also frightened by the one-sidedness of it. She has nothing to give back.

"Good. I'll see you both tonight." Tasya gives Claire one more squeeze. "It will be late-ish. Have a good day. And I hope your brother does too."

And she is gone.

Claire watches Mia untie the laces of her shoes. "Did you go for a run or something?" She says "run" as if it's a dirty word. She hates running. Why do it unless someone is chasing you?

"Yep. With Blue. Helps wake me up."

"That's what coffee's for, stupid."

"Yeah, yeah." Mia gets up. "I'm going to shower. Are you going to the hospital this morning?"

Claire nods. Where else would she go in visiting hours?

"I'll walk with you. I'm meeting Pete at the library to go over biochem."

"Sounds as thrilling as my day."

Mia smiles and strides out of the room.

Alone in the kitchen, Claire rests her chin in her hand and shakes her head. She already feels better being here.

CHAPTER 31

On the walk to the hospital, Claire tries one more time to give Mia an out because she's worried Mia might regret this offer her mother made. She is about to take some seriously crucial exams, way more important than Claire's. And having Claire there means she will have someone else in her house, in her room even, taking up her space and time.

"Are you sure you don't mind? I won't be in the way of your study?" she asks.

"God, Claire, of course not." Mia knocks her elbow against her arm. "You're my friend. I want you to stay, so stop worrying, okay?"

"Okay then." What else can she say?

With the matter decided, they settle into peaceful silence. As they turn onto the traffic-choked road, Claire looks over to the monolithic glass and steel structure of the hospital and thinks about the day ahead. She'll have to go home at lunchtime and get some clothes. And Cam is having his first proper physio session in the afternoon. She wants to be there for that.

He will move to the new ward today, too, if he hasn't already. It was so nice of Lorraine to call and tell her, even if it was the thing that set off that embarrassing little crying jag in Mia's room. Claire doesn't want to think about those tears again because it makes her cringe, mortified at the memory of losing it like that in front of someone. Even Mia.

But Lorraine was trying to deliver good news, and Claire feels as if she wants to thank her properly for going out of her way.

"Do you know if there is a nice florist around here?" she asks Mia. "The hospital one is kind of tacky."

"Yup, I do." Mia nods and checks her watch. "I'll take you to the one Mum uses. It's great."

"You can tell me where it is." Claire doesn't want to take up any more of Mia's time than she already has these last twenty-four hours.

"No, I'll come. I love it."

"Of course you do." Claire grins. Such a geek.

When they enter the tiny shop, Claire can instantly see why Mia and her mother love it. It spills over with all kinds of flowers organised by shade, starting with jars of muted pastel blooms at her feet and ending in shelves over her head in explosions of the most vivid shades of crimson, orange, and yellow. And where there aren't flowers, there are plants— leafy ferns hanging from hooks on the ceiling, a trailing vine framing the window. She has never seen a florist like this before.

She gasps. "Wow." She tries to take in the profusion of colour.

"I know." Mia waves at the small, white-haired woman behind the counter who is busily working at tying up a bouquet of purple blooms. "It's amazing, isn't it?"

"Uh-huh." Claire turns in a slow circle, completely overwhelmed by the assault of scent and colour and choice. "I have no idea where to even start. Help."

"Sure. For your brother, right?"

"What? No." Claire pulls a face and shakes her head. "His only gift is my presence."

Mia laughs. "Who are they for, then?"

"For one of the nurses." Claire stares at the selection and tries to guess what Lorraine might like.

"The one with the hair?"

"Yeah, the one with the epic hair."

Mia takes another step into the depths of the store and stares up at the top shelves. She digs her hands into her pockets. "I'm thinking something bright but traditional." She nods to herself as she looks around.

Claire smirks at the seriousness of Mia's assessment. "Uh, okay, nerd, but I have no idea what that means in flower." She elbows her in the side. "But you sound like you have a pretty good fallback as a florist if you don't get into medicine."

She points at some bright yellow roses. "Maybe those?"

"Nah." Claire shakes her head. "I hate roses."

"Who hates roses?"

"Me." Claire continues to search the shelves. She does hate them. It's a Brendan thing.

Then she sees them, a cluster of rich orange lilies in a shade crazily similar to Lorraine's hair. They are half open, nestled among wide leaves of a deep, lush green.

"Those," she announces as she points at them.

Mia follows her finger and nods. "Definitely those."

* * *

"I'm bored," Cam whines. "Talk to me."

Claire looks up from her book and rolls her eyes.

The nurse tending him chuckles. "First sign a patient is getting well." He places a piece of spotless white gauze over the wound in Cam's leg. "They start crying boredom."

"I liked it better when he slept all the time," Claire grumbles and puts her book on top of her bag. Actually, she doesn't mind the distraction at all. She is currently so sick of the sight of her French culture textbook, she'll take anything, even Cam's complaints, over revising another chapter.

"But you're my visitor." Cam is petulant. He looks like he did when he was ten and realised he'd finished all his Easter eggs before Claire, again. "You're supposed to entertain me."

"No, I'm your sister. That means I'm duty bound to be here with you. Entertainment is what the TV is for. That's why Mum and Dad paid for the premium deal, idiot."

"Don't worry, hon. He won't be bored later." The nurse winks at Claire as he lifts Cam's leg and deftly winds the bandage around it. "You've got physio this afternoon," he tells Cam. "That's going to hurt."

"Is that a threat?" Cam winces slightly as the nurse fastens the bandage.

"No, it's a promise." The nurse lays the sheet carefully back over Cam's leg and grins at him. "Believe me, no one gets thrown from a car, then lies completely still for a couple of weeks in a hospital bed, and enjoys being made to move. You won't be doing much, but you will suffer."

"Well, I'd just like to thank you for single-handedly ruining my anticipation of the day ahead. I had one thing to look forward to. And now, nothing." Cam shakes his head and puts on a woeful, betrayed air.

The nurse checks something off on Cam's chart and heads for the door. "Happy to be of service."

Claire gives Cam her best malevolent grin, but he ignores her. Instead, he picks up his remote control, turns up the volume a little, and flicks through the channels. She kind of understands why he's complaining, though. Even with the good TV package, there's still nothing to watch. Premium gives him a slew of dated movies, mediocre television on repeat, and sport, sport, and more sport.

"I can't wait to get home to my Xbox," he says, still flicking.

"Just please don't make me watch golf again. I may stab myself in the eye. Or you."

"You know, don't you have anything better to do than hang out with me and complain about my choices in viewing pleasure?"

"Yes, Cam, in fact I do," she grumbles as he settles on a basketball match. She automatically picks up her textbook. "But you know how it is, as the only representative currently in town, this Pearson must do her family duty and supervise your whole not-dying thing."

"Yeah, yeah."

His not dying is actually going incredibly well today. He's upright for the first time, bolstered against some pillows. He looks relatively human, too. The grazes on his jaw and face have mostly healed, and his hair has been washed and brushed. From the neck up, she can't really tell there's anything wrong with him.

"Mum called this morning." He stares at the screen. "Just checking in."

Claire nods, not even looking up from her page.

"You know, she got all weird when I told her I can't really remember her being here."

That makes Claire look up. "You can't remember?"

He shakes his head and flips over to a hockey match and then straight back to the basketball. "I mean, I know she was here, and I remember knowing that and remember the nurses talking about her. But I just can't really remember her. Then, I don't remember much, really."

"What do you remember?" She's curious now.

"Just little things, like the doctors talking about me. I remember feeling really weirdly heavy, like I weighed more than usual. I remember pain. I remember not being able to speak. And I remember you telling me about the accident. And I remember how pale you were." He turns and glances at her quickly and then looks back at the screen.

"I'm always pale."

He smiles, but it fades to a frown. "But I just don't remember Mum."

"She would not like that."

"No, she would not." Cam shakes his head and grabs a pen. He shoves it down the top of his cast, scratches at his upper arm, and frowns. "When I told her, she did that thing, you know, where she's kind of angry but trying to pretend she's not because she knows it's not cool to get angry about it?"

Claire nods. She knows that one exactly. "Guilt," is all she says.

"Yeah, I guess." He continues to slowly work the pen in and out of his cast.

Claire watches him as he stares at the screen and scowls when a player misses an easy shot. She crosses her legs and taps her pen on her mouth. She knows her mother feels bad about leaving them here. She wouldn't call so much if she didn't. She wouldn't harass the doctors all the time. She wouldn't organise for their aunt to bring Cam his favourite foods so he doesn't have to eat the shitty hospital food. Of course, she hates that Cam can't remember her being here when, for a while, she was so intensely, irrepressibly here. She almost feels sorry for her. Almost.

"Thanks for hanging out," Cam suddenly says. "I know you've got a lot going on, with exams and everything, and—"

"Cam?"

"What?"

"Shut up."

She tells him to shut up because that's the only way she knows to tell him that of course she's here with him. Of course there's nothing more important for her right now than sitting in this room.

CHAPTER 32

Mia pokes Claire in the side with her foot. "That's *all* you are getting."

Claire pushes away the foot "And this, Mia, is *all* I require."

She undermines her aloof response with an involuntary giggle. She can't help it; the photo is stupidly cute.

They lie end to end on the bed again, with Mia up against the pillows and Claire with her head at the other end. Her socked feet rest on the wall above the bed. Even though it's getting dark and Mia has turned on the lamps, they've left the curtains open and the window raised. The balmy evening air washes in, bringing smells of grass and early dinners being cooked in neighbouring apartments. Every now and then, a passing headlight lays bright tracks along the wall, and as she studies, Claire can hear the sounds of footsteps and doors slamming as people come home from work.

They are on a break. Together they have plotted out the perfect study system, one hour of intense, silent study time, and then twenty minutes to relax and talk, make a snack, or take Blue outside. It works well.

It's Claire's third night at the apartment, and they have worked steadily together every night after Claire gets back from the hospital and Mia returns from the library. Tomorrow Claire's parents will return from Canberra, and she will go home.

She knows she's going to miss it here. It's cosy and lively, with neighbours coming and going, and friends dropping around for tea. It's a world away from Claire's house.

And an added bonus is studying with Mia, who's completely and utterly focused on her work, means that Claire's probably as prepared for the exams as she would've been if Cam hadn't been hurt. In fact, the harder they study, the calmer Claire feels about these coming exams.

Now she's back on track, she's sure she can manage whatever will be thrown at her.

Mia, however, seems to be the opposite. The more she studies, the tenser she becomes. It's not overt. She still acts like regular Mia, but Claire can see the fear winding tighter inside her in the ways her brow tightens when she talks about the tests, or in the way Claire catches her staring off into the distance between bouts of note taking, with a lip-chewing look of consternation on her face. And she knows, Mia is terrified of these exams. And she looks so damn miserable in those moments that during these breaks, Claire tries to distract her from thinking about them. She tells pointless stories or talks about nonsense topics, all to make Mia laugh. It seems to work, mostly.

And this is her latest means of distraction, spurred by genuine curiosity. She lays her head back against the pillow and holds the picture above her face.

It's so unmistakeably Mia, even if she's dressed in the girliest clothes Claire has ever seen her in. She wears a knee-length, floral, party dress with matching ribbons in her hair. Her hair is wrapped in a wreath of plaits around her head, and stray strands fall around her face and neck, exactly the same way they do now. She's laughing in the photo, her mouth open and her arms akimbo as though she were completely in motion when the shot was snapped.

Claire holds the picture a little closer. "How old were you?"

"Maybe six or seven, I think."

It was taken here in this flat. Claire recognises the living room. She almost doesn't recognise Mia's father, though, young and beardless. He is sporting a moustache, though. She must remember to pay him out about that one day.

"Who's that with your dad?" She looks at the small, slender woman with long, honeyed-blonde hair standing next to him. It's definitely not Tasya. Whoever she is, she's laughing with her arm around Mia's neck as if holding her in place. "And why is she strangling you?"

"Who's strangling who?" asks Tasya.

Claire jumps. Tasya leans on the door frame. Claire immediately takes her feet from where they are on the wall. She doesn't want to look too at home.

"Claire wanted to see a photo of me when I was little. I'm showing her that one of Lila and Dad."

"Ah." Tasya nods as though she knows the photograph well. She enters slowly and sits down on Mia's desk chair with a sigh. She leans over to stroke Blue, who is stretched out on the floor as usual. "Then she was probably holding Mia still. You always had to do that for photos. Most of the pictures we have of her under the age of ten, she's being held in a headlock by someone trying to keep her in the frame."

Claire laughs. "A bit hyper, Mia?"

She grins. "I hated being in photos."

"And you hated standing still even more," Tasya adds. She reaches for the photo. "May I?"

Claire passes it to her and watches as Tasya stares at it, a shadow of a frown on her face.

"You were going to turn seven that year," she tells Mia. "It was your dad's thirty-seventh birthday." She smiles at the photo. "I always forget how beautiful Lila was."

"Who's Lila?" Claire turns over on her side, resting her head on her hand.

"John's sister." Tasya takes one last long look at the picture and passes it back to Claire. "She died of cancer two years later."

"Oh." Claire stares at the woman in the photo. She can't be older than thirty. And she is lovely.

"She was Mia's only aunt."

"I'm so sorry. That's so sad." She wonders how well Mia remembers her.

"This was hers." Mia holds up the silver chain she always wears around her neck.

Claire nods. She wondered why Mia always wears the same necklace.

Tasya smiles and sits back in the chair. "I remember taking that photo. I was trying to get a picture of the three of them to send to Rosa, John's mother. And Lila was trying, as usual, to get Mia to stay still. But of course, she wasn't having any of it. I was taking too long to work the new camera, and all she wanted to do was go to the park because Lila had promised to take her."

"Where are your shoes, Mee?" Claire asks as she notices that, despite the fancy party dress and hair, Mia's feet are bare and grubby.

Mia laughs and looks over at her mother as if she knows what's about to come.

Tasya chuckles. "That, Claire, is a question that has been asked often in this house. As a child, Mia had this uncanny ability to divest herself of shoes within minutes of putting them on, even when she was a baby. We'd get in the car to go shopping, and she'd be wearing them. By the time we'd get into the supermarket, they'd be gone. The child could barely crawl, but she could lose a pair of shoes in minutes. I remember once when she was five, some friends found her pair of little white shoes under the bridal table the day after a wedding in Shepparton. We had to leave the wedding with her in bare feet because we couldn't find them anywhere. They had to post them back to us."

Mia laughs. "I hated those shoes. They were ugly."

"And then sometimes she'd simply come home without them." Tasya shakes her head. "I don't know how many times I had to call the school or other parents to figure out where you left them."

"How do you not notice you have no shoes on?" Claire asks, baffled.

Mia raises her hands. "I don't know. I don't lose them anymore."

Tasya laughs. "I wish I'd known the answer to that question when she was a child, though, Claire. I would be a richer woman for it. Some never appeared again. And some turned up in the oddest places. Like on the kitchen windowsill, once." She shakes her head. "The *outside* kitchen windowsill. Of a second-story apartment."

"Mr. Hatsis once found a pair in his yard that I'd dropped on the way home, remember?" Mia's still a little pink but smiles as though she's committed to her embarrassment now.

"Oh yes, that's right. Do you remember that letter you wrote to them? About their yard?"

Mia nods. "Yes. My stroke of genius."

"It really was." Tasya turns to Claire. "When Mia was eight, we would never let her go around to her friend Kristen's unless one of us walked her there. And of course, being an only child, she always wanted to go there and play.

"She lived on the street behind us," Mia explains. "But it was kind of a long block to get around."

"And there was a busy main road on the way," Tasya adds. "So we didn't like her going by herself."

Claire nods. She pushes her book away and rolls onto her side, thoroughly entertained by this nostalgic indulgence. It's way more entertaining than reflexive verbs.

Tasya continues, "Of course, we weren't always able to walk there with her when she wanted to go, not straight away. Which drove her crazy."

Mia laughs. "I would get so impatient. I remember you'd tell me that you'd take me in fifteen minutes, and I'd just sit there and watch the clock and wait for it to move. It felt like an eternity."

Claire smiles. She remembers that feeling when she was a kid. A minute took a day, and an hour took a year, especially when she really, really wanted something to happen.

"And with John it actually would be an eternity," Tasya says. "He'd tell her fifteen minutes and then get completely absorbed in what he was working on and forget."

"Yeah, and he thought he could get away with it, that I couldn't tell time on his study clock yet." Mia shakes her head. "He forgot he taught me how the numbers worked when I was five."

"So what was the letter about?" Claire asks.

"Well, after getting tired of constantly waiting for us to walk her around to Kristen's house or begging us to let her walk alone, which we told her she couldn't until she was ten, Mia masterminded her own solution."

Claire turns to Mia, curious. "What did you do?"

"I finally figured out that if I went over the back way, I actually only had to go through one backyard to get to Kristen's house—their next-door neighbours', the Hatsises. So I wrote them a letter explaining who I was and asking for permission to cross through their yard. And then I got Kristen to put it in their mailbox for me. I even put a stamped self-addressed envelope in it." She laughs, shaking her head. "I don't even know how I knew to do that."

Claire giggles, impressed. "That is kind of genius."

Tasya nods. "It was. Mia had it completely worked out. She even suggested an exchange for manual labour, offering to work in their garden or wash their car in return for safe passage," Tasya adds. "And then they wrote this very nice note back to John and I saying Mia was welcome to use their yard as a thoroughfare and saying what a polite little girl she was. We, of course, had no idea what they were talking about."

Mia shrugs. "I figured I'd wait and see what they said first, before I pitched it to Mum and Dad. I thought they'd be more likely to say yes then."

"And how could we not?" Tasya says to Claire. "We were so impressed at our child's astonishing initiative. And highly amused, of course."

"And it meant you didn't have to spend all your time listening to me beg for you to walk me around the block," Mia adds.

"What would you have done if they still didn't let you?" Claire asks, because *her* mother probably still would have said no just on the basis that *she* didn't think of the idea.

Tasya chuckles. "Probably created some sort of PowerPoint presentation explaining the pros and cons of letting her go on her own. With interactive maps. She wouldn't have given up. Anyway," Tasya slaps her hands on her knees and gets up, "enough of my distractions. What did I come up here for, anyway? I swear it wasn't just to share embarrassing stories about my daughter—although I thoroughly enjoyed it," she adds. She leans on the desk and taps her fingers on her lip, thinking. "Oh, that's right. Mia, I spoke to your grandmother Rosa today, and she wants you to call her before your exams start."

Mia nods and grits her teeth. "Exams." She sighs.

Claire watches as she immediately begins to frown, just that one word setting her off again.

Tasya wearily shakes her head as if she's used to this level of anxiety from Mia. "You'll be fine. You've worked hard."

Mia doesn't even respond. She is too busy backsliding into her quiet panic. After watching her shift in and out of this escalating terror for the last few days, Claire sees what Pete meant when he mentioned Mia and her attack of crazy, because her pre-exam nerves are kind of extreme.

Tasya turns to Claire, her brow furrowed. "Do you get this anxious over your exams, Claire?" She tips her head toward Mia, who is now chewing her lip, brows knitted. She stares into the middle distance and ignores them.

Claire shakes her head. "I get nervous, but nothing like this. Yes, your daughter is nuts."

Tasya laughs, but Mia doesn't even register. "She'll do well. She always does," Tasya says. "But it doesn't stop her jitters." She takes one more affectionate look at Mia and trudges slowly out the room, one hand on her hip. "I'll see you two later for dinner."

"Okay. Thank you, Tasya," Claire says. She turns her attention back to Mia.

Mia chews at her lip, trapped somewhere in the mire of her inner high-achiever panic.

"Hey, Mia," Claire calls out to her, louder than she needs to.

Mia jumps a little. "What?"

Claire taps her pen on her leg. "Breathe," she tells her. "Don't. Forget. To. Breathe."

Mia looks at her, her blank stare slowly shifting into a rueful smile.

"It going to be okay," Claire assures her.

Mia frowns. "How come you're allowed to say that and I'm not?"

"Because," Claire says airily. "Just because. So breathe."

Obediently Mia takes in a deep breath, sighs it out, and returns to the page in front of her.

CHAPTER 33

Nina passes around the bag of leftover muffins Robbie brought from work. "How is everyone doing? Y'all freaking out?"

Claire groans and leans back on her hands in the grass. "I never want to see my French group again after this exam. Bunch of freaking uptight nut jobs." She spent her entire morning watching as they argued about the way one guy pronounced a word. As the other two argued around him, he sat there, bright red, and too weak to stick up for himself. Claire stared out the window and waited for it to end.

They're sitting on the university lawn, surrounded by anxious students hunched over their books and clutching flashcards and coffee. They've all met up for a sly hour, to perform a small farewell of sorts before they march off into their different exams and final assessments. Except for Nina, of course, who claims she's about to march into total social abandonment for the next week or two.

Claire rolls onto her side on the shady stretch of grass and looks at Mia. She's staring intently at a sheath of photocopies covered in different coloured highlighter marks and notes in lead pencil.

"Hey, Mia?" she calls and grins slyly. "How are *you* doing?"

Mia shakes her head. "I have no idea."

Claire smirks. Good to see nothing has changed since she left Mia's place. Claire looks over at Pete. He grins and nods as if he knows exactly what she's thinking.

Claire hasn't seen Mia since she left to go home on Wednesday morning. It's Sunday now, the last day before the two-week exam period starts. Claire is first up, with her French group conversation exam tomorrow, and then her solo one the day after. Victorian Novels is in the second week. Mia has her first three clustered at the end of the week, and Robbie's essay is due on Tuesday. Claire spent her lunch going over it in the café with him. Just as she expected, it's a good essay. His points are clear, and he backed them up. His work just needed some shuffling and a proper conclusion—easy fixes.

"Hey, when's your final exhibition, Robbie?" Nina asks.

"The weekend exams finish. Then a friend from class is having a party after. She lives right near the gallery. We should all go and celebrate being finished."

"Not quite over for us," Pete says. "Mia and I have our postgrad interviews the week after."

Mia holds out her hand, palm extended in his general direction. "You wouldn't believe how much I don't want to think about that right now."

Pete laughs. "Sorry."

Robbie smirks, takes the lid off his coffee cup, and drains the last drops of it onto the grass. He flattens the cup in his hand and sighs. "God, I wish we were all rich and could go away on some exotic, totally debauched holiday when this is all over."

"Oh, that sounds amazing," Nina says and sighs. "I don't even have exams, but I'm doing shifts for everyone who does have them."

"It would be good." Claire rolls onto her stomach and yawns. All she wants after exams is to lie around and not do a thing. And she'd really love to do it someplace far from her mother.

"We could do something," Nina says. "Go away somewhere. Camping, maybe?"

"Camping?" Claire wrinkles her nose. That does not sound relaxing.

"But it would be cheap."

Robbie shakes his head violently. "I'm terrified of snakes."

Claire holds up her hands. "Who isn't terrified of snakes?"

"That guy in that documentary who loved them," Nina says. "And he ended up getting poisoned by one."

"See?" Robbie flops back onto the grass. "Not going camping."

"A friend of mine found one in his tent once, when he was camping by the coast," Nina adds.

"What if you rented, like, a cabin, something sturdier than a tent, that snakes can't get in?" Pete suggests.

"That'd be better than camping," Robbie concedes.

"Uh-huh," Claire chimes in, although she doesn't even know if she likes camping since she's never done it. She's willing to bet she doesn't, though. All her nature time has been spent at the holiday house, where there is the great outdoors, but there is also a hot shower and all the necessary white goods when she's ready to leave it behind. "Oh my God." She sits up. Of course. The holiday house.

"What?" Nina asks, breaking a muffin in half. She holds out the other half to Claire.

Claire absently takes it. She pulls out a chunk of chocolate chip and pops it in her mouth, mulling over the idea. She wonders how likely it would be for her parents to let them have it. "We could go up to the lake."

"We could," Robbie says slowly. "If we knew what the hell you were talking about."

"My family has a holiday house."

"Really?" Robbie raises his eyebrows. "Well, aren't you the landed gentry, missy?"

Claire ignores him, breaks off another piece of muffin, and stuffs it in her mouth. "I'd have to see when my parents are using it, but if they aren't they might let us if we promise not to break anything. They let Cam have it a couple of years ago for a birthday trip."

"Awesome." Nina claps her hands. "Can I pretty please come even though I didn't do exams?"

"Of course, stupid."

Nina grins and raises her fist in the air. "Yes!"

"And can I bring Eli?" Robbie asks.

Claire shrugs. "Sure."

She looks over at Mia. "Hey, Mia?"

"What?" she says absently as she pushes up her glasses and continues to stare at the page in her lap.

"Did you actually listen to any of that?"

She looks up, blinking. "Um, no." She smiles apologetically.

"Listen, space cadet." Robbie throws a piece of muffin at her. "We're going to see if Claire's parents will let her use their holiday house after we've finished school. Up for a post-traumatic holiday?"

Mia nods. She turns to Pete. "Definitely. We could go up after our interviews?"

"Oh hey." Pete raises his hands and blushes slightly. "I'm not sure I'm invited."

Mia looks over at Claire.

"Of course you are," Claire tells him. "You should come." And she means it too. She likes Pete. He's nice, and he's chilled and not annoying.

"Thanks." He smiles at her and turns back to Mia. "I could drive us up after."

"So, what?" Robbie says as he counts them off. "Us five and Eli?"

Claire nods. "That's probably enough, though. My parents are more likely to say yes if it's just a small group."

"Oh my God, yes!" Robbie sighs dramatically. "Light at the end of the tunnel! This is going to be amazing."

"Amazing," Nina chimes in and flops down next to Robbie on the grass.

It will be, Claire thinks, chewing her lip, as long as she can get her parents to agree.

CHAPTER 34

Claire decides to send a message rather than call. She doesn't want to bother Mia if she's studying. She texts, *So, how did it go? First two down...*

The moment she puts her phone back down on the bed, it starts ringing. She looks at the name, smiles, and answers it. "Hey."

"Hi!" Mia sounds breathless, as though she's in a hurry.

"So?"

"Okay, I think I answered everything. I just don't know how well."

"Oh, you killed it." Claire pushes her book off her lap, slides down the bed, and lies against the pillows.

"I doubt it," Mia mumbles. "And now I feel really bad. You already had two exams, and I didn't message you or call."

"So what? Let's be real here, Mia. I do okay, and the result is I pass French and my group doesn't hate me. You do well, and you get into medicine or forensics. So, you know, I'm not exactly offended, okay?"

"Still," she mutters.

"Seriously, I don't care. Besides, you've probably been too busy rocking back and forth in a corner to think about anything else."

"Oh shut up," Mia says. But she laughs. "I think even Blue is a bit dark at me because I haven't been taking him for his usual walks this week."

"Are you going to be completely catatonic by the end of next week?"

"Possibly. You might want to call and check in every now and then."

Claire can hear the smile in Mia's voice, so she teases, "Make sure you get over it before we go away. There's no attic to lock you in at the holiday house."

"I'll do my best. Have you asked your parents yet?"

"Not yet. It's all about timing, Mia. Oh yeah, and actually laying eyes on them. Where are you going right now, anyway? You sound like you're running a marathon."

"Going to meet Pete at the library. Last-minute anatomy session."

"You know, that sounds vaguely dirty when you say it like that. Geek dirty, but still kinda dirty."

Mia laughs. "It's really, really not."

"I know. Anyway," Claire sighs, "I better get back to it. I'm working nights at the bar this weekend, so I'll only have the days to study."

"When is your last exam?"

"Tuesday morning."

"I'll call you after."

"You don't have to. Really."

"So?" Mia tells her. "I'll still call you."

"Whatever, Mia. Remember to breathe." She hangs up before Mia can answer.

* * *

It actually feels good to be back at the bar.

Even if it's not her idea of a perfect Friday, it beats the hell out of another night in her room, trapped in endless study. Or there's the option of watching Cam fall asleep on the sofa while they take in whatever crappy movie she let him pick just because he's an invalid.

It feels good to be doing something mindlessly physical, too, after the mental slog of revision. She studied so much her brain is resisting all new knowledge. It's nice just to be out in the world again, even if it is only the shambolic, drunken little world of the bar. For once, the customers aren't annoying her much, and Nina is slavishly grateful for her company after a week without her friends.

"Hey, there."

The voice comes out of nowhere, but it's familiar.

Claire looks up from the beer tap. It's him, Guitar Boy, from the drunken night of the borrowed bed. He leans against the bar, his arms folded on the surface, smiling. His light-brown hair is wavier than she remembers, but that grin and those cheekbones are the same. "If it isn't the girl who used my bed and then never answered my calls."

"Uh, yeah, sorry, busy." She puts the beer in front of the girl who ordered it and takes her money. The girl smiles as she hands her the note, a smile that says she's been listening and wonders how the hell Claire's going to get out of this. Claire ignores her and returns her change.

"Yeah, right." He takes his arms from the bar. "Busy."

She is about to shrug and walk away, whatever-ing it, but then she turns back. He doesn't really deserve that kind of brush off. He was kind of cool on that awful hungover morning. Especially considering she apparently invited herself into his bed and then told him not to touch her the minute she got in it. Not her classiest behaviour, that's for sure.

"Seriously, sorry," she tells him. "Things have been crazy."

He nods, still smiling as if she doesn't have to explain. She can't tell, though, if it means she doesn't have to explain because he doesn't care, or because he doesn't want to hear excuses.

Either way, she's up for a little torture.

But before she can say anything, Nina comes over and puts two beers in front of him. Her eyes flick between the two of them, clearly curious why Claire is giving a customer the time of day.

She waits for Nina to walk away before she continues. "Like I said, sorry. I've had exams and stuff. Oh yeah, and my brother nearly died in a car crash."

His eyes widen. "Whoa. That's awful. Sorry."

"He's fine now. I just wanted to make you feel bad."

"It worked." He sips his beer and then puts it down with a frown. "Hey, how come I have to feel bad, anyway? You're the one who didn't call."

Claire shrugs. She's bored of the conversation now. "How's your guitar practise? Still a two-chord wonder?"

He laughs and holds up three fingers. "I got to three before my friend took his guitar back."

"Impressive."

He picks up the beers and smiles at her. "Anyway, I better get back." He nods in the direction of the booth, where a lone girl is sitting, staring at her phone.

Claire looks over at her, raises her eyebrows, and nods. "Yeah, you better."

Nina is on her quickly. "Who was that guy?" she asks in a break between customers.

"A guy."

"Do you know him?"

"Kind of. Maybe. No."

"Thanks for clearing that up. He's hot."

"I know." Claire starts to clean a section of the bar, ignoring Nina's curiosity.

"God, you're annoying."

"What? Because I won't tell you every single thing that goes through my head?" Claire asks. "That's your thing, not mine."

"Yeah, definitely not your thing. Blood from a stone, Claire, blood from a stone." She shakes her head. "You know, I've never had a *friend* who plays hard to get before."

Claire laughs and throws the cloth in the sink before walking away. She probably would have told Nina about him eventually. But now that she knows how much it tortures her, it's more fun not to.

The next time he comes to the bar, Claire serves him.

"Just a pint, please, and two shots of...what?" He scratches his head.

Claire raises her eyebrows and hands as if the answer is completely obvious. "Tequila."

He laughs. "Tequila then."

After she pours the drinks, he pays for them and pockets the change. Then he pushes one of the shot glasses toward her, smiles, and holds up his own. She doesn't take it, though. Instead, she looks over at his table. There are three girls sitting there now, all hunched over the original girl's phone.

"Uh, shouldn't you be drinking with your harem over there?"

"My little sister and her twit friends?" He raises his glass higher. "I think not. She's a one-pint screamer." He leans in closer. "Are you going to make me do this alone?"

She purses her lips and glances around. No Andrew to be seen. And it *would* be rude to make him drink alone. She touches her glass to his, meets his eyes for a split second, and downs it.

CHAPTER 35

They edge around the crush of bodies inside the front door.

Claire senses it immediately, the shrill energy of a room full of people determined to slough off this last tense fortnight. To let go after the marathon of output. Now, whatever happened, everybody gets to throw up their arms and stop caring because there is nothing they can do about exams anyway. As she stands there, Nina by her side, Claire senses a thread of something bordering on hysteria in the air. Everyone is wired on the mutual thrill of finishing. And she feels the same.

Claire spots them from across the living room. She grabs Nina by the sleeve and hauls her through the crowd to where their friends are clustered around the kitchen counter. Already the room is awash with empty bottles, puddles of spilled booze, and abandoned plastic cups. Nina launches herself onto Pete's back and hangs off his neck.

"It's over!" Robbie hoots as she gets closer and pulls her into a tight a hug.

"Yep." She grins. Even though she had her last exam three days ago and has had a little time to get used to the newfound feeling of summer freedom, it still feels pretty damn good to be here and to have them all back in the land of the living again.

"I'm so sorry I couldn't come to your exhibition," she tells him, genuinely remorseful. "We had this family thing to welcome Cam home."

"It's totally fine." Robbie waves her apology away. "Anyway, how is he? How was it?"

"Cam's fine." Claire rolls her eyes. "Fell asleep straight after dinner. He got off scot-free."

"But didn't you say the poor guy has to, like, lie around for a month now before he can do anything?"

"Yeah *and?*" She raises her hands. "What's so bad about that?"

"Right now, nothing." He swigs his beer, puts it down on the bench, and claps his hands together. "And we're going to be doing that up at the lake next week! Thank God your parents said yes."

Asking her parents hadn't been too bad in the end. She played it the smartest way she knew how and presented it to her mother while she was right in the middle of a phone tangle with the hospital. She did exactly what Claire hoped she'd do. She waved her away and told her to ask her father. Surprisingly her father agreed easily. It looks as if the guilt of leaving her with Cam on her own paid off. He told her she deserved a break after these last few weeks, and that they were welcome to go up there if they promised to look after the place and not upset any of the neighbours.

Robbie grabs her around the waist again, lifts her up, and swings her around. "It's going to be so amazing!"

She thumps him on the shoulder. "You are nuts tonight!"

"I'm happy." He picks up his beer again. "I am so happy that I kicked ass on my feedback, and I'm happy because I even did pretty well on that essay."

"Of course you did." She takes the beer Nina passes to her. "I helped."

"Yeah, you should never do modesty, Claire." He shakes his head as a girl skips up and grabs him by the arm. "It wouldn't suit you." He grins, a parting shot before he throws his arms around the girl. "Oh hey!"

Claire smiles. It looks as if Robbie is going to hug the whole world tonight.

She turns and steps into the loose circle made of Mia, Pete, and Nina. Pete gives her an exuberant kiss on the cheek.

Mia jumps off the bench and leaps over to her. "I missed you!" She enfolds Claire in a hug.

Claire laughs, returns the hug, and blushes. They don't usually hug. Well, Claire doesn't usually hug. Except with Robbie because she has no say in the matter. "You know, I actually missed you too."

"Aw *thanks.*" Mia rolls her eyes and laughs as she steps back. Tonight, Mia seems happier than she has in ages. And different. She looks different.

"What's changed?" Claire narrows her eyes and looks her up and down.

"Hair?" Mia suggests. "I got a celebratory haircut this afternoon. But it was only a trim."

Claire looks her over again. It might be her hair. It does look good, glossy and rich. But it's not just that. It's all of her. Claire tries to figure it out. She's still wearing her basic uniform—jeans, boots, and a tank. Maybe it's a more sophisticated version of her usual look. Her top is black, made of a silky material, showing off her already tanned shoulders, with a cutout pattern along the neckline. She wears her aunt's pendant and large silver hoops in her ears too. She's a shinier version of Mia.

Mia frowns and runs her hand self-consciously through her hair.

"Oh no, you look really good," Claire tells her quickly when she realises she's made Mia uncomfortable. She takes a swig of her beer and then offers it to Mia.

Mia shakes her head and laughs. "No, I need a break, I think, if I am going to last. I've already had a few too many tequilas."

"You did earn it."

"Yeah." Mia smiles wider, her freckled nose crinkling. "You know, I really did miss you, though. Study breaks were no fun on my own."

Claire smiles back at her. She wishes she'd been there for that last slog too. Her mother took some time off when Cam arrived home and got immediately busy with one of her intense maternal spells, an obvious attempt to make up for the lost hospital week. She'd constantly knock on Claire's door and ask if she needed anything. Sometimes it would be just an inane question. Other times, she'd offer Claire food. It happened so often, it felt as if Claire's irritation had just calmed from the last invasion when there would be another knock. It was so much calmer at Mia's house. The energy is different there.

She's just about to ask how Mia's parents are when she feels a hand on her shoulder. She turns. It's Jeremy, Guitar Boy, a six-pack of beer under his arm. He smiles as he tucks his hair behind his ears. "Hey, I made it."

"You made it," she agrees as she tries to hide her surprise. She completely forgot that she invited him along—after a few tequilas—the other night at the bar.

Sick of his sister and her friends, he hung around the bar and chatted to Claire and Nina while they packed down the place. He was just like he was that morning she woke up at his place, fun and chilled, with that wry, easy sense of humour. She can see how she ended up in his bed. Well, not in his bed exactly, but how she went anywhere near him in the first place. He's nice and he's funny. And definitely hot.

Still, for a second she's a little thrown by his sudden appearance in this kitchen. She smiles blankly at him, not sure what to say.

So he takes over. "Hey, I'm Jeremy." He holds his hand out toward Mia.

"Sorry," Claire mutters. "This is, uh, Jeremy."

"Yeah, got that." Mia shakes his hand. "Mia."

"Hey, Mia. That's my sister's name."

"Is it?" Claire raises her eyebrows. "The one from the other night?"

"Nah, another one." He turns back to Mia. "What do you know, huh?"

"Hmm," is all Mia says to that revelation. Then she looks between the two of them and kind of smiles again.

"Did you just finish exams too?" Jeremy asks.

"Yep." She sighs. "But I plan on forgetting them now. Tonight, there is no such thing as exams." She nods, decisive. Then she reaches out and threads her arm between them. Claire steps aside as Mia takes the shot being passed to her. She holds up the glass in their general direction. "Cheers," she says and throws back the shot before they can even lift their beers in response.

Claire smirks as Mia winces. So much for the break. Mia looks back and forth at the two of them, presses her lips together for a second, and puts the glass on the bench. She throws her arms in the air and says, "Right, I'm dancing. See you." She smiles briefly and squeezes between Claire and Jeremy. "Robbie, let's dance!"

Claire watches as Mia departs for the living room turned dance floor, her arms still in the air and a sway in her hips as she slides between bodies and into the crush. Robbie is close behind. Claire shakes her head. Clearly, Mia is totally committed to partying tonight.

"Did you want to go and dance too?" Jeremy says in Claire's ear.

She shakes her head. Maybe she does, but considering she invited him, it'd be kind of rude to ditch him when he just walked in the door. She takes over Mia's perch on the edge of the counter and downs the last of her beer. He pulls two out of his pack and passes one to her.

"Thanks." She eyes Nina and Pete as they continue to chat at the other end of the bench.

"I don't know what these are like." Jeremy inspects the label. "I found them in the fridge at work. Colombian, I think."

"Where do you work that you find random Colombian beer in the fridge?" She raises an eyebrow as she unscrews the cap with the sleeve of her top.

"A music studio."

"How very rock and roll."

"Not really. It just sounds it." He taps his beer gently against Claire's and takes a sip. "Me and my three chords, we just supervise. We don't play."

"Still, it's kind of cool."

"Nope. You know what I actually do? I manage the bookings for recording spaces for people who couldn't organise a drink in a brewery. They're the kind who inevitably turn up late or at the wrong time no matter how many times you email or call to confirm the times they requested. And then I clean up after them. And let me tell you something, Claire, musicians pretty much live up to their reputation for being pigs. So, not the prettiest job in the world."

She tips her head to one side and concedes it does sound less appealing now.

He pulls himself up on the bench next to her, and they sit there in the swampy thoroughfare of the kitchen, drink surprisingly good Colombian beer, and compare life notes while the party escalates around them. A ceaseless flow of people parade past, from the dance floor to fridge and back door. As the house fills, it becomes steamy and hot, and the whole house smells like beer breath and sweat and something vaguely hippie. Like incense.

Despite the constant flux, she doesn't see her friends for a while. Pete and Nina disappeared at some point when she wasn't looking. She hadn't thought of that particular potential. Nina and Pete. It's about time Nina dated a non-idiot.

Part of her would like to go and find everyone. She hadn't really thought this through when she off-the-cuff invited Jeremy to come along. She forgot she'd be somewhat responsible for him. It's not that she doesn't like him. She does, in some kind of benign, unsure-yet way. But she also wants to celebrate with her friends tonight, and instead, they are all scattered to the high winds of this party.

It's not long, though, before Robbie appears, pushing his way through the back door. Claire has no idea how he made it around the house, but he has.

"Hey, you guys, come here!" He beckons furiously, unable to get much closer than a few feet away before the push of the crowd forces him back as if he's caught in a riptide.

"Where?" Claire calls.

"Just come!" He gestures over his shoulder as he drifts back toward the door. "And bring whatever drinks you have."

Jeremy raises his eyebrows at her and picks up his beer. "Are we going hiking or something?"

She shrugs. She has no idea what's happening. But that's Robbie for you.

"Shall we?" He grabs the rest of his beers and jumps down off the bench.

They fight their way outside and follow Robbie through the small, crowded courtyard and around to the side of the house to where Eli waits. They walk down the side of the house, along a path sandwiched tightly between the wall and a thick leafy hedge.

"What the hell are we doing?" Claire holds out her arm as she tries not to get scratched in the face by wayward branches.

Eli stops suddenly at the foot of a tall ladder. He points upward. "We're going on the roof."

"Why?"

Robbie lets out a huge sigh. "Claire, did you ever see that show *The X-Files* when you were a kid?"

"Yeah, why?"

"Remember when Scully was being all doubty and stick-in-the-mud and Mulder would turn and look at whatever crazy shit was happening and say, 'Just go with it, Scully.' You remember that?"

"Are you calling me a stick-in-the-mud?" Claire punches him in the shoulder. Hard.

"No, but I am telling you just to go with it." Robbie leans in, kisses her on the cheek, and then puts his foot on the first rung. "Because why not, you know?"

Claire shrugs. While they watch Robbie climb, Jeremy introduces himself to Eli, and Claire once again mutters her apologies for not doing it earlier. She's feeling kind of behind the ball tonight, introduction-wise.

As soon as Robbie gets to the top, Eli turns to Claire and holds a hand out toward the ladder as if it's a game show and the ladder is the prize. Claire looks at her nearly full beer, wondering what to do with it.

Jeremy reaches for it. "Here."

"But then what..." she starts to ask, but he takes both their bottles and stuffs one each in the deep front pockets of his jacket.

He holds out his hands. "Ta da!"

She laughs and puts her foot on the first rung, glad she's wearing boots and even gladder she didn't wear a skirt. She takes a deep breath and begins the climb. It's a long way to the top, and by the time she's halfway, she really doesn't want to look down. Instead, she takes another breath and slowly inches her way up until she reaches the top.

She clutches the sides of the ladder and peers over the flat rooftop. Pete and Robbie and another guy are already up there, huddled near the brick chimney several feet away, where part of the roof starts to slant upward to meet the next house.

"You made it alive!" Robbie laughs. He trots over, takes her hand, and steadies her as she steps carefully onto the tin roof.

She straightens and grabs Robbie's other sleeve to assuage the vertigo that sweeps over her as the rest of the world seems to fall away in front of them. They are surrounded on all sides by factories and warehouses. A tall, brick silo shoots up into the night sky. Here and there a few houses like this one sit scattered amongst the industry, and through a break between two warehouses, the lights of the city beam. And way, way above the city haze, she can see the star struck sky.

Robbie loops his arm through hers. "It's amazing, isn't it?"

"Kinda." Claire breathes in the cooling night air and stares. It is.

Jeremy's head appears at the top of the ladder. He grins, puts the last couple of beers in his pack onto the roof, and finishes the climb. Eli isn't far behind.

Claire lets go of Robbie, steps a little further from the edge, and turns a full circle. She takes in their surroundings on all sides—sky and stars and the faintest wafts of cloud. Sounds of the party downstairs, the voices, hoots, and laughter, filter up around her. The bass from the dance floor thuds under the soles of her boots. It *is* amazing.

They park themselves in a circle next to the chimney, spread Pete's coat on the roof, and lay out the drinks they managed to carry in a ridiculous, alcoholic parody of a picnic. Jeremy pulls her beer from his pocket and passes it to her.

"Thanks." She looks around at the other few small groups of people up there, hanging out in small circles or pairs, keeping to themselves.

"Ooh, guess what I've got!" Robbie rummages in his bag. He pulls out a tiny tealight candle and a pack of matches, leans over, and tries to light it.

"I want to ask why you have it." Claire laughs. "But the answer will probably never be as good as the fact that you randomly have a candle in your bag."

"And you would be right." Robbie chuckles as he tries to coax a flame by cupping his hand around the flimsy little needle of fire coming off the wick. It flickers wildly, throwing weak, dancing shadows across the roof.

She sits next to Jeremy with her back against the chimney, pulls her knees to her chest, and zips her jacket up to her neck. It's not exactly the warmest of nights for rooftop picnics, especially the kind of roof not designed for picnics or even inhabitants. But she doesn't care. She loves it up here. It feels as if they are survivors of some great flood, huddled above the world together.

Robbie reaches into his bag and places his half-full bottle of tequila on the "blanket" and pulls some shot glasses from his pockets. "We may have to drink in shifts. I only have four glasses."

Claire shakes her head and laughs, remembering that first party with him when he'd done the same thing. "Seriously, you are like some sort of a mutant Boy Scout. Always totally prepared."

Robbie laughs, pulls out his phone, and reads something on the screen.

"Yeah, prepared for mayhem," Eli adds with a chuckle.

Robbie puts his phone down and pours a round of shots. "Tell me you don't appreciate my Boy Scout talents right now, huh?"

"Oh, we appreciate it," Pete assures as Robbie pushes a glass toward him.

"And I am keeping it classy," Robbie insists.

Claire laughs at that, leans forward, and takes two glasses. She passes one to Jeremy.

Robbie holds his own aloft in the air. "To the end, to the beginning, to whatever." He slings back his shot.

"Totally deep, man," Pete teases as he raises his glass.

Jeremy turns to Claire, and they sombrely clink glasses and drink. The heat courses down her throat and into her chest. She winces and leans against the chimney. Yep, she still loves tequila.

The shrill sound of an eighties pop song bursts into the air, overriding the music belting out from the house below. Robbie pulls his phone out of his pocket and answers it. He listens for a second, shakes his head, and grins. "No, I am not joking. Yes, seriously, the ladder by the wall down the side. I told you, just do it." He hangs up laughing.

Next thing they know, there is a shrill, shrieking laugh coming from the top of the ladder. It's Nina. She gets to the top, spots them, and screams at Robbie, "This is what I do for you! I'm terrified of heights. Now someone has to help me."

Eli laughs and goes to the ladder. He helps haul Nina up onto the roof as she cackles loudly. She clings to Eli's jacket and shields her eyes from the view with her hand as they walk.

When she gets to them, she drops her hand and looks around at them all. "Claire!" she squawks. She totters over and drops onto the roof next to her. Clearly, she's pretty drunk.

Claire smiles at Nina's sodden little grin. "Yes, Nina?"

Nina pokes her affectionately on the nose. "My evil friend."

Claire swats her hand away. "What have you been doing?"

"Nothing," Nina sings as she leans against Claire's side and rests her head on her shoulder. "Drinking. Christ, I'm going to have to sober up before I go back down that thing." She turns and points at the ladder as if it's the one making life difficult instead of all the alcohol she's clearly been consuming. Then she turns to the group and looks around. She points at Pete and his friend. "I know you. You're Pete." She squints into the darkness and turns the finger directly on the other guy. "But who are you?"

He laughs and holds up his hands as if to protest his innocence. "I'm just Dan. Nothing to see here."

She continues to point an interrogative finger at him. "Are you a nice guy, Dan?"

"I think so. But you'd probably have to ask my grandmother."

"I'll take your word for it." Nina uses Claire's shoulder to help herself up and unsteadily tiptoes over to him. She plonks herself down next to him and holds out her hand. "I'm Nina."

He sombrely takes her hand and shakes it.

Jeremy turns to look at Claire, one eyebrow raised. She laughs and shrugs.

"Hey, has anyone seen Mia lately?" Robbie asks. "She is MIA."

Eli pats him on the shoulder. "Mia is MIA. Hilarious."

Robbie laughs. "I didn't actually mean that."

Nina turns from her inquisition. "I've seen her. That girl is dancing," she declares as if she'd willingly testify in a court of law on the topic if she had to. Then she turns back to Dan and continues to fire questions at him.

Claire shakes her head and smirks. Nina is such a delightful idiot. And, of course, Mia's on the dance floor. Claire considers going to find her. She was looking forward to hanging out with her tonight. Problem is Claire has a feeling the climb down is going to be infinitely more terrifying than the climb up. Nope, she's not braving it now. Not after tequila.

Instead, Claire sits back, beer in hand, and listens as Pete and Jeremy begin to compare notes on trips they've both made all over Asia. She doesn't join in, sure her family's overly planned little European holidays won't impress much here. These guys have been all over the place. They have stories about strange encounters, spurious border crossings, and near misadventures in out-of-the-way places. Stories to tell all your life. And she's envious. She wants to have adventures like that. Memories like that.

A few shots later, when the edges of the night smudge into drunkenness, more people discover the ladder.

"Welcome!" someone shouts grandiosely from the other side of the roof every time another new person arrives.

Claire watches as heads pop up over the edge, invariably excited when they see the private little party they've found. One couple slow dances, laughing hysterically as they waltz clumsily around a flat section of the roof, nowhere near in time with the music playing below.

A girl with short black hair clambers up and struggles with her long dress as she tries to get her leg onto the roof. When she finally makes it, the hem gathered in a bunch in her hands, she kneels and calls to someone below. Another person pops up behind her, head tipped back, laughing in response to whatever the girl has said. It takes Claire a moment in the semi-darkness to realise the second head is Mia's. Claire watches her step from the ladder to the roof somewhat more gracefully than her companion, her long legs making the climb easily.

As she stands at the top of the ladder and stares, transfixed by the sweeping view like everyone does when they get up here, Robbie clearly spots her, too. He lets out a loud wolf whistle, and as if she knows exactly who it is, Mia turns, locates him in the semi-darkness, and waves. But she doesn't come over.

Mia follows the girl over to the side of the roof facing the front of the house. They clutch each other's arms as they cautiously step to the edge. They sit unsteadily with their legs hanging over and their shoulders nearly touching.

For a second, Claire feels a flash of envy at their easy intimacy as they sit and talk and laugh right in her eye line. Then she immediately checks herself for being so possessive. It's not as if Mia is exclusively her friend. Mia's the kind of person who will attract new people all the time, so there is no point in being jealous. Mia can talk to someone at a party.

Maybe she's jealous because she stayed with Mia when her parents were gone. Claire's stupidly started to think of Mia as her person, somehow. She shakes her head. Not smart. Mia has got her people already, like Robbie. And then there's her best friend, Kristen. Maybe it's just because Claire wanted to hang out with her tonight. After that intense stretch of being in each other's company, being each other's support, Claire felt almost bereft when she went home.

It doesn't really matter though, because they'll all be going to the lake in a few days. They'll have plenty of time to hang out then. She turns back to the conversation. Pete and Jeremy are talking about medicine now. Pete is mid story, something about a botched operation he heard about at school, all guts and goo and stupid mistakes. She tunes out again. She's had enough hospital gore of late.

She looks up in time to see Mia and the girl stand and step back from the edge of the roof. The girl says something to Mia and throws up her arms and laughs. She overbalances, and Mia quickly grabs her arm to steady her, though the girl was at no real risk of falling. As the girl regains her footing, she grabs Mia's waist. And Claire stares as that hand stays right where it is on Mia's waist as they continue to laugh and talk. Claire feels a blush creep up her face as she comes to the sudden realisation that the hand on that waist means maybe this isn't Mia making a new *friend*. She bites her lip, looks away, and takes a swig of her beer, trying to stem the flush. She wasn't expecting that.

Before she can stop herself, she surreptitiously glances at them again. The girl no longer has her hand on Mia, but she is standing really close and saying something. Mia nods slowly. Then the girl reaches over, rests her fingers briefly on Mia's stomach, leans in, and says something to her again. And then they turn in unison and walk toward the ladder. The girl goes over first, with her dress looped over her arm. Mia pauses at the top, crouched by the ladder, and looks in their direction before she swings her foot over the side of the roof. Claire wonders fleetingly if she called out, would Mia come back to them? Just as quickly, Claire turns away, back to the huddle by the chimney. Why would she do that? That's insane. Let Mia do whatever it is she's doing with that girl. It's none of her business.

CHAPTER 36

Within the hour, the temperature drops, then the wind picks up and blows out their tealight candle. What was a cool, starry night turns much less hospitable. They decide to leave their rooftop kingdom to hunt down some warmth.

Eli clambers down first, and then Robbie stands above, supervising Nina's wobbly, screeching descent. Claire accepts Jeremy's hand as he steadies her first, vertiginous step down from the roof onto the ladder. Slightly drunk and wary, she tests her foot on each rung before she puts her weight on it. Once they're all on land again, they wander back through the courtyard and into the swampy heat of the kitchen.

The party petered out in their absence. The dance floor died and only the dregs are left, sprawled across couches and beanbags in the lounge. Whiny music plays in the background. Two guys play a game on the Playstation with an audience around them. Claire wrinkles her nose. Who does that at a party?

"Yeah, this is our cue to leave." Eli sighs. "When the gamers come out, the night is over."

Everyone grabs their things and gathers at the door.

"Hey, should we find Mia?" Pete asks as he buttons up his jacket.

Robbie pulls on his scarf. "No, she's fine."

And that's when Claire realises that he probably saw what she saw.

"I'm just going to say goodbye to someone," Robbie says.

While they wait for Robbie, Claire crosses her arms and leans against the wall impatiently. She suddenly feels incredibly over this party. All she wants to do is lie down and maybe watch TV. She wants to find some quiet.

When Robbie returns, they step out into the street, and the others turn, headed toward the main road. Jeremy stops in the middle of the pavement and turns to Claire. "Hey, you know, if you need a place to crash, you're welcome to stay." His smile is wry. "Not trying to lure you into my bed, or anything. I just know you live pretty far. I have a couch, too. And I think I proved myself a gentleman in such a scenario before. Or we could go get another drink or something?"

She chews her lip, not quite sure what to say. This time is nothing like last time. She was drunk then. Very drunk. She knew not what she did. This time there would be the expectation that she'd be making decisions, and she's not sure she's in the mood to make any decisions regarding him or anything else right now.

He waits, hands in his jacket pockets, and kind of leans forward over his toes.

She takes a deep breath. All she wants is to get to Nina's and sleep. She feels so graceless and fed up right now. She wants this night to be over, but she doesn't know quite how to make it be over.

Then, before she can stop herself or question the move, she rises onto her toes and kisses him once, briefly on the lips. She knows it's a dumb move, even as she's doing it. It's a deflection more than anything, a way out of this night without being an asshole to him.

So, before he can say anything, she tries to excuse herself. "Sorry, I'm really tired. And I said I'd stay with Neen. She just broke up with her boyfriend, and she's really drunk and—"

He holds up his hands. "Hey, it's okay. You don't have to explain. It was cool hanging out with you again, though. It was fun. And, you know, maybe we could do it again?"

"Yeah, sure." But she knows she doesn't sound as enthusiastic as she should. And she knows she should because he's being lovely.

"Or not," he jokes.

"Sorry." She tries to smile at him. "I'm just really tired. Call me or something? Next week? I mean, if you want."

He nods. She doesn't know which message he's getting. But then, she's not sure which one she intends to send either.

"Okay, sure." He kind of hugs her with one arm, but that's it, as if maybe he's already figured it out. He jerks his thumb behind him. "Anyway, I gotta go that way. So I'll talk to you later, okay?"

"Yeah, sure." She sways back and forth slightly, feeling incredibly gauche.

"Thanks for inviting me on your rooftop adventure. See you."

"Yeah, see you."

He stuffs his hands in his back pockets, turns on his heels, and strides down the street, shoulders hunched.

She watches him walk away and lets out a breath. What the hell is she doing? She shakes her head and turns back toward the others. They are rambling up the street ahead of her. Even from here she can see the boozy lilt in their collective gait. She digs her hands into her jacket pockets and hurries after them.

Nina turns around just as Claire catches up to them. "What are you doing?"

"Hey, can I still stay at yours?" she asks quietly.

"What?" Nina squawks. She stands stock still on the footpath, her hands on her hips. "You're coming with me?" She turns and looks down the street, toward the distant figure of Jeremy. "You're leaving that behind for my scummy couch?"

"So what? Shut up. I'm tired." Claire grabs her arm and turns her around. "Let's go."

Nina laughs. "Oh-kay then." She steps off the curb and skips over to join Eli, Dan, and Pete, who, for some unknown crazy reason, are walking up the middle of the road. They follow the white painted lines, playing some weird game of follow the leader. They take turns at the front.

Claire falls into step with Robbie. He automatically slips an arm through hers and holds out his beer.

She shakes her head. She doesn't want anything else to drink tonight. They walk on in silence. The strains of music from another party come from somewhere nearby, and there is a siren in the distance. Robbie lets go of her arm and thrusts his hands in his pockets. It's freezing.

"Hey," she says quietly as they trudge along, watching the others do whatever lunatic thing they are doing.

"Hey, what?"

She gnaws at her lip and wonders if she should even be asking this. But then, because she can't stop herself, she asks anyway, "Is Mia, like, bi...or something?"

He doesn't say anything for a moment. He drains the last of his beer and tosses it into a trash can as they pass. "You know what that sounds strangely like?" He turns and gives her a look.

"What?" She knows she's somehow about to regret asking this question.

"Something you should be asking Mia."

"Yeah, I know," Claire stutters. "I just...wondered..."

He's silent for another long moment. "She's just doing her thing. Figuring stuff out."

She nods and doesn't say anything else, sensing he's being protective of Mia somehow and that she has unthinkingly tested his loyalty. Slightly mortified, both by the asking and the being chastised for asking, she changes the subject. "So, is Eli going to come to the lake with us?"

"He wants to," Robbie says as they walk the last stretch to a main road and, she hopes, toward a cab that will take her to a bed. "If that's still cool?"

"Of course," she tells him quickly. "I said it was."

"Just checking. He's pretty excited. And he says he'll bring food. He's an awesome cook."

"Good. Because I am not cooking." She hadn't even thought of food, actually, but they'll have to eat.

He laughs and throws his arm around her. "Yeah, I didn't picture you as the Nigella type, somehow."

"Definitely not."

He squeezes her closer and holds her there. She knows it's partly his way of telling her that it's okay she overstepped.

She looks at the others. They've given up follow the leader and moved on to piggyback rides. Pete has Eli, and Nina is doing a terrible job of carrying Dan. She picks him up, takes a step or two, and then drops him. Then she does it all over again as she laughs hysterically. Claire shakes her head.

Robbie laughs. "Maybe we should invite this Dan guy. Nina seems to quite like him."

"I was just thinking that too."

"Hell yes!" Nina yells suddenly.

"Can she hear us?" Claire giggles, baffled.

"Nope, that was some other can of crazy, I think."

And he's right because Nina suddenly gives up trying to pick up Dan, spins around, and trots over to Claire and Robbie.

"Karaoke!" she cries. "We're going to Chinatown to do karaoke. How fun will that be?"

"Um, none?" Claire shakes her head.

"Oh come on!" Nina pleads, hands clasped together. "It'll be hilarious!"

Robbie shrugs. "Why the hell not?"

"Come on, Claire," Nina begs, grabbing her shoulders and shaking them.

But Claire shakes her head and digs the toe of her boot into a crack in the pavement. She doesn't have karaoke in her tonight. Or any other night, really. "Sorry, but listening to you guys duet your little hearts out is not my idea of a good time right now. Lying down and watching shitty television, however, is."

Nina pouts at her. "Killjoy."

* * *

When Claire gets back to Nina's empty, messy flat, she gets exactly what she wished for, a little peace time. She curls up on the couch with a blanket around her and watches an awful new modelling reality show Nina recorded. It's as heavenly as it's going to get tonight.

She should really sleep, but it's after four, and she's wide awake. Tired but wired, her mind turns over everything that happened from when she left her house to now. But mostly, it turns inexorably back to that moment on the roof, to Mia and that girl. To that hand on Mia's waist.

How did she not know this? Or, more confusingly, what is it exactly she should know? Why has this potential for Mia to be into girls never occurred to her? Why didn't she ever consider that their kiss might not have been a first for Mia or maybe even that unusual for Mia? That would explain that moment of crazy. Maybe Mia kisses girls all the time, and Claire just never knew.

She rests her head against the sofa cushion and bites her bottom lip. That can't be it. She'd know if that was usual for Mia, wouldn't she? Claire knows about the guys in Mia's life. About Pete. About the ex-boyfriend she cheated on at a party. And just a week or two ago, Mia told her a story about a guy she dated for a year in her last year of high school. Surely girls would have come up if there'd been any. Maybe Mia's not the most forthcoming about her love life, but she's not that secretive either. She clearly wasn't that secretive about it tonight, not if Claire and Robbie could both figure it out.

Claire's not sure why this new piece of information has thrown her. It doesn't change anything, does it? It's not as though Mia being with a girl should toss any kind of spanner into their friendship. But for some reason seeing her with that girl tonight and witnessing what was clearly a current of something between them has weirded Claire out. And she's not sure if it's envy because she wanted her friend all to herself, or if it's something else.

The something else, she knows, is the fact that they kissed once, drunk at a party. And now, knowing what she might know about Mia after tonight, that kiss has taken on a new shape in her mind. It's bigger and maybe more important in a confounding, as yet unknown way. She can't figure out the dimensions of that part yet, though.

When she thought about it before, she put that kiss down to the intoxicated giddiness of their newfound friendship, combined with a lavish amount of hysterical laughter and tequila. At least that's what she thought. But now she isn't sure. She wishes she could remember that moment better, but she'll probably never get that night back in full.

What she does know is Mia treated the kiss like no big deal. And maybe it wasn't. Maybe there's no connection between that drunken moment and what happened tonight. Not for Mia, anyway. But Claire can't help feeling a kind of sharp awkwardness. It's as though something shifted and became charged with a feeling she can't explain. She doesn't know how to re-orient herself around this new knowledge about Mia.

She sighs, shakes her head, and turns up the television as if it might drown out all these stupid, confounding thoughts. Why the hell does she have to have feelings about this anyway? So Mia might be bi. *So what?* Claire is irritating herself with her overthinking.

She is saved from it, though, by a key turning in the lock. Nina charges in, somewhat drunker and surprisingly sans Dan. Claire is thrown by that. She thought that was a sure thing.

Nina kicks off her shoes, grabs a cushion from an armchair, and throws it against Claire's leg. She curls into a foetal position, her head half on Claire's lap.

Claire moves the remote and yawns. "No Dan?"

"Nope." Nina shakes her head. "No Dan. I'm trying a new go-slow thing these days. It's all part of making better choices." She leans over and fossicks around under the couch. Then she sits up, book in hand, and offers it to Claire. It's called *Making Better Choices About Love.*

Claire takes it from her and examines the pastel blue and pink cover. She smirks. "So your book told you to go home alone tonight?" She returns it to Nina without opening it. All these self-help books are the same, trite nonsense spouted in upbeat, patronising circles that go on for a couple hundred pages. Her cousin reads all of them and tries to lend them to Claire.

"Yup. At first at least." Nina nods. She flicks through it for a second and then throws it on the floor. "Stupid book." She lies back down.

Claire smiles and stares vaguely at the TV screen. "I thought you might be into Pete." She pokes Nina in the shoulder.

"Nah," Nina says through a yawn. "Not Pete."

Poor Pete, knocked back by both Nina and Mia. And he's so nice too.

"Hey, are you okay? You don't usually go home while the party is still going."

"Just tired, I guess."

"Fair enough." And so is Nina, apparently, because five minutes later she's asleep, snoring against Claire's leg.

Claire tries to wake her, but she won't be woken. She just grumbles and pushes Claire's hand away. So Claire covers her with a blanket and trudges into Nina's room. She turns off the light, falls into bed, pulls the covers over her head, and tries her damnedest not to think anymore.

CHAPTER 37

Claire rests her forehead on the kitchen bench and waits for the welcoming beep that signals coffee is imminent. Sighing against the counter, she wraps her arms around her head in an attempt to block out the incessant chatter coming from the other side of the room. Her mother hasn't stopped talking for the last fifteen minutes since Claire stupidly sat here to wait for the coffee machine's next move.

She prattles about a colleague she's locked into a power struggle with. Claire is sketchy on the details, mostly because she only listens attentively enough to be able to grunt or nod if a response is called for. She will not commit so much that she has to open her eyes or lift her head or do anything that will bring her any closer to actually being in this one-sided conversation. Not until there is a coffee mug in her hand and coherence is once again her friend. For now, she closes her eyes and waits it out like a patient prisoner.

Her mother is still closing in on the point when Claire registers another set of footsteps moving so slowly it has to be Cam. He's been limping around the house like an old man, still hunched by his injuries and the painful burden of being upright.

"Good morning, sweetheart," Christine sings. "Coffee?"

Claire frowns. Of course Cam gets sunshine and an offer of coffee. She was greeted with a comment about the raggedy T-shirt she's wearing.

"Honey, why don't you just throw that thing away?" Christine asked the minute Claire walked into the kitchen. "It's so ugly."

Claire ignored her and made straight for the machine. Her mother simply does not understand the luxury that is the perfectly worn-in T-shirt. Nor does she get that it doesn't matter what Claire wears to bed if she's not sharing that bed with someone. Of course, even though it's a Sunday morning, her mother is already immaculately coiffed, ready for anything from the sudden work call to an impromptu garden party.

Claire lifts her head a fraction. Cam's hair is wet, and a towel hangs around his neck. She grins at him. "Hey, pops, what's new?"

"What do you think?" He glares at her. "*Nothing* is new, Claire. Nothing. I've been lying around. I had a shower. That will probably be the main event of my day."

"Don't forget physio this afternoon," their mother adds.

Cam rolls his eyes. "Oh yay. I get to leave the house."

Claire snickers. Cam is starting to get a serious case of cabin fever. She would too if she had to hang around this house all day.

"And I just got a good look at that leg wound in the shower." He pulls a face. "Are you guys aware that I have a hole the size of the Grand Canyon in my thigh?"

"Yes, I'm well aware, Cam," their mother says briskly as she stands in front of the machine, ready to grab the jug the moment it's ready. "But I would think, considering you got out of that accident fairly lightly, you could live with one bad scar."

Cam gives her a petulant look and plays with the fresh bandage over the wound. Then he turns to Claire and gives her a sly grin. "Wanna see?"

"Ew, no." Claire grimaces. "You know, I caught the nurses cleaning out that cavern a bunch of times. It was revolting." She goes over to the cupboard, pulls a clutch of mugs from the shelf, and puts them on the bench in front of her mother. Anything she can do to speed up the process of caffeination.

"One more. Moira will be here soon," Christine tells her.

Claire nods and turns back to the cupboard, smiling. She forgot Moi was in town again.

"The doctor told me the scar will be *significant*." Cam hangs air quotes around "significant." "What does that mean? How big will it be?"

Their mother pulls the milk from the fridge. "Just be pleased with the fact he said it hasn't damaged much muscle tissue."

Claire sits back down. "Are you upset because bikini season is coming, and the beauty of your pasty white leg will be marred?"

"Shut up."

"Scars are cool." Claire kicks her socked feet against the legs of the stool. "Besides, you know, you're alive, so stop being so precious about a little dent in your leg. At least it's not in your head."

"Yes, you should just be grateful to have come out of this okay and that you will be able to go back to work at all," Christine adds.

"Alright, you two stop picking on me." Cam folds his arms over his chest. "I'm an invalid."

"Okay." Claire grins. "If you stop being such a pussy."

"Claire!" Her mother shoots her a disapproving look. "Watch your mouth."

Cam turns and gives Claire one of those trademark annoying grins he gets when he wins a point against her and then takes the coffee Christine slides in front of him.

Claire grabs hers, shoots him a death stare, and takes as big a mouthful as the heat will allow. She wishes she could go back to sleep for another eight hours. Her ass is still dragging from the party the other night. When she and Nina finally woke up yesterday, it was early afternoon. Then they had to go to work. And the bar was crazy. Some people were having a triple twenty-first birthday party, and the place was packed until closing. Claire decided to go home afterward. She craved the comfort of her own bed and decent sleep. Of course, that went south when her mother decided to start up the vacuum in the hallway at some ridiculous hour.

At least it's holidays now, and she can sleep whenever she wants. If her mother doesn't get in the way. Claire smiles about the glorious stretch of time in front of her when her parents will be at work, and she can sleep as long as she likes and do whatever she wants with her time. Sweet, sweet holidays.

Cam elbows her. "So, when are you going up to the lake?"

"Thursday." She almost whispers it. She's miraculously gotten this far without a conversation about this trip with her mother, and she doesn't want to have one now.

But of course, no dice. Her mother has an ability to hear everything uttered within a fifty-meter radius of her.

"Yes, this little trip to the holiday house." Christine turns from the coffee machine and folds her hands on the counter. "Tell me, just who are you taking up there?"

Claire sighs. How does her mother manage to make everything sound like an accusation?

Cam turns and gives her the briefest flash of a knowing smile.

"Just some friends. Robbie, Mia, Nina..." She trails off.

Her mother frowns between sips of her coffee. "I know of this Nina girl. She's the one who doesn't go to school and just works in the bar."

Claire sets her jaw and tries to ignore the inevitable, rising tide of frustration.

"But who are these other people? I've never heard of the others. I assumed you were going with Michelle and Kate and that other short girl, what's her name?"

Claire shakes her head. Typical. Her mother has known Kerry for years and she never remembers her name. "Kerry. No, I'm going with some friends from school."

"From your course?" Christine taps her fingers against the bench top. She can never sit entirely still when she's on an interrogation roll.

"No." Claire stares out the window and wishes Moi would hurry up and get here and distract her mother from this line of questioning. Why can't she just mind her own business?

"I've met Robbie." Cam jumps in. "He's the photographer kid who took that picture of you, right?"

Claire nods.

"What picture of you?" Christine looks between them, suspicious, as though they have been keeping a big secret from her.

"He took a photo of me. And it was in his exhibition."

"What kind of photo?"

Claire sighs, louder this time. "A portrait, Mum. What did you think it was going to be? A nude?"

Christine gives her another don't-test-me look.

"It was a really cool picture, Mum," Cam tells her. "He sold it, too, didn't he?"

Claire nods.

Christine feigns hurt. "I wish you would have told us about it. We might have liked to see it."

"Sorry," Claire mutters, more to shut her up than anything. She almost told them about it in a brief moment of pride. But she knew they wouldn't come and see it. They wouldn't have spared the time.

"And what about this other person? Maya?"

"Mia," Claire says quietly.

"Oh, and I've met Mia, too, haven't I? With Vito that day?" Cam turns to Claire and winks. "The med student, right?" He dangles it like bait in front of their mother.

"Medicine?" Christine sounds instantly impressed.

Claire rolls her eyes. Her mother is so damn predictable. But at least it makes it somewhat possible to play her sometimes. "She just finished biomed, and she's waiting to see if she gets into medicine."

"Hmm." Christine purses her lips and reaches up to straighten her already perfect ponytail.

Well, that shut her up. Claire smiles into her coffee. She realises her mother still doesn't know anything about Mia—she doesn't even know she stayed with Mia and her family for those few days before they returned from Canberra. Claire didn't tell them, and they were so preoccupied with Cam on their return, they didn't ask.

"Mia seems nice. Normal too. Two arms, two legs," Cam reassures Christine. "Robbie's cool too. Don't worry, Mum. I don't think Claire is taking a band of weirdos up to destroy the place."

"Well, okay." Christine frowns. "But you had better leave it in the state you found it, young lady. The living room rug never looked quite the same after Cam had that party there."

"That wasn't me—" Cam starts to protest, but the doorbell rings and Christine is off her stool like a shot to answer it.

Claire takes in a deep breath and raises her arms in the air, triumphant. The interrogation is over and she's good to go. She turns to Cam. "Thank you," she tells him, grudgingly.

"I figure I owe you for all those hospital hours you put in."

"Hell yes, you do."

CHAPTER 38

"Goodness me, girl," Moi says, after Claire recounts the last few weeks of her life. "You have not had an easy time of it, have you?"

Claire shakes her head. "No." She blinks at her sandwich, grateful for this attention to *her* experience during Cam's time in hospital. Moi already knows what happened. She knows all of it. But that didn't stop her from asking what it was like for Claire the minute they sat down to lunch. And Claire told her most of it. She even told her about going to stay with Mia and her family, about how kind and generous Mia's parent were during that awful week.

Claire picks at the last of her sandwich and bites into it slowly. This is why she loves Moi and why she misses her so much. She possesses this inspiriting combination of warm and loving with honest and brash. And she *sees* Claire, takes the time to actually look at her and listen to her in a way that her parents never seem to.

They are in a café near the hospital. Her mother has taken Cam in for his physiotherapy appointment, and Claire takes this precious moment to spend time with Moira *sans* her mother and her running commentary on everything Claire says.

"So, now that this is all over, how are you going to spend your break?" Moi asks as the waiter comes and clears their dishes. "Have some fun, I hope?"

Claire nods. "Mum and Dad actually let me have the holiday house for a few days. I'm going up with some friends on Thursday to celebrate the end of exams."

Moi raises her eyebrows. "I bet wrangling that was no mean feat."

"I asked Dad, so it was easier. And I think they felt guilty about going to Canberra while Cam was in hospital. That helped."

Moi nods but says nothing. Claire can see the look in her eyes, as if she might have something to say on that matter but is exercising restraint. Just knowing the thought exists makes Claire feel better.

"I'm so glad Cam is okay. I wish I could have been here for you, kiddo." She squeezes Claire's arm. "I wanted to fly over, but Sam was in a bit of trouble at the school, and we decided a fast change might be good." She smiles wearily. "You know, before the school suggested it."

"Is he being that bad?" Claire knew he was getting in a lot of trouble, but she didn't know it was expulsion worthy.

Moi sighs. "I think I just have to accept that for some reason he's hurting more than anyone else, still. He's just angry. And he doesn't seem to know how to stop being angry."

Claire nods. She remembers the beginnings of that rage during that awful period before and after the funeral.

"The other boys are doing great, though. Matt is getting good at the footy thing. It seems I have an athlete on my hands."

Claire grins. "He's such a boring jock. What about Cal?"

Two years younger, Cal was always her favourite. He was the one she spent the most time with after Gary died. The two of them sat in the backyard, hiding from the force of all the grief in the house, and asked each other big confounding questions that they were too afraid to ask anyone else, questions they didn't know if they *should* ask. They freed each other to be openly curious about what happens to bodies and souls after death. And even though neither of them had answers, it was a relief to know someone else wondered those same things.

"Cal is doing great. He goes into year twelve next, and then he wants to come back to Melbourne for university."

"Really?" Claire leans back in her chair. "That would be great. I'll show him around."

"I'll miss him like hell, of course. But I have to let him go, I suppose. Though I'm starting to realise you never really let go of your kids." She looks at Claire. "And your mother, she holds on tighter than most, right?"

Claire rolls her eyes. "Yeah."

Moi reaches for her handbag and for the bill. Claire sits up and reaches for her own wallet, but Moi waves her away. "Don't you dare, girl. Put that away. This is my treat, and it always will be."

"Thank you."

"You are welcome." Moi throws a card onto the dish. "You know, I think Cal might be gay."

"Really?" Claire tries to picture what Cal might be like now, but she can't. She hasn't seen him for four years. She can't even imagine who he might be attracted to.

"But the thing is, I'm not sure *he* even knows it yet. So I have to just wait, either for him to figure it out or for him to decide to tell me."

"He'd tell you," Claire says. Moi and her boys are close. Claire can't imagine Cal not telling her.

"Maybe. It's funny how you can know certain things about your kids before they even know. And I think maybe moving out here on his own will free him a little. He's so different from the other two, and I think he struggles with that already, without having any reason to feel any more different."

Claire nods and wonders what her life might be like now if she went away somewhere to study, away from her parents and their expectations and demands. Would anything change? Would she have a better idea of what she wanted to do with her life or who she could be?

Moira checks her watch and signs the receipt. "We better go. Your mum and Cam will be done by now."

"Thanks, Moi." Claire loops her arm in Moira's as they walk back toward the hospital.

Moira smiles at her, her red curls blowing around her face. "Anything for you, kid." She squeezes her arm. "As long as you promise you'll come and take a look at the new centre next week and consider helping out this summer. We're desperately short of volunteers for the holiday program."

Claire laughs. She should have known Moi would be shilling for her help again. "Okay, I promise I'll come and look when I get back from the holiday house." Claire owes her at least that.

"Good girl." Moira squeezes her arm.

* * *

She leaves Moira at the entrance to the hospital and traipses back toward the university. They're having a "meeting" at the café to discuss the trip and what they need to bring. It was Robbie's idea. Claire would never have thought of it. She would've slung clothes, books, and maybe a swimsuit in her bag and jumped in the car. But no, according to Robbie, they might need food and beer and petrol money for the trip, and they need to work out a time to leave and where to meet. And he's right. She's just happy someone else is willing to be the organised one. She doesn't want to think. She wants to stare off into the great, delicious void of lazy days by the lake and let someone else do the planning. Besides, she's providing the venue. Her job is done.

She enters the café and scans the room. It's busy, but not as busy as usual. Now that exams are finished, all the students are probably as far from the university as they can get. She spots Mia at a table in the corner with her head over a book.

Claire stops in her tracks and slides her hands into her pockets as a wave of weirdness washes over her. She didn't think that she might see Mia alone. She hasn't heard from her since the party on Friday, when she disappeared with the girl in the dress. Claire has no idea what to say or how to talk around the fact that they barely saw each other at that party and why that might have been.

She goes to the counter to order her coffee to buy herself some time, hoping the others will arrive before she's done. But they don't, so Claire reluctantly makes her way over. Mia stares at her phone as Claire walks over to the table.

"Hey." She says it as casually as she can as she sits down opposite Mia and rests her forearms on the table.

"Oh hey." She holds up her phone. "Pete's going to be late."

"Where's Robbie?"

"Not sure. He'll be here. It was his idea." She pulls her coffee a little closer to her. "So, how are you?"

"Fine. You?"

"Good. Glad it's holidays."

Claire nods.

And then there's a silence.

And Claire doesn't know what to do because they *never* have silences like this, so loaded and obvious. In the short time they've known each other, they've never once struggled to find something to say to each other. Their problem has been the complete and utter opposite. They always have too much to say, something Claire finds both awesome *and* strange, considering how little they actually have in common.

But right in this moment, she feels as though she's flailing because she cannot find safe conversation territory that won't lead back to the party.

"How's your brother doing?" Mia finally asks.

Claire looks up at her, relieved. There's always Cam to talk about. "He's okay. He's whining about being stuck at home, though."

"It must be hard. Going from his kind of job to doing absolutely nothing."

"I guess."

And that stilted silence drops around them again as Claire stares into her coffee. She feels even more awkward now that Mia's given her something to go on, and she can't even manage the responsibility of running with it properly.

She sneaks a glance at Mia and she looks apprehensive, too, with the skin wrinkled slightly around her brows. It's obvious that they are both fully aware of this fine thread of unease between them.

Claire plays with her spoon and wonders how to make this *not* uncomfortable. She wishes she could deliver a casual joke to let Mia know she knows about the girl, to break open this weirdness, and to let them be normal with each other again.

The little web of tension is destroyed by the arrival of Robbie. He drops his bag on the floor, kisses them both, and sits down in his usual flurry of Robbie energy.

"Question." He puts down his coffee, pulls off his jacket, and rests his forearms on the table. "What do cats need?"

Mia scrunches her brows. "What do you mean?"

"Need for what?" Claire asks at the same time, relieved by this dose of Robbie randomness to save this uncomfortable meeting.

"You know, to live. I mean, they just need food and kitty litter and those little furry ball things to chase, right?"

"Yeah, I guess." Mia shrugs. "But I have a question, too. Why the hell are you asking?"

He rests his chin in his hand and raises a dubious eyebrow. "All of a sudden I seem to possess a cat. A really, really fat cat."

"What?" Claire sits up. "Where did you find a cat? And why the hell do you want one?" She thinks of their old cat, an irritable, suspicious thing who, in that annoyingly contrary way of felines, hated everyone in the house but her mother.

"I didn't want one. I just kind of got one. It was the neighbour's. Well, it is the neighbour's. This little old lady who lives across the hall. She went off to hospital a couple of weeks ago, and her son asked me to feed the cat. So I did. But she doesn't seem to be coming back any time soon. The son didn't leave me his number or anything, so I haven't been able to ask him if or when she'll be home. Or what he wants to do with the cat, who has kind of moved into my apartment. So..." He sips his coffee. "I kind of have this cat."

"How fat is the cat?" Claire pictures a furry barrel on legs.

"Oh my God." Robbie shakes his head, eyes wide. "So freaking fat. Hang on a minute." He rifles through his bag and pulls out a small digital camera. He turns it on and flicks through it. "Here." He holds the screen out to first Mia, who starts laughing, and then Claire. "Behold, Patty."

"Oh. Wow." That is all Claire can think to say as she takes in the sight of this massive tortoise-shell beast, her head a tiny sphere against the furry generosity of her body. A barrel on legs was not far off, it turns out. Except Claire can't actually see her legs.

"So, anyway, that's all they need, right? Food, water, litter, toys?"

"Yup, pretty much, I think," Mia says.

"I'm thinking *less* food." Claire holds on to his sleeve as he goes to take the camera away, just so she can take in the spectacle of Patty a moment longer. She giggles again and lets go. "And maybe a treadmill. Can that thing even walk?"

"Yeah, *just.*" Robbie takes a last look at the screen and puts away the camera. "Every day is a struggle for poor Patty. I think Helena fed her every time that cat so much as looked at her."

"Who's going to take care of her while we're away?" Mia asks.

"A friend." He picks up his coffee and shakes his head wearily. "God, it's like having a child I suddenly have to worry about."

Mia laughs. "Robbie, I'm pretty sure feeding a cat a couple of times a day is nothing like having a child."

"Whatever. It feels like it." Then he leans back in his seat and claps his hands excitedly. "So, where are the others? Let's plan this freaking trip!"

CHAPTER 39

Later, Claire walks down the darkening streets on her way to work when her phone rings. She stares at it for a second as her stomach does a nervous lurch. She shakes her head. Come on, it's just Mia. She picks up.

"Hey, it's me."

Claire can hear the muffled sounds of the café behind her. "I know. Hey."

"I'm on a break, and I wanted to tell you...guess who came in?"

"I don't know. Michael Jackson?"

"Yeah, Claire, Michael Jackson came back from the dead because he really wanted a soy latte, and he just had to have one from here."

"Well, don't ask stupid questions." Claire grins as she moves to avoid a handful of joggers. "So, who was it then?"

"It was Josh."

"Josh?" Claire wrinkles her nose. "As in Nina's former Josh. King Douche?"

"The very one."

"Why do I need to know this?"

"Because, grumpy," Mia tells her impatiently. "I saw something Nina might like. But I figure you would know better if Nina would enjoy it or if maybe it's too soon?"

"Okay," Claire says slowly, still slightly confused. "What did you see?"

"He came in with this girl and ordered coffee and sat near the window. I only just recognised him. You know, when you do that thing where you ask yourself, 'How do I know that person?' Anyway, next thing I know, I am making coffee and there's someone yelling. Like full hysterical screeching. And I look just in time to see this girl jump from her seat, yell something at him, and then dump an entire extra-large mocha over his head. Everybody was staring."

"No way." Claire raises her eyebrows and wishes she'd been there to witness that little tantrum.

"I mean, who actually does that? I felt like I was in some really bad romantic comedy. Only it was kind of funny because it was Josh, and all I could think was how happy this might make Nina."

"Yeah," Claire agrees. "It'll probably make Nina pretty damn happy. I'll tell her when the customers start driving her crazy at work tonight. It will cheer her right up."

Mia laughs. "Kind of revenge by proxy?"

"Yeah." Claire crosses the street.

"What are you up to?"

"Walking to work."

"Oh fun." Mia sighs. "I've got two hours to go, and then I have to go home and prep for my interviews."

"Oh yeah, the interview." Claire nods. Mia and Pete both have interviews for their postgrad medicine course Thursday morning. Then they'll drive up to meet them at the cottage. "Are you nervous?"

"Yeah. Not as nervous as I was about exams but still kind of."

"You'll be fine. Just be your usual charming geeky self."

"Yeah, yeah. Listen, I better go back to work. Tell Nina for me?"

"Of course. And I'll see you on Thursday, up at the lake."

"Yes!" Mia sounds immediately excited. "Don't have too much fun until we get there, okay?"

"I'll do my best." Claire smiles. It feels good to be able to just banter again. "See you."

"Bye."

Claire immediately feels better, lighter even, at having found this plane of normality with Mia again. Now she wishes she hadn't been so awkward at the café.

Why was she so uncomfortable? If it had been a guy Mia'd left the party with, Claire would have just asked her about it. Or at least cracked a joke. In fact, she probably would already have messaged her the next day and made some silly teasing comment about Mia seeing some action. But this, for some reason, has rendered her speechless. Why? For a second, she wonders if she is just being weird and homophobic. She knows that can't be it. She will never give a crap who people choose to sleep with. Unless, of course, it's someone *she* wants to sleep with herself.

And it's that thought that makes her stop in the middle of the path.

No. She steps blindly out of the way of a frowning woman carrying several shopping bags. The woman shakes her head as she passes as if Claire has ruined her day. But Claire doesn't even react. She's far too busy asking herself what is suddenly a very pressing, very urgent new question.

Claire, do you have a thing for Mia?

But of course she doesn't answer it. She can't answer it. She doesn't know *how* to answer it.

But she doesn't dismiss it either. Because now, suddenly, she's aware there's a question begging to be answered. And the rapid flush of this realisation warms her neck and cheeks against the cold night. She slowly starts to walk again as she holds up this new possibility in her mind and thinks about what she *does* know in order to get her closer to answering this question.

One thing she knows is that the thought of having a crush on a girl has never *ever* occurred to her in her life. She also knows nothing has made her consider the possibility, either. Not until this unsettling preoccupation with Mia and that girl. It has taken up far more real estate in her mind than it should. But does that really mean anything? Couldn't she just be uncomfortable because what she thought she knew about Mia might be wrong, when Mia has so quickly become her closest friend?

Claire takes a deep breath, slows her step, and gives herself a moment before she reaches the rude reality of work. She runs through a list of all the things she knows in her mind.

She knows that there's some sort of pull between them, a palpable attraction she's felt since they first met. It's something that turned them so quickly and easily from being strangers to being so damn very important to one another. Until now, she'd just assumed this instant connection was the beginning of a friendship, one of those intense types she has never had before. And it was—*is*—such a good feeling to know someone like Mia wants to be *that* close to her, to be *that* important to her.

She knows she likes Mia more than she's ever liked anyone before. From the moment they met she never even thought about how she felt about spending time with her. And that was because she simply wanted to be with her. That part was simple.

She also knows she feels a freedom to talk to her in a way she has never been able to talk to anyone. It's as if there's no translation needed between them ever. Mia *gets* her. And she feels as if she *gets* Mia. And that's exactly why today at the café was so weird. She misses that effortlessness.

So why would this one new piece of knowledge about Mia change that? Could it be jealousy?

Claire wonders if something might have happened without her noticing it was happening. When she thinks of Mia, she knows she wants to be around her and that sometimes that feeling is even a need. She thinks of when Cam was in the hospital and Mia was the only person she just wanted to have around her. It became almost a necessity to survive that awful week when her parents left.

But the thought of *physically* wanting Mia? That hasn't even offered itself as an option. Or has it? There was, of course, the drunken kiss. But after that? They have barely ever touched each other. Claire doesn't do touchy-feely. She never has. There was the night that Mia held her as she went to sleep when Claire finally caved to her misery about Cam and her parents and the accident. That felt good. She also knows that it was simply comfort Mia was offering to her in that awful, vulnerable moment, but Claire would never do that with anyone else. And it didn't weird her out either.

She walks straight past the door of the bar because she needs a little more time. She strides past the shopfronts, closed up for the night, not ready to let this go just yet. She thinks of what Moira said this afternoon about Cal, about the potential of not knowing something about yourself, even while it's happening to you. Is that what is happening to her too? Is it possible her brain is just catching up with her feelings? She knows that she likes guys, has liked guys. But maybe she just doesn't know it's also possible to like girls too? Well, one girl, anyway. That would explain why she's being so damn weird about Mia and this girl.

Part of her wishes she hadn't seen it, that she could go back to the blissful ignorance that was last week.

And she wishes she felt closer to answering her question about Mia.

As she chews on her lip, head down, she tries to make Mia immediate in order to answer the question. But Claire can't form enough of a shape of her in her mind. She can conjure her up in parts, little images, the way her lips thin out when she smiles, or the fall of her hair around her face when she's reading and forgets to tie it up. And she can picture the way she lays her hands flat on whatever is in front of her when she's talking out a thought, or the way she crosses her arms when she's listening carefully. But it's not enough. She feels as if she needs her right in front of her before she has any hope of figuring out these feelings.

Claire checks her watch and sighs into the fallen darkness. She needs to get to work. There's no more time for chewing over these frantic thoughts right now. She spins around and walks back toward the bar, ignoring an idiot yelling from his car.

Maybe she is simply overthinking this. Maybe that's all this is, Claire chewing too hard on something that has weirded her out slightly. Overthinking has, historically, been one of her greatest talents.

Before she knows it, though, she's back at the bar. She pauses for a moment under the neon light of the sign. For now, it seems, she's just going to have to sit with this unanswered for a while longer.

She takes in a deep breath, pushes open the door, and steps out of these disquieting new thoughts and into her night.

CHAPTER 40

Claire straightens her bare legs out on the wide wooden railing and listens to Nina and Robbie debate the virtues of the different varieties of grapes as they work their way through a bowl. The two of them are flopped together on the hammock by the door, legs akimbo, arms hanging out as if they are in a boat and could skim the surface of the water as they glide along.

She didn't even know there was more than one type of grape. She just thought there were different colours. She kind of doesn't care either, so she tips her head back against the porch post and shuts her eyes against the beaming sun. It's holidays. She doesn't have to care about anything but the whole lazy day stretched out ahead of her.

"Hey, Claire."

She opens her eyes, and her frown turns quickly to a smile when she realises it's Eli bearing coffee. "Here."

She takes the cup from him. "Thanks."

He places his own on the railing and climbs up to lean on the post opposite her and pulls a book out from under his arm. He doesn't open it, though, just smiles sleepily into the sunlight and rests his head on the post. "It's kind of perfect, isn't it? How these railings are wide enough to sit on."

"Uh-huh." She runs her hand along the weather-smoothed wood by her leg. "Dad did it when he rebuilt the deck. He said he couldn't stop us kids from climbing up here and sitting on them, so he might as well make it easier and safer by putting in wider beams."

Eli looks out at the trees huddled around the border of the garden. "It's such a beautiful place. Do you spend a lot of time up here?"

"Not lately, but we used to come up here every holiday, practically, if Mum or Dad could get time off. Even in winter."

"Well, you're lucky." Eli rolls up the sleeves of his T-shirt so the late morning sun can touch his shoulders. "We used to go to Bendigo for our winter holidays to stay with my grandmother."

"Bendigo?" Claire gives him a pitying look. "Boring."

"And if we were really lucky, we'd get a day trip to the goldfields."

"Thrill city." She smiles.

"Hey, thanks so much for inviting us up here."

She doesn't even open her eyes. "Stop thanking me. Just keep cooking."

Robbie was right. Eli is a really great cook. As soon as they got here last night, he made them dinner, a feast of pasta and salad.

"I'm stunned we even made it up here." Eli laughs. "After yesterday."

Claire smiles. It was an epic journey. What should have been a three-hour drive took all day, and they didn't arrive until the sun was setting. Robbie's grand plans were completely destroyed by everyone else being so damn scatty and disorganised.

The drive up, which her father always tried to do in the most efficient amount of time, was the longest trip Claire had ever taken to get here. Every five minutes they had to stop for something. Nina needed painkillers for her monster hangover headache, then Claire wanted driving snacks, and then they realised no one had brought sun block. Sometime in the afternoon, they ate burgers at a twee little pub on the edges of a tiny town off the highway. Then Robbie made them pull over so he could take pictures of funny signs on an old building on the side of the road, and then they all posed by the car for "posterity." Every time they'd get back on the road for any length of time, someone inevitably had to pee or eat or something, and they'd stop again. Claire didn't care though. They were in no hurry. It was fun and funny, and everyone—even Nina and her hangover—was in an incredible mood as they drove into the sunshine and away from the city.

She has absolutely no idea what time it is now. When she woke, the sun was already high in the sky. It's probably early afternoon, but all they've managed so far is coffee and cereal and to gravitate to the large wooden deck, unable to remain inside while the weather is so seductively good. Not that it matters. They have no plans at all.

Mia and Pete will be here sometime this afternoon. Claire still doesn't know how she feels about seeing Mia. Part of her looks forward to it;

the other part dreads it. She can't help being embarrassed by all this thinking she's been doing as she tries to understand the shape of her feelings about Mia. She hasn't spoken to her since that phone call and that alarmingly revelatory walk to work on Sunday. Now, after days of stewing, she has no idea what it will be like once she actually lays eyes on her. Even though Mia can't know what she's been thinking, it feels awkward and strange as if she won't know how to behave.

It isn't long until she finds out.

Claire hears the car before she sees it. She opens her eyes and looks down the overgrown trail that leads up to the road. Yep, there's a car, and the sound of the motor grows louder every second.

"Who's that?" Nina asks from the hammock, the first peep she's made in a long time.

"It might be the other two." Eli puts down his book and leans over to get a better look down the driveway. "Yep, I think that's Pete driving."

"Yes!" Robbie flings his legs over the hammock and jumps up. It swings violently behind him. Nina clutches the sides and squeals.

The battered green car pulls up next to Claire's silver one, and she can make them out through the windshield. Pete says something, and Mia laughs.

She pulls her legs up to her chest and watches them unbuckle their seatbelts. Eli jumps off the railing on the far side and lands catlike on the gravel below. Pete and Mia climb out of the car, already dressed for summer holidays in shorts and tank tops. As soon as Mia opens the door, Blue shoots out. He dashes in hectic to and fros between people and trees and smells, frantic with excitement.

Robbie leaps over to them. "You're here!"

"Yeah." Pete gives him a hug in that stupid back-slapping way boys show affection. "It only took a few hours."

The others crowd in with greetings and hugs. Only Claire stays where she is, watching the scene unfold below her, glued by her awkwardness to her spot on the railing.

"Well, you're apparently much more efficient than we are. We took all freaking day to get here." Robbie throws his arms around Mia. "How did it go?"

"Okay, I think." She lets him go, hugs Nina, and spins in a slow circle, obviously taking in the view of the low-hanging eucalypts and the flashes of water through the scrub. As she turns toward the house, she spots Claire on her perch and waves.

"Hey!" she calls up to her and smiles her warm Mia smile.

Claire crosses her legs on the railing and smiles back. She knows she should probably get down and greet them properly, but she doesn't. "Hey," she says instead, giving her a kind of awkward half wave, and stays right where she is.

Mia points at Blue, who sits at the top of the track leading to the lake, alert to something only he can see or hear. "It's still okay I brought him, right?"

"Of course."

Pete opens the boot of the car. "We brought beer and food and stuff."

Eli peers in. "Wow, you brought a lot of beer."

"I didn't know how close the nearest shops were. I was playing it safe."

Nina looks into the trunk and laughs. "Very safe. And you can carry them in."

Robbie grabs a knapsack from the trunk and a couple of bags and then looks up, brow furrowed. "Hey, Claire," he calls up to her. "Where are they going to sleep?"

The small house is already full. Eli and Robbie have taken her parents' room. Nina is in the other room. And the minute Claire got there, she put her things inside the sleeping porch, the coveted room around the side of the deck she and Cam fought over every single time they came up here. It's her favourite room in the world, a little nest made of glass and screen that hangs off the side of the house. Surrounded by the green canopies of branches, it feels a little like her own personal treehouse.

"Uh, there's another bed in Nina's room, and then there's the bunkhouse." She jumps off the railing, glad of something to do so she doesn't just sit there like an idiot. "I'll go find the key."

"Just warning you people if you want to share—I snore," Nina announces. "Loudly!"

CHAPTER 41

They all slide off the rocks at once and let out a chorus of gasps and squeals at the sudden tingling cold of the water.

No one suggests it; no one commands it, but they all automatically kick out, slowly headed beyond the shaded shore to the sunlit diving platform, a weathered beacon in the darkest blue-green waters of the lake. Pete carries a six-pack of beer on his head as he swims.

Claire paddles around to the ladder, still holding her towel well above the surface of the water, and climbs up. She stretches out on the far side, her chilled skin pressed flat against the sun-baked wood. She shuts her eyes and listens to them laughing as they climb up the ladder and spread out on the platform. The mood is still festive from Pete and Mia's arrival.

Pete opens a beer and nudges Claire's hand with the last one. "See, we are the perfect number."

She takes it from him, slowly sits up, and rests her feet on the top rung of the ladder. The cool water laps over her toes. She stares out across the shifting water. From here she can see all the houses on the far shore of this small arm of the lake, probably empty until the weekend. It's still early in the summer. Too early for all the jet skis and boats and swimmers, and all the sounds of parties and smoky smells of barbecues that usually fill the place and make it feel alive. In a few weeks, it will be like that again. But for now it's sleepily all theirs.

Robbie sighs. "This is so awesome."

Mia kicks her feet in the water and lifts her long, tanned arms over her head. "It's perfect."

"Look." Nina points back to the shore. Blue is sitting on the closest rock to the water, staring dolefully at them. "Poor Blue."

Mia smiles. "If he were a couple of years younger, he'd probably try and swim out here. He'll be okay."

Eli puts his beer down on the wet wood and leans back on his hands. "How were your interviews?"

"Okay," Pete and Mia say doubtfully at the same time and then laugh.

Robbie pulls off his singlet. "What do they ask you in these things, anyway?"

Pete sighs. "Everything."

Mia nods vehemently. "Seriously, *everything*. You go to all these different mini interviews and do all this different stuff. Everything from why do you want to be a doctor, to tell us about a time you used leadership skills, to how you feel about euthanasia, to what you are like when you get stressed, blah blah."

Claire leans against the ladder post, grinning. "Did you tell them about the hot mess you become at exam time?"

"No." Mia laughs and gives her a look. "Someone even asked me about the last book I read."

"They didn't ask me that one," Pete says. "I did get 'Tell us about a world leader you admire and why.'"

"Who did you say?" Robbie asks.

"Nelson Mandela, like an idiot."

Eli frowns. "What's wrong with Mandela?"

"Nothing, but I bet everyone says Mandela. I wanted to think of someone really cool, but I couldn't think of anyone on the spot. In fact, the only world leaders I could think of were Mandela and Pol Pot for some insane reason. And I wasn't about to say Pol Pot."

"Who's that?" Nina asks.

"Cambodian dictator," Eli tells her. "Killed a lot of people."

"Oh."

"Don't worry, I had to tell them the last book I read was *Best Interview Techniques*." Mia laughs ruefully and sips her beer. "When I probably should have said *My Brilliant Career* or something."

"What did they say?"

"They kind of laughed, actually. Apparently, people don't usually admit that."

"At least they laughed. I just got bored stares." Pete shakes his head. "God, I'm so not getting into our postgrad program. So I just have to pray for Sydney or Queensland. I don't want to go to Western Australia."

"Why not?" Nina asks.

"If I have to move, I can stand to move to Sydney or Brisbane. Perth is too far away. And small and boring."

Mia sips her beer and shrugs. "It won't even matter, though, I guess, once we start. We'll have no life anyway. And maybe we'll both be in Sydney or Perth together. That will make it better."

Claire raises her head and looks at them both, eyes wide. She had no idea that Mia might study somewhere else next year.

"Oh, you'll get in here," Pete tells her.

"Are you kidding?" Mia shakes her head. "It's so competitive. I think maybe twenty people from our undergrad course got in last year."

"You'll get in," he repeats, firm. "I'd bet money on it."

Robbie pokes her in the side with his foot. "You better get in. You are not leaving me."

"It's not really my choice, is it?" Mia says quietly, staring out across the water. "Anyway, can we talk about something else?"

"Yes, let's talk about something really important instead," Eli says sleepily. "Like what we're going to have for dinner."

* * *

They lie out on the platform for hours and soak up the sun and swim, reluctant to leave their little paradise while the sun has chosen to shine so beaming and hot on them. Taking pity, Pete even rescues Cam's old dinghy from under the veranda and brings Blue out on it. As Pete rows, Blue stands at the front, both paws on the bow, staring ahead like a comic ship's captain sighting the shore, which makes everyone laugh. Once with them, he trots excitedly from side to side, his gaze vigilantly fixed on everyone in the water, the most dedicated of lifeguards.

He looks as though at any minute he will leap in after one of them. He stays on the platform, though, until Mia dives into the water. Then he can no longer contain himself and skitters off the edge of the platform and paddles furiously after her. Mia doesn't even notice as she glides away. Laughing, the boys haul Blue back onto the platform, where he jumps and barks excitedly at Mia. As she turns and breaststrokes languidly back, he finally starts to relax. Dripping wet, he vigorously shakes the lake from his fur.

"Oh, don't be such a cliché, dog," Claire grumbles as she pulls her towel over her eyes to shield them from the drops that fly from his sodden coat.

Claire, terrified her sunscreen is wearing off, lies under a towel when she's not in the water. She learned the hard way how quickly her pale skin burns if left exposed to the sun.

She lies with her head at the edge of the float and giggles as Pete and Robbie attempt to create some sort of bizarre synchronised swimming routine. She's not sure how they even got started on it, but it largely involves flapping their hands around in unison, while they spin in circles and try to kick their legs up out of the water. They inevitably sink only to rise gracelessly up again to flail and gasp for air. Eli floats peacefully on his back several feet away, completely oblivious.

Claire smirks. "Truly beautiful, guys. You are poetry in motion."

Pete ignores her and turns to Robbie in earnest. "I think maybe we just need to hone our pirouettes."

Robbie nods and swipes his hair off his face. "Okay, from the top!"

They start their little routine all over again, and Claire smiles and rests her head sleepily on her arms as Mia hauls herself onto the platform, dripping water over the dry wood.

"Jesus, Mia." Nina's tone is all accusatory.

"What?"

"Now you're just being selfish. Who needs all that leg?"

Nina prods Mia in her long, tanned thigh. They are kind of ridiculously long and lean. Embarrassed to be staring at Mia's legs, Claire looks away.

Mia laughs at Nina but says nothing.

Claire looks back at them.

"I mean, it's selfish. You couldn't have left some for the rest of us?" Nina straightens her own short legs out next to Mia's, comparing. Her feet only reach halfway down Mia's shins. "That is so unfair." She shakes her head.

"Nina, it's not exactly Mia's fault that you're height challenged," Claire mumbles.

"No." Mia lowers herself down onto her back and throws an arm over her eyes. "Blame my giant parents. They started it."

Nina turns on Claire. "Yeah, well, how would you know how it feels to be a midget? You're tall too."

"Well, I am sincerely apologetic for my luck in the genetic draw." Claire looks at them both lying stretched out, completely exposed to the sun. "But at least you aren't the whitest person alive. You don't have to hide from the sun like a freaking vampire."

"Hmm," is all Nina says.

Conversation over, Claire closes her eyes again, lulled by the warm toward sleep. She listens to the boys as they work on their routine and to Nina as she tells Mia a story about a river where she and her family used to swim.

Claire still can't believe she never realised Mia might go to university somewhere else. She always assumed she'd be around. Maybe she'd be at a different uni but not a different city. Of all the things they've talked about in these last couple of months, this has never come up. How will she feel if Mia goes to study in another city? Will she feel bereft at not having her around? The thought makes her pull in a breath.

* * *

Claire stands at the edge of the float, wrapped in her towel, and watches them argue.

Robbie jabs Eli in his dark, skinny arms. "I may not be a jock, but I can so take you."

"Neither am I, but no you can't." Eli crosses his arms over his chest, facing him off.

"I can." Robbie nods. "Easily."

"Loser has to do all the dishes tonight."

"Fine." Robbie shrugs. "Because it will be you. First one to swim to that rock there." He points to a wide brown rock back on the shore right in front of the path to the house.

"Sure." Eli grins and stamps his legs a little.

"I'm going to win." Robbie rotates his arms over his shoulder like an Olympian preparing for a race.

It makes Claire want to laugh, though, because his scrawny little shoulders are probably half as narrow as any professional swimmer's. She smirks at their chest beating. She had no idea Robbie could be so competitive.

"Shut up, you two," she says. "And just race."

"Hush you," Robbie tells her. "I don't see you challenging."

She shrugs.

Eli points at him. "*All* the dishes."

Robbie nods, serious now.

"Do you realise this is kind of a win for us," Mia mutters. "Either way, none of us has to do the dishes."

Claire smiles. She hadn't thought of that.

"I hope they draw," Nina says.

"Somebody say 'Ready, set, go' for us," Robbie demands as he steps to the edge of the platform.

Eli stands next to him, his toes gripped over the edge of the wood like a diver, crouched and ready to pitch himself into the water.

Nina scrambles to her feet. "Are you ready?"

They both nod and look at each other, dead serious.

"Set!" Nina calls. "Go!"

Claire steps forward to watch them take off. They dive into the water in a duet of messy-legged, flop-bellied dives that tell her everything she needs to know. She drops her towel and waits a beat after them so they don't know she's coming. Then she dives in, legs neatly pressed together, and gathers distance underwater. She kicks out to the surface and begins a speedy crawl, rotating her arms by her ears as she pushes breath out through her nose. She swims a slight arc around them so they won't notice her coming, too focused on beating each other. She catches up easily, breathing to her left side so she can see them both churn up the water not far from her.

Don't forget your legs. She hears her father's eternal advice in her head. She kicks hard. *People always forget their legs when they race and exhaust themselves early.*

Within moments, she easily overtakes them. As she makes a beeline for the shore, she hits a steady rhythm with her breath and feels that familiar push in her lungs and the dull ache in her shoulders. Her body instantly recognises the sensations from all the times she has made this brief watery journey. It feels so good to swim again.

A minute later, she slaps the rock victoriously with her hand and then grabs a hold of it and pulls herself up a little. She turns around, panting for breath, just in time to see them take their last few strokes. Their hands hit the rock at virtually the same time.

The other three cheer and clap from the landing, and Blue barks excitedly. She grins. That was too easy.

Robbie lifts his head out of the water and shakes it, flinging the hair out of his face. "What?" He gasps, dumbfounded, when he takes in her triumphant face in front of him.

Eli swipes the water from his eyes and stares. "Where the hell did you come from?"

She swims slowly away from them. "It was a draw for second, by the way. Looks like you two are doing the dishes together."

CHAPTER 42

"I win!" Claire throws her hands up in the air and giggles.

"Claire, you can't win with a pair of twos." Pete pushes Claire's cards back at her and gives her an amused but weary look.

She throws the rest of her hand down on the table. "So what?"

"So why bet so much? It's a waste."

"Because, Pete," she sits back against her chair, "it's pretty hard to take it seriously when all I'm going to lose is a handful of Skittles. Take them, they're yours. I hate the yellow ones, anyway." She pushes the small pile of candy at him. He shakes his head at her like a disappointed father. And she smirks right back like a petulant teenager.

Pete's taking this game very seriously. He's even wearing a hat. Because, according to Pete, that's the rules. "You have to wear a hat when you're playing cards," he informed them as he sat at the table in a fishing cap he found hanging in the front hall at the start of the game. "It's lucky."

"Uh, okay," Claire told him as Nina dealt out the first round.

Pete cups his hands over Claire's losing pile of candy, and drags it over to meet his pile. "I'd hate to see you playing for actual money."

"Yeah, no offence, but you are really kind of terrible at this game." Eli grabs up the cards and shuffles them.

"And I do not care." She kicks her socked feet up onto the wooden table, knowing her mother would kill her if she saw it. She loves this huge old table. Now it's covered in cards and candy and empty beer bottles.

They've been forced indoors for the night after a wind picked up and the air became too chilly. So now they're playing poker, lamps lit against the darkness, radio on in the background. The wind pushes at the old windows of the house.

Well, the boys and Nina are playing poker, and Claire is just playing along. They explained how the game works a bunch of times, but she can't be bothered. So she just invents her own version. She bets big, trying to bluff them into thinking she's got something good, when truthfully she has no idea what she's got in her hand.

Eli leans forward, ready to deal. "Claire, are you playing this round?"

"Nah, I've only got red ones left, and I like the red ones." She pops two Skittles in her mouth and chews them quickly, relishing the zing of the sweet and sour candy.

Nina giggles and pokes her arm. "That's not how it works either. You're not supposed to eat your winnings."

Claire shrugs and pops another couple in her mouth. She doesn't care. The only reason she's still in the game at all is because she takes extra Skittles out of the packet and adds them to her pile after each loss. And no one really cares because they'll win them off her eventually anyway. Claire is like their default banker.

Robbie pats her hand. "Ah, Claire, you do march to the beat of your own drum, don't you?"

"Oh shut up." Claire grins and slaps his hand away. As she sits back and watches them consider their cards with their serious faces on, she hears clattering and banging coming from the kitchen. It echoes through the house even over the stereo.

Eli raises an eyebrow at the sound. "What is Mia doing?"

"Cleaning up?" Pete suggests.

"But we already did the dishes," Robbie grumbles as he gives Claire a look. "Thanks to Ms. Olympic swimmer over here."

She laughs. That race was fun. More fun than stupid cards, anyway.

"Never mind, let's play," Nina says, incredibly serious. She's really into this game, and she's surprisingly good at it. She's got the most candy in front of her, amassed into a generous pile over many, many winning hands, mostly taken from Claire.

"Where'd you become such a card shark?" Eli asks as he continues to shuffle. "Vegas?"

"My dad." Nina quickly picks up each card as it's dealt out to her and organises her hand. "He taught me to play when I was, like, eight."

Robbie raises an eyebrow. "When you were eight? What were the stakes then, M&Ms? Soft toys? Sand for the sandpit?"

"Nope. Pocket money."

"What? Really?" Claire laughs, eyes wide. She had to unload the dishwasher and clean the upstairs bathroom for her pocket money. Even when they had a cleaner, her mother still made her do it just to exercise her money-doesn't-grow-on-trees point.

Nina nods. "Yup. He'd hand out our pocket money, and then he'd play cards against us and win it all back." She shakes her head. "I was sucked into it for so long. I kept thinking I could beat him one day."

"Did you ever?" Pete asks.

Nina just shakes her head, rueful.

Claire picks up her beer. "Sucker. Your dad is a genius, though." She leaves them and goes to the open front door. The wind has really picked up, tossing the branches of the trees lining the lake. And even from here, with the sound of the stereo behind her, she can hear the usually serene water lapping at the rocks. It's kind of nice to feel cosy inside.

She shuts the door against the brisk air and ambles through the living area, humming. She stops to pat Blue, who is asleep on the rug, and continues to wander. She feels good, kind of loose and expansive after this day of sun and swimming and being lazy. And maybe a little drunk. She drinks down the last of her beer and turns up the music. It was such a good idea to come here. It's summer, she's with her people, and it's fun.

She calls out, "Who wants another beer?"

"Yes, please," they all respond.

She stops in the kitchen doorway. The room has been transformed into a one-person hive of activity. The bench is covered in flour and eggs and dishes, and Mia is busy with a bowl and a spoon and a measuring cup, a beer close at hand.

"Whatcha doing over there, Martha Stewart?" Claire asks as she heads for the fridge.

"I'm making a cake." Mia takes a slug of her beer as if it's the most normal thing in the world. She has flour in her hair and a smudge of something on her T-shirt.

Claire raises her eyebrows. "You are what? That's...nuts."

"You guys said you wanted dessert," she says, flushed and grinning.

"We did...but..." Claire shakes her head and laughs. Mia looks kind of drunk to be baking. "Just how much have you had to drink?"

"I don't know. Some." She picks up the spoon and points it at Claire. A little flour scatters across to the countertop as she does. "I've finished exams. I've finished my hardest interview. I'm on holidays, and now I am drunk, and I want to make a cake. So I'm making a cake." She nods, defiant.

Claire laughs at this enthusiastic tirade. Mia is cutely combative when she's on the sauce. "And you just know how to do that? To make a cake?"

"Yup. Easy."

Claire nods. She's slightly impressed. She carries a handful of beers into the dining room and dumps them on the table.

Robbie takes one. "Thanks. So what is Mia doing?"

Claire shakes her head. "Being insane. And making dessert. I'll be back."

"Dessert?" Nina asks. "Awesome."

Claire spins on her heels and goes back into the kitchen.

"Have you come to watch greatness in the making?" Mia laughs as she cracks an egg into a bowl and then drains the last of her beer.

"I think I should supervise this little drunken episode." Claire sits on a stool at the bench, happy to feel that familiar lightness with Mia again. It's great to find this ability to go back and forth like this, no matter how freaking confused she actually is. But she doesn't want to think about that right now. Instead, she opens her beer and watches Mia bake, enjoying the cute look of concentration she gets on her face as she expertly measures sugar into a cup and uses a knife to swipe away the excess that spills over the top.

"Ah, thanks Claire." Mia suddenly snatches the beer from her and swigs from it. She puts it next to the bowl and grins playfully at her.

Claire sighs and goes to the fridge to get herself another one. "I can't believe we even have the ingredients to make a cake." She shakes her head, unable to conjure a single instance in her memory when her mother or anyone else might have baked something here.

"We brought up the eggs and butter, and I found flour and sugar and cocoa and stuff in the cupboard." Mia frowns. "That's okay, isn't it?"

"Of course. I just didn't know my mother even knew what to do with things like flour and cocoa."

"Well, they were here. So someone does."

"How do you just randomly know how to make a cake?" Claire watches her sift flour into the bowl and stir it, still pretty impressed by this casual show of culinary skill.

"Dad. He taught me. And it's pretty basic."

"Yeah, for some." Claire sighs and sips her beer. "I can barely scramble an egg. I can't cook anything. And I can't play poker, either, it turns out. I am seriously lacking in the skills department, I think." She leans her cheek on her hand and watches the batter smooth out from a lumpy brown mess to a silky chocolate mixture under Mia's ministrations.

Mia points at her with the spoon again. "That is so unbelievably not true. For one, you are a freakishly fast swimmer."

"Yeah, well, that's what my dad taught me so I wouldn't drown in the lake when I was a kid. And it's not about being fast, Mia." She uses her best gruff-dad voice. "It's about being efficient with your stroke."

Mia laughs and goes on, "And you can insult people in French. In fact, you can read entire books in French." She shakes her head. "I couldn't read a bus timetable in another language if I tried. You have skills, Claire."

"Yeah, yeah."

Mia goes back to her cake.

Claire smiles and watches her work. Typical Mia. She wasn't fishing for compliments or reassurance, but it doesn't matter. Mia gave them to her anyway. Because she's like that.

Mia lifts the spoon out of the bowl, taps it on the edge, and lays it across the top. "One thing I haven't found yet, though, is a cake pan." She leans over and starts hunting through the cupboards under the counter. "Any ideas?"

"Maybe in the pantry?" Claire climbs off her chair. "I think we used to keep some cooking stuff in there." She goes over to the huge, old, walk-in pantry, a little room stacked with shelf upon shelf of cans and packets and jars and kitchenware accumulated through the years. Mia follows her in, and they comb the shelves.

Claire stands on her tiptoes and pushes aside large serving bowls to search behind them. "What am I looking for, exactly?"

"I told you. A cake pan." Mia hunts at the other end of the shelf.

"Yeah, but what does it look like?" She yanks out a large, flat tray. "Like this?"

"What?" Mia laughs as she takes the tray out of her hands and holds it up. "What exactly do you want the cake to look like when it's done, Claire? A doormat?"

"I don't know, Mia." Claire sighs loudly. "I told you, I plead ignorance on this whole baking thing."

"I just didn't realise *how* ignorant." Mia turns on her. Her mouth is serious, but her eyes are laughing. "Really, Claire, you don't know what a cake pan looks like?"

Claire shrugs. She really doesn't.

Mia laughs and continues to rummage.

"Ah ha!" she cries a minute later and reaches deep into a shelf. She turns to Claire and holds aloft a deep round tin. "This, Claire, this is what a cake pan looks like, for future baking reference."

"Hey, no judging." Claire giggles and swats at her jeering grin. "You're the one who is drinking and baking. Keep this up and I won't help you at all."

Laughing, Mia grabs at the hand and pulls it away. She doesn't let it go, but holds it in the air between them instead.

For the longest moment they look at each other as some unnameable something passes between them. Mia bites her lip and then smiles a tiny smile, her face flushed with beer and baking and whatever is currently charging the air between them. She drops Claire's hand but leans slightly closer to her.

Claire stares right back at her. There is a buzzing through her body as she wonders if what she thinks is about to happen really is about to happen.

And then they are kissing again.

Just testing, Claire tells herself as she automatically responds to the thrill by clasping the back of Mia's neck with one hand. And the kiss shifts quickly from something tentative to something deeper.

At first, Mia doesn't touch her. Her hands stay put, somewhere down where she's leaned back against the shelves. But then mouths open, and tongues are suddenly, electrifyingly, involved, and Claire feels a hand ease cautiously around her waist and stop on the small of her back. Mia's fingers rest lightly on the exposed skin where her top has ridden up.

Oh shit. A rush of blood centres on the feel of that hand.

This is going to be a problem.

Because it's the small but somehow mammoth presence of those fingers alighting on Claire's bare skin that answers her question about Mia. It's the place where the thrill starts and radiates outward as they lean deeper into the kiss. It's the epicentre of the newfound truth that she's into Mia in a way she can no longer just fleetingly suspect, let alone try and push away.

Claire reaches out and steadies herself on a shelf. Cans and jars shift as they lean back, but their lips don't part ways for a second. At first, all she can hear is this kind of loud humming in her ears and the sound of their breath as she slides her hand from under Mia's hair and cups her cheek. Those fingers on her back press in just a little harder in response.

They are jolted from this moment when Pete shouts from the dining room.

"Hey, Claire, are you in this round?"

"And Mia!" another voice calls. "Where the hell is this dessert?"

She hears the sound of a chair scraping against the wooden floor. And that's all it takes for that hand—and that feeling—to desert her, and for the charge in the air to evaporate.

Footsteps come toward the kitchen. Claire pulls back, and her eyes go wide as she gulps for air.

When Mia meets her gaze and sees her expression, her face also changes.

Just as Claire is about to smile, to try and say something to keep them in this moment, a look passes over Mia's face. She places a hand fleetingly on Claire's hip, but only to use it as leverage to edge her way out from between her and the shelves. She slips out of the pantry and back into the kitchen, the cake pan somehow still miraculously held, jeeringly mundane, in her other hand.

Claire is left alone to regain her breath and her grip on what just happened and why the hell it *stopped* happening. She tries frantically to assess what that look on Mia's face might mean while it's still clear in her mind. Was it disconcertion or regret?

Mia chats to someone in the kitchen as if nothing of any magnitude even happened, as if there hasn't been a seismic shift between them in the last few minutes. Claire orders herself to pull it together. She takes a deep breath, tugs at the back of her top, and quickly grabs up something she's pretty sure is baking related—some vanilla essence—and brings it out into the kitchen as an alibi.

It doesn't matter anyway. Nina is too busy delightedly watching Mia pour the cake mix into the pan to even notice her. Mia slides the cake in the oven, then takes the mixing bowl and spoon to the sink. She glances at Claire and meets her gaze for the briefest of seconds before she returns to her task. Her expression tells Claire nothing.

Claire puts the small bottle on the bench and walks unsteadily past. She stalks into the living room and takes her seat at the table.

"Good timing." Robbie holds up a bottle of tequila. "We've decided this deal is the tequila deal. Shot?"

"Yes." Claire nods numbly but doesn't meet his gaze. She wonders how many minutes have passed in real time since she left the table. And yes, she'd really like a drink. A serious drink. A tequila-shaped drink.

Then Nina returns with Mia behind her, fragments of that unreadable look still on her face. She sits at the far end of the table. As far away as she can possibly get, Claire can't help noticing.

Robbie turns to her. "Shot, Mia?"

She nods, definite. "Shot."

* * *

Later, thoroughly drunk but unable to sleep, Claire lays on top of the covers and tries to make sense of this night and of the way something partly unconscious has suddenly become very, very conscious.

Just to be sure, she asks herself the question again. *Claire, do you have a thing for Mia?*

This time she's pretty damn sure she knows the answer. *Yes.*

It doesn't matter if the kiss was cut short. It confirmed all she needs to know. There is no point telling herself otherwise. She has some sort of crush on Mia. And it's more than emotional. This truth no longer comprises wanting to talk to her, to be in her radius. No, what she wants from Mia has just as much to do with that kiss and that hand on the skin of her back as it does with as any other connection they've made. There's no other way to explain away what she felt during that kiss.

It explains *everything*, in fact. It explains that strange, slightly sick feeling that rippled queasily through her when she saw that girl first touch Mia and then lead her off the roof. Claire knew full well in the pit of her gut what was about to happen. It explains why she hasn't stopped thinking about it. It explains why she left Jeremy on a street corner instead of going home with him and why she hasn't returned his calls. It explains her awkwardness in the café on the Sunday after the party and her unwillingness to hug Mia this morning, to show affection despite her surge of pleasure at her arrival.

And she knows she would have kept whatever was going in the pantry going if they hadn't been disturbed, and if Mia hadn't backed off like that.

And now, faced with these feelings, she's also confronted by that fact that Mia didn't talk to her or look at her for the rest of the night. And Claire has no idea what this means, or what the regret she thinks she saw in Mia's eyes means. Was it regret that they were caught or that it happened at all?

Even though she has her question answered, Claire isn't sure it leaves her any better off given the way Mia reacted. She crawls into the bed fully dressed and focuses on the nauseous twist of her stomach and the slight spin of the room as she shuts her eyes.

Tomorrow is going to hurt.

CHAPTER 43

Uh-huh. Morning hurts.

Claire pulls the sheet up around her head to block out the insistent light. It doesn't help much, though. The bright sun easily pierces the white cotton and beams doggedly at her eyelids. She woke in that very unsweet spot that is late morning when the sun makes a pass straight through the trees by the lake and hits the sleeping porch at full, early-summer throttle. Usually when they come to stay, she'd be up and out of bed well before this moment of torture. But not today. Not after last night.

All she can hear of the world outside is the distant motor of a boat and the busy, argumentative strains of magpie song from the trees nearby. She feels the makings of a solid hangover in the thrumming ache just above her eyes and the queasy bass notes in her stomach. She eases herself onto her back, drapes her arm over her eyes, and frowns. It would help if the curtains were closed, but she clearly forgot to do that in her drunken lurch toward bed last night.

Last night.

At the very thought, she pulls in a breath, holds it for a moment, and then lets it out in a fitful sigh. Last night was all over the messy place. In just a few hours, she managed to run the gamut of moods. First it was fun and easy, then it was hopeful, and then it was kind of hot and revelatory. And then, somehow it was depressing and uncomfortable.

Claire cannot figure it out. What made Mia veer so dramatically from being that messy, funny, and flirtatious version of herself in the pantry to this closed-off stranger sitting at the other end of the table, who looked anywhere but at the person *she* just kissed, a person she seemed to enjoy kissing.

Claire does *not* get it.

It's the inconsistency that throws her the most. In most other ways, Mia always seems so steady, so composed, and so sure of herself. Except during exam time. Claire didn't think Mia did flighty. But maybe she does. Maybe it's just like last time when she ran. Only this time she has nowhere to run.

Claire stretches her bare legs out against the sheets and sighs. That's the most pressing problem of now—what will Mia be like today?

And how is Claire supposed to behave? Is she supposed to pretend it was nothing, like last time? Is that the cue she should take from Mia's withdrawal last night? With a hangover already determined to render her fragile, Claire doesn't know how she's going to perform if she's greeted with the same confounding silent treatment.

In fact, faced with that potential, she doesn't want to do this day at all.

She rolls onto her side, opens her eyes, and measures the assault of light on her hangover. Nope, it definitely does not feel great to be awake today. She contemplates the idea of staying in bed, of curling under the sheet, and sleeping until this day is gone. But somehow she knows it won't fly with the others. They'll come for her eventually.

She peels herself from the bed.

* * *

It's apparent from the moment Claire stumbles back into the house that Mia is going to pretend it didn't happen. She and Robbie are already in the kitchen, trying to wrangle the coffee machine into producing coffee. They look as shabby as Claire feels.

"Hey." Claire feels a slight flush in her cheeks as she sits down at the bench.

"Hey." Robbie leans over and peers behind the machine to play with cords. "How does this thing work?"

Mia gives Claire a brief, bland smile and looks back at what Robbie is doing.

Claire feels a small wave of sickness. She's not sure if it's more closely related to Mia's obtuse reaction to her presence or to her actual hangover. Either way, it doesn't feel good.

"I feel gross." She shuts her eyes and places her hands flat against the cool kitchen counter in the hope it will steady the turbulent, seasick feeling.

Robbie nods. "So do I. And I need coffee. So pretty please get up and make this thing work, damn it."

"I don't know how it works." Claire presses her fingers to her temples and stares helplessly at him.

"What? It's your coffee machine. How do you not know how to work it?"

Claire holds up her hands. "It's my parents' coffee machine, not mine. Dad wakes so early that by the time I get up, there's always coffee ready. And Eli made it yesterday."

Robbie clicks his fingers. "Of course! Eli knows how to use it. We need Eli. I'm going to wake him." He stalks out of the room.

And the minute he exits, Mia mutters something about a shower and makes her own rapid departure.

Claire sighs into her hands. So this is how it's going to be.

And that's exactly what it's like all day. Mia keeps a purposeful distance from her, quietly ensuring that they are never alone in the same space together. And it makes Claire feel awful. She knows Mia would never deliberately be mean. Claire's pretty sure she doesn't even know how to be mean. Mia does, it seems, know how to stay out of the way if she wants. And she knows how to stick to Robbie's side, or to Pete's, so Claire can't get near her. Not that Claire knows what she would do with her.

So, helpless to do anything else, she does what Mia's behaviour asks of her and spends what's left of the morning on the deck with her book. Then in the afternoon, when the day becomes hot, she goes out to swim in the lake alone. She turns languid meditative laps between the diving platform and the rocks and tries to empty her mind of all these busy, painful thoughts. It doesn't work, of course, but the cool undemanding flow of the water around her makes her feel a little better.

CHAPTER 44

In the hot, late afternoon, Claire wanders onto the porch, restless and bored and tired of being alone. Nina is there, perched on one of the railings, scribbling furiously in a notebook.

Claire lowers herself sideways across the hammock and idly watches Nina. So Nina does write. She has only ever heard her talk about it. She writes quickly, too, covering the page with a big looping letters as her tongue pokes out between her front teeth. Claire smiles at her industriousness, the way she tucks her hair behind her ear, quickly flicks over to the next page, and continues to scribble down a thought. She's never seen her friend so serious.

Settling back against the clinging embrace of the hammock, Claire uses her feet to push it into a slight swinging motion, just like she used to do when she was a kid. Then, as a small wave of nausea rises through her, she puts her feet down quickly to stop it. Bad idea.

Nina eventually looks up. She chews her pen and squints at Claire. "Hi."

Claire gives her a mellow smile. "Hey. What are you writing?"

Nina closes the book. "Nothing. Just something dumb."

Claire nods but doesn't ask anything more. She's curious about Nina and her writing, but she can't be bothered to penetrate Nina's coyness. "Where is everyone?" she asks instead.

Nina rests her head against the post, kicks out her legs, and puts the book down next to her. "Robbie and Eli are at the lake. And Pete's hiking into town." She shakes her head. "Where is town, anyway? Is it far?"

Claire raises her eyebrows. "Yeah, it's pretty far. Why didn't he just drive?"

"I have no idea. I think he actually wanted to walk. Weirdo."

Claire smiles her agreement as she lies there and contemplates the incredible stillness of the day. Usually there is at least a light breeze coming off the lake, keeping the trees restless and the air cool, but not today. The only sounds are the chime of a bellbird somewhere in the trees and that dull clang of the pipes being used somewhere in the house.

"Dan messaged me this morning."

Claire reluctantly pulls her thoughts and her gaze back to Nina. She's smiling shyly.

It takes Claire a moment to remember who Dan is such is the state of her brain today. Then she does. "Really?"

"Yeah, he asked me to go on a date when we get back from here." Nina laughs and shakes her head. "I don't think I've been on a date since high school."

"Hang on; have you seen him since the party?" Claire asks, surprised. She assumed Nina saw him again at some point.

"Nope." Nina shakes her head. "We've talked on the phone a couple of times, but I wanted to...I don't know...take it slow?" she says as if this is still an alien concept she's toying with.

"Wow." Claire is impressed. Nina really does seem to be taking that self-help book of hers seriously. "So, he's into you. And you're into him?"

Nina tips her head to the side and thinks about it. "Yeah, both."

Claire is silent for a minute, wishing she could feel that same kind of simplicity right now. Then she finally looks over at her friend. "That's great, Neen. Really, it is."

Nina smiles and turns her pen between her fingers.

The screen door suddenly opens and Mia slips through it, Blue at her heels. She's in her shorts and a tank, carrying runners.

"Hey." She kind of smiles but doesn't look directly at either of them as she walks past and sits on the wooden step to pull on her shoes.

"Hey," Claire mutters, feeling the instant pierce of hurt.

Blue trots over and rests his snout on the edge of the hammock.

"Hi," Nina says. Then she turns straight back to Claire. "What about you? Have you heard from Jeremy?"

"Yeah, a couple of times." Claire blushes and bites her lip as she strokes the soft fur between Blue's ears. Wow, of all the crappy timing, Nina has to mention *that* now?

Her gaze flicks toward Mia. Her shoes now laced, she stands up quickly and ties up her hair into a knot behind her head. She gives off no sense of whether she took in what Claire just said. As soon as Blue sees her stand, he bolts down the steps of the veranda, immediately on high walk alert. Mia pulls her earphones out of her pocket and untangles the cord.

"What are you up to, Mia?" Nina asks.

Mia turns, holding her earphones next to her ears. "Taking Blue for a run." She jogs a little on the spot as if to test her legs.

"A run? After last night?" Nina gasps and shakes her head. "Is this self-punishment of some sort?"

Mia half laughs and rests her hands on her hips. "No, it actually makes me feel better."

Nina's nose wrinkles. "Really? I don't get it, but I fully support you, Mia. Please don't die out there."

Mia laughs, plugs her earphones into her ear, and gives a little wave. Then she jogs away from them in long even strides as Blue bolts backward and forward across the path a few paces ahead of her.

Nina sighs loudly and scratches her ear with her pen. "Who are these people we came here with? One's hiking into town? Another is jogging? Did we just bring them here to make us feel bad about ourselves? I can't tell if I'm jealous of their wholesomeness or disgusted by it."

Claire watches Mia pace away down the track that leads around to the far side of the lake and nods. "Yeah, they're not like us lazy folk, that's for sure."

"I think they might be like dogs, you know, and we're more like cats."

Claire laughs. "What? Uh, okay. You write that incredible metaphor down, Neen. For later."

"Shut up, Claire." Nina smiles, but she looks a little hurt too.

"Hey, I'm kidding. I know what you mean." Instantly contrite, Claire watches Nina frown as she runs a finger over the cover of her notebook. Claire bites her lip. Why does she always pick on Nina? There's no need to tease her just because Claire's a hot mess today. "I'm sorry. Ignore me. I'm just being a bitch because I'm tired and hungover and..." She stops, not knowing what she could tack onto that sentence that she'd be willing to say aloud. So she starts again. "Well, I'm tired and hungover and this is how I get when no one puts me down for my afternoon nap."

Nina lets her off with a small snicker.

Relieved, Claire sits up and yawns. "So I think I better do it myself." She climbs off the hammock and stretches. "I'll see you later."

Nina nods and opens her book again.

Claire starts to walks toward her room but then pauses and turns to Nina, curious. "Do you think you'll ever let me read something you write?"

"Maybe," Nina replies. She holds the book close to her in a way that tells Claire it would be a big ask.

Claire nods and leaves her there on the porch.

* * *

Alone again, Claire lies on her bed. She stares at the shadows of the trees that lace the white walls with a frenzy of patterns and still feels traces of shame at teasing Nina. She fights a sudden urge to cry. She just feels wrong today, wrong and awkward, and as if she can't be comfortable in her own skin.

And the worst part is she feels like this even when Mia isn't around. The feeling and the distance are there whether Mia is or not. But when she *is* there of course it's even worse. She cannot handle this polite, distanced version of Mia. Something has to give.

Claire sighs and pouts at the wall, glad no one's around to witness her acting like an angsty teenager. She doesn't want to be, but sadly that's how she feels today, like an inexperienced adolescent who has no idea how to behave in front of the person she likes, a person who's busily ignoring her.

Claire's never been this person before. And she's never had to be proactive. Guys have always pursued her, been at the mercy of her whims, her level of interest, *her* decisions about how something would play out. Usually it's been them, frustrated and demanding to know what she wants. Now she's quickly learning the insecurity that comes with being at the other end of this power dynamic.

And she's certainly never experienced this sudden change from friendship to something more either. Never has she experienced this sudden, perplexing shift in the nature of her feelings about someone. In the past, guys were either her friends, or they were more, or they were nothing at all. Those lines never felt blurred. Nor did they suddenly shift when she wasn't looking, throwing everything into chaos.

And to make this even more of a brave new world of weirdness, she's never had feelings for a girl either. That's probably a whole other universe of confusion that might or might not be coming to a town near her. But right now, Claire has time only for the immediate concern of her confounding new feelings for *Mia*. What that might mean in the bigger picture can wait.

Claire stares at the ceiling and wishes she had someone she could ask about how to deal with this mess she's gotten herself into.

The crappy thing is Mia's the one she would probably talk to about something like this. But it's Mia she's getting all deranged about. She can't talk to Robbie. Claire already learned the hard and slightly embarrassing way where his loyalty firmly lies. And Nina's a sweetheart, but she's not really the kind of person Claire can have these kinds of conversations with. And Nina will probably think she's talking about Jeremy and get all excited.

She rubs her hand across her forehead and presses in softly on the site of her headache. That means there's only one person who she trusts and who might be able to make this all a bit clearer. She grabs her phone out of her bag.

Cam picks up straight away. That's the bonus of having him laid up. He's actually around.

"Hey, what's up?" he says by way of greeting.

Suddenly feeling completely ridiculous, Claire just plunges in. "Okay, I cannot believe I'm even asking you this, but I don't know who else to ask, so I'm asking you," she tells him without taking a breath.

"Asking...what?" He sounds wary. He should.

"Have you ever been friends with someone, and then kind of gotten a...thing for them, but you're just supposed to be friends?"

Cam is silent for a second, clearly processing the question. "Hey, this isn't that Robbie guy you've been hanging with, is it? The one I met at the gallery? Because Claire, I'm pretty sure he's not into lady parts."

"No." She rolls her eyes. "I am well aware of that. It doesn't matter who it is. Answer the question."

"Okay, bossy." He's quiet for a moment. "I don't know. I don't think so. I've had girls I liked and gotten friend zoned, but the other way around? Claire, I don't have that many friends who are girls, if you hadn't noticed."

She nods. It's true. Cam is very much a guy's guy when it comes to his friendship group.

"Don't you have some chick friend you can talk with about this?"

"Not really. Not right now." *And that's the problem*, she thinks but doesn't say. He doesn't need the details. "So, if you were in that situation, what would you do? Hypothetically?"

He chuckles into the phone. "Okay, well then, the only obvious solution, sister dear, is to get shit-faced drunk with them and see if something happens. That's what I'd do."

Claire sighs. "Been there."

"And?"

"That's when things happen. But then it's like it didn't happen when we're sober again."

"Oh, well, Claire, I don't know. I think you are going to have to do what we Pearsons love to do."

She narrows her eyes. "What?"

"Head on confrontation."

She groans. That's precisely what she wants to avoid.

He knows exactly what she's thinking. "I know, but if you like him that much, you are just going to have to ask."

"Crap." Claire slaps her hand down on the bedcovers.

"Look, I know you're used to dudes lining up at the door, begging for your princess act, but maybe, just maybe, you've found someone where *you* are going to have to do a little work."

"Shut up."

"I hope he's worth it."

"Well, that was no help." She changes the subject. "So, how are you doing anyway?"

"Okay. And sick of being asked that."

"I won't then."

"But I have nothing else to talk about either." He sighs loudly into the phone. "It's all about physio, bed rest, and TV at the moment. I've got nothing. When are you coming back from the cottage?

"In a few days, before Mum and Dad come up."

He laughs. "Of course. Well, come over and bring me some Ping's when you come back. I'm at Elana's for the rest of the week."

"Really?" Claire rolls her eyes. Why does he keep going back for more?

"Yeah, she loves me again. Seems she likes to play nurse. Anyway, when you get back, I want greasy Chinese food like only you know how to find. Elana keeps feeding me steamed vegetables and rice."

"Ugh, sure. I'll bring it." She smiles and picks at a piece of grass caught on her T-shirt. "Even if you do give shitty advice."

"Well, you have shitty problems."

"Thanks, Cam. No really. See you." She hangs up on him, tosses the phone onto the bed and sighs. Confrontation? That's his advice? She sighs loudly. Does she really have to?

CHAPTER 45

It gets to the point where Claire has no choice. Her need for clarity forces her to act. She must end this day less blindly than it started, so she decides to *make* Mia talk to her. First though, she has to get her alone. She gets her chance much later that night.

She sits on the porch, waiting for her opportunity. The screen door slams, and Robbie stops on the step next her. "We're going for a night swim. You going to come?"

She leans back against the porch post and rubs her eyes. "No, I don't feel like it."

"Okay. See you soon. Hurry up, guys!" he yells over his shoulder.

Nina and the others dash out of the house, towels in hands.

"Come on, Claire," Pete calls out as they take off down the track. "It'll make you feel better."

Claire doesn't answer. Finally, the screen door opens and shuts again, quieter this time, and Mia crosses the porch, Blue just behind her. She smiles briefly but keeps moving. Claire almost lets her pass. But at the last minute, she hauls in courage from nowhere.

"Mia?" Claire says quietly just as she's about to disappear down the path.

Mia stops in her tracks and turns slowly. Her hair is bunched on top of her head, and her towel is wrapped around her neck. She looks as exhausted as Claire feels.

"Yup?" she answers lightly as if she hasn't ignored Claire all day, as if there's no tension at all, as if she hasn't deliberately put as much distance as humanly possible between them. She whistles for Blue, who has already taken off down the path. He trots out of the darkness and begins to weave his way in and out of the scrub nearby.

For a second, Mia's lightness works, and Claire wonders if she's making something from nothing. But if it were nothing, Mia wouldn't have pulled away like that. Claire swallows hard.

"What's going on...with us?" She pulls her knees up to her chin as she asks and hugs her legs. She feels her face turning pink, all her bravery spent in the asking of that one question.

Mia feigns innocence. "What do you mean?"

Claire takes a slow breath, harnessing her growing frustration. She will *not* let Mia play dumb. Her dignity won't allow it. "You know what I mean." She's almost terse. "We kissed last night."

Mia nods, but she doesn't say anything. Instead, she stares at her feet.

Claire tries again. "We kissed last night *again*. And, I don't know..." She raises her hands in frustration. "Now it's weird. Actually, it's been weird for a while, and I..." she falters, helpless to articulate the unspoken current that's running between them. But at least Mia can't pretend she doesn't know exactly what she's talking about.

Mia nods again. "I was kind of hoping you didn't remember," she mumbles.

"Well, I do." And Claire wants to say she wasn't even that drunk last night. Not at that point anyway, but she also hasn't decided if she wants that fact to be known. "And you know, even if I didn't, don't you think I would have noticed that you've basically been ignoring me all day? That you've been avoiding me?"

Mia takes in a deep breath and looks up at her. "I'm sorry." She says it quietly, her eyes steadfast.

Claire blinks. She's not quite sure what to do with an apology. She's not even sure what it is that Mia is sorry for exactly.

Finally Mia takes another breath and speaks. "I mean, I was just drunk, and it was dumb. I didn't mean to confuse things between us or to freak you out."

"You didn't freak me out." It's probably only half the truth, but she's pretty sure they are talking about freaked out in different ways right now. "What freaks me out is that you won't even look at me today."

"I'm sorry," Mia says again.

"Stop saying you're sorry."

"Okay, sor—" Mia closes her mouth quickly, and despite the tension, they smile at each other.

Then Claire leans in and takes a deep breath. "It's just, it's been totally weird with us today, and…I don't know…I just want to know what's going on…in your head. That's all."

Mia bites her lip. "Too much. Everything. I don't know."

"Why?" Claire hugs her knees harder and stares at her.

"I shouldn't have done it." Mia presses her lips together. She looks as uneasy and on edge as Claire feels. She doesn't speak for a minute, but Claire waits it out. Mia digs at the ground with her toe, her arms folded tightly across her chest. "Because I'm pretty sure I'm gay," she finally says and steals a look at Claire before her gaze returns to the ground.

Claire stares at her for a moment and tries to make sense of how these facts connect together in the immediate now.

"You know how little sense that makes, right, Mia?" She smiles, sly, unable to help herself. "Who do you think you should have kissed, then? Eli?"

Mia gives her a tiny smile, enough to acknowledge the joke, but then her expression slides back into tension.

"So, you like girls?" Claire lets go of her legs, stretches them down to the bottom step, and tries to sound as casual as possible, as if this news is not even the slightest big deal. She leans back on her hands and looks up at Mia.

Mia pushes her hands into the pockets of her cut-offs and stares off to where Blue is busy hunting. "Yeah, I think so."

Claire thinks back to the night of the party when she asked Robbie just that same question and what he said about Mia figuring herself out. Clearly sometime between then and now, she figured it out. She asks the question she's wanted to ask for days. "That girl? From the party? Do you like her?"

Mia shakes her head. "No. Well…" She shrugs. "In the moment I did, maybe. We were just drunk, and it seemed like a good idea." She digs at the pebbles on the path with the end of her sandal. "I was just…I don't know…trying to make sense of…" She shrugs again and gives up. "I haven't seen her since."

"Did anything happen with her?"

Mia's face turns pink. "Yeah."

Even though she knows it's none of her business, she can't help herself. "Did you sleep with her?"

Mia stares at the ground for a long moment. Finally, she nods slowly.

Claire blinks, not sure why something she's pretty sure she already knew makes her feel so sick all over again.

"Anyway," Mia says quietly as she folds her arms over her chest. She glances briefly at Claire before turning just as quickly away. "Last night, I was really drunk, and I'm sorry."

For drunkenly kissing me, or kissing me at all? But at the same time, she's too scared to find out. So what she asks is the simplest version of the question and leaves it in Mia's hands. "Why?"

"Because. I shouldn't be doing stupid things like that."

"Right." Claire swallows. She gets her answer anyway. She can feel the tears prick at her eyes.

"I mean, I should probably be going out to gay bars like Robbie says and meeting other lesbians instead of doing dumb things like getting drunk and making out with my friend and making things weird like this." She holds up her hands, helpless, and trails off. "It was stupid and trashy."

Claire stares at her and blinks hard because she doesn't want to do something embarrassing like cry. And what starts as hurt turns quickly—easily—to anger. "Yeah well," she mutters through gritted teeth because those tears are coming anyway. "I have to say that makes me feel *really* good. It's always so nice to be something trashy and stupid, to be something to regret."

For the first time since they started this conversation, Mia looks right at her, and she looks surprised to see Claire's hurt. She shakes her head, her eyes wide. "I didn't mean it like that."

Mia looks shocked. And defeated. Part of Claire feels sorry for her, but a bigger part of her feels sorrier for herself. Mia is one of the few people in her life who never made her feel like crap. Until right now.

"I'm going to bed." She leaves Mia there on the path in the darkness.

As she stalks into the sleeping porch and shuts the door firmly behind her, she hears the slow footsteps as Mia walks back into the house and closes the door behind her.

* * *

Claire drops onto the bed and lets go of the threatening, invading tears.

That went so, *so* badly.

She is such an idiot. A stupid, stupid idiot who's been getting all hopeful about something she has no stupid business being hopeful about at all.

She should have realised what this is with Mia. Claire's an experiment, lumped in with that girl at the party. She's just a part of Mia's drunken solution to figuring it out, some trashy, hot mess placebo to make out with when she's drunk until she finds a real girlfriend. Just a step along a road to somewhere better, to something real.

She turns onto her stomach. God, why does everyone think she's not enough of...*whatever?* Insert desired quality here. She's not driven enough to hang out with her friends who want to be lawyers and bankers. She's not a good enough friend to be trusted to keep her hands off people's boyfriends. And now she's not gay enough or smart enough or normal enough for Mia to consider outside of the shit-faced-drunk zone. It's enough to have a mother who thinks she isn't good enough. She doesn't need everyone else to chime in too.

She wishes she hadn't talked to Cam, that she hadn't gotten so close to the brink of utter frustration that she acted on his stupid advice. But what's most painful and humiliating is the sickening realisation that she should have thought about the reality of this a little more. She should have thought harder about what she was seriously considering that Mia, even if she's into girls, would contemplate her as a possibility.

Seriously. She swipes at another obstinate tear. What was she doing thinking someone as smart and incredible as Mia would think of her as a serious option? Someone like Mia will have all the choices when she actually gets out there properly. Why would she be interested in Claire? Claire's a straight girl with a zero track record in relationships, no life plans, and a shitty attitude.

She pulls a pillow over her head and sniffs. What a stupid, stupid freaking idiot she's been. She squeezes her eyes shut and wishes she were anywhere but here.

CHAPTER 46

When she wakes in the brand new light of the morning, Claire pushes her face into the pillow and shudders as she recalls the scene on the porch the night before. She squeezes her eyes closed and hopes Mia doesn't know the real reason she was upset, that she'll just assume Claire was insulted at being called trashy.

Which of course she is.

But right now that's the least of her problems. Of course, she'd love to be mad at Mia. She'd love to be furious. But she can't. And besides, Claire knows she didn't mean it quite like that. Mia would never say something so purposefully hurtful. Claire might. But not Mia. But to hear her, however unconsciously, dismiss her like that? *That* hurt. And the last thing she needs to add to that pain is the humiliation of Mia knowing. So she decides to combat this the only way she knows how—total avoidance.

As a point of pride, of dignity, she decides she's going to be completely and utterly normal. Claire's going to take on the responsibility of letting things fall back into place as easily as they can. And if it's still weird between them after that, let it be Mia's fault.

Yep, that's what she'll do. Claire will give nothing away, nothing at all. And she hopes that Mia doesn't think too hard about what passed between them last night, lest she realises Claire's feelings have stupidly strayed to places they have no business going. And if she's really, really lucky, Mia won't work it out, and Claire will get to step back from this brink unscathed, unnoticed. And then she'll figure out how to get over this stupid crush so they can be friends again.

She's determined this will be a day when she's going to do her damn best not to have any of these stupid, pointless *feelings*. She will not let them get in the way of finding her way back to normal.

Whatever that is.

* * *

"What are you going to do?" Claire asks Robbie as she puts the phone back on the hall table and steps out onto the porch into the morning sunshine.

Robbie grins. "We are going to fulfil Nina's dreams and take her to a country show. She's never been to one, and Pete saw a sign for that one yesterday when he was walking back from the store. You coming?"

"Much as I'd love to," she tells him sarcastically as they sit on the steps together in the sun. "Dad called and I have to stick around here. Some guy might be coming to check the water heater this morning, and on the chance of that *might*, I said I'd stay around to let him in."

"Poor you. What a missed opportunity to watch me comparison shop for organic pumpkins or something." Robbie rolls his eyes and sips his coffee. "Like the middle-aged man I'm bound to become."

Claire smiles, rubs her grainy eyes, and thinks how good it's going be to have some time alone.

He bumps her shoulder with his. "You okay?"

"Yeah, I'm just tired." She avoids his gaze and watches Pete stride up the lake path, towel around his neck. They say nothing as he grins and scurries up the steps past them. Then Robbie suddenly picks up her hand from her knee and kind of plays with it, passing it back and forth between his own. "You know, I can't figure you out sometimes, Claire." Then he smiles at her. "Or maybe I can."

She frowns, takes her hand back, and folds her arms over her knees. "What are you talking about?"

"Oh well, we'll see." He nods his head gently.

She frowns. She has absolutely no idea what this particular cryptic Robbie crap means, so she decides to ignore it. She slaps her hand gently on his knee and then uses it to push herself off the step. "Have a great time confronting your middle-aged self. I am going to lie around and read."

Back in her room, she changes into what has been her daily uniform of swimmers, shorts, and a T-shirt and listens to the sounds of everyone calling to one another as they prepare to leave. Finally, the car doors slam, the tires crunch on gravel, and they're gone. Silence reigns.

Relieved, she grabs her book and heads out onto the porch. Having this morning to herself is a reprieve, of sorts. She won't have to act for anyone, free to spend a little longer feeling shitty and sad and kind of helpless about all this.

She's about to flop onto the hammock when she hears the door open behind her. She jumps and then turns. It's Mia, a towel over her shoulder and a book in her hand. She looks tired, and her unusually pale skin makes her freckles stand out. She holds up her book. "Snap," she says with a wry, cautious smile.

Claire drops her gaze to her feet. "I thought everyone had gone."

"I stayed. You want to go down to the water?"

Claire bites her lip, turns her book in her hand, and contemplates the invitation. She reminds herself of her promise to return to normal today. "Okay," she says finally. "Give me a second."

She goes back to her room, takes a deep breath, and grabs a towel and her flip-flops. They walk slowly down the steps and tread the path in silence as the sun beams down on their backs. When they get to the end of the short path, Mia moves toward the spot where they have been swimming the last few days.

"Let's go this way." Claire points to where a track, worn down through the years by feet in the grass, cuts away from the path. Mia nods, and Claire leads them to a sheltered spot where a tract of wide, flat rocks sprawl down to the water's edge, surrounded by a fringe of trees. Claire clambers from rock to rock with Mia close behind. She stops at a spot where some of the rocks are shaded, while others bake slowly in the sunlight. Stepping over to a shaded rock, she stands next to one exposed to the full sun.

She lays out her towel, throws down her book, and puts her phone where she'll hear it in case this water-heater guy rings. Easing herself slowly down on the edge of the rock, her toes curl as they greet the cold water below. She sees Mia smile as she realises why Claire has picked this spot where they can both have their needed sun and shade. She lays down her towel on the sunny spot and mirrors Claire. She lets her feet dangle into the water on her own little island next to her. Claire shrugs inwardly. She didn't mean for it all to be so damn symbolic. She just didn't want to get sunburnt.

They sit there in silence for a while and stare out over the lake. Some kids are throwing themselves off the swimming platform. Their shouts and laughter slide easily across the water to them. They are the first kids she's seen since they arrived. Must be weekenders. In a few weeks, this place will be full of them roaming in packs, just like she and Cam did with all the other cottage kids when they were younger.

After a while, the kids disappear, leaving only the quieter sounds of water lapping at the edges of the rocks and the call of birds in the thick scrub next to her. She lies back on her towel, her arm across her forehead, and gazes at the canopies of the trees. It's so beautiful here. She had forgotten how much she loves it. She takes a deep breath, slowly releases the scent of grass and leaves and fresh air from her lungs, and listens to Blue thirstily lap water from the lake's edge.

"Hey," Mia says just loud enough for Claire to hear her. "I'm really, really sorry about last night."

Claire squints at her.

Mia hugs her legs to her and rests her cheek on her knees.

"Me too," Claire mumbles.

"I really didn't mean to hurt you or to imply anything about *you* at all. It all just came out really wrong."

"It's okay." Claire shrugs as if it's nothing. Of course, she's not sure if it's okay. She tells her that because she doesn't want Mia to feel bad, but also because she doesn't know if she's ready to talk about that part of their conversation yet. Or ever. And she tells her that because she just wants them to be some sort of okay, for this all to hurt a little less.

"Do your parents know?" she asks after a minute, changing the subject. Kind of.

Mia shakes her head. "No. I've just been trying to figure things out for myself before I tell them, you know?"

Claire nods. "What do you think they'll say?" She cannot even imagine how her own parents would react.

"I really don't know." Mia shakes her head and rubs her hands along her forearms.

"Who have you told?"

"No one, really. Robbie. Now you."

Claire contemplates this fact. "How long have *you* known?"

"For a little while." Mia lifts her head and looks out across the lake. "Well, maybe I have kind of subconsciously known for longer, but I guess I really figured it out recently."

"But you only dated guys before?"

"Yeah." Mia nods. "And that was kind of what made me feel so weird. I was dating guys, but I was never as into it as they were. Like, you know, with Pete?"

Claire nods.

"I don't know. He's awesome and lovely and fun, and I like hanging out with him. And he really liked me. But I just always kind of felt like I could take it or leave it. I think I thought I wasn't meeting the right guys or something, or I was terrible at relationships because I'd lose interest quickly. Then last summer, I had this total infatuation with this girl at work. Even then, though, I told myself it was a one-off girl crush or something. I didn't really put it together until later."

"What happened?"

"With the girl? Nothing. I knew she was straight. She graduated and went overseas. It was just when I met Robbie, and he figured it out before me. He *told* me I had a crush on her. He also told me, if I did figure out I was gay, not to fall for straight girls."

Claire frowns. Robbie and his annoyingly sage advice.

"But then, I dated this guy last year, and I was actually into him for a while, and it kind of threw me all over again."

"Then what happened?" Claire blinks. "Sorry, am I asking too many questions?"

"No, it's fine." Mia gives her a tiny smile before she turns toward the water. "I want to talk about it with you."

She's quiet for a while, though. And Claire lets her sort her thoughts out.

Eventually, she speaks again.

"I guess what really messed with me is realising what I always thought I knew about myself was wrong, if you know what I mean? And also that now I have to tell everyone? I don't know. It's weird."

"Telling them that you changed your mind. That you want a do over?"

Mia smiles and nods, wry. "Yeah, I guess."

"And because it makes everything such a big deal?"

"Exactly." She's silent for a while; then she turns to Claire. "I mean, I know I'm smart. I don't mean to brag, or anything, but—"

"Mia, it wouldn't be bragging," Claire interrupts. "It's just kind of a fact."

Mia smiles, but it dissolves quickly into a frown. "This is what I mean. I'm smart enough to graduate top of my high school, to get into my course, to get interviews for the top universities for postgraduate courses…" She sighs and shakes her head. "How could I be too dumb to realise this kind of fundamental thing about myself earlier?"

All Claire can do is nod, sympathetic to the experience of sudden, surprise recognition of the obvious. Because isn't that what just happened to her?

"And, you know, having everyone know while you're going through something isn't going to be that fun. I'm twenty-one." Mia shakes her head. "Who has this crisis at twenty-one?" She dips her head, resting her chin on her knees.

"Probably plenty of people." Because if it's possible for Claire to come this far in her life before knowing it's possible she could like *a* girl, surely it's possible for it to never have occurred to Mia that she likes *girls*.

"Maybe." Mia raises her shoulders to her ears for a moment, her eyes still fixed on the lake.

"So don't tell anyone yet," Claire suggests. She wonders why Mia feels as though she has to let the rest of the world know her feelings anyway. Claire would just as likely keep something like that private unless she wanted to tell someone. Whose business is it anyway?

"But that feels kind of dishonest."

Claire shakes her head. Typical Mia, worrying about how other people will feel about her own major life upheaval. "It's not dishonest, Mia." She sits up and wraps her towel around her shoulders. "It's not dishonest to take some time, you know."

Mia shrugs, clearly not willing to give herself that concession. She pulls off her sunglasses. "I don't know." She sighs. "Wow, I'm saying that a lot. *I don't know.* I'm getting in." She quickly pulls off her T-shirt, throws it onto her towel, and slides into the water feet first.

Claire shuffles to the edge of the rock and dangles her feet in the water again. She watches Mia swim in a slow crawl out past the shadows of the trees to where the sun hits the water. She lies back and floats.

Blue emerges out of the scrub and trots over. He sits next to Claire and sniffs the breeze coming off the lake, his eyes fixed on Mia.

Claire puts an arm around his neck and scratches the fur on his chest. "She's okay. She's just hanging out."

He turns and licks her cheek.

"Gross." She wipes her cheek against her shoulder. "Do you not remember that little chat we had a while back about personal boundaries, hound?" He turns and licks her face again. She shakes her head and laughs. "That's what you get for conversing with a dog." She stares out to where Mia still floats with her hands moving slowly at her sides.

Claire frowns. Poor Mia. She thinks of the months she's known her, how chilled and lovely she is, how good she's been to Claire, how completely present she was for her when Cam was in the hospital even though they've only been friends for such a short time. And all this time she has been trying to figure this major life stuff out on her own. She's not sure if she's ever met someone as generous as Mia. She deserves to get as much as she gives.

And as she watches Mia slowly breaststroke back toward the shore, Claire tells herself that no matter how she feels or how much Mia's words last night unintentionally hurt her, Mia needs her friendship right now. She deserves her turn to be listened to, to be heard, and Claire wants to give her that.

"Coming in?" Mia calls out as she treads water close to the edge.

Claire shakes her head. "It's not warm enough yet."

"Get out of the shade then." She laughs and turns a quick back flip in the water and then glides up to the surface again. She shakes her hair. The spray splashes Claire.

"Watch it." Claire swipes the cold drops from her arms. "You're worse than Blue."

"Sorry." Mia slowly paddles over and folds her arms on the edge of the rock next to Claire's knees and stares into the space in front of her.

She looks a little sad, a little serious, and Claire wonders if she should have asked her quite so many questions. Questions Mia's clearly struggling to find answers to. Before she can stop herself, she reaches out and picks up a strand of hair that hangs over Mia's eye and pushes it back.

Startled, Mia looks up at her.

"It's going to be okay, you know?" Claire takes her hand away, pulls her knees up to her chest, and smiles shyly at her. "It will."

Mia grins. "You hate it when people say that."

"Yeah, but it must be true. Sometimes."

They're still sitting there, enjoying this tender, careful peace they've found with each other again, when the others arrive. They noisily join them on the rocks, full of their morning's trip to the show.

Nina tells them about their day, about the jellies and honeys and relishes they bought and about some crazy beekeeper they met. Claire covers herself in sunscreen and then moves over into the sun to get warm. When she's hot enough, she slides off the rocks and enjoys the rush of cool water over her skin.

The others soon follow, and Robbie and Pete swim out into the sun and carry out an encore performance of their ridiculous synchronised swimming routine.

And in the midst of the cheers and laughter and applause, Claire looks over at Mia. And Mia's already looking at her. They share a private smile, and a sharp sense of relief washes over her. Whatever has happened, they are back in some form. She feels as though she can breathe again.

Everything will be okay, Claire tells herself as she swims slowly out into deeper water. She will be okay. Mia will be okay. And, whatever happens, she and Mia will be okay again too.

CHAPTER 47

"So, where to, Claire?" Pete stands on the edge of the rocks and runs his hands back and forth through his wet hair. "Pick a city."

Claire spreads her towel across the rock and lies down on it. "Paris, definitely. A week in Paris. No, two weeks," she corrects herself, already dreaming of that holiday she'll probably never get around to taking this summer.

"Haven't you already been there?" Mia asks.

"Yeah, but with my parents when I was eleven. It wasn't exactly the trip dreams are made of. My mother planned every single second of every single day, and we weren't allowed to do anything else. My brother refused to eat any French food, so they had to keep taking him to McDonald's. Versailles was half closed for restoration work, and Mum made us do the Louvre in one hour so she could go shopping after."

"Yeah, that sounds like a regular, old, family-hell holiday." Pete laughs. "Only in Paris."

Claire watches him scoop up a handful of small rocks at the water's edge. "What about you? Where would you go?"

"New Zealand, for sure." He tosses a rock and watches it skip once or twice across the surface of the lake before it sinks into the water. "Definitely New Zealand. I'll be snowboarding every single snow-covered incline I can find."

"I'll be in Paris with Claire." Eli sighs as he flops onto a rock and uses Robbie's leg as his pillow. "Or maybe Berlin. What about you, Mia? Fantasy destination?"

She yawns into her hand. "Reykjavik."

Nina screws up her face. "Where the hell is Rakyar-what?"

Claire smiles into her towel, glad that Nina asked before she had to. "Iceland."

"And where's that?" Nina asks.

Robbie pokes Mia in the leg before she can answer. "You are such a weirdo. Why can't you go somewhere normal, like Disney World, or Hawaii? The only thing I know about Iceland is that crazy singer who was in that super depressing movie."

"That's one more thing than I know," Claire mutters as she pulls her wet hair from her face and ties it back.

Mia wraps her towel around her shoulders. "I just want to see that crazy-beautiful landscape. Volcanoes, glaciers, jet black rocks. And I want to see people who believe in elves and eat pickled sheep testicles and who have no last names."

Claire shakes her head and smiles into her towel. Mia is such a geek.

"And these things are actual cultural drawcards for you?" Robbie asks slowly.

"Yup," Mia tells him cheerfully. "And if I can't go there, I'm going to Barcelona."

"Oh, maybe I'm dumping you now, Claire, and going with Mia," Eli says.

Claire shrugs. "Whatever, Eli. I didn't say you could come anyway."

He laughs.

Mia sighs. "Really, I'd go just about anywhere, though, if you gave me a ticket. I haven't really been anywhere outside Australia except London to visit Dad's relatives."

Robbie stretches his arms above his head. "Well, I know it's a total cliché, but I still haven't been to New York. So that's where I'd go. And just so you know, I'm probably never coming back."

"Oh well, thanks." Eli reaches up and swats at his face.

"What are you getting huffy about?" Robbie laughs and leans down and kisses him. "You just ran away with my best friend to Barcelona. What do you care?"

"I really want to go to Perth," Nina suddenly offers.

"What?" Claire lifts her head from her arms and stares at Nina. "You can go anywhere in the world in this game and you choose Perth? You don't even want to leave Australia?"

Nina shrugs. "I've never been there."

Pete frowns. "But it's like not going anywhere."

"Um, it's further than New Zealand," Nina tells him. "And you want to go there."

"Not much further."

"It totally is."

"No, it's not."

Eli pipes up. "It's way further."

"Oh God." Claire buries her face in her arms. "Someone Google that, please, just to shut them up."

Mia laughs and shakes her head. "I don't need to. It takes six hours to fly to Perth, and it's four to New Zealand. Have you looked at a map recently, Pete?"

"Yes, I have, thanks, Mia," Pete sasses. "Anyway, at least New Zealand is a different country."

"Yeah, well, I'm not going anywhere any time soon," Nina says and sighs. "I'm too broke."

"And lazy. It was hard enough to get you out of bed and up here," Claire teases.

"Shut up." Nina throws a twig at her. "I was hungover."

"Doesn't matter if you're broke anyway," Eli reminds her. "It's a fantasy game, so you can go anywhere you want to go."

Robbie sits up. "I must interrupt all this game with a very, very important question."

"What?"

"What are we having for dinner?"

Claire smiles. No matter what time of day it is, it seems as if someone is talking about when they'll be eating next.

"We have all that stuff we bought at the market today, remember?" Nina tells him.

"Oh yes!" Robbie rubs his hands together, gleeful.

"Um, by the way, is it weird that we are on a holiday and still fantasising about holidays?" Eli muses.

"Yes, actually, it kind of is," Claire mumbles. She rolls over and stretches her arms above her head.

Robbie laughs and stands. "Yeah, it's just plain greedy. We're a bunch of spoilt brats, clearly. I'm going back to the house to forage. I'm hungry."

Claire sits up slowly. "I'm going back too." She's tired even though it's only late afternoon. All she has done all day is hang out by the lake, but she's exhausted. She pulls her shirt over her head and yawns again. She is going to have an early night. And she is going to finally sleep, damn it.

Robbie steps over to her and holds out his hands. She lets him pull her up, grateful.

He squeezes her hands and then drops them. "You look weary."

"Yeah, all this relaxing is clearly draining." She hangs her towel around her neck and picks up her book.

And suddenly everyone starts to get up and gather their things, ready to go back to the cottage. They traipse up the path in the last of the afternoon sun and plan their meal.

"Hey!" Nina suddenly pipes up in the middle of the debate. "I know where I want to go that's outside Australia. Dollywood!"

"As in that Dolly Parton theme park?" Robbie asks slowly.

"Yep," Nina says. "I love her."

Claire shakes her head and rolls her eyes. Of course Nina, adorable freak, loves Dolly Parton.

"Yeah, well, you're going there all on your own, babe." Robbie throws an arm around Nina's shoulder. "And, Mia, I think Nina might have just pipped you at the post for weirdest holiday destination too."

CHAPTER 48

The crickets are loud tonight, even louder than Claire's thoughts.

It's been a long day at the lake, and craving some peace, she left the others in the house and hopes they'll stay there. She's tired of them. Well, she's not tired of them, exactly, but has suddenly grown weary of the constant talking and laughing and movement of people in and out of rooms. Her nerves are jangled from the endless noise and flux around her. What started out fun has become—just for the moment—too much. It's also because she hasn't slept well the last couple of nights between the hangovers and the noisy mornings and this thing with Mia.

And tonight she hoped for some quiet, that maybe everyone will run out of steam, and they can chill. And it was looking that way until Robbie's friends called. Some people he knows were driving up this way and asked if it was okay if they came by. Of course she'd said yes. And it was today that they called. And of course it was late, and they were stuck and wanted to stay the night in the bunkhouse. Claire said yes to that, too. It would've been too Scrooge-y not to. Their new presence has amped the energy in the house again, and she can hear all the talk and laughter growing louder behind her as they drink the fresh round of beer his friends brought.

But Claire can't face it all right now. She needs a minute on her own. So much has happened in the last couple of days, she needs to take a breath. Here, on the large wooden step, she sits in the darkness and empties her mind for a while. And it feels good to just *be*, to sit peacefully in the hot night air where nothing is moving, not even the branches of the trees.

She gets her little pocket of peacetime—maybe half an hour—before she hears the screen door open and shut behind her. She fights the urge to sigh, not quite ready for the world just yet.

A voice says, "Go on." Then Claire hears the clatter of Blue's paws as he takes off past her, out into the night.

She lets out a breath. It is just Mia. She pads across the darkened porch toward her.

"Hey." Claire smiles at her and turns back to the darkness. Strangely, even though Mia is so much of the reason why Claire feels like this, she is also the only person she can stand to be around right now.

"Can I sit?"

"Of course." Claire slides over on the porch step. "What's everybody doing?"

"I have no idea." Mia settles on the step next to her and stretches out her long legs. "I was doing the dishes. They sure as hell weren't there."

Claire smiles and rests her elbow on her knees, her chin on her hand, listening to the crickets go crazy as they have done every single summer night she has ever spent here in their restive presence.

"You want some?" Mia holds out a nearly full beer.

Claire shakes her head. "I need a break."

"Me too," Mia agrees. "I don't even know why I accepted it." She puts the bottle down on the step near the porch post and leans back on her arms.

They sit quietly side by side, and Claire enjoys this new peace that exists between them after this day of slowly mending whatever it was that was broken between them last night. Everything still feels uncertain, but it also feels slightly less fraught and hurting. And for now, despite the questions that are left unanswered, Claire's willing to take it because it's better than the questions left unasked.

Suddenly, a huge thud and a yell rips through the air, followed by peals of laughter inside the house.

"What...was...that?" Claire asks, wary. If those idiots break anything, her mother will kill her.

"I have no idea. But they're laughing, so I guess it is safe to assume no one needs to go to the hospital."

"I'm more worried they've damaged something, and I am going to get murdered by my parents." Claire frowns as there is another thump and a cheer. "Do you think I should go check?"

"The responsible part of me wants to say yes you should." Mia suddenly sits up, shifts forward, and wraps her hands around Claire's upper arm.

She leans in close so their shoulders touch. "But the part of me that doesn't want you to leave wants to say you shouldn't."

Claire turns slowly, chin still in hand, surprised at such candidness. But before she can complete the smile that starts the moment she hears those words, Mia's mouth is on hers, fixed in a soft, steadfast kiss. And when Mia pulls back, Claire's eyes widen, but she still delivers on that smile.

Mia gives her a shy answering smile but doesn't say a word. She leans in and presses her lips to Claire's again.

Claire automatically lifts her hand and slides it across Mia's cheek. Her fingers come to gently grip her neck as she returns the kiss. This might be the last thing on earth she expected to happen tonight, but there's no way she's going to question it either.

So this is the answer. This is what it feels like when Mia sticks around, Claire realises. She removes her other arm from Mia's clutch so she can reach around and trace her hand over her shoulder. She edges it under the weight of Mia's thick hair to the warm skin at the base of her neck. She closes her eyes and feels a small thrill as Mia's hand skims over her bare legs. She gently clutches Claire's thigh just above the knee, helping to hold them in this awkward sideways pose on the step. It's a position that neither seems to want to abandon, not enough to break this kiss, even to rearrange into something more comfortable.

There is another loud crash. The sound of hysterical laughter and frantic footsteps bursts out into the night.

Claire pulls away, her brows knitted, as a light goes on in one of the front rooms.

"Do you need to check on that?" Mia's voice is husky.

Claire shakes her head, takes a deep breath, and gathers her courage. "I should, but..." She takes Mia's hand and stands.

"Then what?" Mia's face is a question mark as Claire takes her other hand and pulls until she complies and stands.

"Well, Mia," Claire whispers because she knows her voice will come out weird if she tries for any louder. "For the first time, you're not bolting." She squeezes her fingers, enjoying the embarrassed smile her statement provokes. "So I am just making sure nothing disturbs that." Claire tips her head in the direction of the house, where they can hear the sound of laughter and now footsteps coming closer. "So come here." She leads her by the hand up the steps. They tiptoe across the creaking wooden surface, hurry past the lit windows and to the darker side of the porch. When she gets around the corner, in the shadows of the house, she stops, leans against the wall, and tries to put the mess of her thoughts into a semblance of order.

"You know," she says quietly but quickly, still holding Mia's hand. "I inappropriately kiss people sometimes when I'm drunk, yeah. So do you, clearly. But you and me? I think it's more than that. And I just want you to know that I am not just being trashy right now. I'm not drunk, and I want to kiss you." She shakes the hand in hers. "And what I actually was trying to say last night was that I think something is happening with us and to ask if you felt it too or if you knew what it was, you know?" Claire feels almost breathless from the urgency and terror of delivering this short monologue. She's not used to communicating in such a forthright way, but it's necessary. It all feels too vital in this moment not to, in case it all slips right back into uncertainty again.

Mia nods slowly and stares down at her bare feet.

"Hey." Claire tugs gently on the hand, wanting to bring her back from wherever it is she has gone.

"I'm so sorry, Claire," Mia whispers, gaze still fixed on the ground.

"What for?" Claire is suddenly frozen. Is she going to bail again? She can't do this again. *She can't.*

"For being so weird. I've been awful."

"No, you haven't. Well, okay, a bit weird." Claire smiles.

And Mia offers a small smile in return.

Claire reaches out, relieved, and pulls at a length of Mia's hair. Mia steps in closer, close enough for Claire to take a hold of the front of her T-shirt and draw her near. "But it's okay. You've been figuring stuff out. A *lot* of stuff."

Mia looks up at her, right into her eyes. And she looks at Claire for the longest time, so long Claire starts to feel self-conscious, almost as if she wants to step away from its force. Finally, Mia shakes her head and bites back a shy smile. "You're so beautiful."

And just for a second, Claire feels as though she no longer knows which way is upright or how the hell she's going to stay there. So she pulls Mia toward her, an anchor, draws her arms around her waist, and rests her forehead against Mia's, breathing in that heady, light scent that accompanies her wherever she goes.

Eventually, Mia pulls back and looks down at her. Now she's the one chewing on her lip, her face still slightly overcast.

So Claire recovers herself and grins coyly at that tense face in front of her. "I don't know what you're worried about, Mee. You're pretty good at this lesbian thing," she jokes to crash them back down to earth because she thinks maybe Mia needs it. She needs to be reminded of the ease that did, and should still be able to, exist between them. "You definitely know how to compliment the ladies."

"Ha ha." She meets Claire's gaze again and grins.

It worked. Claire lifts an arm and wraps it around Mia's neck. "Well, you're beautiful, too, you know."

And Mia doesn't say anything, just closes in on her with another kiss. And there they stay, taking their sweet time. Claire supports Mia as she leans into her, and the wooden frame of the old house does its bit to keep Claire upright. They linger here in this moment and learn the feel of being in each other's arms, of the way their faces and lips and finally their tongues feel against each other's.

Mia pulls back for a moment and looks at her again, her eyes sleepily narrowed. And there's that feeling again, like the hand on the small of her back. Claire feels insanely, unprecedentedly shy, but happy. *This is happening*, she tells herself.

And the way Mia smiles at her, as though to register her agreement, makes Claire wonder if she accidentally said it aloud.

Claire has no idea how long they stand there and kiss with only the sound of their breathing and the background of crickets for company. And she doesn't know how long they would have stayed either, if they hadn't started at the sudden sound of the back door as it flew violently open, and footsteps ran out onto the porch just around the corner from them. They freeze, hold on to each other, and grin into the dim light, hiding in the shadows of the wall.

"Wait!" someone shouts before they run back inside.

They let out a mutual sigh of relief, and Mia buries her face in Claire's neck with a soft, breathy laugh.

"Should we go back in before they come looking for us?" Claire whispers as she wonders how close they are to getting caught. She doesn't want anything to destroy this new place they've created for themselves. She would rather leave it now and rebuild it later than have it shattered by the outside world and for Mia to back off again.

But Mia shakes her head. "No." She moves in to kiss Claire again, more forcefully this time. "I don't want to go back in. I want to stay here with you."

CHAPTER 49

And it's the desire contained in that kiss and in that declaration that decides it, that makes Claire even braver. She bites her lip, takes Mia by the hand, and leads her to the sleeping porch. Opening the door, she pulls Mia inside. With the door safely closed behind them, she leans against the frame, pulls Mia into another deeper kiss, and slides her tongue against hers.

Mia's only reply is to press herself up against Claire, diminishing any distance between them, and to kiss her right back.

And again Claire has to steel herself just to remain standing. When she's achieved the status of being safely upright, she works her hands slowly up the back of Mia's T-shirt. She starts in the middle and follows her spine downward along the soft sling of her lower back to the waistband of her shorts and then all the way back up to her shoulders. Mia breaks away from the kiss, meets her gaze for a brief moment, and takes hold of Claire's hips. She ducks her head, drops a kiss on Claire's neck where it curves into her shoulder, and again a little higher up. Then she glides her hands around to Claire's front and inches them upward over her top, along her stomach, not stopping until her hands are just under the seams of her bra.

Claire sucks in a breath, leans harder against the door as Mia kisses her just under her ear and smoothes her hands slowly up over Claire's breasts. She kisses her throat before she moves to the other side of her neck. There is a dizzying sprint of blood around Claire's body as she locks her knees and tips her head back against the door to make room for whatever Mia wants to do now.

Suddenly, Mia pauses in her journey along her neck, leans in, and presses her cheek there instead, head bowed. Her hands slide slowly off

Claire's breasts and back to her waist and pause there. She stands stock-still and breathes quietly into Claire's neck.

Claire's hands also come to a halt. Confused by this abrupt standstill, she holds on to Mia's arms and waits for a cue. In this silence, she can once again hear the muffled bangs and yells from inside and the sudden quiet of the crickets.

Claire slides a hand up to the nape of Mia's neck. "Hey, are you okay?"

"Yeah," Mia mutters. "I think I'm just...nervous or something." She kisses Claire's shoulder.

Claire bows her head, brows knitted. She shakes Mia and smiles. "Why are you nervous? You've at least done this before."

"I know, but I was really drunk."

Claire giggles.

"And I didn't *like* her," Mia mumbles without raising her head.

Claire stops laughing as she realises the weight that is possibly contained in that statement.

"And because," she buries her face deeper into Claire's neck, "with you I want it to be good."

"It will be," Claire shoots back without even a thought.

Her rapid-fire, cocky response makes them both giggle, which, for some reason, makes everything so much easier. The air around them lightens.

That's when Claire decides that, even though Mia initiated this, she's the one who will have to keep it going. She will not let this dissolve into uncertainty or slink back into the undefined attraction that it has been for so long between them. They need to make this into what it is. She takes Mia by her T-shirt again and pulls her slowly over to the bed.

Mia, obedient, sits in front of her. She looks up at Claire and bites her lip, clearly trying to hold back the giggles. They can just meet gazes by the light of the porch. It's just enough to light the way, but not enough to confront.

"Don't laugh," Claire orders her although she is smiling herself. She leans down and cups Mia's face, then kisses her and pushes her back against the mattress.

Mia lies against the covers, throws her arms up over her face, and shakes her head, smiling. "I have no idea why I'm laughing." Then a moment later, she looks up at Claire from behind her arms, takes a deep breath, and lets it out. "Yes, I do."

"So stop it."

"Okay." Mia repeats the headshake, but more fervently this time, as though trying to shake something loose. "Yes, fuck it. I'm not going to be nervous."

And now it's Claire who wants to laugh because she realises she has never heard Mia drop the f-bomb before. And if this is the occasion that calls for it, she knows she should feel honoured. "Good," she whispers instead of laughing.

Claire climbs onto the bed slowly, and stops with her knees on either side of Mia. She places her hands on either side of Mia's shoulders. She kisses her lightly once and then dips her head and runs her tongue slowly along Mia's neck, trying to invoke the same sensations for Mia as she did for Claire just minutes ago by the door. And the sound of Mia's rapid inward breath tells her that imitation has been the sincerest form of flattery.

She looks up, and Mia smiles at her again. But this time it's a different, slower kind of smile. And the next thing Claire knows, Mia tugs gently at her tank and pulls it up around her armpits. Claire obediently drops her neck so Mia can draw it gently over her head. It falls onto the bed beside them, and Mia smooths her hands over Claire's bared skin as she explores this new territory of her waist and her back and up over her shoulders. And for an indulgent moment, Claire hangs her head and savours the feeling of those exploring hands.

When she can bring herself to move, she pulls back and sits up so she is astride Mia's legs. She takes hold of the bottom of Mia's T-shirt and pushes it upward. Mia bites her lip and complies, looking self-conscious but willing. She arches her back slightly as Claire slides it up over her torso. Now she knows they are finally ready to admit they want the same thing from each other.

Claire immediately drops her hands onto the smooth, tanned breadth of Mia's stomach. She slowly runs her hand over the skin and around Mia's waist and circles her belly button lightly with her finger as Mia moves her own hands up to rest them at the hem of Claire's shorts.

Claire inhales a deep breath and takes a brief, slightly stunned moment for herself, still not entirely sure how they got from this morning to this moment. She traces the ridges of Mia's ribcage with her index fingers and realises she has absolutely no clue about what she is going to do. It's a fact that might normally be daunting but right now, strangely, is not. For some reason she feels as though the ground is within her depth, as if terrified *can* co-exist with happy. She can command this moment just from the sheer wanting of it.

And when she finally looks down, Mia looks right back at her, the tip of her tongue caught between her teeth, expectant, her face stripped of all that uncertainty of the last twenty-four hours. In this moment, she looks calmly bound to whatever is about to happen. Claire feels a rush of something that's part relief, part tenderness, but mostly desire.

Mia still doesn't move, and Claire—happy to be the instigator—smiles and drops a kiss into the dip of skin just below where Mia's bra meets in the middle, and then another just above. She moves her face over Mia's, thrilling at the feel of their skin pressed together.

Claire pauses a breath away from her and looks down.

Mia gives her the smallest of smiles as a tiny, tense furrow appears between her brows.

"Hey, it's just me," Claire whispers.

Mia reaches up and strokes Claire's face. "It's just you."

And that is as far as they manage to get in the undressing department.

Because the next thing she knows, they are under some sort of bizarre siege. Whatever it is that the others have been up to inside the house seems to have escalated. People spill out of the door and onto the porch, the driveway, and the path around the house. Every thump and every shout sounds closer and closer, threatening to breach the perimeter of their small corner of the world.

There seems to be some kind of game in action, one that largely involves a lot of running and yelling and loud splashes and even the occasional excited bark from Blue. When Claire first hears the sound of water being thrown across the porch, she pauses a moment and lets her mind drift into a brief prayer that whatever they're doing isn't in the house too. Then she simply tries to block it out. But the noise of voices and footsteps and these watery clashes are so close sometimes she feels as though she could reach out and touch the people making the sounds.

It feels perilous to be even semi-topless, to be this exposed with everyone in such close, risky proximity. The glass and screen walls of this room don't offer much more than a mental barrier between them and this calamitous world outside. There is an unspoken consensus between them that the threat of imminent incursion makes it too hazardous to bare themselves any further.

Yet at the same time, she doesn't want to relinquish the territory of skin each has gained. This is not ground she is willing to cede. Not now. So they stay shackled in their remaining clothes and make do because there's no other choice. Claire knows there's nowhere they can go where they will gain any more privacy or distance from the others. But she also knows they cannot stop now. This is not even a question in her mind.

Just as she begins to get used to the noise, getting cocky again as they thread their limbs together and explore new ground, a set of footsteps suddenly runs right up to near the window and comes to a stop. The person pants loudly as if out of breath.

Mia pulls back, and her eyes widen slightly.

Claire stares back and shakes her head, silently insistent. *Ignore them*, she pleads with her eyes. *Ignore it.*

Mia smiles briefly and obeys. She curls her hand around Claire's neck and pulls her into another fervent kiss.

But as soon as the footsteps depart again, on to the next battle in whatever stupid war they are waging, Claire pulls away and jumps off the bed. As quick as lightning, she shoots over to the windows and unties the flimsy cotton curtains on the porch side of the room. They don't offer much in the way of security, but they provide at least a comforting illusion of privacy. She strides over and shuts the glass door and pulls down the blinds, shutting out a little more light from the house. Then she turns to the dimly lit, shadow-spattered shape that is Mia, and steps forward slightly so she can make out her face. She lies on her side on the mattress, her head on her arm, still in her bra and her shorts, with her impossibly longs legs curled against the sheet. She gives Claire a small conspiratorial smile as if she's reeling her back in. Not that she needs to. Claire never left.

She stretches out on the bed. They lie there and stare at each other from this small distance and take a little moment to cement something between them. Certainty.

And before they can even touch again, the outside world invades once more, this time in the loud sound of footsteps and the splash of water as it hits wood, followed by a loud gasp and a laugh. Some of the water penetrates the wire screens and spatters on the floor near the window.

Mia opens her mouth to whisper something, and Claire, scared she is going to suggest they stop or postpone, that this could be brought to an end by whatever this bedlam outside is, halts whatever she is going to say with another long, breathless kiss. She has to. Because if she doesn't do that, she doesn't know how she's going to stop herself from storming outside and telling everyone to shut the fuck up and let them have this precious, new, and slightly terrifying moment in goddamn peace if that's what it takes to make sure it happens. And she knows she probably doesn't want to do that.

But to stop what they have started is not an option. So, adamant that there will only be the two of them in this room, no matter how much the outside world tries to march in and occupy this territory with its noisy clamour for attention, Claire will not allow it. Instead, she cups a hand over the side of Mia's face and anchors her to the moment, sealing them both back into their tiny world together, doing everything she can to renew the urgency again. She presses her mouth onto Mia's and moves her tongue against hers—a silent command for Mia to hold her ground.

And it works. Mia's arm snakes around Claire's neck and pulls her into a fierce, returned embrace while her other hand glides along her spine, down over her shorts, and as far along the back of her legs she can reach. She slides her fingers upward, wraps her hand around Claire's thigh, and pulls it up and over her own.

Claire breathes hard into the kiss and does precisely what that hand asks of her. Mia languidly slides her fingers up and down the sensitive skin at the back of Claire's thigh, up to the hem of her shorts and down again. Driven by this new level of boldness, Claire runs her own hand up along Mia's torso and eases it slowly over the swell of her breast. She traces the edge of Mia's bra lightly with her finger before she replaces it with her mouth.

For a while, they manage to maintain the sanctity of this tiny but fiercely held piece of ground despite the unrelenting chaos of everything that comes at them in the form of thuds and shrieks and shadows that dance along the walls. It's easier now as they delve into this new hot and reckless territory.

They manage to stave off their fear of invasion until the dizzyingly anticipatory moment when Mia has slowly unbuttoned a button and gradually lowered a zip. Claire is breathless and strung between two urges—to accommodate the tentative ease of Mia's hand into her shorts and to not relinquish any proximity between them. That's when footsteps come dangerously close and stop.

And it's also when, as Claire feels the first, vertiginous waves of sensation urged by that hand, that the world crashes back at them in full force.

Because that's the moment there is a loud tap on the door.

Mia pulls her head back, her eyes wide.

Claire, dauntless at this crucial point, locks her gaze to Mia's and says nothing. She shakes her head, hoping it will go away. She pushes herself against Mia's hand and bites at the soft skin of Mia's ear lobe, recalling her to the exigency of her task. And Mia, obedient to this silent command, complies.

Then a voice rings out into the hot night air.

"Claire, are you in there?"

Claire draws herself as close to Mia as she can, burrows her face in her neck, pulls in a breath, and holds it. Mia's free arm closes around her head, a flimsy but welcome protection against this latest invasion.

Nina calls out again. "Hey! Are you asleep?"

That's when Claire finally takes a deep, furious breath, pulls her head back, and yells into the night. "Yes! Go! Away!"

And that's when the footsteps retreat without another word.

"Fuck." Claire releases a drawn out, frustrated moan and presses her face into the pillow for a moment. Eventually she lifts her head. Mia raises her eyebrows and lets out a breathy laugh.

And Claire smiles sheepishly and again pleads, in a silent entreaty with her eyes, for Mia to stay with her. And just in case Mia considers straying, Claire mirrors her. She reaches around and slides her own hand teasingly up Mia's thigh and inside the leg of her shorts, giving her no choice but to forget whatever is going on out there and to stay deliciously here with her. And the perceptible gasp tells her it works.

And from this moment on, the world is reduced to the simple but all-consuming sensations conjured by just one hand and the hot press of Mia's mouth on her neck. That hand and those lips are enough to shrink the world entirely around her. This is all she requires to keep her in this dizzyingly hot place.

They are enough and they are too much at the same time too. So much so that it feels as though it's only minutes before she pushes her face into the soft inward curve where Mia's neck meets her shoulder and tries to quell the sounds coming from her in throaty gasps. At the same time, she refuses to surrender her own project of bringing Mia to this place with her. And it turns out that Mia isn't far behind her. She presses her face sideways and breathes out her own orgasm into the pillow.

And then the room is filled with the quiet sounds of their breath hollowing out. They become the hushed eye in the storm of thuds and bangs and shouts that surround them. Paralysed by the product of their own daring, they are capable only of a weak but insistent clutch of limbs, bound together into a slightly shocked silence. Claire blinks heavily, closes her eyes, and presses her lips against Mia's shoulder, unnerved by the hair-trigger nature of the desire that got her to this place so soon. She has rarely felt so instantly kindled and *never* so quickly sated.

That was…unexpected.

Everything about this is unexpected, of course. But most of all it's the unbelievable effortlessness of this call and response they've just discovered in each other.

Now, it has rendered her bashful, this first ardent display of wanting. It's left her too afraid to lift her head and acknowledge its passing. In the past, she's always been quick to brush off sex, slightly embarrassed by the intimacy of the aftermath, no matter how much pleasure it brought. She's always needed to close out the moment with something quippy or sassy, something that would end the silence and haul the moment back to reality. But right now she cannot. Not now and not with Mia. Not yet.

In the end, it's Mia who breaks the silence. But she breaks it *in* silence. She pulls her head back and waits until Claire meets the relentless fix of her gaze. Mia smooths the hair from Claire's cheek and smiles, that cute, tender crinkle at the edges of her eyes recalls Claire back to familiarity. *It's just Mia.* And Claire smiles sheepishly back, astonished by both the simplicity and the intensity of the feelings this girl provokes in her. Why did it take her so long—both of them so long—to be aware of this possibility? She tucks her head back under Mia's chin, breathes in and out slowly, and notes the sudden quiet outside.

"You okay?" Mia whispers as she slides her hand under Claire's hair and curls her fingers against the base of her skull.

Claire nods, presses her lips against Mia's collarbone, and runs her hands along Mia's side. She's not willing to break the silence just yet. So they lie there a little longer, entwined in a bundle of limbs and awareness. Their breath eases in and out, flowing over each other's skin.

Suddenly, the newfound calm outside is ruptured by the crash of the back door as it flies open and the thuds of footsteps from the house. They thunder across the porch and down the steps. Someone says something about the water. They must be going for a swim. She listens as footsteps dash down the path and voices call out into the night.

"Thank *God*." She sighs as their voices fade away down the lake path. She rolls onto her back, grabs Mia's hand, and clasps it between them on top of the sheet because she still needs to touch her.

Mia follows her anyway, turning on her side. She presses her face into Claire's arm and looks up, grinning. They dissolve into giggles over the ridiculous duel just fought between the clandestine intensity of what was just happening in here and the utter chaos of everything that surrounded them. Now the storm has passed, they are free to find the incongruence of the scenario completely hilarious. And they do.

"That was...interesting," Mia whispers as her giggles abate to breathless hiccups. She pulls Claire over and kisses her.

"I have never wanted to murder someone more than I did just then," Claire mumbles. She rolls on top of Mia and luxuriates in the way their legs instinctively tangle together in a delicious slide of limb against limb.

Mia laughs again and folds her arms across Claire's back. "You weren't supposed to have murder on your mind."

"Just for a minute." Bashful, Claire pushes her face into Mia's neck. Then she groans loudly as she imagines the potential carnage in the morning. "Oh God, do you think they have trashed the house completely?"

Mia runs her hand through her hair. "Don't worry. We'll get it cleaned up, okay?"

"Mmm, we have to. Or my mum will kill me." Claire frowns as she slides her hand along the undulated stretch of Mia's side, from hip to underarm and back again.

"Shh," Mia tells her. She dips her hands into the back of Claire's shorts and then runs them all the way up Claire's back. "Don't think about it now."

"Okay." Claire sighs, agreeable, unable to stop the relentless sweep of her hand up and down the sleek landscape of Mia's skin. These hands are, it seems, thoroughly addicted.

She draws in a breath, unable to shake her shock at this beautifully strange turnaround. She cannot quite believe that not so long ago—not even an hour ago, probably—Mia came and sat beside her on the steps and kissed her out of a seeming nowhere. And now they are lying here, halfway to naked, sealed together in this tender aftermath. And Mia's skin under her hands is her proof that this is actually happening.

Claire lifts her head and looks down at her, needing to *see* Mia as proof to further believe it. She rests her chin in her hand and stares. She notes the way the light from outside reproduces itself in small pinpricks of light in Mia's pupils and how one eyebrow raises just slightly in response to her stare. But Mia doesn't say anything at first, just obediently subjects herself to this scrutiny. Eventually though, when Claire has clearly stared at her for too long, a small, nervous half smile crosses her face.

"What?" she whispers.

"Nothing," Claire says quickly. She shakes her head and smiles. She has no idea how she could possibly explain any of these feelings, so she isn't even going to try. Instead, she kisses her.

And it's only now, in the safety and privacy of this moment, they are freed a little and are able to become bolder. Now they get to go back and take the remedial lessons they were forced to skip during that urgent, covert little scene.

This time they get to revel in those fun baby steps they missed, like the simple but provocative striptease of removing clothes. She relishes the delicious baring of skin and how it feels as if they're now showing off for each other, confident that swagger will be met with desire in return. They linger in these moments and make slow new acquaintance with this as yet unmet lay of the land. It's new and hot and even a little graceless sometimes when clothes won't cooperate, or teeth clash, or she momentarily loses her way.

But even those awkward moments, moments that would usually embarrass Claire or make her feel clumsy, don't. Because this is happening with Mia, the one person in the entire world who makes her feel *not* awkward and *not* stupid and *not* embarrassed. And, most of all, she's stunned by this almost electrifying new knowledge that Mia is the person she most wants to feel desired by. It's also during these lessons that Claire learns valuable and highly flattering little trinkets of knowledge about Mia. And these trinkets are as much derived from sight as they are from feel. She notes and relishes the smallest flicker of reaction on Mia's face and in the undivided attention she attracts when she sits astride Mia and slowly, and just a little flauntingly, removes her own bra. She studies the way Mia's eyes narrow slightly, how she bites her bottom lip as she reaches for the flesh now laid bare, her immediate response to Claire's little show. And Claire gets to craft her own lessons in the shape and feel of different tracts of Mia's newly bared skin as together they remove what is left of her clothing. And later, and even bolder, she learns the reflexive ripple of desire that runs through Mia's body when Claire kneels over her, presses her knee between her legs, and dances her tongue along the underside of her breast and then up to her nipple. Then she learns the small, intimate sounds of Mia's desire as she yields more vocally to Claire's touch again, evoked this time by a series of slower, playful, and less clumsy cadences of hand.

And this indulgent slowness is the best part for Claire. With the threat of any imminent encroachment gone, they take the time to learn the valuable lessons that can only be learned by starting right at the beginning with the need for urgency and secrecy gone. These are lessons in how to take their sweet damn time.

It's as though they go backward in some ways. But it doesn't matter because it's a thrilling, heady backward, and Claire never wants to stop. The only reason she lets it end in the early, silent hours of the morning is because she knows it will still be here tomorrow. So she takes in her final lesson for the night as Mia curls herself around Claire's back. She listens as Mia's breathing peacefully evens out and then turns away to fall the rest of the way into sleep on her own. And when Claire hears the others make their whispering way back into the house, she pulls the light cotton sheet over them and follows suit, landsliding into sleep.

CHAPTER 50

Claire wakes to a new day, the day of her twentieth birthday to be exact. Before she even forces her eyes open, she knows it's still early. She can tell because the sun hasn't made it around to the porch yet, and they are still bathed in that filtered grey light. The kind that doesn't assault her eyelids and tells her it's closer to dawn than to full-fledged morning. They are safe from the sun for a spell.

They. She smiles and opens her eyes.

But the smile dissipates when she finds an empty pillow next to her where Mia ought to be. She closes her eyes again, throws an arm over her face, and sighs, immediately nervous. Mia is not in the bed. What does that mean? Claire thinks back to last night, to Mia's unprompted kiss on the steps of the porch, and to the sweet, deliberate explorations they made of each other's bodies into the early hours of this morning. She recalls the spread of their limbs as they made their eventual way together into deep, sated sleep, naked to the hot night air but for a single cotton sheet.

Would Mia want to leave everything they shared behind them? Claire doesn't really think she would. Not after last night.

Her question is answered when footsteps tiptoe across the porch outside and the door squeaks open and closed. Then she feels the dip of the bed and the sheet lift as a body slides in next to her.

"Where did you go?" Claire mumbles into her arm.

"The bathroom."

Claire smiles a small, relieved smile to herself. "I was being a drama queen in my head and convinced myself that maybe you'd run away again."

"No." Mia nudges her with her foot, indignant. "I did *not*."

"Good." Claire turns and looks at her through half-open eyes. Mia lies on her stomach, her face resting in a nest of her folded arms. All Claire can see of her face is one brown, half-closed eye peeking out from the crook of her elbow, and a shock of tangled brown hair. "You are not allowed to run away, Mia. Because I got naked for you."

One half of a languid smile slowly emerges from behind Mia's arm. She lifts herself from the pillow and moves over, her face hovering closer to Claire's. She reaches out and runs a hand over where the sheet covers Claire's stomach. "You did." She smiles down at her, shy but affectionate.

"And, despite popular opinion, I don't do that with many people."

"I feel very, very special." Mia slowly pulls the covers down a little and dips her head to press her lips against Claire's sternum.

"You should," Claire whispers, only half joking.

Mia seems to get that because she looks at Claire for a long time, her cheek resting on her hand and that small smile on her face. Finally, she slides herself across Claire's body and buries her head in her neck and her hands into her hair.

Claire runs her hands up and down Mia's back and lifts the bottom of her T-shirt so she can feel the soft spread of Mia's skin under her fingers all over again. "Why are you wearing stupid clothes?"

She feels the slight reverberations as Mia snickers. "Well, because like you, Claire, I don't get naked for just anybody. And I had to go to the bathroom, which, if you recall, is in the house with all the people."

"I guess that's okay then. But I'm not a fan. Just putting it out there."

Mia laughs quietly and pulls herself up until she's sitting on top of Claire. She quickly yanks off her top and smiles down at her, clad only in her bra.

"Mia?" Claire shakes her head. "Did you put on your bra just to go to the bathroom?"

Mia smiles bashfully and turns slightly pink. "Maybe."

Claire gives her a withering look. But she also finds herself weirdly delighted by this level of coyness in Mia, such a ridiculous contrast to the way they've been in this room together.

"Okay, okay." Mia laughs and reaches behind to unclasp it. She pulls it off slowly, one arm at a time, and throws it onto the floor.

"That's better." Claire reaches up and slides her hands over Mia's stomach and then right up over her small breasts. She grazes her thumbs back and forth over her nipples.

Mia bites her lip, dips her head, and closes her eyes, giving in to the sensation. And eventually Claire stops but only because she wants Mia closer, to feel her skin against her own. She drops her hands and runs them over Mia's legs, certain that Mia will follow them downward. She does. Bending down over Claire, she pulls the sheet away, stretches her body out along hers, and slides one leg in between Claire's.

Claire feels that same instant surge of want as last night when Mia first touched her with tangible, desirous intention. She pulls in a deep breath and runs her fingertips along Mia's side and up over her back.

This morning they're a peculiar combination of bolder but quieter. They are bolder because they have the results of last night's heady explorations in their back pockets. But they are also quieter because, unlike last night, when all the noise told them exactly where everybody was and provided a kind of shield, this morning's silence presents a mystery as to where the others are. So, when it happens, Claire holds Mia's head against her neck as Mia surrenders to an orgasm and helps stifle the sounds that force themselves from her. She tries to prevent them from existing anywhere but in this room. She holds her this way until they have quieted to deep, sated breaths.

And then, when she recovers, Mia makes her way almost unbearably slowly down the landscape of Claire's body and tastes every stretch before she finally stops between Claire's thighs and does what no one has ever, ever bothered to do to her before. Claire bites down on her upper arm to stem the sounds of her own almost embarrassingly immediate orgasm. And when Claire's breath finally quiets, Mia rains slow kisses over her belly and breasts before she returns to lie next to her and nuzzles into her neck. Claire keeps her face buried in her arm, rendered shy once more by the ardour of her reaction.

Smiling self-consciously, Claire turns onto her side, presses her face into the pillow, and reaches back and slides her hand around the leg now curled into the back of her own. Mia lines her body along Claire's back and wraps an arm around her waist.

They fall into asleep again as the sun creeps up and through the porch screens, tangled in each other, arms around limbs, breath on each other's necks, even though it's already getting too hot for so much contact. At some point Claire registers the sounds of footsteps, then quiet voices as a car leaves. Robbie's friends, she guesses. She and Mia remain there, though, skating the surface of sleep. They don't wake completely until there is the slam of the front door and footsteps as someone pads around the porch toward them.

"Uh oh," Mia mumbles quietly. She slides her leg off Claire's and shuffles back to her own pillow.

"Hey, ladies?" Robbie's soft voice comes through the door as he taps gently on the doorframe. "You awake?"

"Hey," Mia calls out quietly to him as Claire pulls the sheets right up around their shoulders. A flush of awkwardness turns her face pink before he even walks in.

The door opens, and Robbie, his eyes still sleepy, pokes his head around the doorframe. "I just came to see if you two were alive." He grins at them as he steps fully inside the room, running his hand through his hair, Blue at his heels.

"We're alive," Mia informs him.

"Good." He strides over to the end of the bed, his hair sticking out at all kinds of crazy bedhead angles. "I missed you."

"Um, you might want to stay there," Mia tells him hurriedly as Claire pulls the sheet even higher.

Robbie rolls his eyes. "A few things, ladies. One," he ticks off a finger, "so you're naked? Freaking duh."

Claire snickers and blushes at the same time. Robbie is so unflappable. And so annoyingly perceptive.

"Two," he ticks off a second finger as he takes a step forward, "it's about time." He sighs dramatically as though he's been waiting to find them naked in a bed together for years. "I covered for you two, you know. People were looking for you, and I told them not to disturb you, that you were having one of those deeply necessary girly girl BFF emotions talks. I think Nina felt a bit left out, though." He lets out an evil laugh. "If only she knew."

Claire pulls the sheet up to her face to hide the redness she can still feel creeping from her neck to her cheeks.

"Thank you," Mia tells him.

He continues to advance on them, holding up a third finger. "And three, you should know by now that the thought of your naked bodies has about as much effect on me as the thought of watching paint dry."

He throws himself on the bed next to Claire and stretches out on top of the sheets. Claire shuffles back and feels Mia's hand settle on her lower back. And just that one small touch, even after all the touching they've done this morning, sets off a little current through her body.

"Hey." Robbie turns and plants a kiss on top of Claire's head. "Happy birthday, honey."

"Thanks." Claire feels Mia pinch her waist gently. And she knows what that pinch is saying. *Sorry, I forgot it was your birthday.* But Claire doesn't care. Not at all. They've had far more interesting things on their minds.

"So, what do you want to do today?" Robbie asks.

"I don't really know." Claire hasn't even thought about it. "Whatever."

He shakes his head. "No, Claire, you can't whatever your birthday."

"It's true." Mia slips her arm around Claire's waist and rests her chin on her shoulder. "You can't. It's against the rules."

"So, come on, what do you want?" Robbie demands. "A girl can't just live her birthday on orgasms alone."

Claire reaches out from under the sheet and punches him in the arm as she blushes again.

"Ow!" He rubs his nonexistent bicep. "I'll let that slide because it's your birthday, but make a decision, woman."

"Okay, okay," Claire grumbles and tries to think about how she wants to spend the day. Basically, she'd like to spend it as they've spent every day, swimming and hanging out. "I want a picnic by the lake."

"Done!" Robbie slaps his hand down on the mattress. He leans over, kisses her cheek again, and sits up. "I shall rally the troops," he says in a terrible British accent. "You two do whatever it is you girls do for a bit longer while I organise everything." He jumps clear of Claire before she can hit him again.

He opens his mouth, but before he can say whatever smart-ass comment he is about to say, the front door slams closed and footsteps approach.

"Claire," she hears Nina whisper loudly from somewhere outside.

Claire freezes and frowns. She's not quite ready to have everyone else in here too. It's okay with Robbie, but she isn't ready to share this naked-with-Mia thing with the rest of the world.

Robbie clearly sees her face because he holds up a hand and walks quickly out of the room.

"Oh hey," Nina says. "I want to wish Claire a happy birthday. She awake?"

"Nah, still asleep," he replies. "Want to come buy stuff for a birthday lunch?"

"Yeah."

Claire smiles. Nina is, as always, up for anything. Their footsteps disappear around the side of the house. She sighs, relieved, and shuts her eyes for a second. Then she turns right over and wraps an arm around Mia "How did he know you were going to be in here?"

Mia shakes her head and turns a little pink. "I think he just figured it out."

Wow, she thinks. Robbie really is just that perceptive. Or they are being way more obvious than she thought. She hopes it's the former.

Mia strokes a hand along Claire's waist and looks contrite. "Hey, I forgot it was your birthday. I'm so sorry. I knew it was today, but I forgot this morning."

"It's okay. I don't care." Claire shrugs.

Mia presses her palms to Claire's cheek and stares at her. "Happy birthday."

CHAPTER 51

Nina pulls off her T-shirt and flinches. "Ouch!" She looks down at her shoulder where a purplish bruise is blooming near the strap of her bikini.

"What happened to you?" Claire asks, but Nina's too busy inspecting her shoulder to answer.

Then finally she lifts her head and laughs. "Oh, I remember. It's from last night. When I ran straight into the doorframe."

"Well done." Robbie leans over to get a look at her war wound. "Excellent spatial awareness there, Neen."

"Shut up. I was trying to get away from *you*." Nina rubs her arm and then lies back on her towel. "And a bucket of water. Remember?"

"Yeah, what the hell were you guys doing last night?" Claire asks from where she clings to the edge of a rock, the lower half of her body submerged in the water. "Other than being incredibly loud?"

"We were playing a game." Eli nibbles on a piece of bread.

"It sounded kind of terrifying for a game," Mia mutters sleepily from her rock.

Claire looks over at her. It's the first thing Mia has said for ages. She's stretched out under the sun with her book over her face. She's been quiet all afternoon. Claire smiles to herself. Maybe she's just tired after last night. "It did sound like you were trying to kill each other." She pulls herself out of the water and wraps a towel around her waist.

"Nah, it was a game," Pete says. "Well, we were inventing it as we went along."

"Yeah, it was like hide-and-seek, but if you won a round, you got tequila." Robbie grins as he scrapes dip onto a hunk of bread.

Nina giggles. "Hide-and-seek for grownups."

"And if you lost, you had to save yourself by running around the house before someone caught you."

"Like, out the back door, around the house, and in the front door," Nina adds.

Claire nods. That explains all the thunderous footsteps.

"And if you got caught, you got a bucket of water thrown at you."

And that explains all the splashing.

"And if you got around the house before someone caught you?" Mia asks.

"You got tequila." Robbie laughs. "Of course."

"Right." Claire pulls a face. "Sounds like the world's most exhausting drinking game."

"Something like that," Eli agrees.

"What the hell happened to you guys, anyway?" Pete asks.

"They were too busy having deep and meaningful girl talk all night," Nina mutters. She picks up a strawberry and munches on it, frowning.

"No, we were hiding from you crazy people." Claire sneaks another look at Nina. She does seem a little bit hurt, as though she feels left out of whatever she thinks was happening in the sleeping porch. At the same time, she also can't believe Nina is accusing her, Claire, of girl talk. But she'll go with it for the sake of avoiding any actual disclosure.

She's about to explain away their all-night disappearance and tell them that Mia crashed with her because they thought Robbie's friends would need the bunks. But as she looks around, she realises no one knows about them or cares. Well, Robbie knows, but he's not saying a word. He's too busy stuffing his face with food. And he's the only person who the possibility of Claire and Mia seems to have occurred to.

"Anyway." Nina inspects her bruise again. "It was kind of brutal, but it was fun." She winces and then sits up and claps her hands. "Let's do presents!"

"Yes, presents!" Robbie brushes crumbs off his hands and reaches for his bag.

Claire stares at them. "Presents?"

"Yes, you know that common custom where people celebrate one another's birth by giving each other stuff?" Robbie winks at her.

She pokes him in the shin with her toe. "Shut up."

He ignores her. "Hey, Mia, did you remember ours?"

She slowly sits up and stretches her arms above her head. "I did."

Eli picks up a large Tupperware container that has sat unopened among all the picnic food and brings it over to Claire. "I don't exactly have a present for you, as such, but I made you this." He squats down next to her and peels off the lid. "Ta-da!"

Claire peers into the container and laughs. It's a birthday cake. But it's completely covered in neon-purple icing and a great big C made from M&Ms.

"Something told me you don't do fluffy-pink icing and flowers," Eli says.

"No." Claire reaches in, swipes off a bit of the icing and tastes it. "Can you tell my mother that?" She smiles at him and turns to behold it once again. "That is an amazing cake. Thanks, Eli."

He squeezes her arm. "Happy birthday."

Pete steps onto the rock, peers into the container and shakes his head. "Wow, what is it with all the baking talent in this group?"

"Yeah, we do seem to like channelling our inner old ladies around here." Eli laughs.

"I think your creation was a little more spectacular than my drunken effort," Mia tells him.

"Yeah, and no old lady is going to ice a cake like that." Nina comes over to Claire and puts a small package in her lap. "Happy birthday, my evil friend." She crouches down and clutches her arm, waiting for her to open it.

"Thanks, Neen." Claire picks up the present and feels the hard square object inside. "How did you even get this here?" she asks, remembering the debacle that was getting Nina out of the house the morning they left. "I packed for you, remember?"

"Smuggled it in Eli's bag. Thanks, Eli." She blows him a kiss.

"No problem, sweetie."

Claire unwraps the package. It is a book—a travel guide on how to get around Europe on the cheap.

"You said you were saving to go away. I thought maybe some inspiration?"

"And it's kind of perfect after our conversation yesterday, too," Pete adds.

Claire nods and flicks through the glossy colour photos of all those exotic destinations inside the middle pages. "Thank you, Neen."

"You like it?"

Claire smiles at her. "I love it, stupid."

"Hey, Mia, where's ours?" Robbie asks.

"One sec." Mia reaches into a pocket of her bag and pulls out a small package. She passes it to Robbie.

He turns to Claire. "This is from both of us."

"We actually saw it ages ago." Mia jumps lightly from her rock to theirs and sits down beside Robbie. "Before we even knew when your birthday was."

"And we thought it was so you," he adds.

"So we went back to see if it was still there last week." Mia gives her a shy smile as Robbie passes it to Claire.

Incredibly curious, Claire turns over the tiny package in her hand, wondering what might be considered "so her." She peels away the thin crepe paper and reveals a tiny card box. She flips open the lid. Nestled inside on a piece of fabric is a ring. The wide band is made from silver, and a delicate engraved pattern encircles each edge of the ring. It's tarnished already, as though it's old.

"It's vintage," Robbie tells her.

She pulls it out, slips it on her index finger, and holds it up. It's perfect. She loves it. It looks like something she's been wearing forever.

Nina leans over her shoulder. "That's hot. I'm jealous."

"Do you like it?" Mia asks.

Claire nods. "I do. It's awesome." She smiles at them, feeling suddenly shy. "Thank you so much."

Mia smiles back.

"Good. Neither of us could really afford it, so we decided to split it," Robbie says as he pulls a large envelope out of his bag. "One more thing from me."

"More?" Claire's eyes widen as she turns the ring on her finger. She's already feeling spoiled.

He passes the envelope to her. "A little bonus."

She opens it and pulls out a piece of folded plain white card. She unfolds it and inside is an unframed photograph, *her* photograph, a smaller copy of the portrait from his exhibition. She stares at it, refamiliarising herself with this version of Claire.

He kisses her on the cheek. "You're going to need this. So when you are old and wrinkly, you can show your grandchildren what a hottie you were."

"Thank you." She smiles at him and then stares at it a while longer, feeling slightly unnerved by the uncanny sensation wrought by this familiar yet strange image. This mousey-haired Claire of a couple of months ago already seems like a different person. She wonders what she was thinking in that moment as she stared out into the bar at the very moment the photo was shot. She can't remember much about that night at all, except that she talked to Robbie properly for the first time. It was, in so many ways, so long ago.

"Is it the photo from the exhibition?" Nina asks. "That was so beautiful. Can I see?"

Claire nods but then stares at it for a fraction longer before she hands it over to Nina.

Pete sighs. "I feel bad, Claire. I don't have anything. I didn't even know it was your birthday until this morning."

"It's totally fine, Pete," she assures him.

"Nah." He shakes his head. "Before we leave here, you'll get your birthday present. I'll think of something."

"Thanks, everyone," she says shyly. "Except Pete, of course," she adds, and gives him a dirty look.

CHAPTER 52

They stay out by the lake all day and graze over the food they brought. They drink champagne to toast Claire's birthday and luxuriate in the last day of their little holiday. Faced with the prospect of their departure tomorrow, they stubbornly remain until the sun drops behind the trees, until the shadows fall across the water, and the chill begins to set in, making the most of the time they have left. Finally, when it's too cold, they wearily carry everything up the track.

"Let's watch a film," Robbie suggests as they pile into the house. Since their arrival, he has been working his way through the old DVDs, mostly Cam's, a motley collection of action and blockbusters. Robbie loves them. For someone who is so artsy, he has an incredible tolerance for crappy films.

The collective mood is tired and mellow, so they all agree to a movie. They put away their stuff, change out of swimming clothes, and slowly return to the living room. Claire grabs a blanket from the shelf and settles on one end of the big couch, relishing the comparative warmth of the house. As she pulls the blanket over her, Nina plonks down next to her, grabs half of it, and drags it over her lap. Claire fights disappointment. She'd hoped Mia would sit next to her.

Without discussing it, they've kept a physical distance from each other today and not put this thing between them on show for the others. Claire knows she's definitely not ready to have her feelings out there for everyone to see. It's too new and too half formed. She doesn't know what it is for Mia, but there seems to be some unspoken consensus that this is how it should be. But now, she can't help admitting to herself, she craves Mia's nearness again.

Instead, it's Nina huddled up next to her, hogging the blanket. Mia's sprawled across some large cushions on the floor with Blue stretched beside her. Instead of watching the opening scenes of the film, Claire watches Mia as she lies on her side, her hand tucked between her head and the cushion, her knees curled up to her chest. She stares at the tanned sweep of Mia's back and wishes she could run her fingers along that smooth, lightly freckled stretch between her narrow shoulder blades. She feels an urgent desire to lie down with her, to shape herself around the arc of Mia's back, and to wrap an arm around her waist as Mia did to her this morning as they fell back into sleep. Instead Claire lets out a small sigh and returns her gaze to the screen. She has absolutely no idea how she has become so suddenly, incredibly smitten.

She tries to focus on the film, but like all action films it has the opposite effect it should on Claire. The relentless speed and sound and danger lulls her somehow, making her want to drift off. So she stares at the screen and lets her mind go elsewhere. It's been such a great day. The best birthday she can remember. Everything from waking to now has been perfect, perfect in ways that not so long ago Claire would never have described as perfect.

And never before has Claire felt as though her birthday truly was the start of a new phase of life, a new age—even though that's what they're supposed to be. Most years, Claire hasn't given her birthday much thought. Or when she has, she's simply felt the inexorable sameness of her life, no matter what new age she becomes. Thirteen felt no different from twelve although people made such a big deal out of it. Sixteen felt like fifteen, and eighteen felt uncannily like seventeen, despite the parties.

But being with these people and waking up this morning to the newness that is her and Mia, it all feels so changed and, in so many ways, so good. Everything that has happened these last few months makes it feel as if something may have palpably shifted in her life—that twenty might somehow be distinctively different from nineteen.

A tiny snore erupts from Nina, yanking Claire from her thoughts. Both of them jump.

"Oh." Nina gasps as she sits up rapidly and rubs her face. "I think I fell asleep."

"You did," Claire whispers, not wanting to disrupt everyone's seeming infatuation with this stupid film. She smirks. "You snored."

"Did I?" Nina reaches up into a long stretch, her skinny little arms arching back behind her. "I think I'm going to go to bed. It's probably only, like, nine o'clock, but I'm so tired. Happy birthday, babe." She squeezes Claire's arm and climbs off the sofa. "Good night."

"Night." Claire watches Nina tiptoe carefully out of the room as if she thinks her bare feet padding along the polished wooden floors could do anything to detract from the racket of the high-speed chase that roars from the TV screen.

Just when Claire, sick of the film, is considering the thought of going to her room, Mia sits up and stretches.

"Bathroom," she mumbles wearily.

Robbie drags his eyes from the film for a second. "You want me to pause it?"

Mia shakes her head and slowly clambers to her feet. She turns and gives Claire a sleepy smile as she passes her.

While Mia is gone, Pete appears from somewhere. Yawning, he flops down in Mia's spot on the floor. Claire smiles. *Thank you, Pete.* Without even realising it, he's delivered on that birthday present he promised.

And when she finally returns, Mia sees Pete in her spot and sits down on the sofa next to Claire. She drapes half the blanket over her, pulls her knees up to her chest, and sits back against the couch. She turns her head toward Claire slightly. "I hate this movie," she whispers into the air between them.

Claire nods. She slowly, timidly reaches out under the blanket and wraps a surreptitious hand around Mia's narrow ankle. And it is mere seconds before Mia's hand joins hers. Her fingers slide over Claire's hand and then her arm, where her fingers stroke the skin of her inner wrist.

Claire bites down on her lip, trying to contain her pleasure at how just that small touch creates a rush of feelings. She squeezes Mia's ankle and refocuses on the film, not wanting to draw any attention to them. But now the night feels complete.

* * *

Claire wonders where the hell Mia is.

She gave up before the end of the movie and, feigning tiredness, she took herself to bed, hoping Mia would know to follow soon after. She hasn't yet.

She rests her head against the pillow and tries to take in the way things have abruptly shifted today. This thing with Mia, she knows, isn't fleeting or small or in the slightest bit insignificant. Not for her, anyway. But it's also new and tender and half formed. And maybe that's partly why she doesn't want the others to know. Because they will make jokes and tease and do the very thing Claire would do if she were witness to a new and highly unexpected pairing. And Claire doesn't want to spoil it with any of that. Let it be precious for a minute. She hopes Mia feels the same.

But now that she's lying in her bed alone, she wants Mia with her now. And it *will* happen even if Claire has to go and get her. She doesn't have to, though, because as she lies there in the darkness and enjoys being cold enough to be under the blankets and cosy, she hears the vibration of her phone. A message. She picks it up and smiles. *Are you awake?*

Her smile grows as she taps her response. *Yes. I'm waiting for you to come here.*

She tucks away her phone, rolls onto her side, and waits. And it's only a minute or two before she hears the quiet squeak of the front screen door, followed by soft footfalls coming toward the room. She smiles into the half darkness. Then there is a tap on the door.

"Don't knock!" Claire whispers loudly. "Just come in."

Mia edges in the door. Claire can make out her bashful grin in the moonlight.

"What are you doing?" she asks, one arm clutching the doorpost. Blue pads inside and immediately flops down on the rug as if he already considers it his room.

"I told you. Waiting for you. Come here."

Mia finally, it seems, needs no further invitation. She tiptoes over to the bed, climbs onto the mattress, and sits next to Claire cross-legged. She smiles down at her. "Hey."

"Hey." Claire feels strangely shy now she has Mia right where she wants her.

"They're all watching another movie. So, did you have a good birthday?"

Claire nods. "Yes," she says quietly, still surprised by this fact. "I really, really did."

Then they just look at each other.

And because Mia doesn't seem as if she is going to do anything but return her gaze, Claire shyly pulls her hand out from under the covers and slides it onto Mia's knee. At that, Mia immediately reaches out and takes the hand in her own and holds it gently between both of hers.

"It was a great day, actually."

"Good." Mia strokes the back of her hand with her thumb. Then she looks down at the blankets between them. That small tense furrow makes an appearance between her eyebrows

"Did *you* have a good day?" Claire asks, slightly unnerved by her tense expression.

Mia nods, and a small smile escapes. Then, as she looks down to their hands entwined on her knee, her face turns straight back to uncertainty. She looks like someone who has been reminded of something she was finally able to forget for a minute.

Claire wants to ask her what it is that makes her look like that, but she also doesn't want to in case it's something that could snap this tender, tentative connection they have made in the last twenty-four hours. But finally she has to ask her something because she feels as though, if she lets her, Mia will sit there and stare at her lap and chew at her lip all night. She squeezes her hand. "Are you okay?"

"Yeah, I am." Mia nods and gives her another more decisive smile as if she has committed to being okay right at this very moment.

Claire has no idea how to respond. But what she does know is that she wants to be nearer to her, that certainty might return if they return to where they were last night. "Lie down with me." She pulls her hand free and lifts the blanket, inviting Mia in with her outstretched arm.

Mia leans back a little, and her eyes narrow slightly. "Are you sure?"

"What do you mean am I sure? Come *here*," she commands, wondering why Mia seems to slip so confusingly between being tentative and being so sure of herself. It dizzies and mystifies her.

Mia obediently shuffles under the covers and lies down next to her. Claire pulls her in against her shoulder, curls her arm around her, and absorbs her into the warmth of the bed. She rests her cheek against the top of her head. Mia's hair smells like grass and like water, like the lake.

"I don't get it." Claire inhales the scent and squeezes her closer. "I tell you to come here, and then you're nervous I don't want you here? What do you want, Mia, a formal written invitation? Because my handwriting is terrible."

"I'm sorry." Mia shakes her head and pushes her face into Claire's neck. "I don't know what it is. I'm not usually so..." She doesn't finish the sentence.

Sighing, Claire pulls her arm out from under Mia and slides down the bed until she faces her. Mia chews her lip, looking more timid than Claire is used to. It makes her seem younger. It's weird; Mia usually acts so grown up, so mature. But right now Claire feels as if she's the older one.

"Well stop it. It's just me, remember?" Claire whispers, echoing the sentiment that seemed to assuage Mia's nerves last night. She brings her face close to Mia's and brushes some of her hair from her face with her fingertips. Then she wraps a possessive, demanding leg over Mia's and grins at her. "It's just stupid me who, despite the fact she is kind of a brat, *you* seemed to like last night."

Mia lets out a short breathless laugh, and Claire decides to take it as agreement.

"So stop being a weirdo." She smiles at Mia to soften the name-calling, then leans in and presses her lips to Mia's and tries to kiss away whatever doubts she's carried into this room.

And Mia wraps an arm around her waist and kisses her.

Satisfied that Mia is finally present in some form, Claire rests her head against hers and lies there in the quiet and relishes being tucked inside their private little world. Over the gentle rhythms of their breath, the raucous soundtrack of another action film emanates faintly from the house. There are voices, too, somewhere further away. Probably some weekend arrivals. Their conversations slide easily over the still lake water.

Mia shifts a little under the blanket and curls her arm further around Claire's waist, breathing softly into the half darkness. Claire shuts her eyes and wishes again she knew why Mia has all of a sudden been wrought so shy and weird and what this small but significant air of tension she has brought into the room is.

She still doesn't even know why Mia abruptly turned around and suddenly seemed to want her last night, let alone does she know anything of what Mia's thinking. Claire feels as though she declared herself in that clumsy speech on the porch last night. But Mia has not explained herself or her actions in any way yet. In fact, she just did what she seems to do— to act but say nothing about it. The only difference is that she has not run away this time. But Claire still can't help but wonder if this silence, this apprehension, might be some form of retreat.

But it's a retreat Claire is just as scared to try and pull Mia back from. Because she's not sure how fragile this thing between them might be right now and what kind of danger she might put it in if she questions it. So she is willing to settle for the fact that right now, in this moment, she has Mia here in this bed, wrapped in this tender limbo with her. It's a quiet, not quite comprehensible version of Mia, but it's Mia.

Besides, the tantalising perfection of right now—of this whole day—is too good to want to spoil with those kinds of questions and whatever unexpected answers they might possibly yield.

Part of her wishes they were on their own here or that they at least had a little more time. Then maybe they'd have a minute to define or cement this thing between them before it's time to return to the crude world of Melbourne and to everything that might get in the way of their doing that. And then there is that equally terrifying prospect: what if it's not the same when they leave here? Unnerved by these thoughts, Claire reflexively holds on to Mia a little tighter. She does *not* want to leave this bubble yet.

But there's no time left. They are leaving tomorrow because Claire's parents are coming up the day after. She presses a kiss against Mia's shoulder and sighs, knowing these silent minutes that are trickling by right now are probably the last moments of peace they'll have together on this trip.

Mia turns her head. "I better go soon," she whispers and presses her face against Claire's cheek.

Claire nods but doesn't say anything. She doesn't want her to go at all, but Mia clearly doesn't want Pete to wonder why she isn't in the bunkhouse for another night. And Claire respects her need for privacy.

But unable to let her go just yet, Claire lifts her head and stares at her. "A bit longer?" She compounds the urgency of the request with a slow, tempting kiss. She knows she's not great at talking or at knowing where to start to make Mia talk, but she's fairly sure she knows how to keep Mia in this bed without saying a word. She slides her hand under the hem of Mia's T-shirt and smoothes her palm slowly up her side as she kisses her.

And it seems to work because Mia's only response is to pull her closer and to kiss her harder. Surfing the rapidly rising tide of her own desire, Claire rolls over and climbs on top of Mia. She lines her torso luxuriously along Mia's, runs her hands up into her hair, and kisses her again.

Claire sits up and looks down at her. "Besides, it's still my birthday, so you have to do as I say. It's the rules." She taps out a playful typewriter on Mia's slender collarbones and grins at her.

Mia just laughs and wraps her arms around Claire's waist. "Really?" She runs her hands under the back of Claire's T-shirt. Claire shivers as Mia's hands roam over her back. "And how is that different from any other day, Claire?" She grins slyly and pulls her down and kisses her.

"Oh shut up," Claire tells her between kisses, but she's not too convincing.

CHAPTER 53

"Ta-da!" Pete holds out his arms.

Claire, still sleepy eyed, looks around the living area and blinks. It's spotless, the cleanest it's looked since they first arrived and unleashed six people's holiday on it. The tables are clear of glasses and mugs, the wooden floor swept, the rug shaken out, and the cushions piled neatly on the sofa.

"I did the kitchen too."

Claire steps into the kitchen. The same again. Spotless. The surfaces are wiped clean, the dishes washed and piled up on the sink. The floor sparkles.

"What have you done?" She shakes her head.

He grabs her by the shoulders. "Happy belated birthday, Claire. Told you I'd think of something."

She can't stop staring. "This is amazing. I didn't even hear you. When did you do this?"

"I woke up early, and I was bored, and I realised we'd have to clean up a lot. Thought I'd get a head start." He hangs a damp tea towel over the back of a chair. "I'm sure there's still stuff to do, but I wanted to help."

"Pete, you're possibly my favourite person in the world right now. Thank you." Claire tells him.

The others wake one by one, each stopped in their tracks by the sight of the immaculate state of the cottage. Instead of spending the morning cleaning, as planned, they throw their bedding into the washing machine, make sandwiches with the last of the food, and take them down to the lake for a breakfast picnic and a swim.

"Pete, you are so my hero right now." Nina pulls the crust off her sandwich and tosses it to Blue. "Thanks to you, we get one more swim."

"I promised Claire a birthday present, and I'm a man of my word." Pete looks at his watch. "I'd better get on the road soon, though. I have a family thing on tonight."

"Oh, I don't want to go home." Eli sighs and lies back against the sun-baked rocks. "And I don't want to go back to work tomorrow either."

"Me either. I don't want to go back to the real world." Robbie pouts. "And just to make my return truly special, I have a 6am shift tomorrow morning."

"Well, I have to work tonight," Nina moans.

"Really?"

"Yep."

Claire tosses the last of her sandwich to Blue. He sniffs it and then snaffles it in one mouthful. "Hey, Neen, maybe you should go back with Pete—if that's okay with Pete, of course. So you're not late? I need to stay another couple of hours and hang out the sheets and towels and stuff so it's ready for Mum and Dad. I don't know what time I'll get back."

"That's no problem," Pete tells Nina. "As long as you don't mind my crappy old car. Benny's kind of cranky, but he'll get us back, I promise."

Nina laughs. "Nah, I love a bomb. Especially a bomb called Benny."

Mia sits down beside Claire. "Do you have much to do? I can stay and help if you want?"

Before Claire can speak, Robbie sits up. "Well, if Mia stays to help Claire, can we grab a ride with you, too, Pete? I have something on tonight."

"Yeah, of course. The more the merrier, Benny says. I'm going for one more swim, and then we can get going." He jumps off the rocks and into the water.

Claire stares down at her hands and wonders how it happened so quickly that she's been granted this unexpected gift of more time alone with Mia. She wonders if Robbie is doing it as a favour or if he really does need to get back. Either way, she's grateful.

CHAPTER 54

Hot and tired from all the work, they decide to spend one more sneaky hour by the lake before they pack up and head back to Melbourne.

She and Mia have spent the last couple of hours since the others left industriously cleaning. They tidied up the bedrooms, cleaned the bathroom, swept the porch, aired out the place—all the jobs Pete didn't get to—with the radio turned up loud and the breeze rushing in the open windows and doors. They haven't spoken much, except about what they're doing. They haven't even touched. But Claire isn't worried. They have some time now. And she's strangely enjoying just being alone with Mia, knowing they have the rest of the afternoon together. Maybe more, if Claire can swing it.

Mia sighs and looks out at the trees as they step onto the path, Blue at their heels. "I don't want to leave. It's so beautiful here."

And that's when Claire presents the idea that's been circling her mind for the last hour. "Hey, do you have to do anything tonight? Back home?"

"Nope." Mia shakes her head. "No plans. I don't even work until the weekend."

"Would you want to, I don't know, maybe stay here another night?" Claire asks, clutching the towel around her neck. "Mum and Dad won't get here until the afternoon, so as long as we left by then?" She feels suddenly clumsy. "Only if you wanted. I just thought..."

Mia turns and smiles at her, but before she can say anything, a couple of kids come sprinting up the track toward them.

Claire steps to the side, expecting them to barrel past. They don't. They stop right in front of them.

The girl, about ten or eleven, wide-eyed and panting, gasps and says, "Can you please help us? Emily's stuck in the rocks."

"Where is she?" Claire asks.

"Down there." The girl points toward the grass path. "And she's hurt herself."

At those words, the boy, who is only about five or six, starts to cry. Mia immediately leans down and puts an arm around him. He kind of ducks his head but submits.

"Okay, come on." Claire puts her hand on the girl's shoulder. "Show me."

The girl takes off down the path at a run, and Claire follows her along the grass path. She spots another boy of about the same age with bright-red hair, looking down at something near the water, and drops her bag down on the ground.

When Claire climbs onto the rock where he stands, she sees what he's looking at. Another girl is down there, sandwiched between two large rocks, half in the water, with her torso draped over the rock. She stares up at them with the wide-eyed look of someone in shock.

Clair kicks off her shoes and slides into the water and flinches at the shock of cold. She wades over to the girl and puts a reassuring hand on her back. "Hey, sweetie, you okay?"

The girl shakes her head.

"Her foot's stuck under the rock," the boy says.

"Does it hurt?"

The girl shakes her head. "My arm," she mumbles.

Claire looks at her arms and immediately notices that the left one is clearly not okay. There's no mistaking the misshapen form of the bone just above her wrist that pushes the skin up and turns it a mottled reddish purple. It's a very broken arm. They need to get her out.

Claire peers into the water, but there's nothing to see but muddy brown and the faintest red wash of blood in the water. "Does anything else hurt?"

The girl shakes her head.

Claire pulls in a deep breath and steels herself, nervous of what she's going to find down there.

She leans over the girl. "What's your name?"

"Rhiannon."

"Rhiannon, honey, I'm going to try and get your foot out, okay?"

Rhiannon nods and presses her lips together, clearly terrified.

"I'll be really careful, but you just tell me if it hurts, okay?"

Rhiannon nods again and shuts her eyes as if trying to block it all out.

"Do you need help?" Mia steps over to the edge of the rock, holding the little boy's hand. The other two kids huddle close to her.

"Maybe. Get ready to pull her out when I get her foot loose, okay?" She looks up at Mia and then at the arm, guiding her with her eyes. "She's hurt her arm, though, so be careful." She doesn't want to say the word "broken" out loud.

Mia flicks her eyes over the girl and looks back at Claire. Her eyes widen slightly.

Claire crouches in the water and follows the girl's leg with her hand along her shins to her ankle as she tries to keep her face above the water. She fishes around on the muddy, pebbly bottom and locates Rhiannon's small foot. It's half under the rock while her heel is wedged against another. She must have twisted it and got jammed in this tight spot between them.

Claire stays crouched in the water, her hand still on the foot, and tries to figure out how she's going to turn her without hurting her. Finally, she stands up and leans on the rock next to the girl. Her eyes are still squeezed shut as if she is waiting for a needle. Claire puts a hand on her arm. "Hey, Rhiannon, I want you to do something for me, okay?"

Rhiannon opens her eyes. She doesn't nod, though, clearly not ready to commit until she knows what it is. Her good hand flattens against the rock.

Claire strokes the skinny, freckled arm under her hand. "My friend Mia is going to grab you and just pull you up a tiny bit so I can get your foot out."

Claire can already see Mia react in her periphery. She moves close to Rhiannon, one hand still attached to the little limpet boy.

"And all I need you to do is be brave and stay very still. Then I'm just going to turn you around a little bit and get that foot out, okay?"

Rhiannon nods, clearly terrified into obedience.

Claire bites her lip, scared of hurting her. At least she's fairly certain Rhiannon's too shocked to feel too much pain.

"It going to be really easy, okay? And it won't hurt." Claire hopes she's telling her some sort of truth.

Rhiannon nods again, and Claire decides to just get on with it.

Mia lets go of the little boy, which makes him cry louder, and grabs Rhiannon. The girl who accosted them on the path immediately steps in and takes the crying boy's hand.

"Okay, can you lift her a real tiny bit?" Claire asks. "I'm going to turn her toward you."

Mia nods, hooks her hands under Rhiannon's shoulders, and pulls her up. Rhiannon whimpers but remains stoic.

Claire takes a deep breath, ducks right under the water, and feels around for the foot while her other hand reaches up and swivels Rhiannon around a little by her hips. A second later, her foot is free. Claire pulls her head back above the water, pushes her wet hair out of her face, and nods up at Mia. "It's out. Let's get her up."

Claire hauls herself out of the lake and helps Mia pull Rhiannon up and lay her down on the dry, flat surface of the rock. That's when she sees the source of the blood in the water, a big gash along the side of Rhiannon's skinny little thigh. She must have scraped it against the rocks as she fell. It doesn't look deep, but it's weeping and angry.

At the sight of the blood, the little boy starts to wail. The other girl pulls him a few steps back, away from it all, but it doesn't make a difference.

Mia crouches down next to Rhiannon, pulls a towel out of her bag, and places it under her head. "Can you please get that for me?" Mia asks the older boy, pointing at Claire's bag. He obediently grabs it and brings it over to her. Mia pulls out Claire's towel.

Claire places a hand on Rhiannon's head. Her face is ashen.

"It's okay, honey." She strokes a hand through her red curls and tries to sound as soothing as she can. They need to get help, though. She looks up at the boy with the matching ginger hair. "You're her brother?"

He nods.

"What's your name?"

"Liam."

"Where do you live, Liam?"

"Over there." He turns and points across the arm of the lake toward one of the houses near the jetty. Not too far away.

"Are your parents home?" She presses her hand on Rhiannon's head as the girl begins to whimper a little.

He nods.

"Liam, I need you to run home, okay? And tell your parents that they need to drive around to 451 Currawong—the driveway with the blue letterbox on the road, okay?"

"Ambulance?" Mia mutters under her breath.

Claire shakes her head. "Takes too long around here. They'll get her there faster."

She turns back to Liam. "Can you repeat that address?" She tries to sound as light and calm as possible even though the blood seeping from Rhiannon's leg has started to unnerve her.

"451 Currawong, blue letterbox."

"Good boy." She smiles at him. "Tell them she's fine, but they are going to need to get her to the doctor, okay?"

He nods and runs off.

Claire looks at the older girl. "Can you do something for us too?"

The girl nods, eager.

"Go up to the house at the end of the path. The one with the big porch and the silver car outside. Go in the back door—it's open. And on a shelf just inside, you'll see a first aid kit. You know what that looks like? A white metal box with a big red cross on it?"

She nods vigorously. "Yep."

"Good. You grab that and bring it back here, okay?" Claire looks at the little boy, his wails reduced to teeny shredding little sobs. "You want to sit with me and help so she can run fast?"

He shakes his head.

The girl pushes him gently toward Claire. "Stay with the lady. I have to go fast. I'll come right back." She takes off at a sprint across the rocks.

Claire smiles at him in a way she hopes is reassuring and holds her hand out. He takes a few tentative steps forward and grabs her hand.

Claire pulls him to her side gently. "Here, you sit down next me."

He obediently drops into a squat next to her as his little chest heaves.

"Why don't you help, by holding your... is she your sister? Hold her hand?"

"Cousin," Rhiannon mutters faintly as the little boy takes her hand.

Rhiannon watches as Mia bolsters the broken arm with Claire's folded towel. Her eyes widen at the sight of her arm.

"Hey, don't look at that. Look at me," Claire says as lightly as she can. She pulls Rhiannon's face gently toward her with the flat of her hand against her cold little cheek and smiles down at her. "My name is Claire, and you're Rhiannon, right?"

The girl nods.

Claire turns to the little boy. "And what's your name?"

The boy just stares at her and sniffs.

"He's Will," Rhiannon tells her.

"Hi, Will. That's my friend Mia." Claire points over at Mia, who is digging in her bag for something.

"Hi, Will. Hi, Rhiannon," Mia says super calmly, flashing them a warm smile as she pulls a bottle of water from her bag. "And this is Blue." She points at the dog.

"Mia's going to be a doctor some day, so she's going to be really good at looking after you until your mum and dad come."

Rhiannon nods faintly.

"You know what?" Claire leans forward, conspiratorial, still trying desperately to run distraction. "I bet I know what you guys were up to."

"What?"

"I bet you guys were climbing the rocks to see what's around the other side, weren't you?" She tilts her head to the small rocky hill at the point of the inlet, where the lake disappears into the trees.

"How did you know?" Rhiannon gasps.

"Because I have been coming up here since I was younger than Will." Claire wraps an arm around the boy who is fixed on the project of holding his cousin's pale little hand in his tiny brown one. "And when I was younger, I always wanted to know what was around there, too. But our parents wouldn't let us climb those rocks, because they were scared we would fall."

"I fell," Rhiannon gravely tells her.

Claire fights the urge to laugh when Rhiannon states the complete and utter obvious. Instead, she watches Mia unscrew the cap of a bottle of water and pour a little on her leg, washing it clean. It's bleeding less profusely now.

Rhiannon winces, taking in air with a pained little gasp.

Claire smoothes a hand over her pale forehead again. "Well, we used to think there was some kind of magic land around there. But, want to know a secret?" She smiles down at her.

"What?" Rhiannon asks, truly distracted now.

"I've been around there."

"You have?"

"Yep." Claire nods. "My brother and I snuck around there one day when our parents weren't watching."

"What's there?" Rhiannon asks, blinking.

"You really want to know?" Claire asks as the other girl arrives, the first aid kit clanking against her legs. "That was super quick," she tells her. "You should try for the Olympics."

The girl smiles proudly, panting, and passes the box to Mia. She immediately opens it and pulls out gauze and a bandage to wrap up Rhiannon's leg.

Rhiannon doesn't even seem to notice, she's too distracted—as planned—by the carrot Claire dangles in front of her. "What's around there?" she asks, urgent now.

Claire sighs, dramatically. She affects a despondent, disappointed expression. "*Nothing.* Nothing at all. Just more trees and rocks. And some more houses."

"Oh."

Claire wants to smile again but doesn't. Rhiannon looks crestfallen. But at least she's occupied while Mia dresses her leg.

"I know, right?" Claire frowns, sighing dramatically. "It was so boring. But hey, I saved you another trip, right?"

Before Rhiannon can say anything, the sound of footsteps running down the path echoes through the air.

She looks up. Coming at them in great strides is a tall man with a shock of curls that are clearly the genetic source of his kids' extreme gingerness. He bounds over to the rock, Rhiannon's brother at his heels, and crouches down over her.

"Rhi." He pants.

"We think she's okay," Mia tells him. "Just her arm and the leg."

He nods but doesn't say anything, too fixed on his kid. He puts his hands under her knees and neck, ready to scoop her up, and turns to Mia. "Can you support her arm?" His voice is gruff with fear.

But Mia is already doing it. She holds Rhiannon's arm and the towel as he rises to his feet. She gently places the towel on Rhiannon's stomach.

"Thank you," he mutters and strides away across the rocks with Rhiannon in his arms, Liam at his heels. The other girl holds her hands out for Will, who immediately scurries over to her and grabs it. They take off behind the others.

Claire and Mia pick up the bags and set off after them.

Halfway up the track, as the girl and Will disappear, Claire turns to Mia and lets out a breath. The adrenalin dissipates.

Mia matches her sigh with a relieved look.

Claire nods. "Wasn't expecting that this morning."

Mia smiles at her and takes her hand. She squeezes it gently as they stride up the path.

Claire squeezes back, still rattled. And relieved they didn't have to deal with anything worse.

Just as they near the top of the path, Claire spots a flash of black next to a red car through the scrub ahead and stops in her tracks. She drops Mia's hand.

Is that her parents' car?

She stares. Yes, that's unmistakably her parents' car. She stands there, frozen on the spot, and blinks.

"What's up?" Mia adjusts her bag on her shoulder and turns to Claire.

"My parents are here." She says it slowly, not quite believing the words.

"Really?" Mia peers through the trees.

Claire nods, speechless. This is not ideal, to say the least.

"Oh."

Claire doesn't reply as she walks mechanically up the track, already resigned to this weird and highly uncomfortable fate. What are they doing here? They aren't supposed to arrive until tomorrow. And they *never* change their perfectly laid plans.

They come out at the top of the trail, and Claire pauses again to take in the harried scene. The ginger-haired man is packing Rhiannon into the back of the car with the help of Claire's father. A small, thin woman holds the door open on the other side. The other kids are clustered near the car in a tight group, looking cold and still a little scared.

Her parents have clearly just arrived, the doors of the four-wheel drive, which is parked halfway up the drive instead of the usual spot, hang wide open.

Claire's mother trots out of the house, cushions and a blanket in her hand. She comes around the side of the car and hands them to the woman.

"We'll take care of them, don't worry," her mother says as the woman climbs in the back of the car.

The man scrambles into the driver's seat and starts the car as Christine shoos the remaining kids off the driveway and watches him make a turn and speed off down the driveway. That's when she spots Mia and Claire standing at the top of the lake path.

"Sweetheart," she calls out, hands on hips. "Not quite what we were expecting."

Reluctantly, Claire takes a deep breath and trudges slowly over to her, Mia and Blue beside her.

"Hey, Mum," Claire mumbles. "This my friend, Mia. Mia, this...this is my mother. And that's my dad." Her father gives her a wave as he closes the doors of the four-wheel drive.

"Hello, Mia. Call me Christine." She turns back to Claire, straight to business. "They're taking the girl to the hospital. And I said we'd look after these little ones until the aunt comes to get them. She's still a way away." She shields her eyes from the afternoon sun and appraises the little group. She gives the kids her best Christine Pearson smile.

They smile politely back, still huddled in a tight cluster.

"What on earth happened, sweetheart?" Christine asks as Claire's father comes over to join them. He leans down to pat Blue. "Were you with them?"

As she wrings out her wet T-shirt onto the gravel driveway, Claire gives them a brief explanation of what happened.

"Well, it was lucky you were here," her father says. "Good job, girls." He pats Claire's shoulder and then holds out a hand to Mia.

Claire watches numbly as Mia shakes his hand and shivers slightly with cold.

Her mother goes straight into crisis-management mode and hustles the kids into the house, telling Claire that due to a dropped case they had been able to leave a day earlier. Then she busies herself making sandwiches and warm drinks for the kids.

Meanwhile, Claire ducks off to the sleeping porch and digs through her packed bag for her jeans and a jumper, warm clothes she hasn't needed to put on since they arrived. Once dried and changed, she pauses by the door and takes a deep breath before she returns to the house. This is not the day she expected. Nor is it the one she hoped for. Not one little bit.

CHAPTER 55

As the afternoon light wanes, Claire and Mia walk the kids back to their house to change and to wait for the aunt to come and collect them. It's almost chilly now as the sun drops and clouds gather over the lake, and the kids are still in their shorts and T-shirts from the day's sunshine. They hurry along the lake path under the shade of the casuarina trees.

Letting themselves into the large, two-story house, the kids disperse to various rooms to hunt out warmer clothes while Claire and Mia wait in the huge, open-plan living and kitchen area. Claire wonders what Mia makes of the sudden appearance of Claire's parents, of what has happened to this day. For the first time since her mum and dad arrived, Claire makes eye contact with her.

"Sorry about my parents turning up," she mumbles and crosses her arms over her chest.

"Why? It's their house. And they seem nice."

Claire shakes her head. That's not what she meant.

But Mia doesn't appear to be thinking about that. She leans back against the bench, shakes her head slowly, and smiles at her.

"What?" Claire pulls a face at her, rendered uncomfortable.

"You were *amazing* before, you know."

Claire thrusts her hands in jeans pockets and sits against the back of the couch. "Yeah, well, so were you."

"What? No. I just did basic first aid. I learned that at camp. But you, you were incredible." She stares at Claire. "Knowing what to do, dealing with the kids, keeping Rhiannon calm." She shakes her head again. "Seriously."

Claire tries to shrug it off, blushing a little at such praise. "Well my parents taught me what to do in every single possible kind of emergency situation from the age of, like, six. They're big on contingencies."

"Whatever, it was amazing." Mia smiles defiantly at her as if she dares her to protest again.

And Claire is just about to brush it off again when Will comes in wearing a woollen jumper that is far too big to actually be his. His legs and feet are still bare, and he's carrying a large plastic dinosaur. He takes it to Mia and holds it up with a grin. It seems he's forgotten all about Rhiannon's accident.

It's only then that Claire realises she hasn't heard him say a single word yet. She wonders if he can actually speak.

They patiently encourage Will to put on some pants and, despite the rapidly cooling weather, all go wait out on the porch.

The house is situated in a beautiful spot, and the high veranda gives a more expansive view of the lake and the bushland around than her parents' place. Mia sits at the picnic table with Will and the girl, Stella, and plays a board game Will dragged out with them. Liam parks himself on the steps leading to the garden, his freckled arms resting on his knobby little knees. Claire watches him stare out at the lake. He hasn't said anything much since his parents drove off to the hospital.

"Your sister's going to be okay, you know," Claire tells him lightly and sits next to him.

He nods his freckled little face and frowns as though he may not believe her.

"I *promise*."

He nods again and hugs his knees to his chest.

"And you know what?" Claire nudges him gently with her arm. "She'll probably have a cast put on her arm, so you'll get to draw on it and stuff."

But that's not what's on his mind. "Her leg was bleeding *a lot*."

Claire bites her lip. Of course that cut frightened him more than the arm, she realises. All that blood. It looked pretty bad.

Years ago, one of the summer boys cut his foot open on a broken beer bottle on the shore of the lake. At eight she'd been horrified at the way the kid's face blanched at the sight of the blood and how he left a trail of red on the path as he limped back up to the house.

"It was a bit of blood," she agrees casually. "But don't worry, she's got plenty left. There's lots of blood inside you, you know. She can definitely spare some."

He turns to face her, curious now. "How much?"

"I'm not exactly sure. But I bet Mia knows. You should ask her."

"That's okay."

His freckles stand out against his pale skin even as the light wanes.

She nudges his shoulder gently. "Hey, don't worry. It looked bad, but it really wasn't. I mean, don't get me wrong, it was totally gross."

He smiles. A small one.

"But it really wasn't bad. She'll be fine."

He nods again, looking a little calmer. They sit in silence together as the sun drops further behind the trees.

"I wish I could have a cast on my arm," he suddenly says. "Or maybe on my leg. Then I wouldn't have to go to school for a few days, at least. That would be so cool."

Claire laughs.

CHAPTER 56

Christine loves Mia. Of course she does. On paper and in person, Mia is everything Christine desires in the kind of company Claire keeps.

By the time they left the kids with their aunt and walked back to the cottage, it was early evening. Claire's parents both, in a united front of insistence, demanded that they stay the night, unwilling to let Claire drive back to Melbourne so late. Because apparently Claire is not capable of driving in the dark and will most likely kill them both.

In fact, Christine's so determined that they are to stay that by the time they returned, she's bundled Mia's belongings into the spare room and remade the bed in there. And, to make it even more difficult to protest, she'd put the makings of dinner together for them all, so they couldn't really refuse.

Claire knows there is little she can do to convince her parents otherwise when they are both agreed on something, and she barely tries to protest. Mia, clearly dizzied by the whirlwind of energy that is Christine, quietly acquiesces.

So, to Claire's incredible discomfort, they're swiftly and violently submitted to a night with her parents at the cottage. And in one fell Christine-driven swoop, the night that Claire hoped for—a quiet, private night to be with Mia, to possibly make sense of this new dynamic between them—disappeared. Instead, that night, so full of potential and promise, was swiftly exchanged for this highly awkward imposter replacement. And now she's relegated to the charade of Claire and her friend just hanging out at the cottage with Claire's parents. It's the last role she wants to play tonight. Or any other night.

They sit at the dinner table, so recently the site of raucous poker and drinking games and of fun, messy meals. Now it's the site of Claire's almost paralysing social anxiety. And Christine, of course, submits

Mia to the usual barrage of questions that she mistakes for normal human conversation. Nothing is left un-interrogated. She asks about her studies, her career plans, her job, her parents, Blue, where she lives, everything.

And despite the fact that she must feel at least a fraction of the awkwardness that Claire feels, Mia deals with it well. Claire listens to the cross-examination and to Mia's cheerful responses. She politely provides answers to everything she's asked and responds with queries of her own. For a moment, Claire finds herself staring in utter admiration at Mia's open, friendly face as she talks. Of course, Mia is good at parents. No parent has probably ever disliked or disapproved of Mia, ever.

A bonus to this unexpected social arrangement, though, is that Christine is so taken with her new friend, she's too busy to pay any attention to Claire. And Claire is incredibly grateful to be left to herself, to concentrate on the simple hand-to-mouth task of eating, playing the patient listener alongside her father. He leaves the table the minute he finishes dinner. Claire stays, though, and pushes the food around her plate, not wanting to abandon Mia.

Slightly wary of Christine's historic ability to deduct everything Claire doesn't want her to discover, she wonders if there is any way her mother could possibly figure out what transpired between Mia and her. Why they are still here, alone. *Of course not.* Her mother is quick, but how can she see something that can't actually be seen? Besides, Claire barely knows what this thing is between her and Mia. How could her mother know? But just to be careful, she drags her eyes from Mia and doesn't look at her again in case her expression reveals too much.

"Do you have a boyfriend, Mia?" Christine suddenly asks.

Oh god. Claire's fork freezes momentarily on the journey from her plate to her mouth. She bids herself to keep eating, to pretend she hasn't even heard.

"No," Mia tells her lightly. "I don't have much time for a social life," she adds as she smiles and tucks her hair behind one ear.

"Ah, I guess not," Christine says airily. "With all that study you have to do." She places her knife and fork neatly beside each other, done with her dinner. "I don't know what Claire's excuse is, though. She has plenty of time on her hands these days."

And with that double whammy, Claire clenches her teeth and puts down her fork. Dinner is officially over.

"What happened to that musician you met, honey?" Christine throws her napkin on her plate.

"He isn't a musician," Claire mumbles as she stands abruptly. She starts to clear the table, desperate to end this meal and this particularly awkward conversation tangent. Now she *really* can't look at Mia. She picks up the plates and takes them into the kitchen.

* * *

Later, in the safety of her sleeping porch, she lies tucked under the blankets and stares into the darkness, sleepless. Thank God the evening is over. Now they can just pack up in the morning and leave.

After they finished dinner, Christine settled in the living room, with the television on, still busily drawing out every aspect of Mia's life. Unable to cope with any more of her mother's questions or comments, Claire escaped to the porch where her father was going over his fishing gear. Her father, of course, wanted her to retell the entire story of what happened to Rhiannon and the kids, to run through every step taken, to assess how Claire had handled it. Claire submitted to it, though, as the better of two evils. By the time she went back inside, Mia had taken herself off to bed. Claire has no idea if it was tiredness or just a need to escape Christine.

Claire said a quiet good night to them both and bolted herself, using the morning departure as an excuse for an early bedtime. And now, as she lies under the covers, she wonders if Mia is awake, wonders how she feels about this whole turn of events. Poor Mia, subjected to her parents on this most surreal of days.

What also keeps her wide awake long into the night is the realisation of another question that she hasn't yet given a second's thought to. What would they—what would her *mother* especially—say about it if she were to date a girl? Christine will have *plenty* of opinions about it, Claire knows that for sure. But she isn't sure she wants to know what they will be. And she certainly doesn't want to know any time soon.

She's still lying there, turning these thoughts over in her mind, when her phone lights up over on the dresser and emits a quiet buzz. A message. She wonders if it's from Mia. She doesn't get up and look though. Because what if Mia wants to come out here to her? Claire wouldn't dare. Her parents, ever vigilant, hear everything that goes on in this place, and she doesn't want them to hear any sneaking around. But Claire doesn't want to say no to Mia, either, so she ignores it and squeezes her eyes shut and bids sleep to come.

She cannot deal with any of this right now.

* * *

It's just past dawn, but Claire's already up. She leans against the porch railing and watches Blue run around and hunt out scents as the sun lifts itself up over the lake through the trees. She packed her bags, showered, and dressed. And now she's waiting until they can leave and get away from this awkward situation.

She knows her parents are up, too, going about the business of their day; neither able to sit still for long. However, when she finally committed herself to the morning and went inside to the kitchen, she didn't find anyone there, just a half-full coffee pot and an empty room. No sign of Mia either.

The screen door opens quietly behind her. Claire steels herself for the potential assault of her mother.

"Hey." It's Mia.

Relieved it's not her mother, Claire turns briefly, long enough to note that Mia's dressed and ready for the day but not long enough to meet her eye. She can't.

"Hey." She clears her throat and puts her coffee mug down on the railing. "We should get going soon."

Mia comes over to stand near Claire. "Sure, I'm ready."

They stand there suspended in a long silence, and both stare out at the lake and the trees. Claire chews on her lip. She wants to apologise for not answering her message last night, but she also doesn't want to bring it up. Because that will bring all the unspoken weirdness of this last twelve hours into a firmer reality. And maybe if it stays in the land of unspoken, it can be ignored.

"Awkward, huh?" Mia suddenly says. She, on the other hand, is clearly not willing to let the situation go by unmentioned.

Claire nods, not quite sure what to say.

Mia takes a step closer to her. "Are you okay?"

Claire tenses, suddenly wary about the unknown whereabouts of her parents.

"Of course I am." She tries to sound as light as possible. "Let me know when you're ready to go." She picks up her coffee cup from the railing and slips back into the house before Mia can come any closer.

CHAPTER 57

Claire takes a deep breath and dials the number. She breathes as steadily as she can through the short voice mail message, nervously awaits the beep, and plunges in.

"Uh, hey, I'm just calling again to tell you Rhiannon—the little girl from the lake—her mum called my mum. Apparently Rhiannon is fine. She's just going to have to have her arm in a cast for a while. And her mum said to say thank you, again. So...uh...anyway, I just thought you might want to know." She bites down her lip until it hurts, urgently trying to decide which way to go next. "Anyway, I hope your grandmother is okay too. Um, okay, I'm going to go. Maybe call me if you, I don't know, want to catch up sometime?" She cringes and grips the edge of her doona. "Bye."

She hurriedly hangs up the phone before she can say anything else dumb. She pushes her face into the pillow and blushes even though no one else can see her.

Catch up. It sounds so ridiculous given this new direction their relationship has taken—or *not* taken. But she didn't know what else to say in her desperation to sound casual, to not let on just how much Mia's sudden silence has thrown her. She pulls the covers over her head, curses loudly, and wishes she could take that message back and start again.

Maybe if she weren't so hungover, she would have been better at it. And maybe if she weren't so crazily fixed on the fact that she hasn't heard anything from Mia that she can't seem to hold a sane thought in her head, she *might* have come up with something better.

She slowly pulls the covers down, blinks into the muted morning light of her bedroom, and listens to the remote sounds of her mother as she charges around the house. She has a day off, and Claire is supposed to go to lunch with her today. Any minute now, she'll rap on Claire's bedroom door to tell her to get ready. And more than most days, Claire wishes she didn't have to. All she wants to do is lie right here and stew on the fact that Mia didn't pick up the phone when Claire called. Again.

They haven't seen each other since the lake. And it's been six days. Six whole, impossible, nerve-wracking days of Claire putting out tentative feelers and Mia doing nothing in response. Well, barely anything. And it's been six days of Claire freaking out more and more about it.

In fact, they haven't even *spoken* since the day they left the lake, after her parents unexpectedly turned up. That experience was awkward as hell, and Claire knows it's partly her fault that it was so uncomfortable. But how could it not have been? When she'd just asked Mia to stay there another night with her and most definitely *not* to hold hands and play Scrabble. And then her parents show up? And then to turn around and introduce her as a new friend? Not ideal. Claire also knows she didn't do much to make that encounter any easier. But she couldn't. She was too paralysed by their sudden, invasive presence to do anything but merely function.

And that awkwardness stayed with them as they drove back to the real world again, leaving behind the bubble of their short, glorious little holiday. Claire climbed into the car that morning harried and annoyed by her mother's last-minute round of reminders and instructions. It was as if Claire had never made the drive between the lake and home before, as if she didn't know the blind spots on the roads, or she didn't know to disable the security alarm back home in Melbourne or anything else her mother felt the need to remind her of.

She was in a foul mood by the time she got in the car. But once on the road, she took in a deep breath and then turned to Mia and smiled.

"I'm sorry. My mother makes me a little tense."

"That's okay." Mia smiled and stared at the road ahead. "She seems like an intense person."

And that's all she said. And that's all Claire could bring herself to say too. For the rest of the drive home, they didn't talk about anything to do with what had passed between them, let alone touch or look at each other. In fact, they were mostly silent. Claire played music to quiet the silence, but it was still irrepressibly there.

Then, when they finally arrived at Mia's house, and it was time for goodbyes, Mia's father was out on the footpath. They'd given him uncomfortable waves as he approached the car and greeted them exuberantly. He didn't even notice the mood, just asked about the trip and helped Mia with her bag as Blue jumped and whimpered with excitement.

All Mia gave Claire in that moment was a quick smile and goodbye and told her she'd talk to her soon. Then she turned and walked inside with her father without looking back.

Claire rolls onto her back and contemplates getting up to nip her mother's nag in the bud. But she really doesn't want to. If Claire has her way, she'll lie in bed all day and stew and wait. That's all she wants to do right now.

And it feels as though, if Mia has her way, they will just lapse into silence altogether. For the umpteenth time in the last few days, Claire scrolls back over her messages between them since they got back from the lake, the few that there are.

She sent the first one a couple of days after they got back after she hadn't heard anything. Unsure what this sudden protracted silence meant, she sent it to Mia just to gauge her response.

My mother didn't say a single thing about the state of the house. We must have actually done a good cleaning job.

The response was brief. *Ha, I'm glad.*

Then there is another message a couple of days later when, embarrassingly unnerved by Mia's three-word response followed by days of silence, she sent another trivial message.

My mother just used the word potential *in a lecture eight times in ten minutes.*

This time the response doesn't arrive for eleven hours. *Wow. Highly annoying, but actually kind of impressive.*

I know, right?

But then nothing.

As she scrolls through the next couple of days, she only sees messages from Robbie, Nina, and Cam. She didn't hear anything else from Mia until Friday. That was the day *after* Claire cracked and tried to call her. But, getting Mia's brief, cheerful voice mail, Claire backed out and hung up at the last minute.

Later that day, Mia messaged.

Hey, sorry, my grandmother is in hospital, and we had to go up and see her this weekend. Back Sunday night.

That message calmed Claire a little. But it was only temporary because now it's Tuesday, and she still hasn't heard a word. And she's too scared to call again after this morning's clumsy message.

But it freaks Claire out because she knows it's a change. A significant one. She knows if she were to scroll back to the time before the lake, she'd see at least a message a day, if not more, between the two of them. Not now.

She keeps reviewing every single moment they spent together. What does it mean? Is Mia completely regretting it now? Or was it nothing to her? It didn't seem like nothing. And Mia certainly didn't treat it like nothing at the time.

That night at the lake Claire feels as though she went over a precipice and she—maybe stupidly—assumed Mia had gone over with her. But maybe she didn't. Does Mia regret this thing they started? This thing *Mia* started but now seems to have stopped participating in?

Claire thumps her phone against the covers a couple of times, contemplative. These short, polite messages throw Claire. She's not used to such brevity or distance from Mia. And she isn't used to it in her romantic life either. Guys who are interested in her are usually pretty persistent, a response to Claire's knee-jerk cold shoulder act, which is her usual means of testing the water and their interest.

She didn't even think to do that with Mia. But now it seems Mia's doing the silent thing to her. And Claire's fairly certain Mia isn't doing it for the same reason. She's way too nice for that. So, Claire has spent hours turning this over and over in her mind, wondering why. And now she's frightened that maybe this thing isn't as serious for Mia as it feels as though it might be for her.

Claire has stewed over this last message, particularly. The one that said she'd be back on Sunday. Didn't that mean Mia would call when she got back? She hasn't yet. Then she chastises herself for being crazy about it and tries to force herself to chill, which is why she made herself go out with Nina for a drink last night. It was no fun, though. In fact, she was so anxious and despondent, she nearly told Nina everything. But all Nina wanted to do was dance and check out guys and for Claire to join in. And Claire suffered through it, receiving an unwanted phone number and a hangover for her troubles.

And Mia didn't call. So, she *still* feels anxious and despondent. With this hangover, she adds sick and tired to the mix too. And her clumsy message this morning might be the last bit of brave she has left. She doesn't know what she'll do if she continues to hear nothing.

She rolls over on the mattress, too committed to her misery to move. This silence has frightened her in a way no silence ever has before. And she hates it.

At first she thought maybe Mia needed some space or some time away from her after the intensity of those few days. Because it *was* intense. And it's not as though Claire isn't feeling those aftershocks too. Every now and then, between her anxieties over Mia's silence, Claire runs her mind over the fact she's so deeply, perplexingly attracted to a girl in a way she's never been attracted to anyone before. Her thoughts touch on the seismic shifts that this is likely to set off in her life but then abandons them. For now, she can't bring herself to care such is her need to make sense of *her and Mia.* But to do that Claire feels as if she needs Mia in her actual sights. It's a pity Mia's not cooperating with that one.

Fighting tears, Claire squeezes her eyes shut and wishes she could backpedal right into sleep and erase this morning, maybe even erase this week. But when the loud knock on her door sounds, when the call to arms comes, she knows she doesn't have a chance in hell of either of those options.

CHAPTER 58

Before she knows it, Claire parks down the street from the café. Before she can stop herself, she climbs out of the car. And before she can decide whether or not it's a dumb idea, she heads straight for the door.

She sees Mia the minute she walks inside, busy at the coffee machine. An immediate conflicting trill of fear and happiness swirls in Claire's stomach, a sensation so sharp that she knows she has to do this no matter what response she gets.

She orders from the girl at the register and then hangs back with the other customers and watches Mia work. Her face is a study of concentration as she works busily and occasionally swaps a joke or a word with the guy by her side. Her hair is pulled up into a loose knot on the top of her head, and stray strands hang around her neck. She looks hot and tired but still so freaking damn cute.

Claire stares so embarrassingly hard she witnesses the very moment Mia sees her name on the order and then glances up as if she wonders if it's her. When she spots Claire, she looks taken aback for a second, but then she gives her a timid smile. And it's the very existence of the smile that gives Claire the courage to move forward until she's leaning on the counter in front of the machine.

"Hey." She clenches her jaw, surprised by just how nervous she feels.

"Hey." Mia frowns at the milk jug. "How are you?" She reads a ticket and calls out a name.

"Fine." Not wanting to be the only thing standing between "Richard" and his latte, Claire ducks out of the way. "You?"

"Good." Mia puts another two cups on the counter. "Meg!" She gives the customer a smile and turns back to Claire. "Yours is next."

Claire nods and bites her lip. She doesn't care about the coffee one little bit. The only thing she cares about is how weird it is to be making this level of clumsy small talk with the person who, only a week ago, she was naked in a bed with, getting to know every part of her body. Claire blushes. Not just at the thought of naked Mia but at the whole damn impossible awkwardness of this encounter. So, to save face and fear, she cuts to the chase and steps back up to the counter.

"So, um, what time do you finish work today?" She clings to the edge of the counter as she asks.

Mia concentrates on whatever she's doing and doesn't answer right away. Then she looks up and hands the coffee to Claire. "At seven."

"Uh, do you think...could...can I come and meet you then?" She takes her drink and clutches it tightly. Too tightly. The waxed cardboard starts to give under her fingers, and she relaxes her grip before she loses her drink or burns her hand. "If you don't have plans already."

Mia looks slightly flummoxed for a moment. Claire honestly can't tell if it's because she's also shy or because she's trying to think of a way out of it. Then suddenly, she nods. "Sure. Maybe at, like, quarter past, if that's okay?"

"Of course." Claire nods, earnest. "I'll...I'll see you later."

"Okay. See you then." Mia gives her a quick smile and goes straight back to work.

Claire marches out of the café as fast as she can. The heat of her embarrassment drains away, and the cool respite of relief quickly takes its place. She hurries back to her car, places the unwanted coffee on the passenger seat, and rests her head back against the seat. At least that part is over. And the radio silence at Mia's end is over too.

The silence is what made her put herself right in front of Mia and to demand her attention. Well, it paid off. Maybe. She'll know tonight. She still has no idea what's going on in Mia's brain, but at least now she's got an opportunity to find out.

* * *

Mia's waiting for her outside the café, leaning against the window with her bag on her shoulder. Claire pulls over and peers up at Mia through the open window, and another sickening clench of nerves stirs in her stomach.

Mia steps over, smiling, but she looks kind of apprehensive too.

"You want to go some place south side?" Claire leans toward the window. "It might be cooler by the water."

"Sure." Mia climbs into the car. She pulls the door closed and then turns and smiles at Claire. "Maybe nowhere too fancy, though. I'm not really dressed for it."

Claire looks over. Mia changed into a new, non-work T-shirt and brushed her hair out, and it hangs around her shoulders. She's made some effort. What does that mean?

She pulls onto the road and shakes her head. "Don't worry. I don't do fancy unless I have to."

* * *

They sit in the busy front terrace of an old, crumbling pub across from the water. A light breeze comes off the bay, butting gently at the hot, still air of the day.

"How was work?" Claire nervously contemplates the menu but more for somewhere to fix her gaze than anything. She's too edgy to be hungry.

"Hot," is all Mia says and sips her beer.

"Is your grandmother okay?"

"Not really." Mia rests her chin on her hands. "She had a stroke."

Claire leans forward, mouth open. "What?"

"A minor one," Mia adds. Her gaze meets Claire's for a moment before she looks the other way. "She's okay. But now, of course, the doctors say there's the risk she'll have another one. A major one."

"That's scary."

"Yeah." Mia nods, staring at the menu. Then she sits back in her seat and shakes her head helplessly. "Can you pick something? I can't think."

"Sure, of course." Claire looks down at the menu for a moment but then decides she'll just wing it at the counter. She goes inside and ends up ordering them both fish and chips. It makes some sort of sense because they're at the beach. Well, across the road from it. When she returns with a handful of cutlery, Mia is chewing on a nail and staring out at the wide stretch of water.

"I'm really sorry, Mia," Claire tells her.

Mia gives her a small smile and returns her gaze to the view. And Claire can't think of anything else to say, so they sit in silence as the tables fill up around them.

"It was just so weird to see her in hospital, you know," Mia suddenly says. "It's so not like her. She's *never* sick."

"Really?" Claire thinks of her own grandparents who always seemed to be suffering from something in the years before they died.

"No, she's crazy tough." Mia smiles. "And not very grandmotherly."

"What do you mean?" Claire leans her elbow on the table, glad that Mia finally decided to talk.

"I just mean she isn't all doting and sweet like most people's grandmothers. I stayed with her nearly every school holidays—my parents had this thing about getting me out of the city as often as possible—and she'd put me to work as soon as I got there. And she always spoke to me like I was a grown up. She's kind of a botanist. Well, she wrote books about flowers. I grew up knowing all the Latin names for them instead of the usual ones." She smiles. "It was kind of confusing. I'd be saying narcissus and hedera when other people were saying daffodils and ivy."

"Kind of perfect for you, really." Claire takes a sip of her drink and gives her a sly grin. "Geek speak."

Mia concedes a smile at Claire's tease. "It was the same with Dad. He says he grew up being able to name any flower seed just by looking at it."

"Wow." Claire shakes her head. Her own grandmother taught her how to blanket stitch and to play 'Frère Jacques' on the piano, neither skill she ever used again.

"You know, she doesn't even let me call her nana or grandma."

"What do you call her?"

Mia smiles. "Her name. Only ever her name. Rosa."

"And your grandfather?"

"I never knew him. He died when Dad was seventeen. In a car accident."

"That's awful."

"It was for Dad." Mia leans forward and plays with the pepper shaker. "He lost his sister and his father already. And now he's scared he's going to lose Rosa."

"Of course he is." Claire stares at Mia. And Mia's scared too. She can tell. She reaches out and places her hand on Mia's arm. Mia starts at the sudden touch.

"I'm really sorry, about your...about Rosa." Claire quickly removes her hand and blushes, not sure if she just gave Mia a fright or if Mia doesn't want Claire to touch her. Either way, she can't help but feel as if she's done something wrong.

"Thanks." Mia reaches over and squeezes Claire's wrist briefly. And Claire knows it's to make up for whatever just happened.

The waiter strides over and slings their plates on the table with a cursory smile.

Mia sits back without touching hers. "You know, it's just hard to watch her stuck in a bed when she's so used to looking after herself, tramping around her incredible garden with the dogs, wearing her big garden boots, and working all day to scare off snakes with a shovel." Mia grins and shakes her head. "She doesn't spend a minute of daylight inside. Then she just comes in at night to write."

"She sounds pretty cool." Claire takes a chip from her plate, an effort at the charade of eating.

"She is." Mia nods and picks out a piece of tomato from her salad. Then she puts it straight back down.

"I hope she'll be okay."

Mia stares at her food. "Me too."

"And you too," Claire adds. "I mean, that you'll be okay too," she clarifies, blushing.

"I am." Mia sighs. "It's just sad realising she's getting old. It's like I didn't notice or something. And now I have."

Claire nods. "Both my grandpas died before I was twelve."

"Really?"

"Yeah." Claire stirs her straw in her drink. "My mum's dad from cancer when I was seven, and my dad's dad of a heart attack when I was eleven. I remember my mother saying to my father something about they arrived early to 'that age' where their parents are starting to die. Can you ever imagine getting to *that* age?"

"No." Mia shakes her head, eyes wide. "I really can't."

CHAPTER 59

They're getting closer to Mia's flat, and Claire grips the steering wheel a little harder and urges herself to speak into the deadening quiet that reigns between them since they got into the car. They're both fully aware, she's sure, that the unspoken words between them are still obstinately unspoken.

And Claire, for one, cannot—will not—let that go. She cannot finish this night, this charade of normality, and return to another prolonged silence from Mia. And she *cannot* go back to her own resulting insanity. And Claire knows it's up to her to say something because she has no way to know just how willing Mia is to let another opportunity to address what has changed between them slip by.

She reaches over and slowly turns down the music. "Mia?"

"Mm?" Mia stares out the window as the night slides by outside the car, encased in her own thoughts, whatever they are.

"You know that thing, not that long ago, when we were naked and... stuff?" Claire tries to say it lightly, to throw it out like a joke. But the minute it's out there and makes contact, she feels the slight stilling of the air and how Mia's stare out the window shifts from relaxed to deliberate.

"Yeah?" Mia finally says in a small voice.

"What happened with that?"

"What do you mean?"

"You know what I mean." Quietly determined, Claire turns onto Mia's street and stops the car across the road from her flat. She keeps her hands firmly on the steering wheel, looks straight out ahead of her, and takes in a deep breath. "I mean, I know you went to see your grandmother and maybe it's just because of her being sick and everything, but that was before, and now you've been home for days, and I haven't heard from you. And I don't really know what's going on with you, I guess..."

She trails off, not sure how to say what she really wants to say. "Like, if you're trying to avoid me, I'm *sorry*?" She suggests, helpless. "Maybe I'm just being too in your face? I don't know."

She feels completely stupid now but decides to turn off the ignition anyway. It's an unspoken message that she doesn't plan to leave until she's less in the dark about all this, even if it's just to hear Mia say she doesn't want to do this anymore, that sleeping together was a mistake. She deserves to be *told* that, at least. She turns to face Mia, biting her lip.

Mia echoes the move and turns slightly. She keeps her face pointed downward, avoiding Claire's eyes. Her fingers worry at a small worn spot on her jeans. She has that apprehensive, uncertain look again.

Claire sighs. Why is it so difficult to erase that look?

Mia finally shakes her head. "You're not in my face. I mean, I *want* you to be. I was just giving *you* space. I didn't know...if that was..." She pauses again, lifts her hands helplessly, and then drops them back down to her jeans. "You know, just a holiday thing, something that stays up at the lake, or—"

Claire smiles in spite of herself. "We went to the lake, Mia. Not Vegas. Or Tijuana."

Mia gives her a small smile. "You know what I mean." She draws in a deep breath. "And it was so weird, after your parents showed up. And we never really talked about it. Anyway, I didn't want to assume you were into this being more than just—"

An overwhelming burst of exasperation makes Claire sigh loudly. She clenches her fists on her lap.

Mia looks slightly unnerved.

But Claire's too frustrated and too tired of this weirdness. "Mia, for crap's sake. It's just..." She turns and stares out the window. "Yeah, I know it was weird when my parents came up, and I'm really sorry for that, but it's not like I haven't tried to talk to you since."

Mia continues to stare at her lap. "I know. I'm sorry."

"And I don't know how else I'm supposed to show you that I like you. I don't." Claire shakes her head, her gaze fixed on a lone man as he walks his dog down the dark street. "I really don't. I got naked for you. I practically *dragged* you into my bed the next night even though you were being weird. And after we left, I called you. I messaged you, repeatedly—

until my dignity wouldn't let me any more. I stalked you at your work and made you come to dinner with me tonight." She holds up her hands and raises her shoulders. "And I did it even though I have, like, zero idea what you're thinking." She pulls in another breath and grips the steering wheel. She feels much closer to tears than she wants to be. "And you know, I don't do this. I don't chase. And I don't really even know how to have these kinds of conversations. I've never had to, but I'm doing it because you're confusing the hell out of me." She turns slowly back to Mia. "I don't know what I'm supposed to—"

Mia leans forward and claps her hand against Claire's mouth, halting the rush of words. "I know, I know, I'm *so* sorry." She looks Claire in the eye. "And I'm really sorry I disappeared for a minute there."

Claire grabs Mia's wrist, pulls her hand away, and glares at her. "It wasn't a minute, Mia. It was nearly a *week*."

And Mia puts her hand right back over Claire's mouth and leans in closer, eyes insistent. "I know, and I am really sorry. I was just..." She bites her lips and shakes her head. "I don't know why I did that. I wanted to talk to you, but I didn't know what to say. I didn't know if this was just...if this was something that was, I don't know, real."

Claire goes to say something, but Mia's hand is still over her mouth. She holds up her hands again and raises her eyebrows at her.

Mia smiles and drops her hand. "Sorry."

"Thank you. May I speak, Mia?" she asks, imperious.

Mia smiles repentantly. "Yes, you may."

And now Mia's eyes are shining again, and Claire isn't even sure what it is she was going to say. She isn't sure she cares either. "Actually, fuck it, I don't want to speak." Suddenly sick of the inexact, frustratingly impossible art of finding the right words to say about all this, she gently clasps Mia's neck between both her hands and kisses her. Because if that doesn't tell Mia this is real for her, she doesn't know what will.

Mia instantly reciprocates. She leans into her, holding them in the kiss. Relief rushes through Claire as she wonders who the hell this version of herself is lately, this girl who keeps finding it in herself to do these incredibly bold things. She shocks herself with her willingness to put herself on the line for this girl, this beautiful but frustrating girl who sits across from her.

But Claire also knows there's only so many more times she's going to be brave enough to put herself out there. But now, *maybe*, she might not have to.

Mia suddenly breaks from the kiss but only to pull back and stare at Claire for a moment. She gives her an affectionate little smile, places a hand on either side of her face, leans in, and gently meets Claire's lips with her own again.

Claire closes her eyes and lets her other senses do the work. When she kisses Mia, it's as if a rush of warmth—a thrill—starts in her stomach and radiates outward through her whole body. It's not just lust. It's more than that. But she has no idea what to call it either.

Finally, they break the kiss. And then they sit there for a long, silent time, foreheads pressed together, hand on necks, in hair, on faces, as they re-acquaint themselves with this proximity.

A small burst of tentative happiness wells up in Claire at finding this place with Mia again—with finding that Mia *wants* to be in this place with her. She seriously started to doubt if Mia wanted this at all. She sits back a little and watches as Mia rests her head against the headrest. She runs her fingers in a lingering trail along Claire's neck and smiles shyly at her.

"You are such a dumb ass," Claire tells her witheringly as she reaches out and affectionately pulls at a strand of Mia's dark hair.

Mia laughs quietly and looks contrite again. She takes a hold of Claire's hand and kisses it. "I know." She stares at her, her eyes wide. "I *know*."

"Good."

"I really missed you." Mia tenderly presses Claire's hand between her palms.

Claire takes back the hand and crosses her arms, still stinging a little. "Well, that's your own stupid fault. I was right here." She stares out at the quiet street as tears loom again.

"I know," Mia whispers. She wraps her fingers around Claire's forearm and pulls her arm back. She takes Claire's hand again and holds it firmly in her own lap. "I'm so sorry, Claire. I really, really didn't mean to hurt you. I was just being an idiot. A freaked-out idiot."

Claire doesn't say anything, but she turns to face her.

Mia gives her a small, hopeful smile. "Why is it you're even more beautiful when you're mad?" she teases. "That's not fair."

And that's it. That's all it takes. Claire's done.

She gives Mia an eye-narrowed glare that slowly dissolves into a smile like she knew it would. Because she's done making Mia feel bad for now. Because Mia's cradling her hand between both of hers once more. Because she's staring at Claire with that diffuse, cinnamon warmth in her eyes. Because she's calling her beautiful again. That's enough for now.

She knows all she needs to know, for now. But she wants more too. "Are your parents home?" she asks, hopeful.

Mia ducks her head and looks through the window into the darkness. "Yeah." She turns back to Claire and frowns.

Claire lifts her free hand and smooths her finger over the dip where Mia's collarbones meet. "That's annoying."

"It is."

"Have you told them anything yet?"

She shakes her head. "It wasn't the right time with Rosa sick."

Claire nods. Of course not.

"You know what I wish right now?" Mia asks her as she leans in.

"What?"

"That one of us had our own place."

"Me too." Claire sighs and rests her forehead against Mia's. "God, me too."

And it's not just about sex even though that concept *is* taking up a lot of real estate in her mind too. She'd also just like somewhere quiet, somewhere private to just *be* with Mia alone, somewhere that's not a car or a pantry or a room surrounded by people threatening to invade at any moment. Somewhere they could just take a minute with each other. Somewhere they could actually have some precious alone time to figure out the nature of this thing between them and what it means.

The stroke of Mia's finger across Claire's cheek draws her away from her thoughts "I had better go," she whispers. "I start at six tomorrow morning."

"Ouch."

"Yes, ouch."

Claire sits up and draws in a deep breath. She has one more thing to say before she lets this girl get away from her again and she returns to whatever it is that happens to her ideas about the two of them when Claire isn't right in front of her. Something that might make the next time they see each other less confusing, less about having to tentatively find their way back to each other. Something that might mean Claire doesn't have to work quite so hard to convince Mia of what she wants this to be.

She reaches out and grabs Mia by the scruff of her T-shirt. "Okay, but before you go."

"What?" Mia looks nervous.

"Stop looking like that!" Claire growls and shakes her and laughs. "I just need you to know that when I see you again, which will hopefully be very, very soon, I'm going to want to kiss you again. I'm going to want to kiss you *still*. So *know* that, okay?"

Mia's smile is radiant. She nods slowly.

Claire lets her go and sits back against the door of the car. "And you know, I don't know..." Claire says in a small voice. "Maybe *you* could call *me*?" She shrugs, trying to look more relaxed than she feels. "You know, whenever, if you want to."

Mia stares at her for a long moment. Then she suddenly sits up and nods. She unbuckles her seatbelt and she leans forward. "I have to go."

"Um, okay."

"See you." Mia drops another light kiss on Claire, then abruptly turns, and climbs out of the car.

Claire takes a breath and re-buckles her belt. What was *that*? Then, unable to stop herself, she turns and watches Mia bound up the steps to her apartment, open the front door, and disappear inside. She sighs. Why does she feel as if she never quite knows what's going on with Mia?

She drives home without even turning on the radio as she mulls over the night. A least now she knows Mia is still into her. That's a start. But Mia's shyness? Her reticence with this? Claire still doesn't completely get it. It feels as though whenever they part she seems to find some kind of misgiving, an uncertainty she hasn't wanted to—or been able to—explain to Claire. Hopefully she will. And soon.

Claire remembers Mia on the night of her birthday, how even just after that day, she'd somehow retreated a little. As if she was unsure of what they should be together despite everything that happened the night before, everything Mia instigated. And Claire gets the feeling it's not because she wants to, but for some reason Mia seems to think she should.

Claire pulls up outside her place and parks out on the street. Just as she pulls the keys out of the ignition her phone buzzes on the dash. She picks it up, wondering who is calling this late. It's Mia. Claire frowns. Why is she calling now? "Hey. What's up?"

"Nothing. You told me I should call you."

There's a smile in her voice. Claire smiles right back, relieved. "I didn't mean straight away, stupid."

"No, actually, you told me to call you whenever I wanted to," Mia corrects her. "And I got inside and I wanted to talk to you."

"And why do you need to talk to me now, Mia?" Claire asks. She doesn't really care though. She just wants to keep her talking, glad to hear that gentle smart-ass tone of Mia's has returned and that it seems to be alive and well. *It's Mia.* She leans her head against the seat, smiling, and wishes Mia were still in this car with her.

"You didn't say I had to have anything to say either," Mia reminds her. "Just when I *wanted* to call you. I missed you. You're very missable."

"Oh okay. Sorry."

"Yeah, so I've got nothing unless the fact that I'm sitting in the kitchen drinking a cup of tea is of the slightest bit of interest to you?"

"Milk? Sugar?"

"Neither, actually. It's mint. Fascinating stuff, hey?"

"Truly."

They sit there in a protracted but comfortable silence.

"So, when can I see you?"

There's a slight turbulence in Claire's stomach, a surge of pleasure at Mia's sudden forwardness. But that doesn't stop her wanting to torment her, either. "Well, might I remind you that you could have seen me any time already?"

"I know," Mia says in a small voice. "I wa—"

Claire interrupts her, over the need to torment. She just wants to see her. "When are you working?"

"Every day but Friday." Mia sounds relieved. "You?"

"Every night until Sunday."

"Then I guess I'll see you on Friday? During the day?"

"Okay."

"But you know what?"

"What?" Claire asks.

"I'm probably going to call you before then. At least once, but maybe even twice."

"Good. You owe me. Night," Claire sasses. But she hangs up smiling.

CHAPTER 60

As soon as she hears the doorbell, nerves hit Claire's stomach at full throttle. She trots down the stairs and through the living room in her bare feet. Somehow, in the hours since they spoke to each other this morning when they arranged to meet here at the house, Claire has become increasingly tremulous about this impending afternoon visit. But she doesn't really know why. She's talked to Mia plenty since their dinner. Mia kept her promise and called Claire whenever she felt the slightest inclination. And now it's Friday and she's here, ringing the doorbell finally.

Maybe the nerves are about Mia coming to her house. It's not ideal, that's for sure, but there wasn't really any other option. They can't go to Mia's. Her mother is on holidays. And there seems to be a mutual, silent agreement they don't want to meet somewhere public. Today they need some sort of privacy, space to find their place with each other properly.

They only have a couple of hours, too, as Mia had to go to a promised but forgotten lunch with her mother before coming, and Claire's parents could be home any time from five onward. And Claire has to work later, too.

She draws in a deep, steadying breath and yanks open the front door. Hot summer air floods in, and Mia's standing there in cutoff shorts and a tank top, fanning herself. She looks sweaty and uncomfortable, her hair bunched messily at the back of her head.

Mia smiles wide as she walks in. "Hey."

"Hey," Claire replies quietly. She moves aside and lets Mia into the relative cool of the house.

Mia swipes her face with her forearm. "Sorry, I'm a sweaty mess. The air con in Dad's car seems to be broken. Either that or I just broke it. Still want to kiss me?" she teases, eyes twinkling.

A shy nod is all Claire can manage, and she wonders where all her confidence—cockiness even—from the other day has gone. And she wonders where Mia found hers.

"Good." Mia leans in and drops a light kiss on Claire's lips.

Claire watches her as she wanders into the living room and feels strangely exposed with Mia in her house all of a sudden. And against her better judgement too. This is the part of her life she could live without Mia seeing for a while longer, this boring, suburban version of Claire, who lives in beige-washed blandness in Nowhereland, Melbourne. It already bears little connection to the person she wants to be or to the way she wants to present herself.

But Mia doesn't say anything. In fact, she barely seems to notice the living room as she crosses the sea of neutral carpet. She stops briefly to glance at a photograph, and then, like an insect attracted to light, she walks straight over to the glass doors that look out into the back garden. Claire watches as she folds her arms and gazes out to the backyard. Yes, it definitely feels odd to have Mia here in her house.

As though Mia has somehow heard her anxious thoughts, she turns around and smiles at Claire. "Now that's an advantage to growing up in the suburbs. Room for a pool."

Claire plays with her earring and stares across the room, still somewhat paralysed. "True, I guess."

Mia turns and considers her. She reaches back and lifts some hair that has strayed down onto her neck and wraps it into the knot of her hair. Then she tips her head to one side. "Are you okay?"

Claire nods and folds her arms across her chest. She stares at the beige carpet and rubs at the pile with her foot. "Yeah, I think so."

"Let's go outside," Mia suggests as if maybe she can tell that the house might be playing some part in stifling Claire's ability to act normal. She slides open the door.

Claire follows her onto the small terrace. It's hot and windless outside, but most of the garden is in shade. The afternoon sun has already fallen behind the tall trees that line the fence. They stand side by side and both contemplate the backyard. Claire hasn't been out here in ages, not even to swim. She recalls how her father talked about removing the pool the last time she was out here with him. It's a round, above ground thing, built in the partial shade of a stand of tall birches, a planting decision her father bemoaned every time he had to clean the leaves out of it.

Mia shades her eyes. "In fact, another great thing about living out here, a backyard in general. Our apartment is pretty big, but we don't even have a balcony."

"Yeah, but you got to grow up downtown," Claire counters. "Close to everything."

Mia shakes her head. "Right now, nothing you can say will convince me that it was better. Not when I am this hot and I'm standing here looking at your big beautiful backyard with its swimming pool."

"*Okay*, Mia."

"In fact, Claire?" She takes Claire's hand in hers and shakes it.

"What?"

"I think I have to get in your pool."

"Is that so?" Claire squeezes her hand.

"I am so hot and so cranky right now I don't think I can actually focus on anything, even you, until I have been in that body of cold water."

"You don't seem that cranky. But by all means, if that's how you feel, Mia, then you should get in the pool." She lets go of her hand and pushes her away.

That's all the invitation Mia needs. She marches over, climbs up the short ladder and down the other side, and lowers herself into the water without even flinching.

Claire watches her stand frozen for a moment, arms outstretched before she dives under. She steps off the terrace and walks around to the shaded stretch of lawn under the birches. Leaning on the rim of the pool, she watches Mia kick out under the surface and reaches over and trails her fingers in the cool water.

Mia finally rises above the surface, pushes her hair out of her face, and smiles part bashfully, part triumphantly at Claire.

"Feel better?"

Mia bites her lip, grins again, and ducks straight back under the water without an answer. Claire turns away, flops down on the shaded grass, throws her arm over her face, and listens to the splashes as Mia continues to swim. She smiles. She doesn't know quite why, but she feels much better now that Mia has made herself right at home.

Finally, she hears Mia climb out and footsteps pad across the grass, but then she hears nothing. She lifts her arm from her face and looks around for her. Mia is a few feet away, holding out the bottom of her top and wringing it out onto the grass.

"Come here," Claire demands.

"I'll drip all over you."

Claire holds out her hand. "I don't care."

Mia comes over, takes her hand, and stands over her. She smiles as drops of water plunge from her hair and clothes and onto Claire. "I told you."

Claire smiles. It's actually hot enough that the water feels good. "And I told you I don't care. Come *here*." She says it more sternly this time, squeezing Mia's fingers.

Obedient, Mia complies. She steps over Claire and drops down so her knees are on either side of Claire's legs.

Claire reaches up and traces her finger along Mia's collarbone. She loves that spot, so angular and fine. "I'm glad you're here."

Mia leans in closer. "And I'm glad I'm here."

"Good." Claire blinks and wipes her face where a drop of water has landed.

Mia quickly sits back and shakes her hair out behind her. "Sorry."

"Never mind." Claire, impatient now, grabs Mia's tank top and tugs her toward her. "Come *here*."

This time Mia more than complies. She leans right over Claire in a press of wet fabric and dripping hair against her skin. Claire flinches slightly and Mia laughs. "Not sorry," she teases.

But Claire really doesn't care because that's when Mia kisses her, first chastely, in a languorous meeting of lips, but it slowly becomes fiercer, and it's all she can focus on. Mia catches Claire's bottom lip gently between her teeth, and then she slowly drops down to kisses her neck and chases the chilly splashes of water with trails of hot breath on her skin.

Claire inhales in a sudden, involuntary gasp, and reaches up and pulls Mia's torso right down against her. One arm winds around Mia's neck, the other pushes up the wet tank top and glides her hand across the water-cooled skin of her slender lower back. She urges Mia's face up over hers again, pulls her down, and slides her tongue into her mouth.

The part of her that's still capable of rational thought tells herself that doing this right here in the backyard, when she has no idea when and if anyone will be home, is probably not one of the soundest decisions she's ever made. But the other part of her, the part that has waited this long to be able to do this with Mia, to touch her again, the part with zero self-discipline, is incapable of bringing this to an end.

But it doesn't matter, because Mia does just that. She sits up, her expression suddenly disarmingly sober.

"What?" There is an instant, encore flicker of nerves in Claire's belly.

"I'm sorry." Mia holds a hand up in the air between them, brows furrowed. "I just...I want to tell you something...to talk to you, first."

"Um, okay." Claire wishes the plunging, ominous feeling would leave her stomach.

Mia climbs off her, lies on her back on the grass next to her, and tucks an arm under her head as if she needs some distance to say whatever it is she thinks she needs to say. Just when Claire starts to think this is going to be something bad, Mia reaches over, takes her hand, and pulls it over toward her on the grass. She weaves her fingers through Claire's.

And Claire can breathe again.

"First, I *am* really sorry that I didn't answer your calls or messages after the lake." Mia turns her head slightly toward her as she speaks. "That was not great."

Claire doesn't answer. She can't because she can't say it's okay. Because it wasn't. And Mia already knows it wasn't. Instead, she chews her lip, nods, and waits nervously for Mia to go on. She knows she needs to let Mia finally tell her about whatever it is that has been happening with her this last week or two.

Mia tightens her grip on Claire's hand slightly. "I didn't really explain it to you the other night. But I really don't know why I didn't call you. Because I really, really like you, and I think I probably really, really liked you from the moment I first met you even if I didn't realise it at first." She turns to look at Claire, her lips pressed together, her expression timid. "Well, maybe that's exactly why I reacted like I did to everything. Because I *really* like you."

Claire stares right back at her. "Oh, so you *do*." She's snarky, unable to help herself despite the tide of warmth that surges through her at these words. "Sometimes you don't act like it."

"Of course I like you." Mia rolls over onto her side, rests her cheek on her upper arm, and stares at Claire. "You're incredible." She is wide-eyed and emphatic as she speaks. "You're feisty and sweet and brutally honest, sometimes all at the same time. And you're so smart and beautiful, and you make me laugh, and you have—"

"Okay, okay!" Claire grumbles. She turns over on the grass and hides her face against Mia's arm, mostly to hide how ridiculously, incredibly good this flood of declarations is making her feel. Wow, when Mia finally decides to let someone know something, she *really* likes her to know.

"And I'm sorry I've been so weird," Mia whispers. Then she's silent for a moment. "I guess I just wasn't completely sure I was *allowed* to like you, and...well...like you as much as I do. Claire?"

Claire, wrought shy still, keeps her face pressed against Mia's arm. "Mm?"

"I didn't mean it at all, that night, that I thought you were trashy or not worth it or anything even remotely close to that. I just didn't think you and I, in the way I wanted you and I to be, was an option. At the time, I thought that we were just supposed to be friends, and that the drunken kissing thing was just that, drunken kissing, for you, and that you just wanted to know why it was happening. So I pretended it was the same for me. But really, kissing you when I was drunk was the only time I was brave enough to do anything about it." She's quiet for a moment. "I don't know. When I'm scared about something, sometimes the only way I know how to do anything is to just barrel in. But I don't always have the courage to follow through." She reaches out and plays with Claire's hair for a minute, clearly gathering her thoughts. "And I wasn't sure if you were seeing that guy from the party, but I didn't want to ask about it either in case it was obvious why I was asking."

"I wasn't," Claire mumbles and turns to meet Mia's gaze.

"And I guess...I really didn't think you would seriously like a girl or someone like me. And besides," Mia smiles weakly, "Robbie kept telling me, after I had that crush on that girl at work, not to fall for any more straight girls."

"Someone like you?" Claire lifts her head, frowning, and pinches Mia's arm. "You're an idiot."

Mia releases a great big sigh.

"And don't listen to Robbie. He's an idiot too."

"Well, clearly I didn't." Mia grins. "Because then, you know that night at the lake? I was washing the dishes, and I was thinking about the night before, in the pantry, and that day and about us and how I should tell you how I feel about you—how I should have just told you the night before when you asked me what was happening with us. And the more I thought about it, I just got this feeling that maybe, just *maybe,* there was a chance that the reason you were upset at me was because you might be into me, too, even just a little, and that you could like me too. I mean, you *did* kiss me back."

Claire smiles a bashful smile. "You noticed."

Mia smiles back. "I noticed. Eventually."

"So, in summary, you were kind of stupid *and* brave."

Mia raises a quizzical eyebrow.

"Brave enough to kiss me out of the blue but too stupid to register that I was kissing you back?"

Mia exhales a rueful sigh chased by a tiny acknowledging smile. "I guess."

"Stupid in the nicest possible way, of course."

Mia smiles and stares up at the trees above them. "So then I just thought, 'Stuff it. I'm going to go find Claire, and I'm going to talk to her and see what happens.'" She bites her lip and takes in a deep breath. "But then instead of talking, I kissed you again. Because *apparently* that's the only way I know how to communicate. I didn't really think much beyond that, in case you didn't realise." She turns and looks at Claire. "But that was pretty much the bravest thing I've *ever* done."

"And look, it worked out pretty well for you."

"It really, really did. But then, I don't know, I was so nervous and so freaked about it, I still just kept doubting it for some reason, doubting that this was something you would think is real too. And all the next day I just kept thinking, 'Don't get too excited, Mia, because this could just be some fun, holiday fling thing.' And then the next night, your birthday night, I really, really wanted to talk to you about it, but I was too scared to." She smiles sadly. "See? I told you, no courage for follow through."

Claire takes her hand again and squeezes Mia's fingers gently. She frowns. She would never have imagined Mia to be this unassured, this lacking in confidence. "For future reference, Mia, I don't know much about how you lesbians roll, but I think it is pretty safe to say if a girl makes out with you and then she cries when you say you are only doing it because you are drunk, she likes you a bit more than a fling."

Mia laughs. "Yeah, I figured that out eventually too."

"What? Like, two days ago?"

Mia nods, smiling, but then her expression shifts slowly back to serious. "I was so convinced that even when you messaged me after we got back, I would tell myself, 'Oh, it's just Claire being nice, trying to make things normal again so we can still be friends.'"

Claire tugs at her hand. "But why didn't you ever just *ask* me? I wish you'd answered my calls, talked to me, instead of deciding all this weird insecure stuff in your head. Based largely on nothing."

"I don't know." Mia chews thoughtfully on her lip for a minute. "Too scared of the answer?" she finally suggests.

Claire sighs and looks at her. Stupid, beautiful, doubting Mia.

Mia rolls over onto her stomach and runs her fingers through the manicured, green grass. "I guess it was all so unexpected, and I thought maybe you were just—oh, I don't know..." She draws in a deep breath and releases it slowly. "I'd always thought you were just into guys, and you're so beautiful, and you could date anyone. Even up at the cottage I just couldn't help feeling like any minute you were going to turn around and be like, 'What the hell am I doing?' I guess I thought it was better just to be your friend than to lose you completely by pushing for something you might not be into in the same way."

Before she can stop herself, Claire sits up in the grass and punches Mia in the arm.

Mia winces and rubs her bicep. "Ouch. What?"

"Well, aside from being kind of pissed at the fact you think I am going to descend into some crazy gay panic, I really don't get why you think that at all?"

"I know. I'm sorry." Mia shakes her head fiercely and rolls over. "That's the thing. I know it's unfair because it's not actually about you or about *anything* you have done or said. It's just about me being weird, mostly because this is all new, and maybe because the one other time I really liked a girl, she was straight, and because maybe that has made me totally insecure. No." She sighs. "I don't even know if it's that. I can't really explain it." She shakes her head again and presses her lips together, clearly on the verge of tears. "I'm sorry," she mumbles.

Claire pulls her knees to her chest, wraps her arm around her legs, and stares down at Mia, contemplating what she's telling her. Basically, she's been freaking out. And part of it is that she's been freaking out because she thinks Claire's going to freak out. Which is really just Mia freaking out. And so she's gathered up every single insecurity she could possibly have about them, about herself, and about Claire, and she's stewed on them. And now she's throwing them at her one by one.

But Claire is going to hold her ground, damn it. Because now, in a sudden, needed gift of clarity, she finally gets it. Mia has been so petrified that Claire doesn't feel the same way that she tried to protect her heart at all costs even if it means talking herself out of something she wants.

It's this realisation that stops Claire from being angry. Yes, what Mia is saying about her freak-out potential is kind of presumptuous and even a little insulting, but it's not about what she thinks of Claire. It's about everything she can possibly imagine that might go wrong, that could go wrong. All that's really in their way is a random bundle of doubts that Claire needs to find some way to assuage. Because it looks as if Mia had no luck doing it on her own.

And now Mia lies there with tears in her eyes, looking like a sad, lost stray on the grass next to her. And if there's one thing Claire can't be angry at, it's that, because it turns out she's a sucker for a Mia-shaped stray.

Even though the fact amazes her, Claire knows she can handle what's being thrown at her because now she finally knows for sure Mia's in this as deep as she is. Because that's all Claire has ever needed to know.

She's trying to figure out how she can reassure her when Mia says, "And you know, maybe it's actually *me* having the gay panic."

Claire watches her chew her lip and stare into the air just beyond Claire.

"It's just…with this, it all feels so real now or something," she whispers and turns to Claire with a timid, vulnerable expression.

Claire blinks. A wave of tenderness courses through Claire. She hadn't really considered how their relationship might throw Mia. *Of course* she's freaking out. Because for Mia this consolidates something bigger, and it's life changing in some major ways. It's a stepping off into a new sense of self. And Claire has to admit it makes her feel a bit melty to comprehend the possibility that Mia's feelings for her are strong enough that they've thrown her into a spin.

She takes hold of Mia's hand again. "Basically you're just having a giant freak out?" She smiles at her.

"Yeah, I guess." She looks at Claire, frowning. "And maybe I'm just a bit overwhelmed by all this?"

Claire blinks, and her stomach drops a little. "Too overwhelmed?"

Mia shakes her head. "No. Suitably overwhelmed. But definitely overwhelmed."

Claire lets go of her knees and shuffles closer to Mia, contemplating all of this. Then she climbs over her and sits astride Mia's legs. "Mia, I'm going to tell you this." She places her hands on Mia's stomach. "Even if you are an insecure asshole, and you think I'm trashy and—"

"Claire." Mia grabs her hands and holds them tight. She glares at her.

"What?" Claire counters with a grin. "Don't interrupt."

Mia grasps her hands harder and yanks at her arms, frowning. "I do not think you are trashy," she says, completely serious, her brown eyes fiercer than Claire has ever seen them. "I have never thought you were trashy. *Ever.*"

"Okay, whatever." Claire shrugs, but is secretly pleased by her ferocity. "But you do seem to think I'm some straight girl who's going to turn around and freak out about being with a chick. And you've decided this without even talking to *me* about it because you are an insecure asshole who refused to return my calls for *nearly a week.*"

Mia tries to interject, but Claire gives her back some of her own treatment from the other night and covers her mouth with her hand. "But you're actually very lucky you're saying this to me because being an insecure asshole is something I do very well. So even if you are kind of making me angry with these random unfounded accusations, I can also sympathise. In fact, it's mildly entertaining seeing it thrown back at me. And I also get it. But you should also know, if we are going to do this, you *cannot* continue to be this high maintenance, Mia. Because *I'm* the high maintenance one in my relationships." She grins. "That's my thing. So pull yourself together, okay?"

She can feel the movement of Mia's cheeks as she smiles under her hand.

"Also, you know, for one, what does it matter who I have been into in the past? I am into *you* now. Right now." She grabs Mia's arm with her free hand and shakes it. "Secondly, why would I not want to be with you? Have you met you? You're kind of a babe. An awesomely geeky babe, but a babe." She takes her hand off Mia's mouth, which, once freed, shapes itself into a wider smile. "So," Claire whispers as she leans closer, staring down fixedly into her dark-brown eyes, "listen to me. I am not going to back out. I am here. So please, please, please stop freaking out, okay?"

Mia's face dissolves into a tender smile. "I'll stop. I promise." She pulls Claire down by the sleeve of her T-shirt.

Claire obeys and folds herself into Mia's arms.

Mia's hands slide over her back and pull her into a tight embrace. "I promise," she whispers in Claire's ear. "And I'm so sorry."

"Okay, shut up now. You're sorry. I get it."

Mia laughs and squeezes her tighter.

Claire is held captive by a rush of feelings, an intense welling of attraction. How can Mia not get it? That it's not even a question that Claire wants to be with her? She lifts her head and runs a finger lightly over the skin above Mia's eyebrow, tracing its arc. "You really are amazing," she tells her.

Mia's dark-brown eyes shine as Claire presses her lips against hers. Claire lifts her head again, gazes at Mia, and checks for any more doubt or anxiety. But it's not there. Mia's smile is a blend of relief, happiness, and something else directed right at her that makes Claire feel almost unbearably happy. She has no idea what she wants to do with the rest of her life, but she knows she wants Mia and that Mia wants her, and that's good enough for now.

Claire lowers her head and kisses Mia again. It starts slowly, but within moments they're back where they left off, before Mia brought things to a swift halt with her confession and apology, back in that hot, wanting space, hungrily laying claim over each other.

But this time it's Claire who stops it as she reluctantly lifts her wrist and checks her watch. She presses her face into Mia's neck and sighs loudly. "Crap."

"What?"

"I have to leave for work soon. And Mum and Dad could be home any minute too."

Mia runs her hand along the back of Claire's neck, under her hair. "Crap," she echoes.

"Mmm," Claire moans into her neck. "Why can't we just have some time?"

"I know." Mia draws her arms around her and kisses the side of her head.

"I need to move out."

Mia chuckles. "I don't want to pressure you or anything, but right now I really want you to as well."

Claire kisses Mia again and climbs off her.

Mia sits up. "I should go. Let you get ready for work."

Claire pouts.

Mia pouts right back. "I know. We'll figure it out." She reaches out and strokes Claire's face. "We'll find a minute."

"Promise?" Claire grumbles.

"Promise. Or we'll run away or something equally dramatic."

"Deal."

They walk slowly back to the house together, out of the heat and back into the cool, still living room. At the front door, they stop and turn to each other. Mia slips her arms around Claire's waist. "Bye."

"Bye," Claire replies, just a touch sulkily. She wishes again that they had more time to wallow in this newfound security of finding themselves finally, out loud, on the same page.

Mia doesn't move to leave, though. Instead, she pulls her in closer and rests her forehead against Claire's. Breathing in slowly, Claire runs her hand up into Mia's drying hair, aware that the minutes she should be spending getting ready for work are trickling away. But she doesn't care. She doesn't want to move just yet. Instead, they stand in the doorway, arms wrapped around each other's waists, and stare at each other, wallowing in this first precious moment of mutual certainty.

Mia smiles and takes a deep breath. "So, you and me? Does this mean we're..."

Or what Claire stupidly thought was certainty.

"Oh, Mia." She throws her head back, rolls her eyes, and laughs. After all that, she has to ask?

"What?" Mia laughs, bashful, clearly completely aware why Claire is rolling her eyes.

Claire pushes out a weary, purposefully melodramatic sigh. "Clearly you need this spelled out for you, what we're doing here, right?"

Mia nods, looking shy but maybe a bit mischievous too.

"I don't want to put a label on it or anything," Claire tells her, faux casual. "But in my head, from here we're, like, an item."

"An item?" Mia laughs and raises an eyebrow. "How quaint."

Claire gives her a superior look. "Well, call it whatever you want, Mia. But considering you seem to be kind of lagging in catching on to this whole dating a lady department or even the whole knowing if she likes you thing, I'm going to explain what that actually means, okay?"

Mia nods, obedient, her eyes twinkling.

"For starters, this thing we have going, whatever it's called, is going to involve hanging out a lot. A *lot*. Can you handle that, Mia?"

Mia pulls Claire a little closer to her. "I think so."

"There'll also be lots of making out, feeling each other up, getting naked." Claire kisses her lightly and continues, "Then there'll probably be some serious debate at some point over who gets to be the little spoon if we ever get to, you know, actually sleep in the same bed together again. By the way, it's *me*, just so we're clear, okay?"

"Um, *okay*." Mia chuckles.

"You're taller. It simply makes logistical sense."

Mia rolls her eyes. "Okay, Claire."

"Also, I'm probably going to tease you a lot about what a hot geek you are, pick on your nerdy ways. I'll also get jealous of your friends and sulk when you don't pay me enough attention, that kind of thing. And you," Claire steps back and takes both Mia's hands in hers, "are probably going to be really nice to me even though I'm a pain, because you are, like, ridiculously lovely. And you'll probably also make me feel bad about being a pain by being generally awesome. Like, for example," she runs her hands along Mia's arms, "if you ever bring me flowers, you'd never bring me roses because you're the type of person who will remember that I told you that one time that I hate roses. You remember that, don't you, Mia?"

Mia laughs. "I remember."

Claire raises her hands and gives her a look as if to say "see?" She goes on. "But you'll also pick on me plenty in that nice but smart-ass way you do, so that I'll know you're completely aware that I'm a jerk, but also that you can't help liking me."

Mia nods. "Sounds about right."

"So, in summary, I guess, whatever all that means to you, we're doing that, okay?" Claire folds an arm around Mia's neck and kisses her fiercely. "You up for it?"

Mia tips her head back and laughs. "Strangely, yes."

END BOOK ONE

THE STORY CONTINUES IN:

THE SUM OF THESE THINGS
COMING IN WINTER 2015

About Emily O'Beirne

Thirteen-year-old Emily woke up one morning with a sudden itch to write her first novel. All day, she sat through her classes, feverishly scribbling away (her rare silence probably a cherished respite for her teachers). And by the time the last bell rang, she had penned fifteen handwritten pages of angsty drivel, replete with blood-red sunsets, moody saxophone music playing somewhere far off in the night, and abandoned whiskey bottles rolling across tables. Needless to say, that singular literary accomplishment is buried in a box somewhere, ready for her later amusement.

From Melbourne, Australia, Emily was recently granted her PhD. She works part-time in academia, where she hates marking papers but loves working with her students. She also loves where she lives but travels as much as possible and tends to harbour crushes on cities more than on people.

Connect with Emily online:

Website: www.emilyobeirne.com
Tumblr: http://it-used-to-be-fun.tumblr.com/
Goodreads: http://tinyurl.com/goodreads-Emily-O-Beirne

Other Books from Ylva Publishing

www.ylva-publishing.com

Departure from the Script

Jae

ISBN: 978-3-95533-195-5
Length: 240 pages (approx. 52,000 words)

Amanda isn't looking for a relationship—and certainly not with Michelle.

She has never been attracted to a butch woman before, and Michelle personifies the term butch. Having just landed a role on a TV show, Amanda is determined to focus on her career.

But after a date that is not a date and some meddling from her grandmother, she wonders if it's not time for a departure from her dating script.

Turning for Home

Caren J. Werlinger

ISBN: 978-3-95533-323-2
Length: 345 pages (approx. 85,000 words)

When Jules goes home for her grandfather's funeral, the visit unleashes a flood of memories and sends her on a lonely—and familiar—path. Her partner, Kelli, feels Jules slipping away but can't figure out how to pull her back. In desperation, she turns to Jules's oldest friend—and her ex—Donna. When a lonely girl reaches out to Jules for help, the past and present are set on a collision course.

The Caphenon

Fletcher DeLancey

ISBN: 978-3-95533-253-2
Length: 374 pages (approx. 165,000 words)

An emergency call to Lancer Andira Tal has shocking news: there is other intelligent life in the universe, and it's landing on the planet right now. The aliens sacrificed their ship to save Alsea—temporarily.

Alsea is now a prize to be bought and sold in galactic politics. But Lancer Tal is not one to accept a fate imposed by aliens, and she'll do whatever it takes to save her world.

Mac vs. PC

Fletcher DeLancey

ISBN: 978-3-95533-187-0
Length: 148 pages (approx. 32,000 words)

Computer tech Anna Petrowski is used to people assuming her advice is free, even on weekends. Elizabeth Markel catches her eye precisely because she needs that advice, but doesn't ask. It's the beginning of something special...except Elizabeth is not what Anna thinks.

People and computers have one thing in common: they're both capable of self-sabotage. But computers are easier to fix.

Coming from Ylva Publishing in 2015

www.ylva-publishing.com

The Sum of These Things

Emily O'Beirne

This summer Claire has learned a few things already. Like falling for a girl is easy. Now comes the hard part, though: learning to trust. Then there's the question of what to do with her life. Claire's new job offers a potential future, but will her pushy mother like it? Now, the biggest lesson Claire must learn is to not let anything get in the way of her happiness. Especially herself.

All the Little Moments

G Benson

Anna is focused on her career as an anaesthetist. When a tragic accident leaves her responsible for her young niece and nephew, her life changes abruptly. Completely overwhelmed, Anna barely has time to brush her teeth in the morning let alone date a woman. But then she collides with a long-legged stranger...

A Story of Now
© by Emily O'Beirne

ISBN 978-3-95533-345-4

Also available as e-book.

Published by Ylva Publishing, legal entity of Ylva Verlag, e.Kfr.

Ylva Verlag, e.Kfr.
Owner: Astrid Ohletz
Am Kirschgarten 2
65830 Kriftel
Germany

www.ylva-publishing.com

First edition: July 2015

Credits
Edited by Sheri Milburn & Jennifer Moorman
Cover Design by Streetlight Graphics